by

AUGUSTA GOSLING

MW01600673

Copyright © 2022 Augusta Gosling

Ebook Cover: Images and Cover Art Illustration by Period Images, Pi Creative Lab and Edgar Design 3

All rights reserved.

ACKNOWLEDGMENTS

Thank you for picking RED ROSE I hope you'll enjoy it as much as I've enjoyed writing it.

The story on the Wars of the Roses inspired me to write this book because it is my favorite period in History.

However, I took the liberty to replace the character of the Earl of Warwick with the Earl of Hampton, who is a fictitious character, mainly because it suited the purpose of the Series. I hope you will forgive this. You will see familiar players in this period and new characters I have created across the Series.

RED ROSE is the updated version of ROYAL, previously published under the pen name of Dana Arpquest.

I would also like to thank my wonderful daughter, who has been supportive throughout the writing of this book.

If you would like to keep in touch and find out about the next books, please join me on Tiktok @augustawrites, Twitter or Instagram @augustagosling; I'd love to hear from you.

Thank you. Keep reading and I'll keep writing,

Augusta

PROLOGUE

France, Plessis, November 1472

Hampton gulped the fine Burgundy when the door swung open. His heart was racing, and his mouth went dry in anticipation of what news the messenger might bring.

"Have you had any news? Hampton asked, jumping onto his feet as soon as the messenger walked through the door to his solar, giving the man no time to close the door behind him.

The messenger nodded and headed straight for the fireplace, shaking off any snow that had attached to him along the way. He couldn't help himself; the warmth was just too tempting.

"So?" Hampton asked again, placing his goblet on the table.

For a brief moment, the messenger hesitated and stared at his feet before looking towards the door. The man took a long pause, then turned to face Hampton. He looked at the ground for what seemed like an eternity, lost in thought, or perhaps the news that was too disastrous to reveal. After a while he finally raised his head and locked eyes with Hampton.

"Have you heard from her?" With a bellow, Hampton bashed his fist on the desk. "Answer! Is she all right?"

"She is well, my lord. But there are rumors about the countess of Dudllan all over London." The man stopped, as if expecting Hampton's outburst.

"Speak!" Hampton said, swiping the desk with a wave of his hand, sending a stack of parchment flying across the desk.

The messenger stepped back and gazed towards the door as he said, "People say she is the king's mistress."

Hampton kicked the armchair, which landed near the fireplace, and the black velvet cape that rested on it caught fire. The messenger darted to it, pulled it out of the fire, and trampled on him to put out the flames.

"Monseigneur, if I may say so, you cannot blame lady Alys. She was told you had been killed eighteen months ago. You can't expect her to be in mourning all her life."

"Do you have proof of these slanders? Did you see her yourself with Edward?"

The man shook his head. "My lord, if you care about her so much, why don't you tell her you're alive - I'm told she's still trying to raise funds for your cause. She-"

"That's enough. Keep your opinion to yourself and get someone to prepare my horse. I'm going to England." Hampton strode out of the room, his spurs clanging against the flagstones.

CHAPTER ONE

September 1471, Dudllan, Alys

Hundreds of dead bodies covered the field like poppies in the summer. The mist that swirled over the valley turned into a thick fog, soaking my clothes to the skin. At each step across the field, I tripped over a corpse or an injured soldier. The shrieks of the wounded, the shouts of the battle, and the sound of metal clanging from the men still fighting for their lives pierced across the field, frightening a throng of starlings which flew out of a nearby bush. I ducked just before they passed over my head. I wished the fog would not only bury the sight but also the shouts of the commanders' voices echoing as they tried to rally to their troops.

As I kept walking, I reached a point where I could no longer put a foot on the ground without treading on a body. Not a single inch of the field uncovered. And the putrid smell of death, mixed with the earthy early morning dew over the soil, invaded my nostrils.

Everything was chaos. Men were attacking their own camp. The commanders called their men to withdraw, but it was an order that came much too late for most. Incapable of proceeding any farther, I stared at a shadow that somehow seemed to be able to walk across the field. It advanced towards me. At first, I noted the man's blade dripping fresh blood. As I looked around for an escape route, I strived to shift my feet. I could not. Then, as the man reached nearer, I recognized Hampton.

Without caring about the soldiers beside me, I dashed towards him. No one seemed to notice my presence: I even shoved a soldier accidentally, but he did not react. It was as if their weapons could not harm me. As I raced to Hampton, a man-at-arms grazed my arm with the tip of his blade. Not a drop of blood escaped my body. They were like ghosts.

Hampton had almost reached me when he let his sword fall to the ground and opened his arms. I rushed to him like to a sanctuary. Nose to nose, we stared at each other, desiring each other: no more soldiers, no more shout, no more battle. Around us was just an empty field on a dazzlingly sunny day. It felt as real as the blood surging within my veins. My hand fondled his face, slowly savoring our reunion, while his hand slid along my back, and then I gazed into his bright blue eyes.

In a trice, blood slithered from the corner of his right eye, covering his entire face in no time with a bright red, viscous liquid. His piercing scream was insufferable. As I held out my hand toward his shoulder, I noticed the tip of a broadsword coming out of his heart, and then Hampton collapsed in my arms, showing the weapon that had been thrust through his back. Even if the sun was high in the sky and the fog had vanished, everything became cold. I bawled for help to the point that no more sound came out of my mouth. No one came.

THEN A DAMP CLOTH OF linen pressed on my forehead, and a whiff of the unfamiliar scent of rose water and lavender lingered in the air. For the last few months, I had survived with the bare minimum and using perfume, or scented water, was not in the habit of anyone in my entourage.

"The fever has returned. Get the doctor," a woman's voice said.

I held out my arm to stop her. I was not the one who needed comfort. "He will die. Someone, please, help!" I screamed, and then again, a calming hand rested on my arm. The place was dark, but I could just make out the candle's flickering light in the chamber's corner.

My eldest son, Geoffrey, whose eyes betrayed his fear, stood by the bed. Mayhap he saw the sword that pierced Hampton's chest.

"Get Fauconberg. Your father needs help," I said, levering myself on the bed.

"Lady Alys, can you hear me?" Lysbette's soft voice asked as she patted my shoulder.

Lysbette? Then I opened my mouth, but no sound came. I had no strength to summon her to rush for succor, and it frustrated me that she stood still, just staring at me. Enraged, I punched the mattress with my fist.

"Mother, are you feeling all right?"

"I..." Then the room came into focus, and I realized I had one of those nightmares again. Since I came back to Dudllan in May, I'd had a dozen troublesome nights. Every time Hampton appeared out of the fog, walked to me, and every time I ran to him and woke with a fever... and he was still dead. Murdered. Assassinated by Robert Woodville because of Margaret of Anjou, leaving me alone with four children and one to be born soon.

Shivering, I put a hand on my swollen belly, reassuring myself that my babe was safe. That pregnancy had turned out to be more challenging than the previous ones, and Hampton would not be present to support me with the childbirth. The thought of having to face this ordeal alone made me anxious.

How would I get through without him to hold my hand? He had been there for my four boys. All those years, Hampton had been my rock, and now he was no more in my life. Even if on several occasions I could have sworn I had seen Hampton lurking in a corner—only to disappear as soon as I called.

My belly was plump as if about to burst, and as if my skin was not strained enough, I received regular kicks from the inside, revealing the footprints of my little captive—another boy, for sure. And a fiery one, like his father.

"I am fine," I finally said. "Just another nightmare." Grateful for his presence, I took my son's hand in mine. Poor Geoffrey—at scarce ten years old, he already had lost his father, and I expected the thought of losing his mother, too, distressed him.

All the same, I smiled, showing him that my ravings were now in the past. However, Lysbette's presence confused me, as I did not recall her arrival at Dudllan, nor having welcomed her at all. As I tried to sit up in the bed to grab the potage Lysbette was holding, an acute twinge crossed the lower part of my abdomen. The common strain of childbirth. My sweet warrior wanted out earlier than planned. Promptly, I moved, desiring to reach the birth chamber which was next to my bedchamber.

"No, stay here. We can't risk you getting worse. I'll fetch the midwife," said Lysbette who, like me, noticed the pool of blood on the bedsheets.

I squeezed Geoffrey's hand. "Wait outside, my son. Lysbette will inform you when your brother is born."

"I had to call for Lysbette," he said. "I did not know what to do. You were rather unwell."

"Have I been bedridden for so long?"

"Almost a month."

"You've done well," I said, hiding my concern. "Do not fret. I'll be fine," I continued, earnestly hoping this was the truth as the contractions grew stronger.

Geoffrey kissed my forehead and bowed before leaving the chamber. As he reached the door, he turned; our gazes met, and I saw the tears in his eyes. My health had not been good for a while, but I did not recall being in and out of a fever for so long. My sons were still young, I could not abandon them. The blood on the bed increased my fear that childbirth and delirium would aggravate the situation. I could not desert my children, not so soon after the death of their father! Geoffrey was too young to care for his brothers, and Arthur was not even a year old. I clung on to life like a leaf on a tree at the end of the summer. All it needed was a powerful gust of wind, and it would be all over. Every day I missed Hampton, but I was not ready to join him yet.

The recurrent waves of pain drew closer and tortured me more frequently with enhanced intensity.

At least the chamber had not been entirely barricaded with tapestries as was the practice, but then there wasn't much comfort at Dudllan. We did not have the means to obtain additional objects, like tapestries, for I had received no revenues from my trade with Master Parker for a little while now, and as regards to the fabric business, Master Cloppelin only sent, three months ago, less than a quarter of what we used to make. Anyhow, since my people knew I detested being in the dark, and even more so since the death of Hampton, as soon as they heard I was awake they cleared away the wooden board from the windows, letting in a shaft of light through the glazed dormers.

The other insubstantial income we had came from the fields. However, few people worked the land nowadays, as we had lost many lives during the battle at Tewkesbury, and most of the survivors fled to France with Robyn, Jasper and Henry Tudor.

Even though Dudllan was not the most luxurious place in the kingdom, it was our stronghold, and it protected my sons and me from the vileness of the court. One day, I vowed, I would make Dudllan as magnificent as Hampton castle. Despite that, I did not know how to create a substantial income from the earldom in which the king had held me prisoner for months. The only consolation I had from this war was that, after the victory of Edward, old King Henry was no more—the version of Edward's detractors was that the king and his brothers had murdered old King Henry, but Edward's allies tattled that the old king died peacefully in his sleep. In fact, I doubted that no one would ever find out what really happened.

During the battle, Anjou's son was killed. When she was informed of her son's death, Margaret of Anjou found Sanctuary in a convent and would forever be forgotten. She was finished, at last. With no one to fight for anymore, she was suffering as much as I did. Margaret of Anjou finally received her comeuppance for all the evil she had spread throughout the years.

Edward's triumph helped me get rid of one enemy, but there were plenty more, and Edward was one of them. Never would I forgive him for what he had done to Hampton. Edward had denied being responsible for Hampton's death, but he had done nothing to prevent it. The Woodvilles, the queen's family, still held their heads high at court and were even more potent than before. And I heard that George and Isabel paraded through the streets of London as if no bloodshed soiled their consciences. George had betrayed Hampton with the help of Isabel, Hampton's own daughter.

The thought of them strengthened the pain in my belly until I no longer felt it. The discomfort I had fought for so long sucked the strength out of me. Everything became distant as if all my senses vanished one by one. First, my vision became blurred, then my entire body felt numb. The words spoken by the surrounding people sounded fuzzy, incomprehensible. The doors of Purgatory opened before my eyes to give me my eternal penitence. Death would have to stand by a little longer, for I was not ready to cross that bridge. My boys needed me. Still Death held my hand and dragged me slowly to her side while my children pulled me together to keep me with them. My love for them was strong, and I would not let the faceless cloaked monk prevail, not this time.

After hours of suffering and fighting delirium, fever, and pain, I gave birth to a girl. At first, I must admit that I tried to disguise my disappointment. Hampton would not have wanted another daughter. But the moment the midwife put her into my arms, I stared at the fruit of my womb, and when she opened her eyes and looked at me, my heart melted. Mayhap I did not need another son; I already had four to remind me that once Hampton and I had loved each other very much.

Remembering how he used to call me his son-maker made me smile; for now, I had failed my mission by giving him a daughter.

"I am disappointed with you, Alys of Lochlainn," was what he would have said, with his suave voice.

Without a fortune, girls were useless in this world. But lost in the depth of her stare, I fell in love with my daughter.

"What shall I call you, lady feisty?" I asked as she kept staring at me with a severe face, her fists clenched tight together. Judging by how many times she had kicked me from the inside, I guessed she had Hampton's character and needed a name worthy of such a temperament. Then I recalled some of my readings and she reminded me of Alienor of Aquitaine, the grandmother of all kings. "You shall be my Alienor."

For a long time, I cradled Alienor in my arms, letting tears roll down my cheeks, and then Lysbette approached and took her from me. "You cannot feed her yourself; you must rebuild your strength. The fever's not yet gone."

Reluctantly, I agreed, for I knew Lysbette was right. It was a miracle that I was alive. To recover faster, I would have to give my body a rest.

A WEEK LATER, AS SOON as my condition permitted me to do so, I went out, breathing in the fresh apples' scent ripening in the orchard. When I came back from the stables, where I spent all afternoon hugging and grooming Tristan, I walked past the solar where my steward frowned over some documents. Although it was a splendid day out there, the windows were shut, and piles of rolled ledgers blocked the natural daylight. No wonder he was squinting so much. However, it was not the squinting that worried me, but the lines on his forehead.

"Is everything all right?" I asked.

As he lifted his head from the papers, he started and pushed some parchments under a large pile of documents. "My lady, are you better now?"

"Yes, thank you. Tell me, what makes you frown like that?"

For a long moment, he did not respond. He hesitated. Finally, he said, "The king has raised the taxes again, to cover for the losses the war has caused, and-"

"The king or the Woodvilles?" I cut in as I entered the solar.

"Isn't it the same, nowadays? I'm afraid the king gets a poor reputation, regardless of who makes the decision."

"And we cannot afford to pay our taxes, is that right?"

"We could, but there would be little left once we've settled our debts. If you want to survive until spring, lay off some of your guards. You are under house arrest; you do not need all of them."

"Those men have been faithful to me. I cannot ask them to leave. Besides, where do you suggest they go? Dudllan is as much their home as it is mine. Find the money elsewhere!"

"In that case, I will dismiss the domestics and your ladies, and mayhap you could manage without my services."

I lifted my eyes. "If that is the only solution, my ladies can return to their households, but I wish to keep the servants, they rely on their wages. And you... well, I could not do without you."

"My family needs feeding too. Without a wage, I could not work for you; as much as I'd like to, I cannot."

"How long have we got to find the money?" I asked, pulling papers from the desk and disturbing a cloud of dust.

"Just over two months."

"We'll find a way. I shall think of something... Try not to worry too much, I'm sure we will be fine."

"On this occasion, I doubt you'll succeed, Madam," he said.

CHAPTER TWO

October 1471, London, Estrilda

The bells stroked the seventh hour. Estrilda lifted her gown to avoid soiling the hem with the mess that covered the cobbles of the streets.

"Hurry, Estrilda. The queen does not appreciate waiting," said lady Jane Spencer, her friend and, like Estrilda, a lady-in-waiting to Queen Elizabeth.

Earlier that day, the queen had sent them on an errand in Thames Street, but now night had fallen over London, and they knew she'd wonder why they hadn't returned sooner. Although Queen Elizabeth was a humble woman who prayed a lot, a faithful wife, and a very attentive mother, she had a weakness: she loved gold. One of her contacts from abroad had brought a unique necklace from Venice. Most of the time, lady Spencer and Estrilda were to meet the man on his arrival.

The queen's caskets and coffers were already full of beautiful jewels, but she always wanted more. Estrilda did not know how she hid them from the king. Lady Spencer and Estrilda reveled in going on regular errands for the queen, but today had been a lengthy one. Shortly before noon, they'd arrived at the wharf, and they waited for hours before the ship, which had been delayed by the weather, docked at the port. Once the deal was done, they headed back to the castle.

After dusk, London became more dangerous: although the streets were still bustling with merchants and all kinds of people, the falling night attracted the rabble, and lady Spencer and Estrilda did not enjoy hanging on too long in the city when it was dark. Especially now they possessed a most precious jewel whose price could have fed hundreds of people for at least a couple of months. At first, Estrilda had hoped that on the way back from the collection, she would have been able to stop by Master Cloppelin's storehouse, but it was far too late to allow herself an impromptu visit. They had to return to the palace.

Since King Edward's victory over lord Hampton and Margaret of Anjou's army, England found peace — almost. In the north, the king of Scotland thought it an opportune time to attempt an invasion, yet again. King Edward had sent his younger brother to restore order, and tonight a special banquet took place to celebrate his triumphal return.

Evenings at Westminster were always full of life and rather joyful; in fact, anything was an opportunity to feast, which did not please everyone. Margaret Beaufort, one of the wealthiest women in the country and another lady-in-waiting to the queen, stated that Westminster and the Tower were the Sodom and Gomorrah of England. She'd even tried to convince Bishop Wallbrooke to put a hold on all extreme celebrations but in vain. He never missed a feast which didn't stop him from preaching every day about humility, abstinence, and giving their time to God. As soon as he entered the great hall, the bishop enjoyed the banquet as much as the king did.

On the one hand, he publicly agreed with Margaret Beaufort, and on the other, he acted the opposite way. Chastity and fidelity were not part of his daily activities. On several occasions, Estrilda had witnessed ladies going into his bedchamber, and rarely the same ones. Still, his position gave him the privilege to act as he pleased. Penance only seemed to apply to non-clergy people.

Lady Spencer and Estrilda rushed through the service door, and as they neared the great hall entrance, they adjusted themselves. Though they had no time to refresh their clothing and bodies, which smelled of the town and the long hours spent in the crowd. But, before going in, Estrilda assured herself that the necklace was secured in the bottom of her cloak pocket.

Mingling with the guests under the buzz of the conversation and clatters of goblets that covered her footsteps, Estrilda approached the top table, from which the queen shot her an inquisitive glance to ensure they had taken delivery of her goods. Estrilda acknowledged her, and the queen smiled, which was a relief as none of the women ever wanted to anger her. When Estrilda took her place next to her husband, everyone had begun to eat. Her husband shot her a reproachful glance, and before he spoke, she said: "The queen sent us to Thames Street." Famished after the long walk, Estrilda ripped a piece of the roasted goose and partridge and placed them onto the trencher. The meat melted in her mouth as she started to eat, filling in her entire body and mind with pleasure and relief.

The hall was heaving with revelers, some from the old noble families but were mainly the queen's relatives. At the top table was a young, charming man Estrilda did not recognize at once. Then she overheard someone mentioned his name: Richard of Gloucester, the king's brother, who had forced the Scotts out of England.

Further to the chatterers, Richard of Gloucester was a great chief-commander. He booted the invaders out in only a few weeks and, to prove his valor, he had brought back the sword of the Scottish king to Edward. Hence, this festivity was to celebrate his victory over the fierce enemy. Much happened since she last saw the duke of Gloucester. Not that he knew Estrilda — she wasn't even at court then, and they were both children — but now by the king's side stood an incredibly handsome man. So elegant, indeed, Estrilda couldn't keep her eyes off him. Thankfully, he did not notice her insistent gaze, and neither did her husband.

With her eyes still set towards the top table, Estrilda savored a little of the malmsey wine. Then her husband put a hand on her knees, and Estrilda's cheeks warmed up with shame.

"England is invincible. That's what the king said and mark my words, it won't be long before he sends troops over to France and claims the territories his predecessors have lost through the years."

"Why would he do that? Haven't too many people already died after so many rebellions?"

"It's only my opinion but look at the king; he's boasting as if he was the one who booted the Scots out. He's got the heart of a conqueror but fret not, tonight is the time to rejoice at our victory."

"Oh yes, I've yet to attend a banquet that is not delightful. The king is spoiling his courtiers."

"Be careful not to let him spoil you more than you aspire," he said.

When Estrilda criticized Bishop Wallbrooke, she was a hypocrite, for she was no better than him, at least in thoughts. Her husband's remarks made her wonder if he had noticed the way she stared at the duke of Gloucester, who did not pay the slightest attention to her. Their eyes met once or twice and she fell for him instantly, but his eyes flicked elsewhere, as if he hadn't even seen her; or perhaps he had, but to him, she was just another insignificant lady in the crowd. What was she thinking? She was a nobody, and he was the brother of a mighty king.

"Wife, could you stop gawking at the king? You're disgracing yourself," Thomas whispered through clenched teeth.

To be caught like that caused Estrilda great shame. Pretending she hadn't overheard his conversation with his table companion earlier, she said: "Oh, no... I was only wondering who is the man sitting next to the queen. Who is he?"

For a fleeting moment, Thomas looked embarrassed and then said: "That is the king's brother, the duke of Gloucester. Have you not met him before?"

"No, I don't believe I have," she said, trying to mask her guilt.

"Then I must introduce you," her husband said.

"I am sure the duke is not concerned about meeting me. I wouldn't like to bother him," she murmured, conscious that her feelings might become visible if she were to stand less than a foot from him.

"No, it is important that you meet him," he said. "If I may confide, I am indeed relieved that it was him you were looking at. For a moment, I thought you were seeking to tease the king's attention, like most ladies at court."

"How could you think that of me, husband?"

"I have seen how he looks at you, and I know of no lady who has refused him."

An infamous lady had once rejected the king but mentioning her name at court was prohibited, lady Alys of Lochlainn, now the countess of Dudllan. Once a grand lady but according to the gossips, now a She-Devil who had ill-influenced many men, including the king. A foe to Queen Elizabeth. Thus, ladies-in-waiting were not permitted to speak of Alys under any circumstances.

Fortunately, no one at the palace knew about Estrilda's previous relationship with lady Alys, apart from her father-in-law, who, Estrilda knew, would never speak of it to anyone. If words of her previous connection with lady Alys were to come out, Estrilda would be banned from court, and her life would turn into a calvary—back on the streets. No one would put her in that plight. Estrilda was a lady-in-waiting to the queen, and intended to stay at court, serving the queen, and to be the best attendant the queen had ever had.

One would have expected that lord Hampton's death would have eased the queen's mind, but it wasn't so. Queen Elizabeth held a grudge against Alys of Dudllan and her sons, and against anyone who had been seen at lady Alys's or lord Hampton's side at any point. It was as if the queen would not find peace until all her enemies have paid for their misdeeds. When lord Hampton killed the queen's father, Estrilda was still young, but rumors were that the queen had sworn to avenge her father's death. However, Estrilda could not understand how Queen Elizabeth could think of hurting children for revenge.

Even lady Alys had cared for the queen's daughters the year before. When lord Hampton had discovered it, Estrilda was the one who took over from Alys and brought food and missives to the queen while she was in Sanctuary. Since that day, Estrilda had served Elizabeth. She must admit that at the beginning, her loyalties did not lie with the queen but lady Alys. However, matters had changed.

Her husband stood and took her hand, getting her out of her thoughts. "Come," he said, and as Estrilda rose and put a hand in his, she trembled a little. Together, they walked toward Richard. All the same, the idea that someone would notice her burgeoning affection for the duke petrified her.

"Can we please retire to our bedchamber? I am a little fatigued," she said as she tried to stop him.

Thomas smiled and shook his head. "It won't be long, and then we'll go to our chamber."

Trying her best to avoid showing reticence, Estrilda forced a smile, and, like a faithful spouse, she followed a few steps behind her husband.

"Your Grace, I am so pleased to see you've returned victorious. My wife and I would like to congratulate you on your prowess," Thomas said and stepped to the side to let her face the duke.

Lost in the depth of Richard's emerald eyes, Estrilda almost forgot she was married and that her duty was to give her husband an heir — which, so far, she had failed to do.

Estrilda's mother-in-law checked regularly her bed for any traces of her course. Each time, although she'd never openly expressed her dissatisfaction, Estrilda knew the woman was blaming her. It was not as if Estrilda did anything to prevent from being with child. She always opened her door to her husband for his regular conjugal visits. But God hadn't consented to bless their union with a child. Sometimes Estrilda wondered if it was God's way of punishing her for having lied about her origins. The lie never was her idea, but lady Alys's.

Estrilda was given no say on that matter, and the thought of it being a bad thing or even a sin hadn't crossed her mind until now.

God sees everything.

Now it was too late to speak up and ask for forgiveness. Besides, what would happen if her husband were to find out and if he were to change his mind about their marriage? Worse, what if the queen were to find out? The reason Estrilda was at court was through lady Alys, to spy on the queen. Well, this was before, when King Edward was exiled. Now, things were different. But if she knew, the queen wouldn't trust Estrilda anymore. People disappeared daily in London, and Estrilda did not want that to happen to her. The confession of her sin would have to wait until extreme unction time.

"Lady Stanley, how very nice to meet you," Richard said. Terrified to look at him, she kept her eyes on her feet.

CHAPTER THREE
November–December 1471, Dudllan, Alys

When I returned from the village, a bitter wind blasted the last leaves out of the elm trees surrounding the stable yard. To prevent my hood from flying away, I held the side of it with one hand and my reins in the other and dashed across the courtyard. In a haste to see my beautiful daughter, I asked Gérard to look after Tristan, before rushing into the dwelling.

Although I had recovered from the birth, worries destroyed me from the inside, keeping me awake well into the night. Each day, I tried to figure out how to find the funds to aid us in getting out of torments. But pride was stopping me from writing to Edward to beg for his clemency. As I cradled Alienor, I stared out the window. My poor boys, they were no better than peasants. Geoffrey and Edmund dashed under the rain across the courtyard after having worked in the farmyard all morning. Not that it affected their mood; for them, this was a game. Still, my heart squeezed at the thought of what they had to go through. As I rocked Alienor in my arms, I noticed she had fallen asleep, so I put her back into her crib and sat at the desk.

For the next hour, I examined our books again, hoping for a miracle, hoping my steward had missed something that could save us. I had to find the money somewhere but selling any part of my estate or the remaining livestock was out of the question. My trades in London had brought no revenue, and until a few days ago, I had been too unwell to explore that matter.

Lost in my thoughts, I stared at the flickering light of the half-melted candle and started when Lysbette knocked on the door.

"I must return to London; my husband needs me," she said.

Half listening, I perked up at the sound of the name of Willem and rummaged into the heap of papers on my desk trying to recover the proof of when I'd last received my proceeds from Willem Cloppelin.

"Is everything all right?" she asked.

"Be honest, Lysbette. How is the fabric business doing?" I asked as I found the document. "Willem has not honored our contract. He owes me a lot of money," I said, waving a paper. "June! The last time I received my proceeds was in June. It's now December. Tell him I demand my dividends. Just because I'm house-jailed does not grant him the right to exploit my predicament. I shall speak to the king if he doesn't honor our terms."

"Hmm." She sat down without being invited, and I stood up and walked to her. Her face became paler as I approached, and she stared at her feet.

"Are you hiding something from me?" I asked, noticing her sheepish attitude.

"You weren't well, and I did not want to disturb you with more troubles than necessary. The king has seized all your trades, and Master Parker was arrested three weeks ago. I received the news just after the birth of Alienor."

Doghearted flap-dragon!

My legs quivered, and I put my hand on the chair to steady myself. "Master Parker has always been faithful to the king. Why would he arrest him?"

"For trading with you. Oh, lady Alys, I know you've been good to us, and we are very grateful. Please do not think we aren't, but..." She paused, and I waited, squeezing my hands together. "Lord Hampton is no longer behind you with his power and fortune — you've no influence at court anymore, and I'm sorry, but Willem can no longer do business with you. If he were to continue, I fear he too would be arrested."

"What reasons would they give to imprison him? All the same, should Edward order his arrest, I promise I would not let him do so."

"Lady Alys, until the king lifts your sentence, you have no rights. Besides, your intervention could put us in more trouble than necessary. You have been defeated, and you must submit to the king's orders. And so should we."

"Which side are you on, for goodness' sakes?" I asked as I shot her an indignant glare.

"On my husband and Estrilda's! What makes you think I would choose you over my husband and daughter? And while we are talking about Estrilda, I can't help worrying for her. You know that living at court is not good a thing. I'll never forgive you for having put her in that position."

"How can you be so ungrateful? Considering where Estrilda comes from, living at court is the best thing that could have happened to her, even if it means living with

Queen Elizabeth. Estrilda has a husband whom she loves and who loves her. What makes you think she is not content at court? I am certain she would not let the queen abuse her."

"That is where you are mistaken. You do not know her as I do. Estrilda is a pliable young lady who sadly has always venerated you, and that is not a model I'd like her to follow."

"Charming!"

"No, you don't understand; I fear that someone might discover where she comes from, and that day..." She paused and wrung the hem of her tunic with both hands and looked down, then continued. "She has not visited us for a while. I hope she will not follow your example."

"What do you mean?" I contemplated the paper, and then my mind was distracted by a robin that landed on the windowsill.

"She might feign to be someone else to gain the queen's favors."

"Nothing amiss with that. Besides, we've instructed her never to disclose her origins. She must have the queen's full trust if she wants to serve our cause."

"Your cause has been lost along with lord Hampton. You are defeated, and Estrilda is still at the queen's mercy. How do you explain that she has not visited us for a few months?"

"I can't say. Frankly, I thought you saw her regularly," I said, trying to ignore her not believing in our ideals anymore.

"She comes to buy textiles quite often, and she sends us many ladies from court."

"Oh, so you do get a lot of interest from the court. Business must be thriving then."

"We..." she started, then abruptly stopped.

"Go to London and tell your husband to send me my shares of this lucrative trade. Be careful, Lysbette, you might be my friend, but if I discover you have tried to delude me, being house-jailed will not stop me from taking revenge. I will not let Willem swindle me because I am a woman and no longer have Hampton behind me."

"No, you misconstrue my meaning."

"Not from what you've said," I snapped back.

"I did not say the business was flourishing; I've only said that Estrilda was sending us some clientele, but not that much, and Estrilda hasn't visited us privately for a while. Something is wrong, I know it."

"I cannot help you. The last time Estrilda wrote was..." I stopped as I recalled the last letter I had received from Estrilda. A few days before Hampton was taken from me! "Estrilda is a grown woman now. You shouldn't worry about her. She probably enjoys life at court... If there were anything we should know, she'd inform us. I doubt it not."

"Perhaps... but something isn't right. A mother feels when something is amiss."

In fact, Lysbette was only Estrilda's adoptive mother, but both women grew close to each other; Estrilda had no mother and Lysbette no daughter, which naturally created a solid bond. My relationship with Lysbette had been good, most of the time, though many times we did quarrel, but even if we both liked each other, we were never that close.

"I miss her so much," she continued, "and I'm terribly afraid to leave my husband alone in London with the latest developments."

"If you must go, then I will ask one of my men to escort you, but I would appreciate if you were to return soon," I said to soften the tension.

"Uh! You did not care for my company when you had lord Hampton by your side," she reminded me bitterly. "And if your son had not called for me, I don't believe you would have ever contacted me."

Mayhap that was true. When Hampton was by my side, I needed no one else in my life. He was my world. Now, my world was this cold castle, my prison. There was no jailer, but I was not free to leave. And if my suspicions were right, Hampton was still alive and thus I would not give up on hope that one day he would return, but I would never give up on Lysbette—I never did, even if I had been somewhat distant at some point. Lysbette's voice sounded agitated, and she went on and on about my devoted fealty to Hampton and then I heard her say, "... now we have nothing left, not even our daughter."

"Are you chiding me for this?"

"No," she said, but her tone revealed that she was. I had not forced Willem to follow me in that venture. When I first proposed to trade with France, once Willem understood there was a lot of money to make, he conceded with no discussion. However, I chose not to mention that detail. Her sudden openness hurt. Mainly because what she held against me were past stories, things I had paid for years ago. But the most hurtful accusation was for the deeds I had not done. What I did for Estrilda was because I'd judged it was best for her.

"Pack your trunk! Someone will accompany you," I snapped, picked up my daughter, and rushed out of the study before my chin quivered.

All this was a little too much for me; I had lost Hampton and my liberty. Now, thanks to the queen's ambition, I had also lost my trades and a friend.

When Lysbette left, I did not show my face, not willing to give her the gratification of seeing my pain. Of course, it wasn't the first quarrel we had, but somehow, I sensed it was the last one.

After her departure, I returned to my study and wrote to the only ally I had left. Not caring I hadn't heard from him for a long time, I prayed that he would still be someone I could count on. It was now time to continue the unfinished work of Hampton.

My dearest King Louis,

As you are probably aware, I am under house arrest at Dudllan; however, I need your help on a matter of urgency.

King Edward has seized my trades and imprisoned one of my associates. Please, I beg you not to supply England with any goods until King Edward has come to reason. I recognize that with my request you might face a momentary loss; however, once Edward agrees to the terms of my trades, we will increase the prices and you will soon recover the temporary loss and gain more. England will not hold long without French goods, especially since the queen's favorite wine is one of your great Malmseys.

In the meantime, please grant me some gold, and in return for the immediate funds, I will oblige to return the deeds to the lands you kindly offered my sons a few years back. I will pass them to your messenger the day I take delivery of the money you will send me.

Your desire to control England is no secret and thus, there is another matter I wish to discuss with you: Henry Tudor. The time for you to challenge King Edward has come, and I have the firm conviction that you should give your support and help to Henry. He must defy Edward. With your help and army, victory is assured. I recognize that Henry Tudor is still young, but his uncle Jasper is a wise man. The Yorks and the Woodvilles must be overthrown once and for all; they are ruining England and the old noble families who supported lord Hampton and yourself.

Please consider this as a matter of urgency. Also, this would be an excellent opportunity for you to restore Calais under the Fleur de Lys.

Your humble servant,

Alys of Lochlainn, Countess of Dudllan.

CHAPTER FOUR
October 1471, London, Estrilda

As Estrilda spread the queen's soft velvet new gown on the fur cover over the bed, she spotted a piece of parchment on the floor at the foot of the bedside cabinet. She could not help but take a peek at it. When Estrilda saw it concerned Lysbette, she picked it up. The message was not signed, but it mentioned that Lysbette had visited lady Alys to assist her in giving birth to a daughter. The letter made Estrilda wonder why there were spies at Dudllan—lady Alys was house-jailed with no wealth, no influence, and no advocates. However, the fundamental question was: why would Lysbette's visit to Dudllan be of importance to the queen?

Estrilda's initial impulse was to inform Lysbette and lady Alys, but she hadn't written to Alys for months. No doubt she would have thought Estrilda was an ungrateful coward for not contacting her. Mayhap she was, but she loved her life at court, and would do nothing that would compromise it, or risk losing it all.

Being sent back on the streets was Estrilda's biggest fear. Yet, she was conscious it was thanks to lady Alys that she was alive and a wealthy woman living at court. Shamefully, she'd never thanked Alys for what she did for her.

For a while, Estrilda assessed whether it would be safe for her to contact Alys while the secret of her origins would be preserved. After all, what if lady Alys suddenly revealed Estrilda's secret to protect herself? Perhaps Estrilda was an egoist, but since she served Queen Elizabeth, there had been many times when she had doubted the trustworthiness of lady Alys, who told them many awful tales about Queen Elizabeth. However, Estrilda only saw a dignified woman who cherished her husband and children. A loyal woman to the crown and one who was always sympathetic to Estrilda. Could it be that lady Alys had ill-advised her and the Cloppelins so they would be on lord Hampton's side? After all, lady Alys had followed and supported lord Hampton whatever he did. Whether he took good or bad decisions, lady Alys had invariably stood by him. Had she approved of the dreadful things he had accomplished? Lord Hampton had executed many men without a second thought, and from what Estrilda had picked up, he was a ruthless man who only cared for himself. More than once, he had slaughtered innocent people because they did not back his cause or because they had shown sympathy to the queen. If lady Alys had concurred with him, then the queen was wise to call her a behemoth. Some women said lady Alys was a She-Devil. Had Estrilda been wrong all her life to think otherwise?

Her heart was telling her that lady Alys had always been good to her, but Estrilda had to devote herself to her husband and his family, and they were serving King Edward now, so that was where her allegiance had to be.

Her husband's father was quite ambitious, who, seeking to be as close as he could to King Edward, had secured a small position at court for his sons and himself. Now that the enemy of the York family was dead, England could finally prosper with no more conflicts—unless the Scots resolved to invade England again. Still, Queen Elizabeth struggled to find peace within her soul. Even if she had given England an heir to the throne, she always worried about King Edward and saw enemies in everyone, close to the king or not. Besides, jeopardizing her situation was not something Estrilda should have attempted, and thus she concluded it was in her interest not to tell Alys or Lysbette about the message. If there were spies at Dudllan, they could intercept any letters.

SOMETIMES BEING IN the queen's suite meant putting up with her temperament, which could be very unpredictable. Estrilda had learned that. All the same, it did not bother her, as unlike the other ladies-in-waiting, she grew up in rougher conditions than one could have ever imagined. She never had the chance to meet her mother or father; her first memory was of the streets of London where they ran barefoot regardless of the weather, where they hid in the church at night when the wind blew gales. Then her next recollection was when she met lady Alys who used to dress like a man then.

Estrilda stared at the letter. Her heart was torn, and then there was Lysbette; she was like a mother, after all. Footsteps in the corridor made Estrilda startled. She immediately thrust the paper under the bed and headed out of the chamber.

LATER THAT MORNING, the ladies of the queen assembled in her private chamber, stitching shirts for the king's men. As every day, they chatted joyfully while carrying out their duties, thoughtless of what was going on elsewhere. An extraordinary fracas interrupted the cheerful atmosphere, and suddenly they heard soldiers' footsteps rushing into the corridors.

Without lifting her head, Estrilda attempted to eavesdrop. Then she dared cast a glance at her companions; all showed worry on their faces, but no one spoke. As if anticipating danger, the queen dropped her needlework on the floor and hurried out of the room.

"What is going on?" Estrilda asked lady Spencer.

Before replying, Jane glanced around and then moved closer and whispered, "The queen has ordered the arrest of a merchant's wife."

"Oh! and why is it causing that much of a fuss?"

"It is normally the king's decision. Something happened this morning—not sure what exactly, but the queen was furious. Didn't you hear her scream?"

"No."

"Anyway, she told the guards she wanted that person to be arrested promptly."

"Who is it? Some of our acquaintances?" Estrilda asked, trying to hide her apprehension that it might have something to do with the letter she saw earlier.

"Yes. It's our fabric supplier, Mistress Cloppelin."

"What! But why?"

"Probably another one who has fraternized with the lord whose name we cannot mention and a certain countess from

Wales," she whispered, without daring to pronounce their names in case someone would overhear the conversation.

"Will the queen ever forget about them? It's becoming worse than an infatuation."

"Shush! Keep your voice down. The day lord Hampton killed her father and brother, she vowed to revenge their deaths, and thus every single person who has anything to do with it will pay for it."

"But Mistress Cloppelin has nothing to do with her father's death."

"There are rumors that Mistress Cloppelin spent the last few weeks in Wales. Being seen with the countess of D. is not acceptable. I don't understand why a woman like Mistress Cloppelin is consorting with this evil countess. Shame though, Lysbette was a nice lady, but if you want my opinion, she'll never go back to the shop. The queen's men are already there."

"We must do something. We can't let this happen."

"Oh, come now, Estrilda, she's only a merchant's wife. It's not as if London's lacking fabric suppliers. Someone else will take over the business. Don't worry, we won't run out of linen."

Unwilling to appear too involved, Estrilda said no more, but she could not let this happen! Lysbette was the only mother she'd ever had. And even if Lysbette's disappearance would keep Estrilda's secret safer, she could not abandon her.

As casually as possible, Estrilda focused on the stitching while figuring out how she could help Lysbette. She was not as bright as lady Alys, so finding a trustworthy ally would not be easy. There was no need to ask lady Spencer for her help; Estrilda could see she would not do anything. Then she recalled that her husband's father was now very close to the king. Incapable of doing further work, Estrilda asked to be excused in order to see her husband.

She rushed from the queen's private chamber, crossing the long galleries, then part of the gardens to reach the White Chamber where she was hoping to find her husband. Despite herself, she worried a little, for her father-in-law was not the most approachable person. Unless one would offer him either a lot of money or some very high favor, he was somewhat disdainful.

"Thomas, Thomas," she whispered from behind a column and beckoned her husband to join her.

"My dear wife," he said, opening his arms. "What a pleasure to see you. Has the queen sent you? Is everything all right?"

"No, she isn't aware I am here," she whispered as he joined her. "I must see your father urgently. Do you know where I can find him?"

"He's with the king and the lords of parliament, and I'm afraid they cannot be disturbed at present."

"Please, as soon as he comes out, tell him I'm waiting for him in the gardens by the menagerie. This cannot wait."

"Is there anything I can do?" Thomas appeared concerned and placed a hand on her arm.

"I'm afraid not."

Her husband ignored her origins, and he would not understand why she wished to speak to his father. Conscious of the time she was allowed to get away from her duties, Estrilda headed for the gardens and waited.

THE SUN SLOWLY GAVE way to a duller sky and daylight became dimmer as the entire city seemed to become quieter. Every footstep that echoed across the peaceful garden started Estrilda. Eventually, when a light breeze cooled her neck and shoulders, after having paced the alley between the menagerie and the fountain many times, and as she was about to return to her duties her father-in-law appeared at the corner of the gardens.

Relieved to see him, Estrilda stood and curtseyed. "Lord Stanley."

"Thomas said you wished to see me. You could have come into my solar to speak."

"No. What I have to say cannot be heard by others."

"Oh..." he said, but he did not pressure her to learn any more. As if this simple gesture would help her find the right words, Estrilda twisted her kerchief, but after a while he coughed as if to remind her of the little patience he possessed.

"It seems the queen has ordered the arrest of Lysbette Cloppelin, is this true?"

He nodded. "It was I who stamped her request," he said and strolled along the alleys of the gardens, and she followed.

"But why? You know Mistress Cloppelin is a good subject. What has she done to deserve that?"

"She and her husband are traitors!"

"Her husband? But no one mentioned anything about her husband."

"He was arrested last week."

Somehow, Estrilda wished she had not requested to speak to lord Stanley and heard the news about Willem. Her knees wobbled, and she sat on the closest bench and attempted to steady her breathing.

"Look, Estrilda," he said and sat next to her. "You are now a Stanley, my son's wife, and your duty is to give me a grandson. Forget about your past life and the Cloppelins."

"But they are the only parents I have ever known, and they have always been generous and kind. It's unfair."

"Perhaps, but you have a family now. Soon you will have many children with whom to direct your concerns. Go back to your chores. Your loyalty now must lie with our king and queen. No one else."

"You will help Mistress Cloppelin, won't you?"

"Certainly not. I must obey the queen's orders. She doesn't like people to contradict her. Out of all people, you should know that. In the future, we will never speak again about the Cloppelins. Do you understand?"

Nodding, Estrilda curtseyed and plodded back to the queen's chamber.

THE NEXT MORNING, THE queen was in a fouler mood than Estrilda had ever seen her, and she was in a no better one herself after the discussion with her father-in-law. Not that long before, lord Stanley had been on lord Hampton's side, and now he was in favor of King Edward. Estrilda doubted the king knew that lord Stanley had been on the opposite side during the last insurgency, but lord Stanley was nothing but an opportunist who changed sides to gratify his personal wealth, and a cunning one, too. If people had wind of her past, they'd probably think that she too was a side-shifter. Before the downfall of lord Hampton, the thought of not being on lady Alys's side had never crossed her mind. Truth be told, Estrilda was grateful for what they did for her. But now that lord Hampton was dead, and lady Alys under house arrest, unlike her father-in-law who had changed sides to gain more fortune, Estrilda had no choice but to protect herself. The queen was the only person who could help her now. So, whatever happened, Estrilda had to be seen as a faithful and loyal servant, and she must admit that she grew a little fonder of the queen each day.

LATER ON, DURING VESPERS, the office got disturbed several times by a man's loud cough. The sounds reverberated against the walls of the church and covered the Latin words of the priest who shot a few angry glances at the assembly. The poor man's struggling cough was quite sickening. He must have known he was disturbing everyone; however, he did not leave. Estrilda looked around a few times to see who the offender was, then she realized it was her husband. Even though she tried to beckon him to stop, he did not pay attention. So, as soon as the service was over, when people gathered outside and the bells of the church covered the conversations and the buzz of the throng, she wandered over to meet her husband.

"Thomas, are you unwell? You sound like you should be in bed," she said as she took his ice-cold hands in hers and walked beside him.

"We were out hunting with the king yesterday, and I caught a cold," he said as they walked side by side towards the main hall. His voice was rather raucous, and she felt pain for him.

"You mustn't stay like this. You must lay in bed at once. I'll send the doctor."

"No, the king needs me," he said then coughed again.

"Please listen," she said and put a hand on his forehead. "You are burning. Go to bed," she said as the dreadful idea of... No, it was just a cold and there was no need for her to imagine what was not. Estrilda forced a smile. "You must look after yourself, my dear husband."

"I will be fine. Don't fret; it's only a little cold."

"You are tenacious, Thomas Stanley. Don't call me in the midst of the night if you have delirium. I have warned you."

"Go, before we are both in trouble. The queen is waiting for you," he said and gestured towards Elizabeth and her ladies waiting for her by the entrance of the hall.

She kissed his forehead. "I shall see you tonight at dinner," she said before scampering off to meet the queen.

"What is wrong with your husband?" Elizabeth asked.

"He caught a little cold while out hunting. Nothing to worry about."

"It did not sound like a little cold. Has he seen a physician?"

"Not yet, your Grace. He said he will be fine," Estrilda said as the church bells continued chiming.

"Then do not let this disturb your duties," she said and beckoned her ladies to follow to her receiving chamber, near which many peasants, merchants, and beggars queued to have a chance to request the queen's favor.

DURING THE NIGHT, THOMAS'S condition worsened, and her father-in-law called for Estrilda. When she arrived in the bedchamber, the physician had been and gone, and before leaving the room, his father asked her to call him if Thomas's state were to deteriorate. Lord Stanley was expecting the worst, for he had already summoned the abbot, who was hovering by the door like a bee waiting to land on a honey jar.

Thomas was fast asleep, still regularly moaning. Estrilda sat on the side of the bed, clasped his icy hands in hers and prayed. But after a little while, the air smelled like a butcher's stall, and it was rather unbearable, so she reached in a cabinet to get some lavender water where she also found some burning salts which she immediately threw onto the fire, hoping it would refresh the stuffy and sick atmosphere. Then she returned to Thomas's side.

Everyone had given up hope of a recovery, but she refused to admit it was the end. Between a couple of Ave Marias, she sponged his head a few times and put more faith in her prayers, but like everyone, she began to lose hope. And then Thomas opened his eyes.

"I knew you'd get better. Do you want something to drink or eat?" she asked, but he did not reply. Although his eyes were open, his regard was absent, as if already in another world. He smiled, and she saw contentment in his gaze. "Thomas, Thomas," she said, shaking him and almost yelled at him. But despite her prayers and efforts, he was gone.

"No, please don't leave me! I need you."

For a while, Estrilda prayed for his soul to go to Heaven but also for her own safety. She was in no rush to inform anyone. While people ignored his departure, she was still someone, she was still his wife and had a potential future. However, she could not keep this to herself and eventually she resigned to send someone to inform her husband's family of their son's passing away.

Her father-in-law put a hand on her shoulder and shoved her to make her move away from his son, her husband.

Now that Thomas was gone, Estrilda was just a widow with no children, no land, and no fortune. Would she be sent back to where she came from? Which meant into the streets, as she could not go to Flanders, as most thought that's where she came from, but she knew no one there. Estrilda had no one here either, apart from Lysbette.

Oh, my Lord, have mercy on us and spare Lysbette from the queen's wrath.

"What have you done to my son?" Thomas's mother yelled as she entered the chamber and pushed her way past Estrilda.

Startled by her entrance, Estrilda hesitated for a fleeting moment, then she wiped her tears and walked to her mother-in-law compassionately, but instead of comforting Estrilda, the woman slapped her as if it was her fault. At least now Estrilda had the confirmation she was dreading: she would never be welcomed in her husband's family. Taking one last look at Thomas, she left him with his mother and father.

Had their marriage been fruitful, this would have assured her safeguard and the safekeeping of her secret, but now Estrilda was more vulnerable than ever. She did not want to go to her bedchamber, nor did she want to go to her duties. She wanted to hide, to keep her secret forever.

What if lord Stanley decided that Estrilda should be arrested for treason, for having grown up with the Cloppelins? But, if he were to speak, he would then have to explain to the king how he had received payment from lord Hampton and lady Alys. Lord Stanley was an opportunist, but he was not an idiot, and he was a proud man who would never admit to having had financial difficulties. So perhaps that would keep him quiet. Estrilda was no traitor. The queen knew that Estrilda had stood by her side when she needed her; Estrilda would not let her father-in-law or anyone else push her away from court. If she were to fall in disgrace, she would ensure they would fall with her,

FOR A FEW HOURS, ESTRILDA hid in the gardens, reminiscing about the past, recalling the day when Willem Cloppelin had announced her betrothal. It was the happiest day of her life. Tears rolled down her cheeks, but shamefully, this was more because of the uncertainty of her future than to the anguish of being a widow. Also, she wept, for she was a bad spouse. An unfaithful wife. Not physically, but she'd had thoughts about another man. The Father in Heaven said, "Thou shall not covet other people's property." The duke of

Gloucester was not married, but he was not for her either. God had seen another of her sins, and he punished her for what she had done.

"What are you doing out there on your own? We've been looking for you all over," said lady Spencer. Then she sat next to Estrilda and put an arm around her. "I have heard about your husband. I am sorry."

"Oh Jane, what will become of me?" Estrilda said and embraced her.

"You'll get over it, and you'll marry again," she said as if she thought nothing of Estrilda's husband's passing.

"No one will want to marry me."

"Of course, you will find another husband. You are a lady-in-waiting to the queen, that alone attracts many suitors. I did not marry until I was twenty-eight. You're only seventeen, you still have plenty of time. Come inside before you catch your death out here."

Lady Spencer and Estrilda had been friends from the moment Jane had arrived at court. She used to serve a family in the North, not that she admitted it, but Estrilda guessed it was a family who supported lord Hampton. When King Edward was restored, she and her husband moved to London, and he managed to get her a position in the queen's suite. But that was all Estrilda knew about her past. Though, lady Jane Spencer was rather nosy when it came to other people's lives, she was very secretive when questioned about hers.

It was only the day after Thomas passed away that Estrilda found the courage to return to her duties. As she took her place alongside the other ladies-in-waiting, the queen beckoned her to approach. While terrible thoughts went through her head, Estrilda neared her chair and curtseyed.

"I am sorry for your loss," said the queen. Estrilda sniffled and tried to smile. Then Elizabeth continued: "Do not worry, my child, you are still young; your pain will soon ease."

"I fear my situation might become worse, Your Majesty, for I suspect you might soon ask me to leave," she said in a trembling voice.

"What makes you say such nonsense? You have been so kind to me when I was no longer a queen, and now that I am back on the throne next to my husband, you've shown me nothing but respect and loyalty. I need people like you on my side; I will not let you go."

"Thank you, Your Grace. I am very grateful." Estrilda kneeled and kissed her hand, then she stood up, and as she was about to leave, the queen called her back. "Estrilda, there is one more thing, though. The time might not be very appropriate, but I am afraid it is of high importance. I have heard that you have been regularly visiting a certain merchant's house in London. I would appreciate it if you avoided dealing with Master Cloppelin and his wife or any of their acquaintances. As a matter of fact, you must find another supplier for your fabric, as Willem Cloppelin has ceased trading and will soon face trial. It would be unfortunate if the king were to discover that one of my most faithful ladies has been dealing with a traitor, for I could not protect you. I hope you understand it is for your own good that I am requesting this of you," she said.

Estrilda blanched, and for a long moment she stayed silent, worried that the queen might have discovered her secret. "Master Cloppelin always has the best fabrics in London," she heard herself say. "Where else would I get the same quality?"

"Perhaps, but he has not always been faithful to my husband's cause. He has dealt with lord Hampton and his harlot, and I do not wish to contribute to their prosperity. They do not deserve it."

"Very well," Estrilda replied and curtseyed.

Still shaking, Estrilda left the private chamber. She did not know what to do. Her visits to Willem and Lysbette had been sparse over the last few months, but that did not mean she loved them less. Lysbette and Willem were like mother and father to her. How could she tell them she was no longer allowed to see them? She had to warn Lysbette. Thomas's sudden illness had taken her mind away from Lysbette, and she had almost forgotten about her imminent arrest.

Hopefully, Lysbette was still at Dudllan, and no one had been there to arrest her yet. Poor Lysbette. She did not even know about Willem.

As soon as Estrilda returned to her bedchamber, she kneeled before her cabinet, opened the bottom drawer, and pulled out a box. Everything she possessed was in this little coffer: a few valueless jewels that her husband had offered her, some letters he had written, a little rock she'd picked by the Thames, a feather from the garden, and a well-worn fabric doll. Instinctively, Estrilda picked it up. She remembered the day lady Alys gave it to her; she was about five or six years old then—no one knew when she was born—it was the physician who had guessed how old she was when she was younger. That was when she was happy, and then lady Alys left for Middleham. What a miserable day! Although Alys had promised to come back for Estrilda, she never did. She had sent money to Lysbette and Willem for Estrilda's keep, but she only did it out of duty or pity. At least that's what Estrilda thought.

Sometimes, it hurt to think that Alys never loved Estrilda the way she'd loved her. Perhaps the queen was right about lady Alys, she was a heartless person who had frozen blood running through her veins. Lady Alys was part of Estrilda's past. She scrambled to her feet and threw the fabric doll into the fire and watched it shrivel to nothing, hoping the smoke that permeated the chamber would dissolve the memories of lady Alys.

Queen Elizabeth was her only ally now, but still, Estrilda had to warn Lysbette. She had to leave Dudllan, go to Flanders and never to return to England.

My Dearest Mother,

Pardon me for writing to you while you are at Dudllan, but I have no choice. The queen has ordered your immediate arrest.

Do not return to London, for you will be arrested when you enter the city. Go to Flanders. As soon as I can do so, I will send you some money. However, I, too, am currently in a precarious situation for my husband passed away a few days ago, and I must show the queen my full support if I do not wish to return to the streets of London.

Do not inform lady Alys of what is happening, for I fear she has never been on our side. I know from unimpeachable sources that she is responsible for all our woes. You must not help her anymore. Please leave Dudllan at once and do not let lady Alys know about this letter. If you were to stay with her, you would put your life in even more danger.

You will be in my heart always,

Your dearest daughter.

Having no seal, Estrilda let the candle wax melt over the side of the letter and waited for a little for it to cool, then she pressed her finger over it, ensuring the message would not fall open before it reached its destination.

In the middle of the night, when everyone in the Tower was fast asleep, she slipped out by a service door and took a barge up the river to the Steelyard quarter, and then she ventured through the streets of London to find a messenger who would not betray her. Estrilda had never dared go out on her own at night before. She prayed to God that no one would notice her absence and that the queen would never find out about her little escapade, for Elizabeth would not have understood.

CHAPTER FIVE
January 1472, Dudllan, Alys

D odging the pork leg and bunches of onions that hung on the ceiling near the entrance, I emerged in the kitchen where I started when I saw my children sitting quietly at the table while they relished fresh, lukewarm goat's milk. All of them were absorbed by the tale Gérard recounted about his life in France. But when I overheard parts of the story, I could not believe my ears.

"The man put a rope around the children's necks and hung them on a sidewall. He left them long enough, but he took them down before they died and gave them a brief respite. Only when they thought they were safe, the man sliced their throats in..."

"Doghearted flap-dragon, stop!" I shouted. "What are you thinking, telling my children those horrors?"

Gérard had arrived at Dudllan a few days before Christmas— Jasper Tudor had sent him to protect us. At first, I had declined his offer; I still had Hampton's men, but Gérard was persistent and stood his ground like all Frenchmen. Quickly, he proved useful, especially at poaching on the Ratcliffe family's land. For that reason alone, I granted him leave to stay. Besides, he brought in food and cost me nothing.

"True story," he said.

"Gibberish."

"Oh no, this one is real. It happened when I was still a boy. I recall our governess telling us about it."

"Stop scaring my children. You're fortunate enough it was Jasper Tudor who sent you here; otherwise, I would have sent you back to your barbaric land."

He nodded and bit his lips as if he tried to suppress a smile, which fueled my anger, and then said: "They're not scared. They love to hear—" A messenger interrupted our conversation.

"Message for Mistress Cloppelin."

I moved forward and held out my hand. But the man whose clothes and boots were spattered with fresh mud brought the letter closer to his chest.

"You're the countess of Dudllan, aren't you?"

"I am, indeed. Now, give me the letter. I'll pass it to Mistress Cloppelin," I said, doing my best to control my growing irritation.

"Forgive me, but I've received explicit instructions to deliver it to Mistress Cloppelin only."

"She isn't here, but I expect she'll return soon. You can trust me."

"Sorry, ma'am, I was told to give it to her, no one else," he insisted.

"The letter is for Mistress Cloppelin, not for the Pope. Give me the letter!"

"I've received orders. I cannot give you this message."

His foolish loyalty alarmed me. Someone did not want me to see the contents of that letter. No messenger would have been that stubborn unless they were plainly directed not to hand the letter to me, which of course made me also think that the message was about me.

"Well, you are a trusted servant," I said, doing my best to appear calm. "You must be drained from the long journey. Please sit with us and have a malt beer and some pâté. You can wait for Mistress Cloppelin here if you wish," I said as I poured him a cup of ale. "Keep an eye on him. Don't let him go anywhere," I whispered to Gérard, and then I left the room calmly. But I knew Gérard wouldn't have to do much, for my boys had already started to question the messenger about where he came from and what he had seen on the way.

Reassured that he would not be able to move from the kitchen for a while, once I passed the door, I rushed to the guards' quarters.

"Come, I've an intruder in the kitchens. Subdue him and bring me the letter he's carrying."

Immediately, my men headed towards the kitchens, and in no time, they took control of the messenger and handed me the letter while I ordered my children to return to the solar with Gérard.

I had to read the letter a few times to ensure that the sender was indeed Estrilda. Lysbette had worried that Estrilda might have changed, but she was far from the truth. And she was wrong. The only model Estrilda was following was the queen. After all I had done for that ungrateful idiot, she had changed side and had let the queen manipulate her. Estrilda was a brainless coward.

If the letter had mentioned Willem's arrest, it would not have surprised me, but it was about Lysbette. Undoubtedly, the queen would stop at nothing to get revenge. It seemed that she'd continue until all my friends and allies have been vanquished, until no one was left to raise a rebellion, until she'd taken all the wealth of England for herself and her enormous, commoner family.

Oh, Estrilda... what lies did the queen tell you for you to turn against me?

The more I thought about it, the more my heart was torn and bruised by Estrilda's betrayal. I had done her no wrong. I would have understood her hatred if it was otherwise, but I had always ensured she had everything she needed.

"What should we do with the messenger?" one of my guards asked.

"Lock him up for a week and then release him. We do not want him to return straight to London to alert the sender that his letter did not reach the recipient."

As they took him away, I walked to the fireplace and threw the letter on the burning ashes, letting the fire shrink the paper and melt the ink as if it would make it all go away.

"Mother, something is going on outside," said Geoffrey as he rushed back into the kitchen.

"What is it now?" I said as I followed my son to the courtyard.

Dusk had settled, and the few torches around the courtyard were not bright enough to allow me to identify the face of the visitor, but I heard Gérard talking to a man behind the portcullis. "The countess wishes to see no one."

"You don't understand. If you tell lady Alys who I am, she will want to see me," the man replied.

That voice! I knew it... Covering my shoulders and neck with my shawl, I hastened to the entrance. My heart thudded hard as I moved nearer and recognized the man: "Let him in, let him in," I yelled, and before the portcullis was fully raised, I slipped under it and jumped to embrace Fauconberg.

Being in a man's arms made all my fears melt with one stroke on my back. It was awkwardly pleasant, even if he did not smell particularly fresh. Fauconberg's embrace was the haven I had needed. For a fleeting moment, I wished he was Hampton, and I closed my eyes. As he moved back, his unshaved, bushy cheeks brushed mine, and I lifted my eyes to him, still holding him, and then as if to bring me back to my senses, a hint of his odor wafted in my face, and I moved out of his arms.

"I thought they got hold of you," I said. "That... you were dead."

"They've tracked me like an animal, but they will not catch me so easily."

"Look at you, Captain! You're all bones. When was the last time you had something to eat? Come," I said, taking his hands. He looked ashamed and lowered his eyes.

Comforted by his presence, I led him to the kitchen where I prepared a tray with some sugared fruits from the orchard, as well as some leftovers of boar, smoked herring, and bread and cheese, then I placed it on the table. As soon as I sat in front of him, he grabbed the food with no manners.

"I am so pleased to see you're safe," I said.

"If it had been possible, I would have come earlier, but I was abroad," he said with a mouth full of bread.

"Is that where you left your manners?"

Promptly, he wiped his mouth and straightened on the bench. "Pardon me, I'm ravenous."

"Think nothing of it. I'm only tormenting you... go on, eat and drink as much as you'd like and use both hands if you wish. Who am I to give you an etiquette lesson? I am just a prisoner."

Fauconberg picked up a piece of herring, and I was not willing to interrupt him, for he evidently was starving. He was a man who had always served Hampton with pride, and now it was as if he had none left. Once he had finished, I took him to a bedchamber.

"Were you in France?" I asked as we climbed the stairs of the north tower.

"Yes, it was the only place I would have been safe."

Fauconberg was not a man to cover from insecurity, and so I could not accept his response. He'd had no purpose for going there — unless it was to join Tudor, but that made little sense. Did he intend to continue Hampton's work without involving me?

"Please get a maid to prepare a bath and fetch some clothes of lord Hampton," I asked one of the domestics as we approached the bedchamber.

"No, I cannot accept. Not his clothes. This is too much."

"I don't believe he would have minded. Furthermore, it would take too long to wash those," I said, gesturing at his filthy tunic and breeches. "And it would be quite inappropriate to have you parading around naked for a few days."

He glanced down and blushed; only then I realized what I had done, but shaming him had not been my intention, on the contrary.

"Stay in those clothes if you feel more comfortable, but Hampton won't need them anymore."

"You're right; I could do with a bath and some fresh clothes. It is just that..."

"I understand... No need to say it..." Then I chuckled. "I remember that once, a long time ago, you were the one waiting for me to wash off the smell of the beast. Do you remember?" We both laughed.

"Years have gone by since then," he said as he pushed the door open.

"Ten long years. Sometimes I wish I could go back." I paused for a short reminiscent moment, then I continued: "I'll leave you to rest. You can tell me all about your French adventure in the morning. Good night, Captain."

"Good night, my lady. It's good to be back."

IN THE MORNING, LIKE every day, I was up with the dawn and paid a visit to Tristan, but as we were about to go out into the woods, I saw Fauconberg leaving the castle by foot. Curious, I followed without making him aware of my presence, but when Fauconberg entered the village church, I turned around, slightly disappointed. What was I expecting? A dream? A miracle? Fauconberg, still a good Christian, was only attending church, and there would have been no opportunity for him to do so at the castle, as it was long since there had been a chaplain at Dudllan. People had been talking behind my back for that reason, and because I had not continued the religious education of my children. But God had abandoned me, and even if many times I had feared to go to Hell, I could not bring my heart to God, who had taken so many people I loved in the past. After Mass, Fauconberg joined us in the solar where my children and I were reading the Round Table story. It has always been my favorite, and now it was the boys' favorite, too. Not that Arthur could understand, but the illuminations in the manuscripts seemed to fascinate him.

"Geoffrey, do you remember our dear Captain Fauconberg, your father's cousin and confidant?" I asked, closing the books as Fauconberg stepped in.

"I do," he said, and then he turned to Fauconberg and thrust himself forward as this would dissuade Fauconberg to approach any closer. "Where were you? Mother needed you and you abandoned her like a coward! I doubt that my father would have been proud of you."

"Geoffrey!" I shouted.

"Let him speak, my lady. Young Geoffrey is right, for I've failed to keep my promise to lord Hampton. I should have been there for you and not run to France. Pardon my cowardice."

"You'd be dead if you hadn't run. What is done is done!" I stared at the man I could hardly recognize. A man that war and England had broken. "I'm afraid I've more bad news; Master Parker has been arrested, and the queen has ordered the arrest of Lysbette. She has probably been arrested now; she left Dudllan a few weeks ago. The warning letter arrived last night. Edward must feel terribly insecure to think that we are preparing another rebellion. Sit down," I said as I gestured for him to take the sit opposite me.

"With what? We've no funds, and there is nothing we can do. We've lost."

"Oh no, you're wrong, Captain. We've only a lost a battle. That's what Hampton would have said. Now that you're back, we can continue, and this time we will win... for him."

"No one will rebel against Edward now that King Henry and his son are dead."

"Have you forgotten that there is still someone else who could challenge the king?" I said as I let Arthur to the floor.

"Don't tell me you are thinking of..."

"Indeed, I—"

"But he has nothing; no one will follow him. This is a lost cause."

"Henry Tudor is still young, and although I receive no news of him, I know he's in France." I stood and crossed the room to pour some wine into cups. "I've already written to the king of France, whom I'm sure will give us his support. Didn't you say you were in France? Surely you must have heard that Henry and Jasper retreated there."

"I... No, I've heard nothing about them," he said and crossed his arms, burying himself in the chair.

Alienor started to cry, so I picked her up from her crib. Fauconberg told me he was in France. How could he not have heard about Tudor when Robyn, his protégé, was there with them? Fauconberg was lying, but why? He had never lied to me before. Was it because he did not trust me anymore? He had known me for years, and I had always trusted him. Why was he lying now? But I did not have the heart to argue with him.

"Well, I'm sure that king Louis will be in touch soon," I said as I rocked Alienor against my shoulder.

Fauconberg laughed as if I was not someone to be taken seriously.

"We can continue. We must."

"Forgive me, I do not wish to offend you, but no one will follow a woman. I regret to say this, but you must admit defeat. The king of France is no longer your ally, and he does not wish to be involved in the conflicts in England."

"How do you know?" I asked, but Fauconberg did not respond. "Why are you giving up on everything Hampton fought for? Why did you bother coming back if it is only to take my hopes away? You might as well be dead; it would make no difference," I said, and straightaway regretted it. Fortunately, he did not seem affected by my words.

"Believe me, if I still had men behind me, I would continue. But I'm alone; I will never be able to raise an army. I don't have the means, and neither do you."

"We need time, that's all. As I said, I've contacted King Louis. And regardless of what you think, I know he will send me the funds. I know how he thinks, and most of all, I know what he wants. King Louis works with promises."

"You seem pretty sure of yourself. Why would he do that?"

"I've offered him something he cannot refuse."

Fauconberg looked at me quizzically, waiting for more, but I gestured towards my boys who, although they pretended to be busy, were listening to every word. "I'll tell you later," I said as I put Alienor back in her cot. Then, as I went to sit at the desk, I realized I still had the ring he had left me after we were told about Hampton's death. I took it off and handed it back to him.

"You've kept it!"

"Of course. Take it back, it is yours."

He picked it up and stared at it. "Any news from Robyn?" he asked.

"Last I've heard, he was in France with Jasper and Henry. Robyn is not one to stay in a quiet place like Dudllan. He prefers the rough life of a soldier to the comfort of a castle, not that Dudllan has much to offer."

"I'm here, my lady," said the nursemaid as she entered.

"Thank you," I said and then turned to Fauconberg. "Want to go for a ride?"

He nodded and followed me to the stables.

"YOU'RE STILL HERE," Fauconberg told Tristan as he entered and patted his neck as Tristan's inquisitive nose sniffed my hands in the hope to find some treats.

"My most faithful companion for the last sixteen years. He'd never leave me to go to France like you or Robyn did," I said.

"Robyn's a good lad; you should call him back. Besides, I don't believe I will stay here much longer; you need someone who can fight by your side, and Robyn's your man."

"I have my sons. They are still young, but Geoffrey is feisty, and I also have Gérard, the Frenchman who stopped you from entering last night," I said as I released Tristan's rope.

"You need someone who was trained by Hampton or me, not a suspicious Frenchman. How do you know he is not working for the Woodvilles? Which horse am I riding?"

"Take Ginger. He has not been ridden for a while, though." I gestured towards Tristan's stable companion.

Fauconberg approached the horse. "Promise me you will write to Robyn and order him to come back."

"No, he is not mine to order. Robyn is a free man."

"A faithful one who will forever be in your debt."

"I refuse. Robyn owes me nothing, and I will not blackmail him for something I did over ten years ago. Just like I once released you from a promise, I have released Robyn from any oath he would have made to Hampton or myself." I led Tristan out of the stables and tied him to a hook in the stable yard.

"But who will look after you and your sons?" he asked as he followed me with his horse.

Dudllan stable yard was usually the liveliest place in the castle, as this was where the men spent all day, constantly training as they used to when Hampton was alive, though they had seen little action for the last few months. At least it meant that the day we'd raise a rebellion, they'd be ready and eager to go to battle. Sometimes I felt a little ashamed of how the whole place looked decrepit, more like a village square than a castle courtyard.

"We've managed for the last few months; I am sure we can continue. One day I'll get back the money from my businesses. Until the king of France sends his help, we're selling our crops."

"Your income is just enough to cover your taxes. You might not have enough to feed everyone. How do you expect to finance a rebellion? What can I do to convince you it is over?"

"Captain. Not you! You cannot give up. You've always been one for battles and rebellions, and you always supported Hampton. Whatever decision he took, you never questioned him. Why have you changed your mind? You are not the man I once knew."

"Lord Hampton had men behind him, men ready to fight and die for him because he had plans to put someone else on the throne, because he had noble families ready to rebel against the king. He had an endless fortune. With all due respect, you are nothing."

I shrugged and brushed Tristan's mane.

"Please do not think I am disrespecting you, for this is not what I mean to do. I shall always be faithful to you, but this is the truth."

"I agree, I am nothing, but my son is the earl of Dudllan."

Fauconberg lifted an eyebrow and said: "Geoffrey is only ten years old!" A groom brought Fauconberg a saddle and bridle.

"Please, what must I do to convince you that I will not give up?"

"There is nothing more you can do. You must abandon all idea of revenge and accept your fate." Fauconberg had hardly finished his sentence that a loud rumble resounded in the sky as if God himself disagreed with his statement.

"As a prisoner? No, I will not accept this. It is not my fate. I will fight for the wheel of fortune to turn in our favor. It always does."

"Do you want your saddle, my lady?" Gérard asked as he came into the stable yard. "I was about to go hunting if you want to join me," he continued and shot a glance at Fauconberg.

"That's an excellent idea, isn't it, Fauconberg?" I said, as low, heavy dark clouds accumulated in the sky and usually, January storm were not the kind to bring a warm, refreshing rain.

"Not really," he said. Then as Gérard entered the saddle room, Fauconberg whispered: "Why is this man here?"

"Jasper Tudor sent him."

"How do you know?"

"Because he told me."

"And you trust a Frenchman?" he asked as he passed the bridle around Ginger's head.

"Do you care to join Gérard and me, or do you prefer riding on your own?" I asked, exasperated by his endless questioning. Then Gérard returned, and I took the saddle from his hand. "Thank you, I'll tack Tristan myself."

"Let me help, my lady. It is always a pleasure," Gérard said, and I saw him glancing at Fauconberg. I was not quite sure why Gérard played that game, but I found it somewhat distracting and flattering.

"Isn't Gérard wonderful?" I told Fauconberg.

"Indeed," he said. Then between clenched teeth, he asked: "Has he tried to court you, too?"

"Would you care if he had?"

"No. Anyway, we were having a conversation before we were rudely interrupted, and my reply to this is that I will see what I can do."

"I knew I could count on you," I said, securing Tristan's bridle. "But I hope you are not doing this just because you are jealous of a Frenchman."

He shrugged, and I mounted Tristan. Then I bent towards Fauconberg. "Although it pains me to do so, we can always ask Margaret Beaufort for her support. She is one of the wealthiest women in the country now, and she'd do anything to have her son back in England."

"And you forget that she is also a woman who hates you as much as the queen does."

"In battle, it is better to join forces; that is what Hampton taught me. As long as we aim for the same goal, we can put our enmity aside, at least for a little while," I said as I bent in the saddle to be closer to him.

"I will deal with her. In the meantime, gather funds. As much you can, and we'll just have to pray that the king of France will give Tudor his support, but it might take a few years before the boy is ready."

"Patience is a virtue we should all have. I couldn't live with the idea that Hampton died in vain, so a few years waiting for victory is good enough for me."

"Hampton was right when he said you should have married Edward. You would have made an amazing queen." Fauconberg patted Tristan's neck, and then he stepped back.

"Well, this is in the past, and Edward is no longer a friend. I am house-jailed because of him."

"Then you will have no objection if he becomes a prisoner of France."

"None at all."

As we passed under the portcullis, I twisted in the saddle to look at Fauconberg. I could not believe he had agreed to help because he was jealous of a Frenchman. Not jealous because he loved me the way a man loves a woman, but like a brother protects his sister, or perhaps more like a brother would defend his brother's property.

For the first time in a long time, with the canter through the forest and the hope that Fauconberg had brought, life had returned slowly within my veins, and I smiled all the way to the river. Edward and his wife were in for a big surprise, hopefully soon.

CHAPTER SIX
March 1472, London, Estrilda

All morning people had been in and out the service gates by the road and by the river, with carts full of game, barrels and crates of all kinds of victuals. Almost a whole winter's worth of provisions would be consumed in one single evening. The king's anniversary, a day to enjoy. Also, an excellent opportunity for Estrilda to put her mind at peace and push aside the recent troubles. There was still hope.

Even if she was still mourning, she wasn't keen on constantly wearing black; it did not particularly flatter her complexion. However, vanity was not something Estrilda could afford at the moment; besides, she had to be as invisible as possible to keep her father-in-law content and to avoid attracting attention to herself so that he would forget about her, about her past, and let her live at court in peace.

"Hey, watch where you're going, my lady," shouted a kitchen wench when, lost in her thoughts, Estrilda nearly tripped over a bucket full of animal guts.

"Sorry," she replied absently.

Then she rushed through the gardens to avoid the backyard, full of feathers after the kitchen domestics had plucked crested pheasants and hazel grouse all morning. As she came face to face with the duke of Gloucester, Estrilda froze and then she became flustered. The palpitations of her heartbeat sped up when Richard acknowledged her presence. As if guilty, she immediately lowered her eyes, feeling his gaze on her.

Many times, Estrilda had dreamt about the duke when her husband was alive, which of course was a sin. And now she was a widow and still not allowed to long for someone else, so she curtseyed to Richard and continued. The queen had wanted her to stay in her service, which was fortunate, and so she had to ensure that everything she was doing was as per Elizabeth's expectations. After all, she had been kind, and in a way, she had soothed Estrilda's pain. Thus, Estrilda was adamant: she would not dishonor the queen. Besides, her situation did not allow her to think of pleasure. She pushed the thoughts of Richard aside and scurried across the gardens without even stopping by to enjoy the beautiful sunrays that illuminated the daffodils.

The entire palace was in preparation for the evening. From the queen's private chamber, they could hear the clatter of pans, the scraping of trestle tables and benches that the domestics were transporting to the great hall. As they were finishing the last adjustments to their garments for the evening festivities, they heard raised voices in the corridor. It sounded like Lysbette, but it was impossible. Estrilda had told her to go to Flanders. Then Lysbette forced her way through the door and prostrated herself before the queen.

"Your Majesty, I beg you to intercede with the king to release my husband; he has been arrested, but he is innocent."

"Who are you?"

Lysbette stood up and curtseyed. "Pardon me, your Grace, my name is Lysbette Cloppelin."

"How dare you show yourself before me on a day like this? We have a warrant for your arrest. I could call the guards and have you arrested at once."

"I know you've a good heart, which is why I came to you. My husband is innocent."

"Your husband has been dealing with the countess of Dudllan, and he has supported lord Hampton's rebellion."

"Your Grace, the information you've received is wrong. He is only a merchant. The countess offered him some business, and he saw an opportunity to make more money. But I can vouch that he has never conspired against the throne."

"He helped funding the rebellions."

"Please, you must trust me. My husband wasn't aware they were plotting against our king. What will become of my children and me if you keep him locked away?"

"You can only blame yourself for having put him in contact with Dudllan. I can do nothing, for this is the king's decision. Now please leave before I call the guards."

"Estrilda, please say something," Lysbette begged.

At once the queen shot Estrilda a dark glance. "What is it with the familiarity?" she asked Lysbette.

"I... I have been a faithful customer for a while, and Mistress Cloppelin and I spent many hours talking fabric," Estrilda replied. Then Lysbette looked down, and Estrilda shot her a furious look for not having listened to her advice. Lysbette should have left the country. Estrilda could not believe Lysbette almost blew her secret in front of the queen.

Lysbette did not realize how tenuous Estrilda's position was: a word misunderstood and unintentionally wrongly placed, and the queen could have turned her fury against Estrilda.

"Well, Mistress Cloppelin, just because my ladies-in-waiting spend their wages at your stall does not allow you to be so familiar. There is a certain rank you should respect. The countess of Dudllan might have allowed you to think you were equals, but that does not mean you are permitted to do this with other members of the nobility." Then the queen turned to Estrilda. "Please bring me the pearl necklace of my mother. You will find it in the royal garderobe storage room. The rest of you, please leave us," she said, and Estrilda knew this was her way of requesting to be on her own with Lysbette and to keep Estrilda further away.

Putting her work aside, Estrilda curtseyed and left the chamber. Then she rushed through the many corridors that were already full of the aroma of roasted meat and strong herbs. She stepped down to the cellars, crossing the dark and humid corridors that led to the other side of the palace. The outbuilding where the king and queen kept the items they were not using on regular basis was not a place Estrilda frequently visited. To avoid catching a cold in these wind traps, she wrapped her shawl around her shoulders. After a long walk through the dark and cold gallery, she finally noticed faint daylight from under the door.

"The queen has sent me to get her mother's necklace," Estrilda told the guard as she reached the door, and so he moved aside to let her in.

The room was full of treasures and coffers, statues, gowns, and valuable jewelry. Beautiful ones. Fascinated,

Estrilda scrutinized the room and then spotted the coffer that used to be in the queen's chambers. Tiptoeing wasn't enough, thus she stretched out to reach the top, but she was still a foot too short. She glanced around for a chair or something to climb on. There was nothing. Then she studied the cabinet for a moment. It looked strong enough to support her weight; however, she was not an agile person.

Even if the queen had only used the necklace as an excuse to get Estrilda out of the room, she had to return with it. Especially after Lysbette's remarks, Estrilda ought to do her best to stay on the queen's good side. As she lifted her gown, she attempted to put a foot on the side of the cabinet, which proved rather difficult if not almost impossible.

"Let me do, my lady," she heard someone say. Thus, she removed her foot from the cabinet and turned to look at her savior. Her back brushed his torso. Apologetically, Estrilda thanked him. But when she realized it was Richard, she immediately stepped back and curtseyed.

"Please rise. There is no need for this formality. No one else is here."

A little embarrassed, Estrilda smiled but did not dare speak. Then he asked: "Will you come to the banquet tonight—lady Stanley, isn't it?"

"Indeed, your Grace. All the queen's ladies will be present tonight, for we have prepared a small performance for the king. I hope he will be pleased with it."

"Knowing my brother, I'm certain he will rejoice in the spectacle. You must do me the honor of a dance after the banquet."

"I'm still in mourning, your Grace."

"I'll ask permission for you. After all, this is the king's special day, everything is permitted tonight."

Their hands gently brushed. The warmth and softness of his palms aroused her desire to touch his cheeks, to have his smell on her skin a little longer. Estrilda refrained from smiling and misbehaving. What would people think of her if they were to see her? A disgrace! But it was stronger than her self-control. She could not keep her eyes off him. As soon as their eyes met, guilt burned her cheeks. It wasn't the moment to let her feelings go: Lysbette was in danger, and she dared to think about romantic matters. What a terrible daughter she was.

"I must get the pearl necklace to the queen. I presume it is in the coffer over there," she said, pointing at the top of the shelf.

Even for Richard it was a little high, but after a slight effort, he grabbed the coffer and handed it to her.

"Thank you," she said as she opened it. There were many necklaces, but she immediately recognized the one she needed; it was laid on top of the others. "I must go," Estrilda said as she put the necklace into her purse.

"Wait! Take this." He held out a sprig of dried lavender which he took out of his pocket.

"This is beautiful, thank you." Estrilda brought it to her nose and breathed in the well-needed soothing fragrance before heading back to her duties.

WHEN ESTRILDA RETURNED to the queen's chamber with the necklace, Queen Elizabeth was on her own, staring out of the window. Lysbette was no longer there, but Estrilda dared not ask where she was, for Estrilda wanted no one to suspect that she cared for her. Acting as normal as possible wasn't easy, but somehow, she managed. Now Estrilda had to hide her thoughts about Lysbette and so to distract her mind from Lysbette, Estrilda gently squeezed the herbs Richard gave her and replayed what had just happened in the Royal Garderobe. For a brief instant, she wondered what it would be like to be married to a duke; that would certainly stop her father-in-law from revealing her little secret. Estrilda even caught herself imagining entering the great hall as the duchess of Gloucester. She beamed. Her smile was probably too broad for the queen asked what was causing her to smile so idiotically.

"Nothing, Your Grace," she lied clumsily.

"Up to a few weeks ago, you were constantly sitting with a long face which is comprehensible after what happened. But recently, you've looked happier; you are smiling for no apparent reason. In fact, you've got that gleam in your eye, and it isn't because I've ordered the arrest of that merchant's wife," she said, looking at the necklace and putting it on the top of her desk.

At those words, Estrilda tried to hide the horror and surprise that just crossed her mind and understood the reason Elizabeth'd asked them to leave. She did not want her ladies to witness the arrest, for she was not acting on the king's orders, but most certainly against his decision.

To take all anger, regret, and guilt out of her mind, Estrilda repeated the name of Richard in her head, and somehow this brought back a smile to her face.

"My dear girl, if I did not savvy you were mourning, I'd say you are in love," the queen said.

Immediately, shame slapped Estrilda in the face and brought her back to reality. The queen was clever, but if she had noticed, someone else might too.

"Oh no, you are mistaken. I've been faithful to my husband."

"You can't hide it from me, Estrilda. I can see what is going on."

"It is nothing. Nothing happened. It is just that I can't help thinking of this particular man. His smile has captured my heart. Even though I should not think of him, I do. All the time."

"Is he married?" she asked as she sat down and invited Estrilda to do the same.

"No, of course not."

The queen suddenly looked more at ease. Did she think Estrilda would have told her if she'd been besotted with the king? King Edward loved his wife very much, but he was also extremely unfaithful. Especially now that he had a son, his visits to the queen's chamber were getting sparser. The king would rather spend most of his nights with his mistresses, and the queen well knew that many of her ladies bedded her husband on regular occasions. That included Estrilda's friend, lady Spencer. Estrilda had not, and that was probably why Queen Elizabeth was kind to her.

"So, who is the fortunate fellow? Do I know him?"

"Please, Your Grace, as you said, I am still mourning. Nothing happened, and I'd rather keep his name to myself if you would allow me."

"Considering you are a widow and that the man in question is unmarried, you have my blessing."

"Thank you, but I don't believe it is necessary, as I could not."

"Estrilda, you are young and beautiful. You will not stay a widow all your life. I'll vouch for you. Do you think I would have married the king if I had not done what was necessary?"

"Even if I would wish to marry him, my husband had no personal fortune, and I am poor. All I have is the allowance you are giving me. I could not marry him, or anyone else in fact."

"Let not the lack of a dowry worry you, I will provide it for you. When I was in sanctuary, you always treated me as a queen. To be truthful, I do not have many confidantes, for people here turn their coats easily, but you have always been there for me, and to have someone loyal by my side is very important. Now, go and find that man. I'll see you at the banquet, I hope you, ladies, are all ready to honor my husband tonight."

"We are. The king will not be disappointed." Estrilda smiled, curtseyed, and left the room.

From seeing such compassion from the queen, Estrilda understood that everything lady Alys had told them about Queen Elizabeth was ignominious lies. The more Estrilda got to know the queen, the more she knew that someone had tried to manipulate her mind, and perhaps the monster was not the one Estrilda had believed to be during all those years, but the one she had trusted. The one who had caused the disgrace of Lysbette and Willem. And it was time she repaired her wrongdoings.

Lady Alys,

Lysbette and Willem Cloppelin were arrested because of you, because you unfairly manipulated them to support lord Hampton's cause against our king. If you still have a little honor in your veins, please write to Queen Elizabeth and explain that both are innocent. They only followed lord Hampton because you ill-influenced them. You might consider you owe them nothing, but both have been, God only knows why, faithful to you. So, you owe it to them.

I'm begging you to act before it is too late.

Estrilda Stanley.

CHAPTER SEVEN
March 1472, Dudllan, Alys

The night seemed so long and after the sight of Hampton's bloody face had woken me, pearling my body with sweat, my heart thumped in my chest. To ease the pain, I drank a goblet of wine in one gulp and returned to bed, forcing myself to recall the good memories of Hampton, in vain. Nothing worked. I turned in the bed, got up again, went back to bed. In the end, just before dawn, I got up, dressed, and took Tristan out. Dawn had not yet arrived, and though there were some eerie sounds in the distance, everything seemed peaceful.

As I crossed the empty streets of the village, wrapped in a heavy cloak, I thought about the few people who had been kind to me over the years, but it was not the same without a man to help me, and being banned from court frightened most people. When Hampton was alive, it was different. In a way, I had his power then. Without even trying, I'd gained people's respect. Now he was no longer there, I realized their loyalty was because they were either on his side, or because they feared him. Everyone had a reason to follow him, and without his presence and power to support me, some people saw no reason to continue their support. Jasper Tudor had left the country, and the Yorks were the victors. I was on the losing side.

As I reached the seaside, a low base of thick, gray clouds swirled above the sea over the horizon like a partition. The sky above the beach was still bright, and the sunrise illuminated the sand, but the murk would soon invade the land. With damp cloak and hair, I cantered along the beach. Riding Tristan with my hair loose, my riding breeches and boots brought me back ten years ago, when I was innocent and yet probably rather stupid. There was not a day where my mind did not take me back in time, back to Hampton. And then I saw the fog coming over me from the sea. I could not see farther than Tristan's ears; it was thicker than ever.

Once the land was entirely hidden under thick, almost charcoal, clouds my heart thumped harder, and all at once, the nightmares about Hampton shifted from the back of my mind, frightening me. Even the forest was hidden. Panicked, I trembled uncontrollably.

"Come on, Tristan, we've got to go back."

When I arrived closer to the castle, I spotted the shadow of an army displaying an insignia. If it weren't for the sound of horses' hooves crushing the undergrowth and the rustle of leather breeches against saddles, no screams or metal clanging, I would have thought my nightmare had come to life, except that it was all more serene.

For a brief instant, I dreamed that Hampton would emerge out of the fog. I recalled him telling me to stop reading romances and to become more responsible, as was my duty. My smile faded when I distinguished the king's livery.

Worried that Fauconberg would be caught by the king's men, I pushed Tristan to reach our courtyard before the king and his retinue. I had lost Hampton because of Edward, and I would not let him take Fauconberg from me. But Edward and his troops arrived at the gate at the same time as I did. Glancing around for a sight of Fauconberg, I shouted as loud as I could:

"Make way for the king!" Hoping that if Fauconberg were around, he would hear and hide. Then Tristan and I entered the courtyard first, and I dismounted and gave the reins to Gérard.

"Rub him down with straw," I said and patted Tristan's back.

"You were out early," he said. "Is everything all right?"

"The king is here. Of course, things aren't all right."

Keeping my angered eyes firmly on Edward while he dismounted and getting my bravery from the twenty guards standing behind me, I waited by the water trough. I had not seen Edward since the day he ordered my house arrest, and it was his fault that I was without Hampton. All my troubles were his fault. I did not bow as he approached; instead, I stood proud and straight.

"My dear lady Alys," he said, opening his arms as if the events of the last few years had not altered our friendship.

"Your Grace," I said, and eventually inclined my head slightly.

"What a cold welcome. Won't you invite your king inside for some refreshments? The air is chilly this morning."

Without a word, I gestured towards the stairs and headed for the keep.

"Would you like us to accompany you, my lady?" asked one of my men.

I looked inquisitively at Edward who, without being prompted, removed his sword and handed it to one of my guards. "That won't be necessary; I do not intend to harm my hostess," Edward said. But my guards glanced at me for approval, and I nodded.

When Edward and I entered the solar, I headed to the side cabinet and took a pitcher of ale and two cups.

"So, what brings you to Dudllan?" I asked as I approached Edward, who took a seat by the fireplace and warmed up his hands over the flames.

"It's almost a year since Hampton passed away."

"Surely you meant to say 'since he was murdered', as you are perfectly aware that he did not pass away peacefully, surrounded by those who loved him to help him on his last journey," I said, filing up the cups with ale.

"It was a tragic accident. But I'm not responsible for what happened to him."

"Oh yes, you are. He would still be alive now if you had not married that witch!"

"That is the queen you are talking about!" he said, leapt to his feet and bounced towards me, his cheeks reddened with anger.

"She will never be my queen. She was never Hampton's either." I handed him a cup that he immediately left on the side of the table.

"Let me remind you that I married her because you broke your vows."

"Only because you had married another woman in secret, or have you forgotten already?" I asked, raising my voice.

"She wasn't important," he said, putting a hand on my arm. All of a sudden, his gesture left me petrified. "I would have married you, and you would have been the queen of England, but you threw it all away. It was your fault. So perhaps the person responsible for Hampton's death is you. None of this would have happened if you had married me as planned." Then he picked his goblet from the tablet and sipped a little out of it.

"It is far easier to blame someone else for your mistakes. I know... for I used to do the same, to suppress any guilt, to feel only anger." He stood so close to me that my nostrils detected a whiff of sandalwood. I stepped away from him.

"The only anger I feel right now is that there are still people plotting against me, and you know who they are."

"How would I? I've not been out of Dudllan for months. Anyway, tell me how anyone could plot against you when you are tracking everyone like game."

"Those people are against me, and I must prevent them from planning another rebellion. I will have no one disputing my authority and my place on the throne, or even being against the queen I've chosen to rule by my side."

"In this case, keep depriving me of my freedom, for I might plot a rebellion when you release me."

He laughed. "Oh yes, you're more than capable, but you will not," he said, trying to put a hand on my forearm.

I stepped back, eschewing his gesture. The idea of him being so close to me brought tension into my spine and rage in my stomach.

"Don't fear me. I never was your enemy and will never be."

"But you will always be mine. Please, Edward, leave Dudllan and never come back. I do not wish to see you ever again." My breathing started to speed up, and I had to draw a long breath to calm my drumming heart.

"Hush, hush... I know you are angry with me, but I'm not responsible for his death... You are. As I said, had you been my wife, he would not have rebelled, and he would still be here now."

That was so cruel; perhaps because it was true. I had killed Hampton because I was an egoist.

"Did you come here to torment me?" I asked.

"Not at all. I was visiting my son at Ludlow when something reminded of you. It has been a long time since I'd last heard from you, and I wondered how you were. Curiosity, nothing else."

"We have been on opposite sides for years now, and I'm your prisoner. Why would you care how I am doing?"

"Isn't it time we put the past behind us? I loved Hampton as a brother, and I will always respect him for what he taught me. I regret what happened, but I cannot change it. England needed peace, and now we have it, we must work towards the prosperity of my country."

"Do you honestly believe it is over?" In a way, the fact that he thought the battles and plotting was over suited my plans.

"King Henry and his descendants are dead. There is no one left to challenge my authority."

"What about your brothers or Tudor?"

"Henry Tudor is no danger, for he has no right to my throne, and with regard to my brothers, they are loyal."

"I would not trust George, if I were you."

"He's happy with Hampton's fortune. He'll never rebel again."

My mood darkened at the idea that George was now enjoying the benefit of his evil deeds. I turned around and paced to the window, incapable of thinking straight. Down in the courtyard, I saw my boys pestering Edward's men, probably asking questions about London. For some reason, every time we had a visitor, they felt the needed to question them. Did they hope to get some impossible news out of them?

"Pardon my lack of diplomacy. I should not have mentioned this. Let's forget about it. Let's go and see your sons. I would be delighted to meet them," Edward said, joining me by the window.

How could I ever forget, Edward? I hate George with all my soul.

To avoid having him standing too close to me, I moved to the door and called for my sons to meet the king. When Geoffrey entered, I noticed his lack of enthusiasm to meet Edward, and his brothers, who were following him like they were his shadow, just took example from his reluctance to bow to the king.

"Young Earl of Dudllan, what a pleasure to see you're well."

Geoffrey only bowed without replying. Had he been older, he would have reacted differently and would have made the most of the opportunity to get rid of the king but getting rid of Edward now was not a wise decision. He had an heir, and should anything happen to him, his son would then be the king and Elizabeth would be even more powerful. I hated Edward for what he had done, but since I had no one on my side and he had made the first step to visit me, I had to ensure that he'd be clement to my appeal. Even though being pleasant to him was painful, I knew that I had to. Hampton had been capable of putting his hatred aside and being sympathetic to an enemy when needed. I had seen it so many times. Thus, I just had to pretend it was a game and it would be so much easier.

"Why are your sons still living with you? They should be placed with other families to learn their duties."

"Geoffrey and Edmund were educated by their father. As for Louis... well, I can't bear the idea of him living with anyone else. He is bright, and in time he'll learn his duties, and Arthur is still an infant."

"Do you expect them to become farmers and find some nice peasant women to marry? They already reeked like them."

The boys spent most of their days outside with the animals, helping where they could and I had actually never noticed, until Edward pointed it out that all of them carried around the smell of chickens and pigs. I lowered my eyes in shame.

"Send Louis to court, he will be a great page, and I will find squire positions for Geoffrey and Edmund, so they can catch up on their education," Edward continued.

"My sons are going nowhere without me."

"Are we going to London?" Edmund asked, reminding me that the three of them had suddenly become silent to spy on the conversation. I turned to them and saw three little sheep, quietly sitting in chairs by the fire side. Oh, these boys- as bad as me when I was their age.

"No, you are not. Now get out of here and stop prying on my conversation with the king." I gestured to the door. "And ask your nurse to prepare you a bath, all of you!" I shouted as they scampered out the door.

"You must be reasonable. I thought you were capable of anything to protect them. Educating your children will help them," Edward said once my sons were out.

Taking the flagon of ale, I refilled the goblets and handed one to Edward. "I also savvy that sending them into families related to your wife will put their lives in danger. I'd rather send them to King Louis than to any traitor in England."

"Traitors?"

"People who have turned their back on Hampton are traitors to me," I said as I contemplated the content of my goblet.

He grinned. "You're impossible. Still like the young Alys of Lochlainn. I thought that Hampton's death would have calmed your ardor, but I can see the same fire is still flowing in that stubborn little head."

THE DAY WENT ON AND Edward was still at Dudllan, so I felt obliged to invite him to stay for the night. The evening meal was no banquet, and the great hall was too cold— it would have taken too long before we could set trestle tables to accommodate the king and his small retinue. Thus, I changed nothing of our habits, and we took our meal in the kitchen where the large oak table could take all the guests in one sitting and the temperature was more bearable. Also, we served nothing extraordinary, only the same food as on an ordinary day: cabbage soup, bread, cheese, freshly caught salmon and sorrel sauce, and salted pork. Not that I wanted to insult the king, but we had to look after the little we had left, and we could certainly not afford to spend more than usual.

"You've arrested my associate, Master Parker, when will you release him?" I asked as we all sat around the kitchen table with the domestics serving our meagre repast.

"Lady Alys, you are not unaware of my admiration for you, but you must also know that I cannot afford to have people becoming richer than I am. People cannot raise armies against me. I will free your associate and let you trade again the day I get your assurance you accept me as your king and will forget about what lord Hampton had pursued."

At last, I could see a glimmer of hope, and perhaps Edward would become amenable to my request. It was now up to me to ensure that by the time he left Dudllan, my fortune would be granted. I sipped the wine, holding his stare.

"I'm a woman with no power, Your Grace. Even if I had lord Hampton's fortune, no men in their right mind would follow a woman, would they? I am no threat to the Yorks' crown," I said, drinking more wine.

"Margaret of Anjou was a woman."

"She was a queen, and she had her own men and supporters. Who do I have?" I asked, waving my hands in the air, and then glanced at my four boys who were gulping down their soup and bread rather loudly, without a care in the world. It was a little sad that our noble blood was now reduced to eat like peasants and dressed like them too. Shame hit me when I noticed the mud stains on Louis's and Edmund's faces—although they did not seem to worry about the future, only to stuff their bellies with as much potage as possible.

"You are not much different. And you might think you are nothing like Margaret of Anjou, but I can see the resemblance between you two; the same determination is flowing through your veins. She fought until she had nothing left to fight for."

"In this case, I too have nothing to fight for either; that means you can free Master Parker and return me my fortune. Let me trade, please. I am no rebel."

"You won't convince me so quickly. I savvy who taught you to be cunning and I would not believe in your sudden loyalty because of your beautiful smile, Countess."

"What proof would you need?" I asked, swallowing another goblet of wine.

Edward did not reply, but his eyes were burning with a desire I thought he had lost years ago. His gaze warmed up my cheeks. This was awkward. I could not stoop to those kinds of feelings, not for him... Or perhaps I could. I just had to control them and make sure I would not fall for him. If I were to give him a glimpse of hope that he could have what he had coveted a long time ago, he would return my patents and then I would have enough funds to bring Tudor to England and challenge Edward. All I had to do was to apply to the letter the rules of courtly love that the countess had so often wished I learned... I had paid little attention when they tried to teach me, so I knew only the basics.

The wine scented the room more than the leftovers on our trenchers. I sipped my seventh goblet slowly, letting its aroma and sweetness go down my throat while keeping my eyes on Edward. Then I said: "If you were to give me a little time, I am sure that I could show my loyalty to your crown."

"How?" he whispered with a gleam in his eyes.

"You might have guessed," I whispered too, ensuring my sons would not notice this sudden courtly tone.

"This will keep me in a good mood for my return journey. With regret, I must leave now. I would have gladly stayed a little longer, but parliament requires my presence in a few weeks, and the queen should not suspect I have been here."

"A king should oversee his own activities. Come back as soon as you want," I said, still trying to keep his interest going, but he moved and beckoned his men to follow him.

Night had fallen a while ago and as the king and his troops prepared their horses for departure, making our courtyard as animated as it was years ago when Hampton used to spend time here, horses were stomping on their hooves, impatient to leave when a messenger reached the portcullis.

"A message for the countess of Dudllan," he shouted as he entered the courtyard.

"For a prisoner, you seem to receive a lot of visits here. I should send your guardian to keep an eye on your activities," Edward said.

I ignored him and walked to the messenger. And without caring about Edward's presence, I opened the missive, but it was too dark to read. Thus, I approached the wall where a torch was burning, and read the letter. My heart almost stopped as I read Estrilda's words, and all the promises to be nice to Edward faded.

"Why did you arrest Master Cloppelin? You want to ruin me? Is that what you are trying to achieve? Do you want me to have to live in a barn with my sons and daughter?"

Edward gave back his reins to one of his men and approached. "Alys, I am sorry; he was arrested a while ago."

"But you must release him. How do you expect me to pay the taxes if you cut off all my income?" I asked, putting a hand on his forearm, and a strange feeling filled my body. I removed my hand as if I had burned it over a fire.

"Do not worry about your taxes. No one will touch your land; I give you, my word."

"What about my associates? I told you I'm willing to show you my goodwill, but—"

"People must see I have authority over everyone. Besides, I don't know if I can trust you, yet."

And then, something came over me—probably caused by the many goblets of wine I had drunk—I threw myself into his arms and embraced him.

"Come back quickly," I said. Edward hugged me against his chest and immediately I regretted my gesture and words. After an embarrassingly long embrace in front of my sons and men, we drew apart. Edward laid a kiss on my lips and then mounted his horse. The taste of fruity wine lingered on my lips for a while, and I passed a finger over my mouth as

I watched Edward leading his men out of the courtyard. As soon as they were out of sight, I released a big sigh. This was not part of my plan; I would ensure I'd not let this happen ever again. What was I thinking, throwing myself into his arms?

As I headed back inside, I saw Fauconberg coming out the stables. "What are you playing at?" he shouted across the yard.

His tone hurt a little, but I was glad to see him. "Oh, there you are. I've been worried about you."

"I can take care of myself, but it doesn't look like you can. What were you thinking of? Throwing yourself into Edward's arms! Have you forgotten which side you are on?"

"I know exactly where I stand, but the king will not return my business and free Master Parker and Cloppelin until he has the assurance of my loyalty." I passed him the letter. "Both Master Cloppelin and his wife were arrested."

"And you think bedding the king will help them?" he asked, not even reading the content of the message.

"I do not intend to bed him. When I look at Edward, all I see is a gory face, and a sword covered with Hampton's blood. I have not forgotten that Edward is responsible for my sorrow. Hampton befriended enemies in the past. If my memory is correct, this never troubled him. I've no ally. For the sake of my sons, whom I cannot deprive of anything, I must appear cooperative. One day they'll go to court with their heads high; they'll lead armies and will be feared like their father was."

"I agree that Hampton was at ease with his enemies when he needed something from them, but I can assure you that he would have never become too familiar with them," he said and grabbed my arm to stop in my track to the solar.

"That was a weapon he did not possess. He had power, money, and men. All I have is this," I said, flapping my hands on my breasts. "Well, at least for a little while, before I am too old."

"Edward might be right to compare you to Margaret of Anjou."

"Why don't you all understand that comparing me to that monster is an insult?" I said as I moved and continued to the solar.

"I know how strongly you feel about it, and I hoped that this would make you realize how low you have fallen. But again, Margaret of Anjou did not sleep with her enemies."

"Captain, why can't you give me your support?" I turned around in the middle of the corridor with my voice echoing against our bare walls.

"You have my support. I am just worried that you might hurt yourself and lose..." He stopped. "Yourself," he continued.

I laughed and clapped him on the back. "I will never lose myself. My blood is too Irish for that, and my head is firmly on my shoulders. Come, let's go in and have a drink," I said, leading inside.

"I suggest in the future you slow down on the wine; it seems you've had quite enough for today. It has gone to your head. I would not like you to do anything stupid when I am gone."

"Are you leaving? Why?"

"Because you've asked me to pursue something, but promise me that when I am gone, you will do nothing stupid, like bedding the king."

"I give you my word that I will never bed the king. So, when will you leave?"

"Only in a month or so."

"Will France be ready to attack by then?" I poured myself a cup of ale.

"King Louis will not give us any support; well, I don't think he will. No, I am going to meet some old friends in the North. You know how King Louis is, and I think he is quite happy with how things are in England at the moment. His protégé lost and Edward never knew about his involvement. We cannot count on France." Fauconberg approached and before I had a change to get a sip of the wheat on my lips, he removed the cup from my hand. "You've had enough."

"And you are not my guardian!" I said, trying to get the cup back—without success. "Anyway, if what you said is true, I might have to go to France and speak to him myself."

"You are still under house-arrest; you will not be able to leave Wales."

"Only if the king finds out."

"If you were to leave, he would easily find out, now that you've enticed his feelings... What if he pays you another one of his impromptu visits? How should your men explain your sudden disappearance? You do not want to put them in danger, besides not only your men would be in danger, but your children too. This is not the wisest idea you've ever had. Besides, I suspect you might have some people spying on you," he said, lowering his voice and taking my arm to walk outside the solar.

"Again!" I said, horrified.

"People are poor and would do a lot for money."

"Who?" I asked as I let myself sink in the chair by the fire. "Can you add a log on the fire, please?"

He nodded and grabbed a log that he threw over the fire, disturbing some of the ashes that flew across the room. "For the spies, I'm not quite sure who they are."

"Do you think some of my men? I mean, they are poor... someone could bribe them."

"They are not that kind of people. You can trust them; they'll put your life before theirs. Come, you need to rest." He opened his arm to invite me to move.

"What a comfort to think that they are men of honor." I stared at the flames in the hearth and, for a moment, listened to the pleasant crackling sound of the fire. My body almost drifting into a peaceful sleep.

"A man of honor would protect you for free. These men are paid," he said.

"I've not paid them for a while. Would it be possible that they will betray me if I don't find the money?" The short-lived sensation of a restful night, suddenly vanishing.

For a quick moment, Fauconberg appeared to be uncomfortable. "Fret not. I shall speak to them."

Fauconberg was different. The man I had known in the past had always been full of confidence and had never hesitated in his actions or speeches.

"Are you hiding something from me?" I asked.

"No, my lady." But even that answer did not seem sincere. Then he suddenly seemed to regain his self-control. "That Gérard... Are you sure you can trust him?"

"Yes. If Jasper Tudor sent him, then I can trust him."

"How do you know this was not a lie?"

"I..." Fauconberg was right. Gérard showed me no proof that Jasper Tudor had indeed sent him. When Gérard arrived, he had mentioned his name, and I'd trusted him immediately.

CHAPTER EIGHT
March- April 1472, London, Estrilda

When the bells chimed for Prime, Estrilda rose to her feet, took her missal, and headed to the chapel. For days and weeks, she had been staring out the windows for a messenger, but none came, and she could not help assuming that lady Alys's silence was pernicious. As if she did not care about Willem or Lysbette. Estrilda'd imagined Alys would have replied to the message or at least sent a letter to the king, but she did nothing. The queen was right, lady Alys was an egoist who only cared for her own cause and no one else.

As Estrilda strode along the corridors, pondering on Lysbette and Willem's cause, she walked past Richard.

"Lady Stanley, how are you? Is everything all right, you look a little sad today. Is it because we did not dance on the king's anniversary? I am sorry. I really wanted to, but my brother'd required my presence more than I had wished."

"Oh... no, Your Grace, it is... I was thinking."

"Mayhap you should not if it makes you sad. I see you've kept my flower," he said as he pointed to the dried flower that she had attached to her brooch. "Would you like to stroll with me in the gardens after Mass, this might bring a smile to your face?"

"I would be delighted, thank you," she said, and they both walked silently to the chapel where she sinned in thought during the entire service.

Afterward, as they stepped away from the courtiers, Richard took her hand, and she followed him outside. She was hoping he would not sense her speeding pulse. For a while they walked silently, admiring the gardens, breathing in the scent of violets and freesia, which always brought joy to her mind, but what she enjoyed the most was the touch of his hand on hers, like silky gloves. The duke had a way to make her forget about everything wrong in this world. In his presence, nothing else mattered than being with him, her savior.

As they passed the corner of the cloister fountain, Richard stopped and brought her closer to him. Her heartbeat sped even more.

"You have turned my head," he said. "And pardon me for saying this, but I would like so much to kiss you."

This shocking revelation left her incapable of saying a word, making her heart rumble through her chest as if knocking on a door that someone refused to open. To warn her. Estrilda should have run away at that instant.

But of course, she did not. She smiled and held his stare, and suddenly he moved forward and kissed her. A sweet, delicate sensation filled her body; however, worried someone would see them, she quickly stepped back.

"Your Grace, please, we must not. What if someone catches us?" she said as she tried to move away, but with a hand he prevented her from going anywhere.

"If this happens, they will see a beautiful couple in love."

"In love?"

"From the moment we were introduced, my heart has bled for you. My thoughts have been for you, night and day. Please, pardon my directness, I-"

"Your confessions flatter me, but I am a widow. This is rather inappropriate."

He brought a finger to her lips to silence her.

"We can be discreet until your mourning is over. Please do not deprive me of your company, unless you do not wish to be with me. I would hate to force you, far from it." He paused for a moment. His declaration was all Estrilda had dreamed of, but she could not admit to it. "I get your sentiments for me are the same... I hope they are," he continued.

She smiled and nodded as she stared at her feet. Suddenly warmth filled her entire body, and it was not the splendid sunlight that shone all over the beautiful blossoms. "Your Grace, this is not proper. Please, I beg you to forget me. I am a lady of the queen, and she would not be pleased."

"The queen does not need to know. No one needs to know," he said and then pulled her closer. The woody scent of his hair and skin wrapped her in an enchanting daydream. "Look," he continued. "Why don't you meet me here tonight after the banquet. I'll show you my favorite place."

"It would be unwise," she said.

A series of drum roll followed by a loud crowd's brouhaha startled them.

"What is it?" she asked.

"Sounds like an execution."

"Again?"

"The king has been chasing rebels all over the country, and he's getting rid of all of them. One by one."

"Who is it today?"

"I don't know. Would you like to attend?"

"Oh no, dear Lord. I've never attended an execution." Just the image of it froze her blood.

"There is always a first time. But I must warn you, this might not be pleasant, but some people develop a taste for these kinds of events. They are bloodthirsty when there's an execution. Come," he said, taking her hand and pulling her hood over her head.

"Rejoicing in someone else's death is a sin," she said as they hurried across the gardens.

"Not when it is the one of a traitor."

Obediently, Estrilda followed him through the gardens, out in the streets, and then they mingled with the crowd and followed the flow of people to the square where the execution was to take place. By the time they reached Holloway Square, they could barely move. People pushed and shoved each other to ensure they secured the best view. Thus, Richard wrapped Estrilda under his arm and forced their way across the square to be closer to the scaffold.

Afterwards, half a dozen soldiers brought a prisoner and pushed him up the steps. And to her horror, Estrilda recognized Willem Cloppelin. He had lost a lot of weight and had black circles under his eyes and a rather untidy beard, but there was no doubt it was him.

"What are they going to do? Don't tell me they will behead him; I couldn't bear seeing that!"

"Don't worry, they will only hang him. To be beheaded is a privilege for nobles. Look, the ropes are ready," he said and pointed to the scaffold.

"Why are there three ropes?"

"There will be other prisoners shortly; this one is the first one. One of the others might have fainted. They normally bring all prisoners out at the same time."

"Who are they?"

"I don't recognize this man, but he's either a thief or a traitor. There are a lot of them out there. Probably a merchant, as we've found quite a few traitors amongst them recently. All of them contributed to the rebellions. If he's a merchant, there will be a fight to get the portion of his business and customers. Merchants are a different kind of people, they help each other, but they are also raptors when it comes to stealing each other's business," he said, lowering his voice a little. "Ah, here is another one."

The crowd jeered louder and threw rotten food at the prisoners. And then a tall and rather broad man placed himself before Estrilda, obstructing the view, and thus she could not see if she knew the other prisoner.

"Excuse me," Richard told the man. "The little lady cannot see a thing."

The big man apologized, and then he lifted Estrilda as if she was a bag of oats and leaned her against his shoulder. "Better?" he asked.

"Thank you," she said and looked at Richard, who shrugged and smiled at the same time while trying not to laugh.

Twisting her head, Estrilda looked toward the scaffold. The other prisoner was Master Parker, who was as pale as the pages of the manuscripts he sold. Estrilda was hoping to see lady Alys cantering at any moment into the square to stop the execution; at the same time, she was also dreading to see the third prisoner. To her great relief, the third prisoner was another merchant, not Lysbette.

Estrilda dared not ask Richard about Lysbette, but she had to mention lady Alys. Why was she taking so long to rescue them, her associates?

"Where is the countess of Dudllan?"

The place was crowded but if she had wanted to come, she would have found a way to shove people around. Surely it was not the repulsive odor of the unwashed bodies gathered in one square that would have stopped Alys.

"Why would she be here? She is under house arrest and cannot show her face in London."

"That merchant, I know him. He has done deals with her in the past," she said without thinking.

"How do you know that?"

The crowd roared and insulted the convicts as the executioner placed each of them in position and then he put a rope around their necks, which saved her from answering Richard's question. Afterwards a priest gave each of them extreme unction. She glanced several times across the square. Still no signs of lady Alys. Another drum roll, the herald announced the reason for their execution:

Treason. He added: "For the last time, reveal where the lords Tudor and Fauconberg are hiding, and your lives will be spared."

None of the prisoners replied. The crowd shouted and cried out insults to the prisoners, and then another drum roll silenced the people for a brief moment. A trap opened and in turn the others did, one by one. The bodies gesticulated, trying to escape their imminent death. Estrilda closed her eyes and put her hands over her ears to cover the sound of the crowd, she could not bear to see Master Cloppelin suffering. Then when the crowd became silent, she dared reopen them. The bodies dangled on the ropes, rocked by the wind. Their souls were on their way to, she hoped, Heaven.

When it was all over, and people had deserted the square, the man lowered her back to the ground, and immediately she found refuge in Richard's arms. The spectacle still shook her, and the visions of Master Cloppelin's body hanging on the rope would never leave her.

"It's horrible. How can you enjoy seeing that?"

"I don't, but people do. As soon as there is an execution, everything stops, and people abandon all chores to assist. They want to see justice."

"But is it? All I could see was cruelty."

"It is justice, but I do not feel pleasure in watching them die. All the same, I do not feel sorry for them either. These men were traitors, and they've received the rewards for their actions."

Even though she disagreed with him, she could not contradict him.

"Come, my lady, we'd better return to the palace before the queen wonders where you have disappeared to."

Hand in hand, they hurried across the streets and slipped back into Westminster's gardens, and as they reached the point where they had to go their separate ways, he brought her hand to his lips and kissed it. "I will see you tonight at the banquet," he said.

Estrilda nodded and hurried through the corridors to return to her duties.

The visions and sounds of the morning's events disturbed Estrilda all day long. Even though she tried to concentrate on her duties, the images crept back in her head, but she could let no one notice her disquietude or the queen would have not failed to question her, and Estrilda was a terrible liar. So, she tried to replace the horrible thoughts with beautiful ones, which then turned into wicked ones, imagining what could be between Richard and her.

All day she had played their encounter so vividly that in the evening when she entered the hall, Estrilda grew flustered when she saw Richard, as if she had been caught out. Not that he could have read her thoughts, but guilt sometimes pushes its way out to become visible to all.

ALTHOUGH TONIGHT WAS an ordinary banquet, it was still luxurious, and no courses were missing, and the entertainment, as usual, had started as soon as the first guests had arrived. The king's laugh echoed across the hall. Even though the evening had just begun, it was clear that he had already drunk too much, and the more King Edward drunk, the louder he became. It was the same almost every night. Estrilda took her place at the table with the ladies of the queen. Most of them were accompanied by their husbands, but Estrilda was next to lady Spencer, whose husband was nowhere to be seen.

Estrilda's mind was elsewhere, and she paid little attention to the conversation, looking for Richard's gaze. When he caught her staring, she smiled, but immediately lowered her eyes, terrified he would find out what had been going on in her head, and then she forced herself not to look at him anymore.

After dinner, people danced. Every single person seemed to revel in the music, the wine, and the dances, but sadness and loneliness overcame her. She wondered where Lysbette was and whether she had heard the news about Willem. When someone placed a hand on her shoulder, she started.

"Madam, please, do me the honor?"

"My widow status does not allow it," she replied as she twisted on the bench to see the person. Immediately, lady Spencer elbowed Estrilda, telling her she should accept. So, Estrilda took Richard's hand and followed him.

"I have been thinking about you all day," he said as they joined the dancers.

Nevertheless, she wouldn't admit that she had done the same; she remained silent, for her voice would have betrayed her indecent thoughts.

"You speak little tonight. Are you feeling all right?"

"I am conscious that I'm still in mourning, and people might talk behind my back."

"Let them talk." He kissed her hand as if to defy anyone who would have dared to stop them enjoying each other's company. "Let's go to the gardens, at least no one will see us there."

Estrilda nodded. They discreetly moved toward the back door, and once they were out, they scurried hand in hand towards the gardens.

As they reached the corner of the moonlit gardens before the menagerie, they stopped and started to laugh like children up to mischief. Next, Richard took her in his arms and kissed her. Suddenly Estrilda did not care about tittle-tattle or even her mourning status. The buzz of the revelers sounded most distant, like they were now in a world of their own. For the first time, her life was complete, or so she thought.

His hands explored her body over her gown, but she had to stop him, as this was slightly going beyond what would have been accepted as pure courtly love. They were in the gardens, anyone could have come at any moment, and perhaps she was a hypocrite, but as much she wanted to enjoy the touch of his hands on her skin, she did not want it to be at the risk of being caught by the queen, or worse, by her father-in-law.

"We cannot," she said.

"I can't help it. I think I am in love with you. Come to my chamber."

"It's not-"

He put a finger to her lips and took her hand while leading her through secret passageways that led to another part of the palace, an area she'd never visited. Her heartbeat louder, but she followed him faithfully and eagerly. Were her lustful thoughts about to become a reality?

ALTHOUGH ESTRILDA ENJOYED the night beyond her wildest dreams, remorse tortured her conscience and thus the next morning after Mass, she stayed behind and requested a confession. Her punishment was not as severe as she had imagined– not that she'd fully told the truth to the priest. A dozen Pater Nosters and fifty Ave Marias daily for four months. And so, Estrilda continued her sinful double life at night without daring going back to the confessor.

After a couple of weeks of nocturnal escapades to Richard's bedchamber, Estrilda became an expert at leaving her chamber without being noticed, and every night Richard waited impatiently for her arrival.

"What is the matter?" Estrilda asked as she caressed his lips, breathing in his woody perfume, and stared at him while she could see some deep lines furrowing his forehead.

"My brother George is causing trouble again," he replied without elaborating, as if either he did not want her to know more or he assumed that she knew what his brother had done. Although Estrilda would have loved to hear more, she did not ask. Letting her hand slide over his torso, she listened as he continued. "I must leave for a while, for I am worried that George will do a thing beyond repair."

"Is the king aware of whatever your brother is doing?"

"Yes, of course, but Edward wants peace and refuses to do anything that would upset our brother. He's probably worried that if he contradicts George, he will turn against him again."

"Our king is a clever man, and it is understandable that he does not wish to disturb the peace in the country. It has been a long time since we've had no war or rebellion." She put a peaceful hand on his torso.

"And if we want to keep it that way, I must do something about it. I shall be absent for a while. Will you wait for me? Promise me you will not let another courtier seduce you while I am away."

"Of course. Will you be gone long?"

"I'll leave in the morning, but I am not sure how long I will be, a month or more."

"May I ask where you are going?"

"Wales."

At the sound of the name, the thought of lady Alys crossed Estrilda's mind, and she became angered. "Not to Dudllan, I hope," she said aloud, then immediately regretted it.

"Why would this bother you?"

"I heard about the countess of Dudllan, Hampton's whore... she is not a lady of good virtue, from what I have heard."

He looked disappointed. "Lady Alys has a noble heart. She has been unfortunate and had a difficult life. You must not listen to court gossip."

"Perhaps if she had not followed a traitor, life would have been more clement."

Richard put a finger over her lips. "You should not talk about people you do not know. As a lady-in-waiting to the queen, I am certain you've heard no praise for the countess of Dudllan or lord Hampton," he said, sitting back in the bed, and he removed her arm as if she had offended him. "Just because you are in the queen's suite doesn't mean you must have an opinion on that matter. This is not as it seems."

"Pardon me, but you speak of her as if she is a close acquaintance. I was told she was house-jailed for treason and that you were her guardian. Has she tried to seduce you, or has she got you under her spell? People talk a lot about witchcraft nowadays, and it may be-"

He laughed, interrupting Estrilda's flow of thoughts. "Ah, Estrilda, you have been working for the queen far too long. The stories you have heard are all nonsense."

"But it is true. I go the market regularly, and some people sell love potions and even inheritance powder... perhaps lady Alys has given you something without you being aware."

"Let's not talk about it anymore," he said. Then he caressed her back and pulled her to him and kissed her forehead.

But Estrilda was no longer in a lusty mood. Lady Alys had mesmerized another man, and Estrilda would not let her take this one from her. What was it about lady Alys that men found so attractive? Estrilda pulled the linen over her shoulder and turned her back on him.

AFTER RICHARD'S DEPARTURE, Estrilda felt a little restless. Instead of concentrating on her duties, her mind tricked her with images of Richard and lady Alys. She was a few years older than him, but so was the queen to the king. Would Richard really leave Estrilda for Alys?

Twice, filled with rage, Estrilda accidentally stabbed her finger with the needle. Everything she did reminded her of Richard, and it made her feel ill.

The other day, lady Spencer had noticed that Estrilda was paler than usual; it's true she had a tendency of being light-headed more regularly, and one afternoon, as they followed Queen Elizabeth across her private gardens, under the trees in blossom, a sense of weakness took over Estrilda's body and she stumbled a few times. At first, she had thought it was because she hadn't broken her fast and that the fresh breeze and the fast-paced walk played a part in her dizziness.

"Have you been drinking brandy in secret?" asked lady Spencer as she grabbed Estrilda's arm to stop her stumbling even more.

"No!"

"What is it, then?"

"I've been exhausted lately. I'm sure it is nothing to worry about," Estrilda murmured as they continued behind the queen, who was trotting as if she was heading for an important meeting. Panting like a messenger's courser as he reaches a destination, Estrilda followed, when all of a sudden, she became thirsty and then she did not recall what happened between the moment she felt the need of a drink and opened her eyes. The queen stared at her from above, tapping her gently on the cheeks.

"I'm sorry, Your Grace," Estrilda said. When she realized she had fainted, she tried to scramble onto her feet.

"Stay there."

"I am fine. It must be the heat."

"I believe you've omitted to inform me you were with child," the queen murmured so that the other ladies could not hear.

"But-"

"Do not worry. This can wait until we are alone. No one else needs to know for now. Go and lie down a little, we will do without you today."

Lady Spencer accompanied Estrilda to her bedchamber and took some smelling salts for Estrilda to breathe, but the bitter smell churned her stomach and she had to run to the privy.

"I am all right," Estrilda finally said as she looked at the horrified look on lady Spencer's face.

For the rest of the afternoon, Estrilda prayed and wondered how she could tell the queen the truth without lowering in her esteem. Estrilda had done something she should not have, and now she was with child and a widow. No doubt this time Estrilda would be banished from the queen's suite, and even worse, excommunicated for being a sinner.

IN THE EVENING, AS all the ladies left the private chamber for the evening mass, Elizabeth sent for Estrilda, and she knew that it was the moment she had been dreading.

"Are you feeling better?" the queen asked as Estrilda dropped in a low curtsey and waited for the permission to rise.

"I do."

"Sit down," she said, pointing to a seat next to hers. "Who is the father?"

Taking a deep breath, Estrilda rose and walked towards the queen.

"Oh, Your Grace, please forgive me. I did not realize that it would come to this."

"You are very naïve, then," she said as she picked up one of her tiny Italian greyhound puppies and put him on her knees.

"When I was with my husband, we have tried to have children for more than a year, and nothing happened. So, you understand that I was not expecting this to arrive after a night or two. I suppose you will ask me to leave now."

"Why would you do that?"

"I thought Your Grace would not want a lady like me in her service."

"When I gave you my blessing, did you not realize I meant you should marry him, not become a whore? Estrilda, you are the most loyal lady I have, but what would people think if they knew I gave my blessing to a harlot?"

"I am not a whore; I love him."

"Then I will speak to the king, and we will arrange a marriage before your condition becomes too visible to all, for I could not do without your help," Elizabeth said, putting a hand on Estrilda's knee.

"I don't think the king will allow it."

"Why not? Is the man dead?"

"No," she replied, without finding the courage to speak his name.

"I am very patient, and you know you have my support, but if you wish me to help, you must trust me and tell me his name. Whoever he is."

"Richard of Gloucester."

The queen did not reply immediately. At first, Elizabeth's silence darkened Estrilda's thoughts, and Estrilda became agitated and anxious, but then the queen stood, let the dog to the floor, and paced the room with the puppy following her, unhappy to have been ignored.

"This explains why he has spent so much of his time at court recently. How stupid of me! I thought he was here to show his support."

"He is. Richard's faithful to the king and yourself. He would do nothing to hurt any of you. I can vouch for him."

"Except following his male instincts. I believe the king has other plans for him, but I will speak to my husband and see what I can do to help you."

"Do you mean you will ask the king's permission for Richard and me to marry?" Estrilda lifted her eyebrows in both surprise and hope.

"I do not think it will be so easy. But I do not want to lose you. However, you cannot have a child if you are unmarried. My ladies and I must show an example to our people, and I cannot have a whore in my suite."

Her words were a little hard to take. Perhaps the queen was being cruel because Estrilda reminded her of lady Alys. Like Alys, Estrilda had not thought of the consequences of her actions, but her situation was different: Richard was not married, and Estrilda was promised to no one.

"I am sorry, my queen. I will do all I can to repair my error, and I promise that it will never happen again."

"Do you think you are fit enough to stay by my side a little longer, or should we send you in the country until you have given birth?"

Immediately Estrilda thought that if she were sent away, she'd not see Richard again, or at least not for a long time.

"I will be fine. I will ensure that I do not faint in your presence. Please forgive me." Kneeling before the queen, Estrilda kissed her hands and suddenly Estrilda began to cry hysterically, embarrassing herself.

"Calm down, I shall have a word with my husband," she said and tapped her hand.

Estrilda wiped her eyes and blew her nose. "Thank you. I will do everything you ask of me."

"We will keep you here until it is no longer possible. When your belly shows, I will send you to one of my sisters where you can deliver your child safely, and then we will find the child a place to stay and you will return to your duties. In the meantime, you will have no contact with Richard, we want no one to find about this affair. Don't you realize what a sin it is?"

What Elizabeth'd said was true; however, Estrilda did not comprehend why the queen was so harsh with her when her husband was unfaithful every single night and she did not seem to reproach him his infidelities or try to hide them from other courtiers. King Edward had fathered so many children that he could have a full regiment with his bastards. The queen treated Estrilda as if she had been sleeping with an entire troop. Estrilda was a widow and free, and her lover was an eligible bachelor. But being called a whore was not the hardest thing she had said. What had hurt Estrilda the most was that Elizabeth had suggested that Estrilda should abandon her child once the baby was born.

However, Estrilda dared not ask if she could leave the child with a nursemaid temporarily instead of abandoning it. She would have hated for her child to grow up like she did. Not knowing where she came from. Had Estrilda's mother been forced to abandon her?

Richard was in Wales so Estrilda could not risk contacting him there, and also, she had promised the queen she would stay away from him until the child was born. But when someone forbids you to do something, it haunts your mind even more.

CHAPTER NINE
April- May 1472, Dudllan, Alys

Like most evenings, as soon as the chill filled the courtyard, I returned to the solar to read stories to the boys and enjoy what was left of our wine under the dim light of a couple of candles and the fading daylight. When footsteps broke the silence in the corridor, I perked up and looked alarmed at Fauconberg, who did not seem to worry at all, and then the door flung open and a man, with a bony face and bushy beard stood at the entrance.

"Who are you? How dare you enter without permission? Guards!" I shouted and bounced from my seat to place myself between the intruder and my children. As soon as I was nearer, I recognized him.

"Robyn?"

"Yes, my lady, pardon my appearance. I've been traveling for days to come to you."

Delighted to see him, I hugged him with all my heart, but since he hesitated to return my embrace, I let him go.

"Come in and sit with us. And tell us all about your travels."

Fauconberg stood up and tapped Robyn on the back.

"Geoffrey, Edmund, please go to the kitchen and ask John to bring food to our guest."

The boys stood up and scurried out of the solar.

"Don't expect too much, I am ruined," I warned Robyn.

Robyn took his satchel, dug in his hand, and got out three large goatskin purses. "We... I heard about that. Hopefully, this will help you," he said.

I opened one. It was full of gold coins—not silver, just gold. Unable to contain my joy, I gasped: "There is a small fortune here. Where did you get it?"

"It is better not to ask," he said, "but this is for you and your sons."

Again, I embraced him. "So, you were in France, weren't you? I thought I'd never see you again. How come have you returned now?" As I said this, I caught him glancing at Fauconberg, and from the corner of my eye, I noticed that Fauconberg shook his head. I frowned. Fauconberg had pretended he had news from Robyn, but that look clearly showed that he had lied and that he was the one who had called for Robyn to return. "So," I repeated. "What made you return to Dudllan?"

"I... life in France was rough. Henry Tudor is not yet ready to fight King Edward. But, when they are ready, I will go back to France. In the meantime, I thought you might need my help." He sat close to the fireplace and rubbed his hands over the flames.

"Really?"

"Yes."

"Did you enjoy the French court? I guess the money is from King Louis, and you are the messenger he sent with the money."

"No, I did not meet King Louis. We were living in the woods, and in the winter, it was not pleasant every day. King

Louis has not denied his help, but he has refused to give us a roof, for he does not want to interfere with English affairs."

"But he gave you that money, didn't he?"

"It's not from him. As I said, I've had no contact with him. Why would the king of France speak to me? I am no noble and no knight either, just a soldier."

"Well, when I am free and allowed to rule my lands as I wish, I will make you a knight and arrange that you have lands, too. But it might take a while."

"Isn't a knighthood for the king to give?"

"No, as the lady of Dudllan, and having no husband, I possess the same rights as the earl of Dudllan. I may grant a knighthood to any man I think deserves it, plus having a knight will bring me more money."

Robyn chuckled before saying, "If it will help."

Then we all chortled as if our nerves were suddenly out of control. Although I was sure that Fauconberg or King Louis had something to do with Robyn's return and the money, I did not mind as I welcomed both.

"So, when was the last time you two saw each other?" I asked both Fauconberg and Robyn.

The response took a long time to come, and it was Fauconberg who spoke first. "Before Barnett."

But then, at that word, a frozen silence felt over the room. None of us liked to be reminded of that awful time. Thanks to my little Louis, our thoughts came back to the present, and I realized that Robyn's arrival had distracted me from my children's presence. Willing to stay up a little longer, Louis had made himself extremely quiet, like I used to when I was his age. Geoffrey and Edmund had not yet returned from the kitchen.

"Louis, it's getting late. Time you go to bed," I said, and then their nursemaid stood up, but as she was about to take Alienor from her crib, I jumped in. "I'll take care of her. Take Arthur!" I said, pointing at him slumbering in the chair. Then I turned to Robyn: "Go to the kitchen and get yourself something to eat; I'll be with you shortly. Oh, if you see them, tell Geoffrey and Edmund to go to bed at once."

Later, after I had put Alienor to put and walked down the stairs to meet Robyn, I crossed my eldest sons. "Where have you been? I clearly requested that you bring food to our guests, not to eat it for yourselves."

"Sorry, lady Mother," Geoffrey said and curtseyed.

"Fine, but next time, I'd appreciate if you were to remember your manners. Come on, off you go," I said after I kissed both on their foreheads.

FAUCONBERG AND ROBYN sat at the top of the large oak kitchen table, drinking ale and dining on small servings of bread and cheese while a domestic cleared the other table where earthenware pots of herbs and salty food were scattered all over.

"Get some meat and fish. It's not with stale bread and cheese that you will get your energy back. I'm sorry that my boys did not bring the food when they were told," I said as I joined them, striding over the sacks of oat and flour to reach the bench on the opposite side.

"The boys have grown up so much. When are they going away to learn their duties?" Robyn asked.

"I do not intend to send my boys away."

"Geoffrey is almost twelve, and he knows nothing about being a page or squire. What is he going to do when he is older?" Robyn drained his goblet of ale and took a piece of poultry.

"Hampton taught him what he needed to know."

"But you haven't continued their education," said Fauconberg. "What happened tonight would not have happened if they had received proper schooling. Obedience is the first thing they should learn."

"Geoffrey spends a lot of his time with our men-at-arms. I've seen them teaching him a few tricks, and Louis does the same."

"Louis has taken the feisty side of both of you. I would not wish to cross him when he's older. I fear he might be a voracious fighter," Robyn said, now cutting a piece of pork.

"Which is a good thing. Ah, my boys could not be more different. Geoffrey thinks he must be serious and be the man of the house, Edmund just follows what his brothers tell him, and Louis is the unruly one who would defy a wild boar if it were to come across his way. Hampton would have been proud of them."

"I'm sure he is proud of them," Robyn said.

"Is?" I queried.

"From where he is, I am sure he watches over his boys and you," Fauconberg said, looking shifty.

"Shame he won't see them grow up," I said as my heart sank, and then I took a deep breath. "In a way, it is better so, I don't think he would have been keen on having another daughter."

"But he would have loved her all the same. This young lady is your spitting image. I wonder what she will do when she is older?"

"Probably marry a gentle farmer if she is fortunate enough," I said, twisting the goblet of wine between my palms.

"Not lord Hampton's daughter. This young lady will have a great life," Robyn said, lifting a hand, and at the same time, a whiff of body odor reached my nose. But unwilling to offend him, and though I wrinkled my nose, I tried to ignore it.

"You speak as though she was betrothed to some great man already," I said. "No one will want to betroth Hampton's children to their own. At least not while the Woodvilles are ruling over Edward. Anyway, Robyn, you can stay here tonight, but tomorrow you'll go with Fauconberg to Tudor's manor. I'm expecting the visit of my guardian any days now; it will be safer if you are not around when he arrives."

"Robyn can stay," said Fauconberg. "His head is not on the list, but mine is."

"No, Robyn's head is too precious, and I will not let them touch him; there is no point in taking unnecessary risks. You'll both go to Tudor's manor. I'll send for you after Richard's visit." A shiver crossed my body at the idea that Edward could try to arrest Robyn.

A FEW WEEKS LATER, as expected, Richard arrived with only a handful of men with the weather on his side. He had visited regularly at the beginning of my imprisonment, but in the last few months, his visits had been sparser. This one was by order of Edward. An unnecessary one, as I had nowhere else to go, no friends, and no fortune, and they knew I could do nothing against them. Not yet, anyway.

"Good afternoon, lady Alys," Richard said, waving ahead from atop of his horse.

"Richard, what a pleasure to receive the visit of my guardian. To what do I ought such an honor?" I asked as I hurried to his side.

His companions followed him into the courtyard, and a few of my men and Gérard came in to assist with their horses. Having visits always reminded me of the past. It was such a great joy to see the courtyard animated and hear buzzes of conversation and the clip-clop of many horses echoing against the cobbled, but the men and horses had gathered lots of dust from the dry road that when they dismounted in a jump, a small cloud of dust escaped from their tunics and hair.

"To nothing in particular except that I need to speak to you," Richard said as he tapped his horse's neck then handed the reins to Geoffrey.

"Have you convinced your brother to free me and return me my trades?"

"No, I have not spoken to him about you. I am afraid there is nothing I can do to help you on that front. I am supposed to be your guardian, not your friend. No one must know that we are friends again. It would cause the queen's wrath," he said, removed his gauntlets, and he took my hand before we walked side by side toward the keep.

"So, you are content to come and talk like in the old days, but too ashamed to tell people you are enjoying my company. What would you do if someone were to report our conversation to the queen?"

Richard smiled. "Visiting you is part of my duty to ensure you haven't escaped and that you are not preparing a rebellion."

"I am only a woman, my friend. How do you expect me to raise an army against the king of England?"

"You are like no other woman I have met. I savvy that you might not like the comparison, but you and Margaret of Anjou have more in common than you think."

"You have no idea indeed," I said as I recalled that once Margaret had also been Hampton's mistress and that she gave him a child, but no one knew, except for the queen's mother who would never speak about it and now that Hampton was dead, I had no intention of bringing this up to anyone. This was a secret now buried forever.

"Actually, come," I said as I swung around, pulling him towards the stables. "We should go for a ride in the forest. It would be a shame not to go out by this weather."

"I've just arrived, and I am exhausted." He tried to stop me in my enthusiasm to lead him to the stables. "Don't worry, I intend to stay a couple of days, so we'll have plenty of time to ride later. I need to give my horse and my legs a little rest."

"Oh, of course. Well, have something to eat, a rest, and then we can go."

The visits of Richard had brought back our friendship to almost as it was when we were both at Middleham—almost, for the ghost of Hampton still stood between us. But I had forgiven Richard for his betrayal since he had never intended to hurt us but to stay loyal to his brother. He had chosen to support his family at the time, and no one could not blame him for that.

IN THE MIDDLE OF THE afternoon, racing across the fields and through the forest like in the olden times, creating clouds of dust behind us, reminded me of Ireland, where I used to do the same with his brother, Edmund. My memories were all I had left of my past, of my mother and brothers, of Edmund, of Hampton, and at least no one could ever take them away from me. The chirping of the birds and the buzz of the bees exploring the heather bushes under the warm sun made it all more pleasant. For a brief moment, I even forgot I was house-jailed and with my guardian.

After we dismounted, we sat next to each other by the river. For a moment, we both stayed silent, enjoying the peaceful sounds of the birds singing and the rustle of the water. Then I noticed Richard staring blankly at the river, watching the water running over the few rocks that attempted to block its path.

"You look worried. What troubles you?"

"George," he replied, looking absent.

"What a surprise! Tell me, what has he done now? Another rebellion?" I sat on the grass and lifting my head towards the sun.

"In his way, yes. He keeps Anne Neville in a convent against her will. George did not even ask the king's permission either, but Edward will do nothing about it."

"Why should this concern you? You've never cared for Anne in the past."

"I did care, but since..." He coughed and shot me a quick glance while plucking a daisy before continuing, "Lord Hampton passed away, George has been living at Hampton castle with Isabel. They've gained the entire estate of lord Hampton since the countess retired to a convent, and therefore keeping Anne prisoner is preventing her from getting married, so George can keep the entire estate for himself. You know how much Hampton possessed. If George gets it all, he will be so wealthy that he could raise an army against Edward."

As rage tried to take control of me, I took a deep inhalation before responding. "You know my feelings for George. I'm probably not the best person to give you advice on this. Having said that, I would hate to see George benefiting from Hampton's death. He does not deserve it. Can't Edward stop him?" I asked. My heartbeat rose by a notch.

"Edward does not want to argue with George. He wants peace, but I think George is-"

"Why don't you marry her? That would stop George from getting the entire estate."

"Me?"

"Hampton always wanted you to wed Anne, and she loved you when you were younger, very much indeed. She is a beautiful lady. Admittedly, she is no longer a virgin, but she is a widow, and you'll have a wife who loves you."

"I cannot marry her."

"Why not? This would solve the problem. I thought you said you cared for her."

"I did, but I've met someone else."

"Oh, and you want to marry that woman?"

Absent-mindedly, Richard ripped some blades of grass from the banks and crushed them in his palms. "I do not think Edward would permit that either."

"But you won't know until you ask. I suggest you take Anne for your spouse and the other lady for your mistress."

"You always make things sound so simple."

"Because they are," I said and stood up, almost exasperated by his negativity, and walked a little further away.

"But what would the woman I love say when she hears I'm to marry someone else?"

"Did you promise that special lady that you would marry her?" I stopped and turned towards him.

"No."

"Is she your mistress already?"

He nodded and gave me a bashful smile.

"If you've not promised her anything, she must accept your decision. Life is not always as we want it. I know that more than anyone else. She'll get over it, and if she loves you, she'll take what you offer. Do I know her?"

"I don't think you do; she is new at court. Her father is a Flemish earl, lady Stanley, but now she is a widow."

Estrilda! No, no, this cannot be. I had almost forgotten about her husband, but I understood why she had fixed her choice on Richard. Deep down, I didn't believe she actually loved him but was looking for an escape from the Stanleys.

Oh Estrilda, you clever girl.

The poor girl feared to go back in the streets, and she tried to reach high to ensure her protection. But I guessed she did not even think about what Richard would say if he were to find out about her origins. If only I had taken care of her education, I would have taught her better. My thoughts were running wild, and I did not notice Richard had stopped speaking.

"Are you all right? You're a little pale," he said.

"Er, yes. Sorry, your love story reminded me of my own. Maybe you should marry the woman you love after all." I sat next to him and put a gentle hand on his forearm, hoping this would give him the courage to chase love.

"No, I think you are right. Being Anne's husband would make me a rich man, and it would stop George. Besides, Edward would not be pleased to have a Flemish widow for a sister-in-law. Anne will be my wife."

"But you will break lady Stanley's heart."

"As you said, if she loves me, she'll take me as a married man. You've done that for lord Hampton."

"My love for Hampton was strong. I would have accepted anything to stay with him."

"Then the problem is solved, I'll head for London on the morrow and will rescue my future wife from the convent."

In my memory, Richard had often been indecisive, but on this matter, he had been quick in deciding; I guessed that either his heart was torn between the two women, or he had already made his mind before coming to Dudllan but wanted my approval before taking half of Hampton's fortune. All the same, I knew it was for the best, as stopping George from getting all the estate was the most important thing to do now. Even though Estrilda had not been as faithful to me as I had wished, I hoped she would not end up with a broken heart. But if this happened, she was young and would get over it.

"Mayhap you could find lady Stanley another husband?"

"What?"

"You can't expect to marry someone else and force her to stay a widow?"

He stayed silent for a while, and then he agreed.

"You know it is the best solution. What about your friend Francis Burley? If I recall, he was a pleasant lad, and I believe he is not married yet."

"Francis is my best friend."

"So, he should have no problem with the idea."

"But Estrilda is a beautiful lady. What if he falls in love with her?"

"What if she falls in love with him?" I replied and let him ponder over it.

CHAPTER TEN
July 1472, London, Estrilda

The queen shot a dark glance at lady Spencer, who entered the audience chamber adjusting her gown and with her hair undone, but although Queen Elizabeth guessed where Jane went, she said nothing. Then lady Spencer sat by Estrilda's side.

"Richard is back," she whispered as she bent to pick up her missal from under the chair. Estrilda's heart almost stopped, and from that moment, she fidgeted restlessly on her chair until the queen released them for an hour of respite. Even if she was not allowed to see Richard, Estrilda kept on thinking about how she would break the news to him. He had to hear it from her first.

When Elizabeth finally dismissed them, lady Spencer informed Estrilda that she would find Richard at York Place and as they were both about to leave, the queen called Jane. Most certainly to reprimand her for bedding the king. Perhaps this was an opportunity that would give Estrilda plenty of time to meet with Richard, for the queen would talk to her friend for a long time, and knowing that Estrilda wanted to see Richard, lady Spencer would keep Queen Elizabeth occupied with her sermons as long as possible.

Grinning broadly, Estrilda descended the stairs and crossed the galleries, and then she dashed across the gardens, lifting her gown. Before entering the hall, she pinched her cheeks a few times and bit her lips so that her colors would be as attractive as possible, then Estrilda peered at the corner of the entrance and noticed Richard. Full of confidence, she stepped into the hall, and as soon as she touched his shoulder, he started. He almost appeared as if he was displeased to see her.

Had anyone told him about her news? Was he unhappy to have heard it from someone else?

"What's the matter?" Estrilda asked.

He took her arm and pulled her further away from his companions. "I cannot speak to you now. I am to be married," he said in a rather casual way, as if the news was of no importance.

The shock and probably the fact that she was with child and sensitive to every single word or smell made Estrilda's throat ache, and then a little wetness built in her eyes. Immediately, she turned to face the tapestry on the wall. "I suppose I am not your first choice," she managed to say without shedding a tear.

"This is not a choice, my love." Then he put his arm around her waist and led her outside the hall into a side room where no one would eavesdrop on their conversation. Once alone, she opened her arms to embrace him, but he stopped her. "I will always hold you dear in my heart, but I am afraid I must marry someone else."

"Why? Has the king ordered it? Is it because of what I have done?"

"What do you mean?"

"Oh..." she said when she realized no one had informed him about the child, and all of a sudden, her courage to tell him faltered.

He hesitated. "I've yet to speak to my brother."

"I don't understand. Where is the decision coming from, and who is she?"

"Anne Neville." He lowered his eyes.

"What! That ugly woman."

"You are unkind to speak with such pettiness. Anne is a beautiful woman. All the same, it is not for her beauty that I'm marrying her. I have no choice. If I don't do this, George will get hold of the whole estate and fortune of lord Hampton, and he could raise an army against Edward."

"Anne always had her eyes on you, but I thought you were not interested, so I was told. Why are you so smitten? Is it because you prefer money over me, or is it because you love her?"

"I... I don't love her. You know that." He tried to hold her in his arms, but she was the one to step back this time. "It wasn't my choice," he said again.

"Leave me alone, please. Since I am not good enough to be your wife, go on: marry that woman, but I'll make sure you will never see your child!"

"My child? What are you talking about?"

"I am with child, and it is yours," she said, feeling sick as the words came out, even though she was certain that the sickness was provoked by the stuffiness in this compact antechamber. On top of that, the smell of dead poultry that the domestics plucked all morning crept into the chamber from under the door.

"Estrilda, listen."

"No, I do not have to listen to you. Besides, I promised the queen not to contact you. I suppose that your marriage to someone else will help me be faithful to my queen."

Estrilda's sorrow was now out of control, and Richard took advantage of her weakness. He wrapped her in his arms; although she tried, she could not fight back.

"I hate you, I hate you..."

"And I love you," he said, strengthening his embrace, and then he laid a kiss on her forehead. "I must go," he said and left her alone in this dark antechamber.

Out of despair, Estrilda let herself slump against the wall. She wanted to die, but God had other plans for her. In any case, she would never have the courage to end it all. She'd be too scared to end up in Hell. So, she returned to her duties.

AS ESTRILDA ENTERED the queen's private chamber, she was somewhat disappointed to see that the other ladies had already taken their seats, ready for the afternoon reading. No one was talking, and the silence, although she had become accustomed to it, was a little daunting, but Estrilda had to speak to the queen.

"Your Grace, might I have a word in private?" she muttered, knowing that her requests would cause her companions to gossip and wager on the conversation Estrilda wished to have with the queen. She nodded and beckoned people to leave the chamber.

"Richard is to be married to the Neville girl; please don't let this happen, intercede with the king for me. I beg you," Estrilda said as she fell on her knees before Elizabeth.

"What!" she yelled.

Estrilda started at her reaction and scrambled to her feet.

"I've just seen him, and that is what he told me."

"Wait here," Elizabeth said, and without warning, she stormed out of the chamber, leaving Estrilda bewildered.

For the next hour or so, Estrilda recited about fifty Ave Marias while staring at the crucifix on the wall, and then she stopped when the door opened. The queen was much calmer but still did not look at peace. She sat down without a word. So, Estrilda kept a low profile and put more intensity into her prayers.

"Estrilda," the queen said. Estrilda lifted her head and approached her. "You know that I respect you for never giving into the king's will. Now I can see why you never did. Your love for Richard is strong, but I am afraid you must forget him."

"Then allow me to leave court forever. I could not bear seeing him at court with his wife. Please, release me from my oath."

"Never! You are too precious to me. Tell me," she said and stood. "Has Richard said anything else?" As Elizabeth walked past, Estrilda had a whiff of the rose water sprayed on the queen's gown. A fragrance that Estrilda found soothing, but which did not quieten her curiosity.

"What else should he have said?"

"Can you tell me what he told you, word for word?"

"He said he had to marry that girl and that he had no choice. So, I guess, it must be an order from the king."

"And why would my husband ask Richard to marry the daughter of his dead enemy when he could use Richard to make an alliance with another king? If you want to know, it is her doing."

"Who? Anne Neville?"

"No, the Whore of Wales, of course. The one who thinks she is still under lord Hampton's protection. It is her doing. She knows Richard is vulnerable, and she must have put that idea in his head when he visited Dudllan. Think about it. Why would he come with that decision only a few days after his return from Wales? Dudllan has manipulated him because she does not want George to get all of Hampton's fortune. She must have convinced Richard to wed the Neville girl to protect her own interests. That harlot is plotting again, and I will find out what she is up to!"

"I'm not sure I understand. What are you saying?" Estrilda asked.

"Richard spoke to the king and requested that marriage and my husband gave them his blessings, but the decision came from Richard."

"It can't be. Before leaving, he told me he loved me."

"Even house-jailed, Dudllan is dangerous. Richard is her guardian and visits the countess frequently. Lord Hampton's death has changed nothing, for even dead, lady Alys looks after his interests. I am sure Richard was ill-advised."

"Why would he listen to her?"

"You are too young to remember, but before I became queen, they lived together at Middleham. From what I've heard, they used to spend a lot of time together. I thought the fact that he refused to follow lord Hampton was a sign that he was on our side. Perhaps Edward had made a mistake when he appointed him her guardian. That woman is evil and cunning."

"I know little of her," Estrilda lied.

"It is better that you don't know her at all. The woman is a She-Devil. People in Wales say that she never goes to church. She is a sinner in more than one way, and that is without counting the horrible things she has done in her glorious time. Sometimes I wondered if she was not the one who pushed lord Hampton to do some of his misdeeds. When he killed her husband, she stood as cold as a grave. People said she did not blink when lord Hampton beheaded her husband in front of her. Some even say she laughed when his head hit the ground. Only pure evil can laugh in front of such a spectacle. The woman has always followed her own interests. She cares for no one." The queen slammed her hands against the armrest of the chair.

The woman she described was not the lady Alys Estrilda had known. But then, it was probably all true. After all, lady Alys did nothing to help Willem. Thinking about it, Estrilda recalled there were things lady Alys had done that Lysbette had disapproved of. Estrilda did not understand. If Alys was that vile, why had Lysbette supported her all those years? Perhaps Lysbette did not know everything about lady Alys; she had never mentioned the earl of Dudllan's death.

"There is something else you must know, Estrilda," the queen continued, recapturing Estrilda's attention. "It is not my place to tell you, but you too will get married, and if you love your unborn child, you will accept it. It is an excellent position and a chance for you to keep your child as you wish."

At the news, Estrilda stumbled a little and had to hold on to her chair. "Who am I to marry? An old man who is twice my age?"

"Not at all, and to be honest, I am rather surprised by Richard's choice. Your future husband is a young and handsome man. I'd say there is a good chance that one day you might even fall in love with him."

"I've learned my lesson about love. This is not something I will ever do again."

"You have not been fortunate so far, but you will survive. My first husband fell on the battlefield, and like you, I thought I would never love again, but I met the king, and I love him probably even more than my first husband. If this is any consolation, I think Richard is suffering from these decisions more than you think. Even if he did not tell you, his heart is broken."

"Who is the man he has chosen?"

"Sir Francis Burley."

"But he is Richard's friend!"

"Francis Burley is one of our most loyal subjects. Fret not, for he'll look after your child like his own, and he will care for you. The king will grant him a new title: Earl of Vancey. That would make you a countess, and you will have lands in the North..."

Estrilda remembered the day she married Thomas Stanley. She was full of hope, and although it was a wintry day, she could feel warmth in her heart. At first, she had worried about leaving Lysbette and Willem for her new family, but lady Alys had chosen well. Even if he was not a healthy man, Thomas and Estrilda got on very well—was not even a man then. Poor Thomas. God had called him before he had a chance to know what it was like to be a man. In a way, it was probably for the best, for Estrilda would have certainly been unfaithful to him, but since she was a widow now, it was, of course, acceptable that she had found a lover in Richard. They would have been so good together, but it was not meant to be. The king could not have a low-ranked lady for a sister-in-law. A nobody could not become a duchess. That was how Estrilda convinced herself that marrying Francis Burley was a good thing.

If only Lysbette were here, she would have advised Estrilda. Then she wondered about lady Alys. Estrilda never knew what happened when she went to Middleham, but Estrilda had heard rumors that Alys was to marry the king and that he had repudiated her because she had become Lord Hampton's mistress. Then all the troubles between the king and lord Hampton had started, which was why the king killed him at the Battle of Barnett.

Lord Hampton had never addressed Estrilda directly when he ruled in the place of old King Henry, but he had never been nasty to me either. The malevolent one had been lady Alys all along. Not that she had ever spoken to Estrilda badly. Oh no, lady Alys was of a more devious kind. The kind of person who smiles to people's face, and when one expected it the least, she'd strike from behind.

But Estrilda had never been disagreeable to her, and she did not understand why lady Alys would have advised

Richard to marry someone else. If they were friends, surely Richard had told her about Estrilda — unless it was because of the letter Estrilda had sent her, perhaps Alys had not appreciated it and convincing Richard to abandon Estrilda was her way to get her vengeance. The queen was so right; lady Alys was a dangerous woman.

Pain affected Estridla's entire body, and appetite left her. She felt like giving up on life. Her sorrow dragged her into a dark place where no joy or hope could penetrate. But she could not let this happen. She had to do something before it was too late. After all, Estrilda had not admired lady Alys all her childhood for nothing. She had seen her bounce back many times. She no longer approved of her, but that did not mean she could not try to follow her example.

My dearest love,

I know that the decision of marrying Anne Neville was taken after your visit to Dudllan. Why did you let the evil countess turn you against me?

The decision broke my heart and even more so when the queen informed me of my marriage to your friend, Francis Burley. You had no right to be so cruel.

Although I would hate to beg, I really hope it is not too late for you to change your mind.

Your dearest Estrilda

As soon as she finished writing, Estrilda folded the letter and scurried outside her bedchamber to deliver the message by hand. Richard was not in his bedchamber, so she left the note on his bed and returned to her chamber before anyone noticed she went out.

The following day after Mass, Richard walked over to Estrilda. He discreetly handed her a letter without even uttering a word.

My dear Estrilda,

The fact that we are both to marry does not stop me from loving you. The countess of Dudllan has nothing to do with my decision to marry Anne Neville. This is a sacrifice I must make to protect my country. I have told you that it is the only way to prevent my brother George from rebelling against our king.

Meet me tonight behind the menagerie.

With all my love, I'm looking forward to seeing you tonight.

Your dearest Richard

CHAPTER ELEVEN
July 1472, Dudllan, Alys

L etting the wind blow in my face, I ducked a few times to avoid the branches scratching my face, but I rejoiced in the freedom of the ride. While Tristan was approaching seventeen years, he still had some fire in him. Twice I glanced over my shoulder and saw Robyn push his horse to catch up, so I urged Tristan a little more, turned off the main path and cantered along the ravine.

"Nooo," I heard Robyn shouting.

He did not want me to take that path because he was nervous about taking it himself. It was narrow and on a steep slope along an escarpment on the right side. I had taken it many times and knew every corner and every ditch on the path. Last night, it had been pouring down; and so, the track was a little more slippery than usual, but I knew how to handle my horse. Tristan and I were one when we were out in the wood. I glanced back up. Robyn followed us.

"Come on, Tristan," I said and spurred him a little more.

"Watch out!" Robyn bellowed, and I turned to peek in his direction.

As I looked again in front of me, a large oak tree blocked the path. Too late to stop. Tristan jumped over it in a straight line, and then I saw my life passing me by — as if time had stopped. The faces of my mother, Edmund of Rutland, the two children I had lost, and Hampton appeared clearly in my mind, and the thought of my sons and Alienor crossed my mind. What would they do without me? My visions stopped when Tristan landed on the edge of the path, but he slipped and tried to avoid falling into the ravine. I stood on the stirrup, helping the weight to go toward the track and away from a certain death. But the mud and leaves took us both in an instant, and we slid down into the sharp slope. I tried to jump off the saddle, but the strap of one stirrup wrapped around my ankle.

The more I gesticulated to unwrap the leather strap, the more it entangled. I heard Robyn's voice, but the sounds of stones and wood sliding alongside my body covered it. While we slid down, I could not see Robyn, only trees and leaves on each side. My face got battered by brambles and thorns. I closed my eyes to prevent them from getting damaged, I grabbed some branches in an attempt to slow our fall, but the leaves came away, leaving green stains and splinters in my palms.

I shook my feet again, hoping I'd be able to slide my foot off, but it did not work. At the speed of the devil, I was taken down the slope with Tristan, who was leading our fall, and the more he tried to fight our fate, the more he created a straight slope. I bounced behind him like a bag of oats that was dragged around, hitting every stump and rock. Each bump was a slap on my head or cheeks, and my hair dragged leaves, mosses, twigs, and mud. Next, the back of my head hit a rock; all I remembered was Tristan's neigh and the fear in his eyes.

When I finally opened my eyes, slowly regaining feeling in my legs and arms, I noticed Robyn kneeling by my side.

At first, I was relieved that I was alive, but I spotted a lot of blood on Robyn's tunic. Without thinking, I checked myself for bruises and cuts before realizing the blood wasn't mine.

"Are you alright?" Robyn asked.

I put my hand on the back of my head, which had a minor bump. "Yes, I think so," I said, and then I twisted my neck and saw Tristan on the ground. He was immobile next to the trunk of a large oak tree, the undergrowth around him colored in bright and dark-red blood.

'Tristan!' I shouted and scrambled up to my feet, but Robyn stopped me and shook his head.

"Nooo!" I pushed him and ran to Tristan. When I saw his neck had been sliced, I glared at Robyn. "Did you do this?"

"I had no choice. Tristan was suffering. He had a broken leg and would have died a long and painful death. I had to; I am sorry."

My legs faltered, and I let myself fall to the ground next to Tristan and hugged him. He was still warm. "Tristan..." I said, as tears filled my eyes slowly as if to bring me to realization. My throat ached as if obstructed. I could not swallow my saliva. My friend, my best friend ever, was no longer alive, and I had not said goodbye. "Tristan, why?" It was my fault; I should not have taken that path... "I am sorry, Tristan... come back, please. Come back!" The air was filled with the smell of blood, earthy leaves, and moss—my breathing was now jerky, and then tears flowed out.

Robyn stayed away, leaving Tristan and me time to say goodbye to each other till I had no more tears to shed. I stared at him with my head against his neck. Dusk came, but I did not want to leave Tristan alone.

"Come, my lady, we must return to Dudllan."

"No, you go back. You've done enough," I said. "Go back and pack your stuff; do not show your face in front of me ever again. Go to France or to Hell, I don't care. You've nothing to do with me anymore. Leave us alone," I shouted.

"Please, lady Alys, I had no choice. I loved Tristan, and I did not want him to suffer. Believe me, I would have asked for your permission, but you were unconscious, and I could not bear seeing him suffer that much. You must understand I did it because I loved him."

"Leave!"

Robyn did not insist; he bowed and climbed back towards the path without looking back.

I returned my attention to Tristan and caressed his head, then I removed his bridle and released the girdle, but I could not remove the saddle. A moonless night had fallen. I got cold, but I did not want to leave Tristan, so I snuggled up against him. But he was getting colder by the hour.

I closed my eyes as if it would dissipate my nightmare. After a little while, I heard noises around the branches.

"Go away," I shouted, thinking it was some predators who wanted to attack my horse. "Shoo!"

But then I looked and saw the light of a torch and a man approaching.

"It's me, my lady," Fauconberg said.

"What are you doing here?"

"I came for you. Robyn explained what happened."

Fauconberg removed his tunic and knelt to be at my level, and he put it on my shoulders.

"Come, you must go back to the keep. There is nothing else you can do for Tristan. It is better like this. Trust me, I have seen some horses suffer. Robyn did the right thing. I would have done the same."

"But we could have tried to save him."

"No, he had a broken leg, and it was the upper part of his front leg. Tristan was too old; he would not have recovered. If he had been under five years old, he would have probably stood a chance, but not at his age. He had a good life, and he was fortunate to have you as his master. You must let him go now."

"I can't leave him here; I must bury him or–"

Fauconberg sighed. "I knew you would react like this." He stood up. "Come on, you," he shouted towards the bushes. "Bring the shovels and dig a hole."

I forced a grateful smile. "I can always count on you, Captain," I said.

"Do you want to keep the saddle?"

I nodded, for I could not speak as I stared at Tristan's body. It was my fault. When the men finished digging the hole, I bestowed one last kiss on Tristan's nose, and then Fauconberg took me further away while the men pushed Tristan into his grave. Before they covered him, I glanced one last time at Tristan, threw a handful of soil over him, and made the sign of the cross. The men covered him. I moved further away and picked up two sticks of equal size.

"Have you got a piece of rope," I asked Fauconberg as I put the pieces of wood over each other to form a cross. I could see he was not happy, but he ripped a part of Tristan's bridle.

"Here," he said.

Tying the sticks in a cross, I recited a short prayer, and then I placed the cross on the top of Tristan's tomb, still not wanting to leave Tristan alone.

Fauconberg put his hand on my shoulder. "Your children need you. They've asked after you all day, please come now."

My throat still ached, and I gazed for one last time at the tomb and followed Fauconberg back to Dudllan. It would never be the same without Tristan.

LIFE WAS NO LONGER enjoyable. The older I got, the more friends I was losing every year. And even my children had difficulty in getting a smile out of me. Tristan had died because of me, just like Hampton, and I worried I would cause other people to die if I was too close to them. I spent most of my days in my bedchamber, which had no luxuries apart from the few books that I amassed over the years.

"My lady, the king has returned. He's in the solar, and he wishes to see you now," said Gérard, as he opened my bedchamber door and waited outside.

"Why is he here?" I asked as I turned to glance at the window. Looking at the position of the sun, I guessed it must have been past noon.

"I don't know, but he looks wrathful."

"Tell him I wish to see no one."

"And you think he will listen?"

"I do not wish to see him."

"Very well," Gérard replied, and I heard his footsteps moving away, but shortly after I heard shouts and then spurs clanged against the floor, followed by Edward who forced the door to my chamber.

"Being the king does not give you the right to break down my door," I said as I moved out of the bed.

"I have every right, especially with traitors."

"What have I done now to deserve such a name?"

Edward moved forward and slapped me, but I did not stumble. It did not matter anymore; he could have beaten me to death, and I would not have run. On the contrary, I would welcome the treatment that would have brought me to Tristan and Hampton.

"You know exactly what I am talking about. Tell me where he is?"

"Who?"

"The traitor you are protecting."

I straightened my head and managed a provocative smile. "Which one, Your Grace?"

I could not tell him that Fauconberg was here. Fauconberg had mentioned that there could be spies at Dudllan. Was it possible? I could see Edward's face going redder by the minute, and I smiled defiantly. "I am hiding so many traitors at Dudllan. If you do not tell me which one you are looking for, how can I answer your question?"

Edward did not reply. His nostrils flared in and out, but he said nothing.

"Fine," I continued, "I will answer for you: the first one stands before you right here. Then there is my son, Geoffrey. Oh, there is also Edmund, Louis, and-"

Again, Edward slapped me. "You are too insolent. Bow in front of your king, and do not taunt me ever again. I am not Hampton! You will not win your way with a smile. For the last time, where is he?"

Crossing my arms, I said: "What will you do if I do not answer? Arrest me? Oh no, you've already done that. I have no account to give you. You took everything I have, but you will not take my dignity. I don't know who you are talking about, but if I knew of one of my supporters' location, I would never tell you."

With no warning, Edward hit me with his fist, as he would have done to a man. I crashed on the floor, face down, and it took me a few minutes before I could move. By then, Edward had left the room.

With my hand over my nose to stop the blood from spurting out, I stayed on the floor. I did not want to move. Ever. It was like I had lost all fire. What had become of me? When I used to argue with Hampton, I was full of spite, always had a word to say back, but he had never hit me. Even if I had thought he would have been capable, he always controlled himself and respected the fact I was a woman. He was a true knight who respected the Code. But Edward had no such delicacy.

Edward re-entered a few minutes later. I was still on the floor.

"Forgive me, Alys; I've acted on impulse. I should not have hit you."

"No, you shouldn't have," I said, retrieving my strength by swallowing the metallic taste of blood in my mouth.

Edward held out a hand for me to stand up and took a kerchief out of his pocket to put against my nose.

"I am sorry," he said again. "But I know the traitor is here. A trusted source saw him coming to your castle. Alys, you are under house arrest and therefore, you are not free to welcome whoever you want here. I could take you to the Tower if I wanted to."

"You only want to arrest him because he is on my side. He has always been faithful, and I will never betray him. You can torture me, but I will not break my word. I told him he would be safe here, and I intend to keep it so."

"Should I send my men to search the place?"

"If it pleases you."

"You are impossible."

I did not reply. Edward stood and poured some water into a basin and brought it closer to me, then he picked up linen and dampened it a little. He brought it to my face.

"Are you feeling guilty?" I asked.

"You have provoked me."

"You're the king and should be able to control your anger. Had I been Anjou, you would not have acted like this."

"Pardon me," he said as he rinsed the linen and wiped the blood on my face again. Then as I watched him trying to erase the mark of his unbridled aggression, he caressed my cheeks, letting the linen fall on the floor, before attempting to kiss me.

Not only I had promised myself I would never be his mistress, but I had sworn to Hampton that I would never let another man come near me, and I intended to keep my promise.

In disgust, I turned my head as the reasons why he was my enemy and why I should not succumb to his charm sprung into my mind.

"What's wrong?" he whispered in a soft and gentle voice.

"Edward, you've lost control, and you've smacked me as if I was a man and now you're trying to kiss! You should know what's wrong. I am no longer a young, innocent demoiselle. If you want my favors, you will need to do much more than wiping away the marks of your onslaught," I said and stood up. Then I paced to the window.

"Once, I told that you will be my favorite mistress. I always keep the promises I make to myself."

I did not respond. As I stared out the window, I noticed my three eldest hovering around Edward's men, admiring their equipment and probably questioning them about London. My heart sank at the sight of my poor boys, who were happy peasants. Edward would pay for all the wrong he did. He would pay for depriving my sons of their youth.

"Leave! You've done enough for one day," I said, without looking at him.

"Not until you've told me where he is."

"I never will. Now leave, you've humiliated me enough."

"Fine, but you know what will happen if I catch him!"

"He will not let you catch him, of that I am sure."

"You still love him."

"Of course I do, he has been my friend for years; without him, I would not have survived Hampton's death. He helped me."

"Who are you talking about?" Edward asked, taking me by surprise.

"Who are *you* talking about?" I asked, now somewhat confused. All the time I had thought it was about Fauconberg, but for a second, I did not think we were talking about the same person. For a brief instant, I even had the feeling that Edward was talking about Hampton. But it was impossible. Perhaps Jasper Tudor had returned, for if it was not Hampton or Fauconberg, I was not sure whom Edward was looking for.

"Never mind," he said and picked up his sword before leaving the room.

I followed Edward to the courtyard. As we both reached the stable, Gérard blocked the way to Edward. "Have you hit lady Alys?" he asked the king.

I realized the top of my gown was covered with blood, and before I had time to tell Gérard to let the king pass, Edward pushed his way past Gérard, who unsheathed his sword.

"No," I told Gérard. "I'm fine. I tripped and knocked my nose on the ground. Put your sword away."

I could see doubts in Gérard's eyes, but he did as he was told and ordered for the horses to be taken out of their stalls. Edward's men were busying themselves in the yards, readying their mounts for departure. Some horses tried to bite the grooms as they attempted to put on the saddles, while other horses were eager to go.

Edward took hold of his horse's reins, and before he mounted, he defiantly kissed my lips in front of my men and placed his hands on my buttocks, which he squeezed.

"Never do this again in front of my people," I said, gritting my teeth and trying hard not to slap him.

"In that case, don't hide traitors and tell that Frenchman that if he wants to stay on English soil, he'd better learn to respect the king."

"I will make sure to tell him not to leave our Welsh soil, then," I said.

Edward shrugged, mounted his horse, and spurred him out of the courtyard.

When the king was out of sight, I turned to Gérard.

"Where is Fauconberg? He must be careful; Edward wants his head."

"Your king is not looking for Fauconberg," he said, avoiding my eyes as if he had said something he shouldn't have.

"What do you know? Who is he looking for, then?"

But before Gérard could reply, Fauconberg appeared.

"Are you all right?" Fauconberg asked as he approached. "What happened to you?"

"Nothing, Edward and I had a brief discussion."

"And the rest," Gérard added between his teeth, and I shot him a stern glance and returned my attention to Fauconberg.

"I think the king is looking for you, but his words were confusing, just as if he was looking for someone else. Do you know who? Is it Hampton? Is he alive?"

"It's me Edward wants," he replied. "I think it is time to confront him."

I put out a hand to stop him. "No, do not provoke the king."

CHAPTER TWELVE
July 1472, London, Estrilda

To avoid having to attend the wedding ceremony, Estrilda pretended not to be well, but neither the queen nor lady Spencer had believed she was ill. Therefore, she had to participate in and get ready like everyone else. This was not to be a grand ceremony. However, there was a lot of fuss about the wedding preparations, which did not rejoice only two people: George of Clarence and Estrilda.

The smells of the flowers, potent herbs and the meat roasting since the morning made Estrilda genuinely sick, mainly with despair but also anger. Up to that morning, she had hoped that Richard would change his mind, but nothing could convince him not to go ahead with his wedding. All that to get a fortune.

"Estrilda, you're resplendent," said the queen. "If I did not know you, I'd say you're trying to outshine the bride."

Her remark made Estrilda blush, which was not a good way to hide that she had deliberately chosen the best fabric she could afford, and she had asked an old friend of Lysbette's to make her this beautiful gown, embroidered with ruby and sapphires.

Then Elizabeth approached and whispered: "It is for the best. Although now, both lord Hampton's daughters will be my sisters-in-law, which far from pleases me. At least it allows me to keep an eye on them. Don't worry, once your child is born, you too will get married, and you will soon forget about it all."

"How could I ever forget when I will have a child to remind me daily of what happened?" Estrilda asked, placing both hands on her belly. The puffiness of it was hidden under clever pleating.

"Hopefully, you've now learned your lesson. You are not an idiot, but you have been foolish on this occasion. I regret to tell you this, but this is the truth."

There was no need to remind her. Estrilda knew she had been stupid, and she would have a child to remind her all her life. But then, love was a silly thing that no one could order or conjure up. It was not like it was that easy to fall in or out of love. When you do not expect it, it lands on you when you are at your most vulnerable point.

Shortly before the ceremony, as Estrilda strode along the long gallery, making her way through the throng of nobles, domestics, and merchants, she passed by Richard dressed in the most elegant finery she'd ever seen him wearing. Estrilda stopped and curtseyed, but although he acknowledged her presence with a smile, he did not address her. This was precisely what she did not need, feeling even more rejected. She supposed this was her fault. She never went to meet him that night, and since then, she'd avoided him. But a short while after their encounter, someone grabbed her arm, pulled her behind a pillar, and kissed her before she spoke.

"What are you doing?" she asked when Richard released his embrace, looking around to ensure no one had seen them.

"I wanted to see you."

"But I thought you wanted nothing to do with me." Her chest fluttered, and she stepped away from his musky scent before she would lose her senses.

"What makes you say that? You're the one who has ignored me."

"You chose to marry someone else, didn't you?" she said, still tensed by the buzz of conversations from the people walking up and down the gallery.

"That doesn't mean I do not want to see you anymore, I do. I need you."

"But tonight, someone else will share your bed."

"It is my duty to bed my wife. You cannot be angry with me for that."

"No, only for abandoning and forcing me to marry someone I dislike."

"Only because you do not know him, but you will see, once you meet him, you will love him as much as I do. I'll introduce you at the banquet." Then he kissed her briefly and left while she stood trying to understand what had just happened.

The ceremony had been an excruciating experience, and the banquet was the most horrible feast she had ever attended. Of course, the food and the entertainment were, as usual, magnificent and people reveled past midnight, but she was alone. Even Lady Spencer paid little attention to Estrilda, and as for Richard... Not even once did he glance at her, not a smile, nothing, as if she had ceased to exist for him the moment Archbishop Wallbrooke had pronounced him wedded to Anne. On the top that she still had not met the man she was to marry. Although Francis had been present.

When she heard someone mentioning his name, she stole a peek; indeed, her future husband was a pleasant-looking man. Nevertheless, a rude one. He could have at least come and introduced himself. But no, he did not.

"PULL TIGHTER," ESTRILDA told lady Spencer as she steadied herself against the post of the bed in her chamber as she attempted to fasten her skirt around her waist. Lady Spencer had come to her rescue as soon as she called for her in the morning when she realized that her wardrobe needed a serious adjustment to suit her swollen belly.

"If I do, you won't be able to breathe." Lady Spencer puffed as if tying the laces of Estrilda's gown was a strenuous effort.

"But I can't go out like this; my belly is showing too much, and if anyone notices, the queen will send me away."

"Perhaps it is time you go," she said and sat on the side of the bed. "Time will pass by quickly, and soon you will be back here as if nothing had happened."

"But my child is not due for another four months. I don't want to leave now. I've never left London," she said, then realized her mistake and swiftly added, "Since I've moved to England, I've never been outside London. No, I want to stay here as long as possible."

"You are quite petite; you cannot hide it much longer."

"What is going on here? Why aren't you ready," said Queen Elizabeth as she entered, making them both jump as she had never ventured into her ladies' quarters before, and then she said: "Oh, I see, the time has come for you to leave the court, lady Stanley."

And so, two days later, sobbing constantly, Estrilda was gathering her belongings, with Jane helping her pack her gowns and the small treasures she possessed.

"You will not need this one," Jane said, extending the gown in front of her. "Can I keep it?"

"I might do," Estrilda said as she took it off her hands and stuffed it in the trunk. Then she opened the cabinet and took out her little coffer full of souvenirs. The dried piece of lavender was on top of all her treasures. Tears ran down her cheeks, and she closed the box. Lady Spencer put a gentle hand on her arm.

"You'll be back soon; it is not Adieu."

"What if I die in childbirth?" she asked, staring out the small, glazed window.

"You won't. You are not the first woman to give birth, and many have survived it many times."

"Easy for you to say," she said, reminding her she had not yet gone through that Calvary.

"It's because I am not as foolish as you."

"Doesn't your husband mind?"

"Of course, he does, but he spends so much time with his many mistresses. There's hardly a chance I will give him an heir one day."

"But with your lovers, how come you've not been with child?"

"I have been many times," she whispered. "I have used potions in the past; now I use other measures. It's the best way to avoid being with child. Try it next time."

"I don't know if there will be a next time. Richard did not address me once yesterday. Now he has a wife, and I am going away, he'll forget about me."

"Don't be so sure," she said, then she dug into her purse and got out a letter. "He asked me to give it to you when you were on your way to the North, but you might feel better if you check it now."

"Have you read it?" Estrilda asked as she noticed the broken seal.

"Only to ensure it would not break your heart," she said, but Estrilda knew it was more out of curiosity than anything else.

Opening the letter, Estrilda glared at her furiously. Then she read it, and as her eyes scanned the contents, her face lit up, and she cried out: "Oh, Jane, he loves me!"

"Without a doubt. Now, hurry! Or the queen won't be happy. I'll keep an eye on him while you're gone."

"Not too close, Jane. I know how you are with men."

As the carriage took Estrilda away from the palace on a splendid summer day, she kept on looking out the window, letting the gentle breeze brush her face while she prayed that Richard would come to bid his farewells.

CHAPTER THIRTEEN

September-November 1472, Dudllan- London, Alys

"Going to London is not a wise idea," Fauconberg said, approaching.

As I turned around, I shielded my eyes from the sun, which only showed me a shadow coming towards me. "It's time I show my enemies that I am still alive. I must go for Hampton's sake; while I live, he will still be in people's minds, and being at court is a little victory."

"Seems like you've made your decision already. You have been living for this moment, and I will not try to change your mind, but please do not take the children to London. It might be a trap. You are strong here, as you have us to protect you, but in London, you will be at their mercy. Some people are waiting for an opportunity to strike."

"Robyn and Gérard can accompany me. Besides, I have no choice. I am ruined, and only the king can provide us with the funds we need. If I listen to him, he will fill my coffers with gold."

"My lady, pardon me for what I am about to say, but a whore would not speak differently."

"Not from you, please. For years people have called me a whore, and you were the only one who told me to ignore them. I am no longer worried about what people are calling me nowadays. But not you, please."

"We've always been honest with each other, and that is why you appreciate me. If I cannot no longer speak my mind, I no longer have a place by your side."

"Captain, you are my friend, and I could not live without you, but I need to know that you still have some respect for me."

"If you want my respect, then do not bed Edward just because you need money."

"I will never bed the king. I told you before."

He gave me an inquisitive look. "That is not what I've heard from others in the castle."

"You know I won't. I am only flirting a little with him. I cannot disappoint him, for he is the only one who can help me in England. Mayhap, it would be wise to remind the gossipers to verify their facts before spreading slanderous rumors about me."

"Well, I still have my doubts that you are telling the truth, but I doubt not that once you are in London in less than two nights, you will be in the king's bed."

"Regardless of what I do, I don't believe this should concern you. Besides, we have tried to gather funds for months, and we have not got very far. You know that I cannot gather enough men if I have no money. Edward won't even notice he is funding a rebellion against himself. But I promise you, the king will never have me."

"Just don't forget who you are."

"How could I? Especially since London will bring back some delicious memories."

"Which is perhaps a good thing, as it might remind you whom your heart and faith belong to. Hopefully, it will remind you who your enemies are, but I fear it will also bring you closer to them. Aren't you worried that your life will be in danger?"

"I fear not."

"I don't think he's worth it. He's been your enemy for years. What has he done to change your mind?"

"For a start, he lifted my sentence. I am now free, and then he promised to return what was stolen from me. All the same, I would insult the king if I were to refuse his invitation."

Fauconberg shrugged and paced to Robyn. No doubt to order him to keep an eye on me. As I approached the stables to prepare my horse, I removed my cloak and tied it on the back of the saddle when I realized we would have scorching days for the first days of our travel.

UP TO THE LAST MINUTE, Fauconberg tried to convince me to stay at Dudllan, but still, he helped me onto the saddle and waved when I passed the drawbridge. Gérard and Robyn did not speak to each other; I was making conversation with one and then the other. The last time I took the road to London, I was with Tristan, traveling without him was strange, but by the end of the journey, I accepted that my life had changed over the years. Tristan, Hampton, Edmund, my mother... all of them were part of my past, and I had to find peace and think about the future. As we drew nearer to London, many memories crept from the back of my mind. The last time I was in London was a week after Hampton's death. It pained me a little to return there, but when I received the invitation to attend a banquet at Westminster and the confirmation of my pardon, I could not resist the opportunity to shine again.

When we approached the city at dawn, we could hardly see the buildings. The mist was thicker than ever, and even though it was still quite cold, the smell was more unbearable than what I recalled. The fog worried me a little, but since both Gérard and Robyn looked relatively serene, it lifted my spirit and gave me the courage needed to go on.

As I entered the courtyard of Westminster Palace, nothing seemed to have changed much. Edward welcomed me with open arms, and the queen, as usual, welcomed with me a frosty smile. She was pale and stood a few steps behind Edward, her face as gray as a statue. No smile showed her pleasure at seeing me. Of course, I was not expecting anything from her, unless perhaps a curse. Out of obligation, I curtseyed. Bowing before her was as painful as pressing on bruised flesh, but I forced a smile.

The king offered me one of the best chambers in the palace, a room where Hampton and I had spent some wonderful time in the past. All the luxuries were an honor that no noble would miss, and it was a proof Edward had pardoned me and reinstated me to my rank, but also proof of his intentions towards me. Fauconberg was right to worry. However, I was determined to stay strong and stick to my plan; after all, this was my victory. I had to ensure I'd make the most of the opportunity even if I was not sure I wanted to celebrate this small victory with these people. I did not know if I could be polite and insincere to those who were no friends of mine. I should have listened to Fauconberg; it was a bad idea. I should not have come to London. The feeling of loneliness increased my melancholy and need for love, but there was no one to love anymore. My heart had dried out.

A few hours after my arrival, I was conveyed to attend the banquet. My wardrobe had not been renewed for a while, so it did not take me long to decide which gown to wear. Although at the time I had bought the fabric, it was the latest à la mode from Paris, the years and the travels had worn out the material and I possessed no embroidery skills that could have helped me alter my old wardrobe into something more fashionable. Deep down, my peasant look alarmed me that people would mock my attire. The fall had been so sudden and lasted for such a long time that now it was as if I had climbed up to the surface and everyone was sorry for me. But in reality, the only person who felt sorry for myself was me. The first familiar faces I saw when I entered the hall were George and Isabel. Inside, I wanted to scream and slap them, but I smiled in the hope of discomfiting all those who were praying for me to trip over an uneven flagstone.

As I walked along the central alley, someone shouted "She-Devil" and then someone threw something which reached my face in a wet and cold slap. With a thud, it landed on the floor before me, and I shot a swift glance at the object: a hand severed from its body—quite a while ago. Not wanting to show weakness, I kept my head high and broadened my smile exaggeratedly before lifting my gown to step over the hand. Only after that, I dared to look in the direction from where the hand came from. The culprit could have been any of them. Robert Woodville? Indeed, he should have known better, but then I did not recognize the people around him. All the same, I continued towards the throne.

The room was silent as if almost empty, the only sounds were my footsteps against the stones and the swishing of my old silk dress. All eyes were on me; some whispered here and there, but I ignored them. I was the countess of Dudllan, returning to court. This was supposed to be my moment of glory, but with my return, I brought the ghost of Hampton and his past actions, which of course displeased many courtiers.

As I neared the throne, only the king had a genuine smile for me. A smile that I was hoping would not betray the little incident that had helped my return. It was only a kiss, but by the reaction of Fauconberg, I knew that people in London would have also imagined the worst. In truth, I did not care that much. I was soon to be rich and powerful again. Even without Hampton, I could hire the best men-at-arms and bribe people to finish Hampton's work, but in the meantime, I had to be a little more patient and ignore my enemies.

Then Richard approached and welcomed me, kissing me on both cheeks. Grateful for his diplomacy, I smiled.

"Where is your wife?" I asked.

"She stayed in our house in the North. It will take her a little time before she comes to court."

"I can't blame her. To be truthful, I'm already regretting coming here," I whispered.

"Whatever you feel, don't show it to people. I remember you used to smile a lot in the past. Try to regain your smile."

"It died with Hampton. It's not the same without him," I said as memories crept in my mind. "Would you excuse me; I would like to retire to my chamber?"

Richard nodded and kissed my hand.

IN THE MORNING, I BRAVED the cold mist, beggars, and other townsfolk to reach the marketplace. Before asking Edward for my business back, I had to find out about Lysbette. When I arrived in front of the thatched timber-framed house, it looked abandoned. All the shutters were closed. I tried the front door, but it was locked, so I slipped through the courtyard, which only a few stray chickens seemed to inhabit. All the horses were gone, as well as the stock of hay and straw. Hopefully, no one had robbed the fabrics in the storeroom. To force the door open, I grabbed an iron bar and pushed with all my strength. When it gave way, I pushed the door ajar, but the sight of emptiness disappointed me. The vultures had stolen the lot. All the fabric was gone. The only thing remaining in the storeroom was the strong smell of dye.

"Hey, you! What yer doing?" someone asked from the side of the courtyard gate.

"I'm looking for Lysbette Cloppelin. Do you know where I can find her?"

The person hesitated, so I continued, "I am lady Alys of Lochlainn, countess of Dudllan. I am a friend of the Cloppelins."

"Oh, milady," the woman said, bowed, then looked around. "Come to my house, I'll tell yer all about it."

Without hesitation, I followed her into her house. We entered a small, dark room where she only had the bare minimum and made Dudllan look like a palace. Recently, I complained that I could not afford luxury or extra tapestries, but here were empty walls, a large pallet on the floor in the corner, a table and a couple of chairs but no cabinet, no meat hanging on the ceiling. It hardly looked like a livable place.

"Willem got arrested a few months ago; fortunately Lysbette was with you. Nasty people, those Woodvilles."

"Do you know the reason they arrested him?"

"'Cause of you and lord Hampton. They're arresting everyone who helped you in the past."

"I heard about Lysbette's arrest. Is she still in prison?" I asked as I sat on the wobbling chair.

"Not sure, she came back from her journey, and when we told her Willem got arrested, she went to speak to the queen. Never came back. I never miss an execution and did not see hers. I think the queen's keeping her locked up somewhere."

"Oh, and what about their sons?"

"Gone to Flanders to live with their uncle; my husband helped them to travel with some goods before the others took the rest." Then the woman grabbed a jug by the small fireplace and a wooden cup. "Want some ale?"

"No thanks. So, you think Lysbette is in prison?"

The old woman put the jug back on the floor. "Probably, what's for sure is that they've not executed her in a public square. If they've killed her, then they done it on the quiet." She spat on the floor in disgust.

"Which would not surprise me at all. And what about Master Parker, you know where he is?"

"Executed a few months ago."

I stayed silent for a while and squeezed my hands tight. It was my fault. How many more people would die because of me? When would the king stop this massacre?

"It's not your fault, my good lady," she said as if reading my mind and placed a hand on my forearm.

"They'd still be alive if I had not asked for their help."

"Nay, you never forced 'em, they wanted to. You probably don't remember me, but I remember the young lady who came from Ireland. The one who wore men's clothing. Do not be too hard on yourself. Willem always dealt with lord Hampton, even before you arrived."

"I entered the storeroom, but it's empty. Have you seen the brigands who stole it?"

"No one stole it. The rascals did not wait for Willem's body to cool down. They got in there the next day with some of the Woodvilles' men and took the lot."

"Who's got the goods?"

"Sorry, I don't know. Someone from Guildhall probably."

"Thank you, I think I will pay Guildhall a visit. They will need to pay their due if they expect to keep my goods."

"No one will pay you anything. They probably paid the Woodvilles to get hold of it, and you won't be able to access Guildhall. Only members can go in."

"I'll find a way," I said and stood up. Then I dug in my purse and took out a few coins. "Sorry it's not that much but take this."

"No, no."

"Please take it and give your husband a good meal tonight."

After a bit of hesitation, she took the coins and kissed my hand.

As I headed back for Westminster, I had the sensation of being observed. I turned a few times but saw no one acting suspiciously, and then I hid behind a door at the corner, and there they were: Gérard and Robyn!

"What are you doing here?" I asked as I jumped behind them, making them flinched.

"Er... going to the market," Gérard said first.

"Ah! Do you expect me to believe you? You were spying on me. Both of you!"

"I am sorry, my lady. Fauconberg asked us to keep you safe, and when we saw you leaving on your own, we had to follow you."

"Well, while you are here, you might as well make yourself useful. Someone from Guildhall stole all my goods. I must find the name of the thief. Go to Guildhall and find out the name."

"Are you going back to Westminster?" Robyn asked.

"Fauconberg was right; coming back to London was a mistake. I'm only going there to get my horse, and then I will go back home."

"I'll go with you," Gérard said. "Robyn, will you be all right dealing with Guildhall? I don't think they'll let a Frenchman in."

Robyn nodded and immediately headed to Guildhall while Gérard and I rushed to Westminster only to leave shortly after we had arrived.

LEAVING LONDON WITHOUT informing Edward roused his rage, and the day I arrived back at Dudllan, Richard came with a few more men-at-arms than usual.

"Are you invading Wales?" I asked as Richard reached our portcullis with about forty men.

"Would you please ask your men to open the gates so that we may come in?"

"You can come in, but your guards are not welcome. Should I remind you that I am now a free woman, and you're no longer my guardian," I said from behind the closed portcullis.

"If your behavior doesn't change, it won't take long before you are deprived of your freedom again. You've angered my brother."

"Why is that?"

"If you don't know, then you are a lost cause. Why did you leave London without telling anyone?"

"Am I not free to come and go where and when it pleases me?"

"Not when you are the guest of the king. Now, would you please let me in?"

"Fine. Open the gates for the king's rascals and his brother," I told my guards and faced the reproachful look of Richard.

"Your men can wait in the courtyard. I don't want them in the hall with their muddy boots," I said as Richard dismounted.

When we entered the solar, the nursemaid took Alienor and left without being prompted.

"Tell me, why has your brother sent you to check on me?"

"He had arranged a special treat for you, and you can imagine his reaction when he was told you had left. You did not even have the decency to speak to him or even leave him a note."

"I did not like the welcome I received. People did not want me at court; that is why I left."

"Are you sure that it's the only reason? Is it not because some of your friends have returned and you have left to join them?"

"Think, Richard! If it was the case, would I be here at Dudllan?" I said. Although I had no idea what he meant. Perhaps Jasper and Henry had crossed the Narrow Sea and were ready to take on England. If it was the case, why didn't they inform me?

For a moment, it seemed that my words reached him.

"Now you can return to London and tell the king that my departure has nothing to do with him or anyone else."

"I am not fully convinced, but I will pass your message to my brother. Do not be surprised if he comes here to check for himself."

I shrugged and invited him out. "I hope you will forgive me for not inviting you to stay for dinner."

As Richard was about to leave, Robyn and Fauconberg approached the gates, and as soon as they spotted Richard and his army, they turned around, but 'twas a little too late, for Richard noticed and immediately glared at me.

"Who was that?" he asked.

"Pardon?"

"You have seen him. Who was that?"

"I am sorry, I saw no one. Must be your imagination." I twirled around to suppress a guilty smile.

CHAPTER FOURTEEN

January-March 1473, Mount Dale, Estrilda

Estrilda's days consisted of praying while being confined to her bedchamber, patiently waiting for her child to be born. The queen's sister was a little older than Estrilda was, but she had been very hospitable. She had treated Estrilda with respect from the moment she'd arrived as if she was already the countess of Vancey. As Estrilda grew heavier and fatter, days seemed to drag, and she longed to see her child.

Then one day, Estrilda felt a sharp pain in her pelvis, so she called for the midwife. Her body felt torn, and Estrilda was terrified of what was coming next. The women who helped her were patient and gentle, but even so, it did not ease her suffering. Hours seemed to have gone by, she pushed all she could to expel the child, but nothing was happening. The midwife and the queen's sister did not give up on Estrilda, sponging her head, rubbing her belly with different oils that filled in the chambers with all kinds of fragrances. One for courage, another for calmness, one to bring luck, and one to ensure she would stay strong until her child arrived. Then came a sudden gushing, and at last, she released the child. Estrilda let her head fall on the pillow, catching her breath and thanking God.

"A fine boy," said the midwife as she passed the wailing, slimy child to her assistant for her to clean him.

At last, she was free. Free of worry, free of pain. It was such a relief, but Estrilda knew that it would not last long, for as soon as she recovered from the birth and reenter society, she would need to return to London to get married. The queen's sister would look after her child until her wedding was consummated. At least she knew that her offspring would be in good hands and well looked after.

SIX WEEKS LATER, ESTRILDA was back in London. Making small steps—as if this would somehow help her—she advanced towards the altar where her future husband waited. Francis Burley, now Earl of Vancey, looked about as pleased as she was, but the queen was right; she was fortunate, as Francis was quite a pleasant-looking man. He was a little younger and taller than Richard, and to be perfectly honest, much more handsome, too. Nevertheless, Estrilda had difficulties in overcoming her feelings for Richard. Therefore, she couldn't see how she would be capable of treating her new husband like the first one. She was no longer an innocent child. Perhaps it would have been easier if she had been.

After their wedding celebrations, she would probably have to leave London and go to the North, where her husband's new estate was. But after having spent a few months in the tedious countryside, she was not keen on having to leave London again. At least, she supposed that her departure would please Anne Neville, for she'd be away from her husband.

The first night of the wedding was the one she dreaded the most, for she would have to share her bed with Francis and let him do his duty. When they arrived in their bedchamber, she shivered. Not that it was cold in the chamber. Oh no. The fire was burning vividly, and even the smell of soot did not bother her, but she dreaded what was coming.

"As my husband, you have every right over me, and I will do my best to honor you, but I hope you are not expecting me to love you," she said, attempting to unlace her gown, ready to go to bed.

"This is not what I am not asking of you. One day, you will come to it without being forced."

"Why did you marry me?" Estrilda asked as he approached to help her with the laces of her gown.

"To obey an order. Besides, I also received a generous dowry, a new title, and land. How could I refuse such a generous gesture? But I must admit that the decision was easy. They could have forced me to marry an old aunt of the queen."

"Is it true? Was it Richard's idea?"

Francis hesitated for a moment, then he said: "Yes, it was Richard's decision. First, the king had proposed that you marry someone else, I am not sure who, but Richard wanted you to marry someone who'd treat you well. And someone who would let you see him now and then."

"And you agreed to marry a woman that other people would call a whore?" she asked.

"I did it because Richard is like a brother to me, but there is one thing I told him I would not guarantee, and he knows it," he said, pushing her gown to the floor and caressing her naked shoulders. She held back a shriek.

"Oh, and what is it?" She tried not to think of his lips on her neck.

"One day, I might love my wife, and that day I might change my mind about her seeing another man. Besides, I have one condition I would like you to respect: you will not bed Richard until you have given me an heir. I want to make sure that the child is mine. I do not know if I can count on you, but I know I can count on Richard to respect my wishes. After that, you will be free to do what you want. I will not care. But until I have an heir, you must honor our vows."

From the day Richard married, things had not been the same between them, and probably never would be again, but the fact he had promised his best friend not to touch her until she had given him a boy deflated her spirit. At least she had her son to keep her will to live.

"Then I must do my duty," she said and lay on her back over the soft fur coverlet on the bed.

Waiting for Francis to get on with his conjugal duty, Estrilda stared blankly at the ceiling when he clumsily climbed over her, she bit her lips to repress a laugh. Then his incessant movements churned her stomach, but she dared not move or open her mouth. When he finished, he tried to kiss her. Estrilda turned her head away in disgust.

"Good night," she said, turning her back on him. A few minutes later, he got up and left the room, and she wept.

Then, unable to sleep, she got up, sat at the desk, and began to write a letter to Richard.

CHAPTER FIFTEEN

December 1472 January 1473, Dudllan/ Nottingham, Alys

Fauconberg and Robyn left Dudllan a few weeks ago. I had received no news until an afternoon when a messenger arrived drenched in freezing rain. The letter wasn't from Fauconberg as I had thought, but it was about him. The handwriting was of someone who was not well lettered, and I struggled to decipher the words.

"Fauconberg-arrested-Nottingham-executed- treason."

Without wasting a minute, I rushed to my bedchamber and changed into men's clothing. When I returned to the solar to grab my satchel and some coins, my son Geoffrey started when he saw me dressed as a man.

"What is it, Mother?" he asked, dropping his book to the side.

"They've arrested Fauconberg. I must leave at once."

"Let me accompany you," he said as he stood and stretched himself to appear taller, or older, or probably both.

"No, this could be dangerous."

"I promised Father I would look after you. I might be young, but I am brave, and I intend to keep my promise." He put a hand on my arm. Admittedly, this was a nice gesture, but he was eleven years old, even if he thought himself much older and ready for battle.

"No, you must stay here and protect your brothers and sister. If I am not back in a month, then you will need to take them to the manor, and you will hide until someone comes on behalf of Jasper Tudor."

"But–"

"You are the eldest, and therefore you must do as I say," I ordered as Louis and Edmund had stopped their little game and stared at both Geoffrey and me.

"Ask Gérard to do it, I'm going with you," he said, almost ordering me.

"Ah, Geoffrey Neville, you are a stubborn mule!"

"I'm your son, ain't I?"

"And you speak like a peasant... perhaps they are right, I've neglected your education," I said as I ruffled his hair. "Come on, then. Get your horse ready," I said as I reached for the door.

"What about my sword?"

"You know how to use it?" I asked. He nodded. My son had grown up a little too quickly for my liking, but I supposed the circumstances of our lives gave him no choice.

I asked the nursemaid to look after the boys and Alienor while Geoffrey and I headed north. "If there's any problem, Gérard will stay with you," I told her before heading to the kitchen, where I packed some food for the journey.

WRAPPED IN OUR WARMEST and thickest cloaks, we left Dudllan before dusk had fallen; the rain had eased a little, but as the night went on, the rain turned into slippery sleet. The horses struggled to move in the deep mud that covered the roads. The first night, we travelled nonstop, and a few times, I dozed off on the saddle. The following nights, we decided to stop at an inn where we could recover. When we finally reached a village close to Nottingham after a good seven days of travelling, news of what happened to our men came to our ears. Fortunately, Fauconberg had not been executed, but we could not find out anything about Robyn.

The following day, we headed to Nottingham, hoping to find the whereabouts of Robyn and Fauconberg. It did not take us long as many people had already gathered on the square, most of them shouting insults at the prisoners. I had a sensation of déjà vu. This was where, a few years ago, Hampton had executed my husband. Those people who had once supported Hampton had now switched their allegiance to the Yorks.

We both dismounted as it was too crowded to ride amongst the bloodthirsty throng. Not wanting to leave the horses unattended, I called a young boy who was hovering about.

"Can you keep guard over the horses? If when I return both horses are still here, I'll give you a silver coin. Can you do this for us?"

"One silver now and two more when you return," the boy said.

I took a coin from the purse and handed it to the boy. "We have a deal. Make sure both horses stay safe."

He nodded. Then Geoffrey and I pulled our hoods over our heads, trying to cover our faces as much as possible—not that people would have recognized us.

It was not the first execution of the day: the thin white coat of snow on the ground had already been covered with red patches all over, as if the master of the Merode triptych had added them with precision to form a harmonious painting. A few bodies were piled on top of each other in the cart. My heart thumped hard as I tried to peek at the corpses.

"There," Geoffrey said, elbowing me and pointing at the scaffold where Fauconberg had his hands tied behind his back and stood between two guards.

Hiding amongst the crowd, I wished there was something I could do to stop the execution. Not my friend, not him! I moved forward, and then someone touched my shoulder. I turned to see who had dared. It was Robyn, and he brought a finger to his lips before I could speak.

"Thank God you are safe. Do you have a plan to save Fauconberg?"

He shook his head.

"We've got to do something. I can't let this happen."

"My lady, you cannot show yourself, or you will follow him. George has declared war on everyone who supported lord Hampton. There is a reason why the execution is taking place here. This town has always been on lord Hampton's side."

"It's hard to believe when you listen to the insults those people are shouting at Fauconberg. It's not fair! We can't let him die. Fauconberg has done so much for me in the past and for you too, Robyn, or have you already forgotten?"

"I know what he did for me, and I am grateful. But we can't do anything, I'm afraid. If we move, we might end up on the scaffold ourselves. Come, we cannot stay here."

But I could not. I freed my arms, ran to the platform, and pushed away the guards who tried to stop me and embraced Fauconberg. Tears were running along my cheeks, and I did not care about offering people a spectacle they did not come to see. Then the guards separated us. I screamed and shrieked as I held my arms towards Fauconberg. I struggled.

Then Fauconberg moved towards me.

"It's got to be done. You cannot stop it, but promise me never to lose your courage or your smile," he told me.

"You can't leave me. You're the one who's kept me going all those years. How can I live without you?"

"You have your sons. Be brave, Alys. Pardon me for being so informal, but my situation permits me a little familiarity." Then he laid a kiss on my forehead. "Hampton is alive," he whispered so low that I did not register the information immediately. Then louder, he almost shouted: "God bless you, Countess!"

I took his hands in mine and hugged him until a guard took hold of him, and another man pulled me away from him. Fauconberg's hands slipped out of mine. I looked back. Uncontrollable tears of pain, rage, and failure blurred my vision of Fauconberg's smile. He then inclined his head to the executioner and kneeled before the block. Then it dawned on me: "Wait! What did you say?" But he shook his head. Did I hear right?

Perhaps he meant within me, as I had been told for each person who had died in the past, "They'll always live on through you." However, that was not what he had said. His words were, "Hampton is alive." The square was full of people shouting and screaming, but I knew what I had heard.

Fauconberg did not look at me anymore; he turned his head in the opposite direction. I walked down the stairs, surrounded by soldiers. They kept hold of me while the executioner did his dirty work. When I heard the thud of Fauconberg's head hitting the ground, my knees faltered. It was not the first time I assisted at an execution, but at the last one, I had rejoiced in the show, for it was when Hampton had avenged our lost child. Today was the first time I witnessed someone I loved losing their life. My strength abandoned me, and I fell on the ground, and then the soldiers let go of my arms.

It was as if everyone around had become quiet. No wind or birds. Total silence. Then the church bells tolled as if to welcome Fauconberg in Heaven. It was all lost, the end of what Hampton had fought for. All those people had died for nothing; they had fought in vain. No one would rise up against the Yorks ever again. Who would dare? Then, as if courage from beyond the grave took over me, I stood up, determined.

I would.

I had to be the one to continue Hampton's battle, at least until his sons were old enough to pursue their father's campaign. Even if I should end up the same way, I was ready to fight to the death.

Fauconberg's last words floated in my head.

Robyn! I had to find him. Fauconberg had given me hope, and Robyn would know if I had heard correctly; he should know. I shoved people, searching for Robyn and my son. There were too many people: all I could see were strangers, peasants, soldiers, but no familiar faces.

Above the buzz of the throng, the order "Seize her!" resounded. Before I had a chance to take another step, two soldiers took hold of me and led me to the front of the stairs of the scaffold where George of Clarence stood. I tried to free myself.

"Kill her," he said with no pity. He was not brave enough to do the job himself. He would have a few months ago, but Edward had stopped him. Perhaps he was worried that Edward would find out he was behind it; by asking someone else to do it, he later could blame someone else when the news of my death would come to Edward's ears.

"I should be judged before being executed. That is the law!"

"You never complained about Hampton's practices when he killed your husband without judgment."

"It was different. My husband was guilty."

George sniggered. "And you are guilty of treason."

"Nooo," shouted my son, shoving people out of his way.

"Get him too," George ordered.

"Leave him out of your grudge; he's only a boy," I said as I could feel the pulse in my temples.

"Who will grow into a man, into a Hampton! It is better to destroy him before he turns too dangerous."

"Take me, but leave my son out of this," I pleaded.

As the guards pushed my son onto the scaffold, a strength that only a mother wanting to protect her offspring would ever find seized me. I pushed the guards, took one of their swords, and pointed it at George, who laughed at me.

"Let my boy go. Now!" I ordered, putting pressure on the blade and feeling my veins throbbing.

"All right, let him go... for now, but you will go nowhere," he said.

"Go," I ordered my son as soon as the soldier released him. As he disappeared in the crowd, I watched him from the corner of my eyes while I kept the tip of the blade on George's neck, willing to press harder on the blade but incapable of taking that action.

"You'll join Hampton and Fauconberg. That's where you belong... in Hell," he said.

"Says who?"

"The queen."

"Oh, you've changed sides again?" I asked, keeping the blade pressed against his neck. "Has she forgiven you for killing her father and brother? Murdering her enemy won't protect you from her witchcraft. Your mind is too weak, George, you will not win against her, and you will certainly not have an ally in her, never!"

A strange sound like a clap of thunder resounded, and a large stone was catapulted into the air; it landed on the side of a building close to the scaffold, crushing a couple of soldiers. Making the most of the disruption, I pushed my way across the panicked crowd and through the loud and unorderly commotion, I ran without looking back. Again, the rumbling sound covered the panicked voices, and then people rushed and ran in every direction. I looked around for Robyn and Geoffrey but could not see them, thus I continued away from the square, then saw the young boy who was keeping our horses.

"Thank you, to be honest, I thought I'd never see those horses again," I said as while on my guard, I handed him the promised coins.

"And I thought you'd never come back either. I was going to wait until dusk, and then I'd sell them, but they're not worth a silver coin..."

I bit my lips to suppress a smile, mounted my horse, and then took the reins of Geoffrey's horse.

"You've not seen the boy who was with me?" I asked the young lad.

"No ma'am."

Before pushing the horses out of the town, I took one last look. The rumbling of cannon was still sounding, and the large stones landed at regular intervals on the square. Then I spotted Geoffrey and Robyn running toward me. I dismounted and embraced my son.

"Come," said Robyn. "We cannot stay here."

"Are you responsible for this interruption?"

Robyn nodded and lifted Geoffrey onto his saddle, jumped up behind him, and spurred his mount. I followed them out of the town, shoving people out of our way.

Robyn slowed his mount to walk as we reached the forest, and I dared release a deep sigh.

"Robyn, is Hampton alive?" I asked.

"Are you feeling all right?"

"Out of all people, you are the last one I am expecting to lie to me. Tell me: is Hampton alive?"

"I saw him fall on the battlefield. I am sorry, he is no longer with us."

"But why did Fauconberg say he was alive?"

"You went to St. Paul's. You saw lord Hampton's body, didn't you?"

"What if it wasn't him I saw? What if it was someone else?"

"I am sure you would have recognized him."

"His face and body were caked in blood and mud. I did not think for a second to check whether it was really him. I thought it was him. The man I saw was very much like him, but that does not mean it was him."

"Do not give yourself false hope, lady Alys. If he were alive, he would have come to you. Be reasonable. Lord Hampton is dead."

We walked on in silence for a while, listening to the birds chirping happily and the breeze gently blowing between the empty branches of the trees. And then, as if the wind had whispered the answer, I said:

"We must go to France."

"Why?"

"I have to see Henry and Jasper Tudor. You were with him; you know how to contact them. Get a messenger to inform them of my arrival at Honfleur in ten days. First, I must go to Dudllan with Geoffrey."

In the first village, without a word, Robyn dismounted and walked towards the inn while Geoffrey and I waited by the church. When he returned, we continued our way to Wales in the unstable January weather.

Then, a dry, pleasant day guided us on our way to Dover, which we reached before sunset. I did not even allow myself some time with my children when we were in Wales, just changing horses.

However, on our arrival at the harbor, no ships were preparing to set sail for France.

"Go to the inn and find someone to transport us across the narrow sea."

Robyn held out his hand, and I took a couple of coins out of my purse. Once Robyn came out of the tavern, he beckoned me to follow him and a couple of drunken sailors.

"Do they know what they are doing?"

"They were cheap," he said, giving me back all the coins but one. "All right, it's not luxurious, but they will take us to France and back."

"Are they trustworthy?" I asked, unable to control the butterflies in my belly.

"We're in no position to be fussy." Then he pulled the hood over my head. "Some men don't like to have women on board. It's bad luck."

After a long, uncomfortable crossing on a fisherman's boat that could only host a dozen people, we saw the French shores. The many hours of jolting and breathing in the gory smell of dead fish had sunk my heart and churned my stomach, and the sight of the shores gave me a temporary relief. I would soon be able to walk on firm land and steady my stomach. I was pleased I had not had much to eat on the way to Weymouth. When our ship docked at Honfleur, I was in a hurry to get on firm land and extremely pleased to notice that Jasper Tudor was hovering on the quay.

Like most of my friends who had escaped to France, Jasper had a very untidy beard, and looked as if the life had been drained out of him. Still, he smiled broadly and kissed my hand.

"Has France run out of game?" I asked as I embraced him. All my long-lost friends seem to be so starved-looking after living in France for a few months.

"It is that we are living the rough life of mercenaries, no banquets or feasts for us. Just the wood to cover us from the rain and snow, and we eat what we can catch. And I am afraid I might not smell too fresh either," he said, but although I had noticed, I did not want to comment on that.

"I feel embarrassed now," I said as we walked along the docks, with Robyn following up from a distance.

"This is not your fault. Come, let's not stay here," he said, waving at the drizzling rain and he beckoned Robyn and me to join into a nearby tavern.

The place was rather empty for that time of the day, and it did not inspire much confidence. Only a couple of men sat at a table at the far end of the inn, playing some dice game and arguing at the same time. Jasper wiped the top of a table with his sleeve and invited me to sit down.

"It's not much, but no one will trouble us here," he said.

"I can't believe I've traveled all the way in the hopes of getting some money, and now I can see that you have as much as I have," I said as I sat down. "King Louis is the only one who can help us now. How is Henry? Is he ready to invade England?"

"He is still too young to be taken seriously. We need to wait a little longer before we can do anything. You should return to Wales, and I promise to inform you in a couple of years. Be patient."

"No, I will not return to Wales without King Louis's word. George has murdered Fauconberg, and he's tried to take my son. I can't let him get away with his actions."

"Why don't you ask Edward for some money? Rumors are that you are pretty close."

"Rumors about me and Edward in France?"

"They travel fast. *Trois pichets de bière*," he ordered as the waitress came over.

"News gets distorted over the narrow sea. I am not sure what you have heard, but I am far from being close to Edward. He does not even know that I am here."

"Aren't you worried he will take his wrath on your children when he finds out you have fled to France?"

For a moment, I realized that Jasper was right. The thought had not crossed my mind. I could have put my children in danger, but at least they were in the capable hands of.

I shook my head. "My children are in safe hands. Gérard is looking after them."

"Who?"

"Gérard, the man you sent to me last year, Gérard du Boisbaudry."

"I am afraid I have sent no man to Dudllan, and I do not know any man that responds to that name."

At those words, I shot an alarmed look at Robyn. "But he said... Oh, Fauconberg was right, Gérard is a spy... I've been so stupid! When he came, he pretended you sent him over to protect me, and he was speaking good French. Besides he has been very useful around the place, and helped us. I did not want to believe Fauconberg. I thought he was just jealous, for Gérard is a typical Frenchman. He likes the presence of a woman and—"

"Is he your lover?" Jasper interrupted.

"Absolutely not! He just happens to be pleasant company."

Jasper said nothing, but I could read his mind: *Lady Alys of Lochlainn has not changed from the innocent and foolish lady who does not think before acting.*

"Right," I said. "Robyn, go back to Wales immediately. As for myself, I will return as soon as I have seen the king."

Robyn nodded and finished his ale in one gulp. Then he bowed and left.

"Jasper, I must meet with King Louis. Can you arrange something?"

"I'll see what I can do."

After spending the evening with Jasper in an auberge near Honfleur and dined on boiled mutton and hot spiced wine, I slept all through the night for the first time in a long time. The auberge was not the quietest of the town, but the few pitchers of wine did the trick. At dawn, Jasper knocked on my door, making me jump out of bed. King Louis was on his way to meet me in the town.

"I was expecting to go to Plessis to meet the king," I said after having refreshed myself the best I could without any soap or warm water.

"For some reason, he offered to travel to meet you. That is a great honor."

"Or does it mean he wants to send me back to England and see me off his land?"

Jasper laughed. "Come, we do not wish to make him wait. I've got horses waiting for us in the stables.

The ride only took us a good ten minutes, and I was pleased the weather in France was a little more clement than it had been in Wales the last few weeks. Walking through the streets of Honfleur brought back the memories of Fauconberg and Hampton, and though I should have been happy that soon the king would confirm his support, I felt sad and reminisced about the past. As we approached the house where I was to meet the king, I stopped.

"What's wrong?" Jasper asked.

"This house... it doesn't belong to King Louis but Hampton. Why is the king meeting me here?" I asked in a trembling voice.

"I don't know. Come," he replied and spurred his horse towards the gates.

For a moment, I dreamed that someone else would be present with King Louis. Perhaps Fauconberg was right. Hampton was alive, and he was waiting for me behind those walls. I pushed my horse to reach the gate first and threw the reins to a groom as I jumped off the saddle.

But as I approached the door, King Louis appeared on the threshold.

"Lady Alys, time has spared you, I see," he said and appeared pleased to see me. Still, even if this was a great honor, I paid little attention, for I had only one thing in mind and expected to see someone else behind the king.

"And you have not changed either, your Majesty," I replied briefly while attempting to look over his shoulders to see if Hampton was there.

"Come in, it is much warmer inside," he said, leading the way. Jasper waited in the hall with some of the king's men while I followed King Louis into the parlor, which I recognized at once, even if all the furniture had been removed but two leather chairs by the fireplace.

As the king invited me to sit down, I was a little disappointed to see that Hampton was not there.

"Why are you meeting me here?" I asked, with my eyes wandering across the room.

"Jasper Tudor informed me that you wished to see me. He also said you would force my door if I did not accept your visit and I believed him, but I must warn you: do not expect me to raise an army against the king of England," he said without replying to my question.

"I am not expecting you to go to battle. A long time ago, Hampton told me that you could win wars without shedding blood."

"Lord Hampton was right when he said you have the wisdom of a man. Tell me, what is it that you want from me?"

"Since the ...." I could not manage to say it, fearing that my hopes would vanish for real if I were to say it. "Since the..."

"Since King Edward has been back on the throne," King Louis said, to ease my feelings.

"Thank you. Edward has stopped my trades, and apart from the crops from my lands, I have no income. Someone stole all my goods. I need to start a new trade with France."

King Louis lifted an eyebrow. "What makes you think King Edward will not stop this one either?"

"Simply because he will not know I am behind it. It will belong to lady du Plessis," I said, using the first name that came into my head.

"Why would Madame du Plessis get involved in this trade?"

At least as far as I knew, there was no lady du Plessis; that was only the name of one of the residences of King Louis. But the king's tone implied that there was a real Madame du Plessis somewhere.

"It's just a name I am borrowing to trade under a different name, and in the position I am, I would be able to discover when information is delivered to Edward."

"Yes, I've heard you were his mistress."

"I..."

He raised a hand to stop me. "No need to deny it. Everyone knows, even in France."

"But–" My response was interrupted by a maid who brought in a tray with a large jug of wine and two goblets.

"ARE YOU GOING TO TELL me you've bedded him with the intention to remove him from the throne?" The king asked as he took the goblet the maid offered him.

"What I do with my life is none of your concern! But I can assure you that I am not his mistress." I shook my head as the maid approached.

"When you request my help for an uprising in England, then I want to be sure you know which side you are on."

"I know on which side I am on, thank you," I replied, clutching the side of the chair.

"Good, then you will have no objection if the king of England is killed in a battle or elsewhere."

"I... I want him off the throne, but I did not say I wanted him dead."

"While Edward is alive, he will not abandon his throne. He will always come back until he no longer lives. Besides, being his mistress puts you in a very convenient position; you could cut his throat during his sleep. Why haven't you done so already?"

"Your Majesty, with all due respect," I said, unwilling to repeat myself, for it was clear that he had made his mind and did not want to listen. "Edward is not the root of the problem, but his wife and her family are. Taking Edward's life would only complicate matters more. His son would be the king, and Elizabeth even more powerful. No, we must replace him with fresh blood. The Yorks and Woodvilles must be defeated together. I can't do that myself; that is why I need you."

"Indeed, you are pretty clever, after all."

"Who said I wasn't?" I asked as I picked up one of the goblets of wine.

"When you leave your children in a vulnerable position, that does not make me think you are the most intelligent person."

At the mention of my children, my heart skipped a beat. "I have not left them on their own but with trusted people."

"Haven't you yet learned not to trust anyone, not even myself?"

"I trust you, your Majesty."

"I am flattered, but you should not." He brought his goblet to his mouth and drained the content in one gulp.

"Oh! Is that why you never replied to my letter? Because you did not want to help?"

"I have received no letters from you, I'm afraid. What was it about?"

"I needed money."

"And you thought I would give it to you, just like that." He clicked his fingers, beckoned the maid to refill his cup.

"No, I had promised you Calais and-"

"Is Calais yours to give?"

I lowered my eyes. King Louis knew I had nothing and was no one anymore, so I stood up and curtseyed. "Thank you for your time, Your Majesty," I said, disheartened that I had wasted my time. And then a thought crossed my mind. "Do you know Gérard du Boisbaudry?"

For a fleeting moment, his eyes darted toward the arras, and then he quickly said: "No, I am sorry, I've never heard that name. Anyway, I'll help your contender reach England when he is ready, but you will need to be a little more patient. In the meantime, I'll arrange for a boat full of French wine to reach lady du Plessis, but I want half of your profits. That seems fair. Also, I do not wish to involve you in any further plans. Edward will be defeated and removed from the throne for good. However, you will know nothing about it."

I lifted my eyes, and my smile broadened. "Oh, thank you," I said, almost wanting to leap across the room to embrace him.

"Now, return to Wales and wait, and if you want my advice, stay away from London and King Edward."

CHAPTER SIXTEEN
April 1473, Vancey, Estrilda

E strilda and Francis had been living in the North for a couple of months, but Estrilda struggled to adapt to living in the countryside every day. Having lived all her life in London with its putrid air, its incessant busy and noisy streets, its banks full of beggars imploring pity for alms all day long, getting used to the peaceful life of the small castle and looking after a household proved rather tricky. However, today was different. Under a timid, early spring sunshine, the courtyard was heaving with people, merchants and villagers, all bringing supplies to welcome the king and queen.

"I will do my best to honor you, husband."

"Be gracious, amuse the queen. She has always liked you, so it should be easy."

Francis Burley was eager to receive the king, even if he did not have a large estate. Anyhow, it was only for a short period, and deep inside, Estrilda hoped that the decision to stop at Vancey came from Richard.

As soon as Edward and his retinue approached the gates, Estrilda's husband and the domestics became agitated. But all Estrilda could think about was how she would hide her joy at seeing Richard again.

However, to her great dismay, Richard was not there, for he had gone to Wales to the countess of Dudllan. The evening entertainment had been entirely aimed at pleasing the king with more food and wine than they could spare. At least, everything went on better than her husband expected.

In the early hours, when every guest had retired to their bedchamber, Estrilda decided to do the same, but as she climbed the stairs to her chamber, the king stepped in front of her to block the passage.

"You are more beautiful than I remembered. Lady Burley, you remind me of-" He paused, grabbed her by the waist, and pushed her in the corner so she couldn't escape. King Edward had drunk a lot of wine, and he probably had forgotten that he was the guest of her husband. Edward moved his face closer to hers. She was petrified. She did not want to offend the king, but she was not willing to become one of his whores.

"Your Grace, please, you have a wife," she said, trying to restrain his approach and turned her head to avoid his lips and his drunken breath. "Don't force me to do this to the queen; she has been good to me."

"I am the king, and you will do as I say." He grabbed both her shoulders and pulled her closer.

"Please, I beg you not to force me. I am married, and my husband is a faithful follower of the house of York… Do not tempt me anymore. My heart belongs to someone else."

"Richard?" he asked, releasing her.

"Yes, from the moment I saw him, I felt strange. Don't tell him, please."

"Your secret is safe with me… if you keep this little incident to yourself." He passed his hand through his hair.

"I will." Estrilda bowed and scurried up the stairs. From the corner of her eye, she noticed the queen moving away as if to avoid being seen. Hence, Estrilda pretended not to have seen her, but she did not want her to think she had done anything wrong with the king.

Therefore, she stopped and turned to face the king. "Your Grace?" she called. He stopped and turned around as if ready to follow her up the stairs.

"Have you changed your mind?" he asked.

"No. I was just wondering if you were still having an affair with the countess of Dudllan?"

Edward blanched but did not reply.

"Good night, Your Grace," Estrilda said and curtseyed before continuing to her bedchamber, knowing the queen had heard their conversation and that she would be furious with Edward, and thus she would do something to prevent him from seeing lady Alys again. After all, lady Alys had stopped Estrilda from seeing her lover; there was no reason Estrilda should not do the same to her. Besides, preventing the king from seeing her would also stop Richard from going to Wales. Lady Alys was too much of an evil influence over Richard.

CHAPTER SEVENTEEN
February 1473, Dudllan, Alys

When I left France, I returned to Wales intending to confront Gérard and kick him out of Dudllan, but he was no longer there when I arrived.

"Didn't he say where he was going?"

"No, Gérard disappeared shortly after he heard you were going to Honfleur. I did not have a chance to confront him myself," said Robyn. "He was gone before I arrived."

"Who told him I was there? I don't recall having mentioned it to him before I left."

"Your son Geoffrey, but you can't blame him."

"Fret not. Of course, I am not blaming my son."

At least it was a relief that my children were all safe, even if I was somewhat disappointed that Gérard had left without an explanation or having told us who he was spying for. Another counsel of Fauconberg I had not followed. Still, I struggled with the idea that Gérard wanted to hurt me. On many occasions, he could have killed me, and he had not attempted it once. On the contrary, there wasn't anything he wouldn't have done. Gérard was always helpful and caring, mayhap it was how he had hoped to gain my confidence, and I had fallen for it without thinking. Now he had most certainly already informed the king or queen about my visit to France. At least he wasn't aware of the reason I traveled there. According to my son, Gérard did not ask why I went to France. All he said was that he had to go, and he left.

A MONTH AFTER MY RETURN from France, I was back in London, summoned by the king. At first, I dreaded that the invitation was to reproach me for my little escapade to France, but Edward mentioned nothing about it. Mayhap he was not aware.

A knock on the door took me out of a pleasant dream. For a moment, I wondered why I had returned to London. Fauconberg was right, I was in danger of losing myself, and I certainly did not want to be Edward's mistress. I did not want people to call me his whore. I was not! Although. it was hard to ignore the gossip floating around and the buzz of conversation stopping when I entered a room.

Edward had given me back my freedom, but he had not returned my fortune, and he certainly could not give me back the most significant treasure I'd ever possessed. That one was gone forever, and it was Edward's fault. I would never forget that, and people were idiots to imagine I could ever love Edward. I wanted so much to trust Fauconberg's last words, but no one else believed me when I talked about his confession. Everyone told me that I had misheard. Robyn was right, if Hampton was alive, he would have come to me.

The knocking on the door became more persistent.

"What is it?" I finally asked.

"Hurry, I have a surprise for you. Put your riding gown on," said Edward as he entered the bedchamber.

"What are you doing in my chamber at this early hour?"

"Get your riding gown on and follow me."

WE ARRIVED AT THE STABLES full of many magnificent horses. Edward took my hand and asked me to close my eyes, which I did, and then he guided me forward. The clip-clop of a single horse echoed against the pavement, followed by what sounded like a lot of movements around, but I kept my eyes shut. Still, I smelled a whiff of the familiar odor of a horse, very close to us. For a second, I imagined it was Tristan. Then Edward stopped and said: "Open your eyes."

A majestic dapple-gray mare of at least 17hh stood in front of me.

"I know you are missing Tristan, so I wanted to make sure this one would be different and special to you."

"She's splendid," I said as I stretched my hand for the mare to sniff it.

"I bought her a few months ago for you. But you disappeared the day I intended to surprise you. She's just past four years old and comes straight from the queen of Spain's stables. I am sure you will teach her everything she needs to know."

"Is she mine?" I asked, unable to hide a smile.

He nodded. "Her name is Boudicca." Edward wrapped his arms around me. I moved back.

"Why are you so kind to me?" I asked, ensuring I was keeping my distance.

"It's not without interest; you'll repay me one day."

I did not have to ask, for it was apparent what he meant, and it was not subtle of him to bribe me with such a beautiful horse. He would want me to become his mistress in return for the gift.

"I cannot accept," I said, stepping out of the stables, dodging a squire who was bringing a brand-new saddle. Without looking back, I dashed inside the building and ascended the stairs to my bedchamber.

STILL ANGERED THAT Edward had thought to bribe me with that beautiful horse, I poured myself a goblet of wine and sipped it slowly. I was lost in my thoughts when Edward entered the chamber. I did not move. I stayed by the cabinet and continued sipping the wine as if I had not noticed him. He was still handsome enough in his early thirties, but there was no attraction. Too many disturbing memories lay between us. Although I knew that he came to convince me to reconsider my decision, I put the goblet down and was about to ask him why he had entered my bedchamber without even knocking on the door.

Before I spoke, he enveloped his arms around me and swayed me over as if we were dancing. I did not resist. The warmth of his embrace was all I needed at that time. I turned to face him, and for a while, we stared at each other without a word. Our fingers interlaced. I was as if paralyzed, incapable but also unwilling to flee, even if reason was nagging me in the back of my head, pleading with me to step away from the king. For the first time in a long time, I wanted him to kiss me.

He caressed my cheeks, and then he brought me closer to him and slid his hands down my back. His lips on my skin burned with passion, and when he pressed against me, I felt his desire to have me.

"That's enough," I said, stepping back.

But Edward ignored me, lifted me in his arms, carried me to the fireplace, and laid me on the floor. He smiled like he had won a battle.

"Remember I told you once that one day you'd be my favorite mistress."

I chuckled. "Yes, I do remember," I said as I propped on my elbow. "But I also recall having told you that this would never happen."

"You did not mean it."

At the time, I meant it without a doubt. Now I was not so sure. But I did not want to tell him, nor did I want to anger him, for I could not afford to lose his interest.

"I am not ready. Please, you must give me more time." I sat and stared at the hearth.

"Is it a promise?"

I remained silent. Then he stood up and invited me to do the same.

"Let's not talk about the past. Come, we must attend the feast and celebrate."

"Must I?"

"Yes, this is an order from your king, and you cannot refuse it. Put on the gown I've sent you; I want you to shine among my guests today."

"I am sure your wife will appreciate this."

Then as we left my bedchamber hand in hand, guilt rushed over me. What was I doing, letting my senses control my mind? I had to remain vigilant, for Edward's company was extremely pleasant and I did not know how long I would be able to resist his tender embraces.

RELUCTANTLY, I FOLLOWED Edward into the great hall, but, unwilling to attract attention, I stood in the corner of the room and watched people dance. Edward sat on the throne with his wife by his side. She took his hand and did not let it go for a long time. Had she scented another woman on it? Had she sensed his unfaithful desire? Although we tried to be discreet, Edward kept on glancing at me, and our eyes met a few times. Each time I turned my head away as if I was not interested in him. But he had given me hope and, dare I say, happiness; he had brought me back to life when I thought I would never find it again. I stared at him. Being loved by a powerful man gave me the impression that I was eighteen again, and it fueled my sense of power. It gave me confidence.

Then an image of Hampton crossed my mind, and I felt sick with myself. Edward was stealing my soul, but I had to take it back. I could not fall for him.

All the same, Edward was a man who could give me the power I craved for... but I had done things that could destroy this power. The king of France and Tudor were preparing the rebellion, and there would be nothing I could do to stop them. Once the time came, and all the people involved would be ready, they'd launch an attack on England. I supposed that being on both sides meant that I would win whatever the outcome, but did I want a court where Margaret Beaufort would reign over her son until he was of age? Speaking of the devil, there she was, still dressed in black, having to mourn her first husband for the last fifteen years. I wondered if I had made a judicious choice when I offered her my support via Fauconberg.

At least I could trust her discretion, for if I was to fall, I would make sure she'd fall with me. Edward had a court full of people scheming behind his back, and it was like he either did not care or did not see it. Did he really believe that people had accepted his wife and her family now that Hampton was dead? As if to bring me back to my senses, the last words of Fauconberg haunted me again. Then, as I quietly minded my own business in the corner of the hall, rocked by the music the minstrels played in the gallery, Robyn gestured to catch my attention.

"Lady Alys," Robyn whispered.

I looked around and followed him to an antechamber.

"Be careful, Estrilda knows you've been to France," he said once I had closed the door behind me.

"How did she find out? She's not been in London for months. Do you think she has spoken to Gérard?"

"No, of that I am sure, but I don't know how she found out. I heard lady Spencer mentioning to someone that Estrilda was thinking about informing Richard."

"Lady Spencer? I don't know her. I should have a word with Richard before someone else does."

"Perhaps we should silence this lady Spencer and also Estrilda; they possess too much information, and they are too close to the queen." Robyn put his hand on his dagger as if ready to act at once.

I lifted my hand. "No. I do not wish to harm Estrilda. I'm aware that her loyalty has changed, but I cannot blame her. It is probably my fault. I'm the one who placed her in the queen's service, and now she has nowhere else to go."

"Or it is that Estrilda's roots are coming back, and she has forgotten who saved her?" Robyn looked disappointed by my clemency.

"Estrilda is not like you, Robyn. I must say that I am very grateful for everything you have done for me. Still, sometimes I worry that you might feel obliged, and I would hate to think that what you do, you do with obligation."

"No, I do what I do because I was taught that doing the honorable thing and being faithful is the most important thing."

"You've not been taught that by Hampton."

"Fauconberg," he said.

I smiled.

"But there is something else? That lady Spencer. You do know her."

"Do I?"

"Remember lady Jane? The one who pretended to be your friend."

I paced to the window. In the courtyard below, a few of the queen's ladies tittered with some of the guards and there she was, Jane! My heart sank. "No. It can't be. Hampton got rid of her."

"He only kicked her out. In truth, he didn't expect her to find a husband who would place her in the queen's services."

"Hmm. Did you say she was a friend of Estrilda?" I asked as I stepped away from the window, having enough to look at the traitorous face of lady Jane.

"Very close. Until the queen sent Estrilda away from court while she had her child, the two of them were inseparable."

"We must get rid of her."

"Leave it to me," he said as we left the room before heading back for to the hall.

"No, if you get caught, it will be the scaffold. I will come up with something," I whispered, and then I noticed Robert Woodville and I hid behind the arras.

"Also, I found who took your goods from Master Cloppelin's storeroom. The fellow's name is Heathcote. He is part of the corporation at Guildhall."

"Then I shall send him a little message, thank you, Robyn. I'll speak to the king."

CHAPTER EIGHTEEN
August 1473, London, Estrilda

As the cart passed the gates of the city, Estrilda took a deep breath and recognized the putrid air typical of London, yet in a way, this brought her back to life. She'd never paid attention to how bad it was in London before, but it was where she grew up and where she felt the most alive. Once Estrilda was back at court, lady Spencer, whom she had missed a lot, filled her in with all the latest gossip at court. Mainly about lady Alys and King Edward.

"The She-Devil is back!" said the queen, pacing the room while twisting the sleeves of her gown.

None of the ladies said a word. Of course, they all had seen the countess of Dudllan around earlier in the week, but lady Alys had not attended any banquets, and no one had dared to mention her presence to the queen. Now Elizabeth was aware of it, her ladies were expecting a jug or a goblet to fly across the room, but instead, Elizabeth yelled: "Leave! All of you."

Without waiting for a second order, the ladies gathered their embroidery baskets and left the room, conversing amongst themselves. Further down the corridor, Estrilda gave her basket to lady Spencer. "Put this away for me, please."

"Why? Where are you going?"

"I must see Richard."

"I regret to tell you this, but you must hurry if you want to catch up with him. He's going on an outing with the countess of Dudllan."

This was the third time this week that the two of them were going out on their own. Being unable to ride, Estrilda was a little frustrated that she could not follow them to find out what they were up to. Were Richard and lady Alys having an affair?

AS ESTRILDA WAS ABOUT to enter the stable yard, she heard laughs. She stopped dead and peered from the corner and saw lady Alys and Richard. Children would not have behaved differently. The grooms brought in their horses, all saddled, ready to go out. Lady Alys was resplendent in her bright red velvet riding dress, and she had a new horse. Rumors were that the king bought this beautiful mare for her—he paid a colossal sum for the horse. Then Richard helped her up on the saddle, and Estrilda did not like how he touched her. Lady Alys had taken Edward from the queen, and now she was taking Richard from her. Estrilda couldn't hear what they were saying to each other, for they were whispering and giggling, which was very inappropriate, considering that there were grooms, squires, and men-at-arms nearby.

Sometimes, Estrilda wondered if she would not be better off staying at Vancey, at least there, she would forget about lady Alys and Richard. But here, she would be the first to find out what was happening between them.

As they passed near Estrilda, she quickly hid behind a pillar, for she did not want to show her face. The warm day had brought good humor to the domestics, who seemed to rejoice in the sunshine that lifted their spirits, but it did not have that effect on Estrilda. The laughs and the hubbub of their joyful conversations, instead of making her happy, sunk her mood in deeper darkness. She waited a long time for Richard and lady Alys to return, but then duty called her, and she had to go back to the queen's chamber.

After a few hours, when she returned to the queen's private chamber, Richard and Alys finally returned, both still looking quite jovial, and the king welcomed them in the courtyard. He even kissed Alys as he helped her out of the saddle. This was far too scandalous. Estrilda felt sorry for Elizabeth, who was still acting as if everything was perfectly normal.

"Why do you let him humiliate you?" Estrilda wanted to ask, but then she realized that she was no better than Lady Alys herself. Even though the affair between Richard and Estrilda was different, they were in love before he married. Lady Alys could not be in love with the king, surely not. She had accused him publicly of killing lord Hampton, and she had rebelled. Estrilda even wondered if she did not pretend to like him so that she could murder him in his sleep one day. But again, Estrilda could not tell that to anyone with no proof.

That evening when Estrilda met Richard, she reprimanded him for his lack of attention, to which he replied with a passionate embrace.

"Do not be jealous," he whispered in her hair.

Needless to say, he and she were much more discreet than the king and his mistress, and at least, they had the decency to hide from the courtiers to kiss. Yet sometimes, even if they did not kiss in public, they could not help looking at each other and dancing like no one else was around. But when lady Alys was around, Richard enjoyed dancing with her more than with Estrilda, and the king even let them do it. The thought of the three of them being together also crossed Estrilda's mind, but she knew Richard. He was gentle and pure; he would never let himself indulge in that sort of devilish, immoral act.

LATER THAT EVENING, when the tables had been cleared and everyone had started to dance, Richard took Estrilda's hand.

"Did you have a pleasant time this afternoon with the countess of Dudllan?" she asked, swirling around him to the rhythm of the music while refraining from being too reproachful; she had to make him realize how hurtful his attitude was.

"Thank you, yes. We rode outside London into the woods. It was a much-needed distraction."

"I wish I could ride, so you could go with me and with not her."

"So, it is true, you cannot ride at all? I had heard about it, but I did not want to believe it. I am surprised that your father had not thought about this."

A few steps to Estrilda's left before she could reply, and then she glided closer to him. "Most of the times, we were traveling by cart in Flanders," she continued, hoping that was enough and that he would not ask any more about her life in Flanders. Then, as they kept on dancing, she changed the conversation. "Did you know that the countess went to France a few months ago?" she asked him.

"No."

"Don't you find it strange? She must be plotting against the king; otherwise, why would she come back to court just after she met the king of France?"

"Don't be so spiteful. Lady Alys has a noble heart. She would never harm my brother."

Estrilda stopped in mid-swirl, letting his arm go, stepped away from the other dancers. There were no words she could have said that would have made him change his mind about Alys. She could do no wrong in his eyes, and it was frustrating for Estrilda.

AS LADY SPENCER AND Estrilda passed the gates and hopped on the barge, Estrilda covered her face with a hood. Since she had been living at court, going into the streets of London reminded of her previous life and putting on a hood was like putting a wall between the present and the past life she wanted so much to forget. She was a lady now, no longer a nobody in rags and barefoot, and neither was she the daughter of a merchant anymore but a lady-in-waiting to the queen, married to a wonderful man. Accompanied by lady Spencer, they rushed along the wharf and avoided the many puddles of urine, rain, and animal dung. Each time Estrilda walked across the streets, her gown was ruined.

On the Wednesday, the day the new fabrics arrived from Flanders, lady Spencer and Estrilda were a little late to get first hands on the merchandise—they should have been there just after dawn when the merchants unloaded their delivery of silks, damask, all sort of furs and velour, but both women overslept after reveling a little too late the night before. Most of the merchants knew they were there on behalf of the queen, and fortunately, none recognized Estrilda as the Cloppelins' daughter, so even if they were a little late, they expected some to have kept the best fabric aside for them. Mainly because the merchants were all hoping that the women would put good words in for them.

"Psst!" Someone hissed, trying to attract Estrilda's attention.

She turned around but saw no one. Then she heard it again as if the sound was following them. As Estrilda twisted her neck, she noticed someone hiding at the corner of the street. Someone or a ghost at that point, she could not tell as the vision had been so furtive, but then Estrilda heard her name.

"Continue without me," she told her friend.

"But, Estrilda, I don't know the way very well, and you are so much better than me at dealing with those merchants. They always give you a special price. They will try to rip me off."

"Tell them I will come a little later, I need to... do something."

Then lady Spencer took Estrilda's forearm and brought her face closer to her ears: "Have you got a new lover?"

Estrilda looked down, pretending to be ashamed. "Please, tell no one."

"You have my word," she said and laughed. "And I thought no one would be able to get the duke out of your head," she added and continued towards the market while Estrilda headed in the opposite direction.

"MOTHER? IS THAT YOU?" Estrilda asked as she approached the corner of the old timber-framed house at the angle of Dyer Street and Cobblers Street.

"Yes," Lysbette said as she moved forward.

"You are alive! I've enquired at almost every jail, and I could not find you." Ensuring that she was not dreaming and at the same time so relieved to see her safe, Estrilda embraced Lysbette with all her heart.

"I was in Flanders. The queen's men put me on a ship to Burgundy, and I had to swear I would never return to England."

"So why did you? You should have stayed there where it is safer. Come, we can't stay here. What if someone sees you?" Estrilda said, put her arms around Lysbette, and walked towards the wharf, which was more crowded, and therefore they could easily disappear within the throng. Not even a bitch could find her pups.

"Estrilda, you must help me see lady Alys. I've tried to go to Westminster, but that boy, Robyn, said Alys did not wish to see me anymore. He's lying. Help me, please. It is important that I see her as soon as possible."

"No, you cannot. If someone finds out you are here to meet her; the queen will have no mercy on you. Mother, there is something I must tell you about lady Alys: she is our enemy, and we have to accept that we were wrong about her."

"If she is the enemy, then why is she parading at court as if she was the queen herself, as if Hampton had returned?"

"Because lady Alys is lady Alys. She does not like being left in the shadows. She is the king's mistress, but we must not speak to her. I am a lady of the queen, and honestly, I am outraged by the king's attitude."

"If lady Alys is as bad as you say, then explain why she rescued you when you were living in the streets. Do not forget that if you are here today, it is thanks to her."

"Perhaps she was kinder when she was younger, but she has changed. Even you said that many times in the past. You said lord Hampton had changed her and that she became cruel and heartless."

Lysbette stayed speechless for a while. She could not deny that, indeed she had had that feeling when Hampton was alive. Now he was no longer here, Lysbette had the feeling that Alys had softened, or at least she thought she had. Perhaps it was just her pitying Alys for having to live in disgrace with five children.

"Lady Alys is a lonely person and needs us. When we needed her, she never abandoned us as a matter of fact. The reason you lacked nothing when you grew up was that she always provided everything you needed."

"You have a soft spot for her, but lady Alys is not what you think. She manipulates people to reach her goal. The proof is that she did nothing to stop the execution of Father, and she knew about it. You've always said she had the same mind as lord Hampton, pretending to be a lamb to get what they wanted. But only her bastards and her dead lover count."

"Never call her children bastards," she said and slapped Estrilda. Not even when Estrilda had misbehaved when she was younger had Lysbette reacted like that.

"But they are," Estrilda said, feeling tears welling up in her eyes, so she stopped and stared at the barges that floated on the side of the water.

"So is yours. Francis Burley might have given you his name, but the truth is that your child is a bastard, too."

Clearing her throat with a little cough, Estrilda said: "Mother! Lady Alys has turned your head."

"And the queen yours! You are no longer the grateful girl I had. When lady Alys brought you into our home that night, I must admit that at first, I was not too pleased. Although we weren't poor, we weren't rich either. But from the day lady Alys left for Middleham, I've loved you, and I would do everything for you. Have I ever treated you differently than my sons?" she asked.

Estrilda lowered her eyes and shook her head.

"You are my daughter, but I feel like I am losing you. I was not happy the day lady Alys decided that you should marry the son of lord Stanley. I was worried that you would be sent to court, and I was right. The court does bad things to people. It changes people for the worse."

"Mother, please do not be angry with me. You must trust me when I say that lady Alys is not a good person and that you should stop seeing her. Mayhap you are right. If she had not sent me to court, I probably would not have seen the other side of her character, I would not have seen what she was capable of, and I would still trust her. Her plan has turned against her." Estrilda walked on, avoiding a group of rough young lads.

"Do you hate her that much?" Lysbette asked as she dodged a drunk lad and a puddle of urine.

"Our duty is to serve our king, and Edward is the true king, but even if she is his mistress, I know lady Alys still plots against him."

"What did you say?" she asked, grabbing Estrilda's arm to stop her.

"She still plots against the king."

"No. You said she is his mistress. That cannot be true."

"I am afraid it is."

"But that can't be! She always said that the king killed lord Hampton. She hated him when I saw her last. I can understand that she might flirt, but his mistress! No, this can't be true. From the moment she fell in love with Hampton, she never looked at another man."

"Hopefully now you realize that what I am saying is true. She is using people. Lady Alys is now the mistress of King Edward, and the queen knows it too, but what everyone is ignoring is that lady Alys is still plotting to remove King Edward from the throne. I discovered that she is in contact with Henry Tudor and his uncle. No one has found the letters, as she destroys them as soon as she reads them, and she uses Robyn to deliver her messages. Everyone knows he would rather die than betray her."

Lysbette sat down on a lower wall, flabbergasted by the news she did not want to believe.

"She went to France," Estrilda continued.

"How do you know all those things? Is the king aware of this?"

"I have only told Richard, but he did not want to believe me."

"But if you hate her that much, I am surprised you have not told the queen or the king."

"The king would not listen to me; he is head over heels about her, and if I tell the queen, she would not be able to do anything, for King Edward would only think that she is trying to spoil lady Alys's reputation, and it would only bring Edward closer to lady Alys. I was hoping Richard would listen."

"The duke of Gloucester might be your lover, but first, he is her friend."

"He is not her friend," Estrilda said, trying to convince herself she was telling the truth. She knew they were spending a lot of time together, but Estrilda was still hoping that he would put her before Alys. After all, she was the mother of his child.

"They've always been friends, and if their friendship has survived lord Hampton's death, then nothing will break it. I'm afraid you cannot trust him when it comes to lady Alys. She will always come before you."

"No. Why would he put her first; I am the mother of his child!"

Lysbette thought about it a moment.

"What is it?" she asked, seeing Lysbette was trying to hide something from her. "Mother, tell me."

"I think he might love her," she said, avoiding her eyes.

"This is ridiculous. I know you disapproved of me having a lover, and you would like that I return to my husband. Believe me, I have tried, but I love Richard, and there is nothing I can do about it. He is always in my thoughts."

"I have not said he doesn't love you, but I believe he is really fond of lady Alys, and I don't believe you can change it."

"Then I shall leave court and take my child with me."

"Now, this is a wise decision. You will be better away from it all and enjoy your son's company," she said and stood up.

"Yes, but that means he will grow up like a farmer. A rich landowner with no manners and no army."

"What do you think is best?"

As they walked along, Estrilda stopped and took Lysbette's hands.

"You are right. I will speak to my husband. Why don't you come to the north with me? No one will find you there."

"No, I shall return to Flanders soon. I only came to see lady Alys, but I guess I will have to return without seeing her," she said, letting Estrilda's hands go, and walked on.

"You did not say what was so important that you risked your freedom to come to London for her?"

"Perhaps it wasn't important at all. I thought it was, but if what you tell is true, then I have indeed been very foolish to travel all this way," she said without elaborating more. "I'll take the first ship out of London."

SEEING LYSBETTE LEAVING again made Estrilda sad and she could not help but recall the conversation and the fact that Lysbette said Richard was fond of lady Alys. Undeniably, lady Alys was a prey whom all men wanted, and was indeed a beautiful lady, but Queen Elizabeth was much prettier, and that did not stop the king from bedding another woman. She tried to understand what men saw in her. Alys had no fortune of her own and had acted like a whore most of her life, and still, men found her attractive. She would not steal Richard from Estrilda. Who knows, when she'd be bored with the king, she might turn to Richard. They spent an awful lot of time together.

Rushing back to the palace, as Estrilda thought about a way to get rid of lady Alys, an idea crossed her mind. Alys must remarry. Preferably someone who'd take her far away from London and from Richard, and Estrilda would have him for herself. He'd no longer have an excuse to visit her in Wales. Immediately, Estrilda rushed back to the market to join lady Spencer and then, once they had the fabrics, Estrilda intended to speak to the queen about her little plan.

LATER ON THAT AFTERNOON, just before Vesper and after dropping the fabric they had purchased on the market in the antechamber, Estrilda joined the queen. Her conversation with Lysbette had troubled her all the way back to the palace.

"Your Majesty? May I speak to you about a delicate matter?" she asked, seeing that Elizabeth appeared to be in a good mood.

"Hmm. What is it?" the queen asked, lifting her nose from the book she was reading. "Have you not got the new fabric I asked for?"

"Oh, no, I have it," Estrilda said. "We have found some fantastic new damask and ermine fur. No, I would like to talk to you about the countess of Dudllan."

Once she'd mentioned the name, she heard a few needles dropping on the floor and glanced at the ladies around the queen's chamber. Fortunately, at the sound of the name of lady Alys, Queen Elizabeth waved her hand, signaling the ladies-in-waiting should leave the room.

"Tell me," she said once they were alone.

"The countess should remarry."

"Why should this concern you?" she asked, closing the book in a loud clap.

Estrilda blenched, and for a second she worried, but she had no choice now, she had to speak. "She... She and Richard are spending too much time together for my liking. If she were to marry someone who lives as far as Scotland, that would put my mind at peace."

"And mine," Elizabeth muttered. "Scotland, hmm, that is indeed quite far. You are right. That is the only way unless we'd consider murder, of course."

Aghast, Estrilda stared at the queen. Estrilda was no longer an admirer of lady Alys, but she would not have gone as far as to murder her. Admittedly, Alys was most certainly capable of doing so herself. Nothing would have stopped lady Alys from killing someone to protect herself or her children, but Estrilda did not want to be the accomplice of anyone's murder. Not even Alys's.

"Surely, you are not considering.... that, Your Grace?" she asked.

"Why not? This would save me a lot of trouble."

"What about her children?"

"They'd be better off without her, or she might turn them into enemies of the crown."

"Not if you take them from her and put them with a loyal tutor," Estrilda suggested.

"Excellent, Estrilda. Excellent. She will suffer more if we take her children from her. Oh, and we should arrange for her to marry as soon as possible And then we'll separate her from her children. That will finish her. I knew you were a faithful person, but I did not realize you could be so sharp but also so devilish. You might need to see your confessor, lady Vancey."

"Oh, no, I did not—"

"Do no fear, for God is on our side; He does not like sinners. I am sure he appreciates us more if we were to bring back a lost sheep on the right path."

"Um..."

"Ah, jealousy... it would cause a saint to betray his companions. Right, if you can excuse me, I must speak to the king about our little plan," she said. "Thank you, Estrilda."

As the queen left the room, Estrilda remained alone in the private chamber, composing her thoughts. Was she right to have suggested that lady Alys should be sent away, that she should be separated from her children? Suddenly a wave of nausea invaded Estrilda, and the urge to confess took over her conscience.

CHAPTER NINETEEN
September 1473, London, Alys

"You've no idea how I enjoy our little outings," Richard said as we crossed the city gates and headed toward Waltham Forest, leaving behind us the bustle of London and its repulsive smell. Somehow, I wondered how I had lived in London without paying attention to it. Now, I could not wait to get out of the city and breath in the fragrance of the oat fields that bordered the woods and the moss that covered the undergrowth of the forest. The sun was still hot, and the roads were dry and dusty. Farther ahead, peasants harvested the field. Their joyous songs- which was probably a way to give them the strength to work from dawn to dusk with very little respite- reached us and lifted my mood even more, giving me the courage to speak to Richard.

"Richard, I need your help. But please do not ask me anymore—just agree or refuse, but do not ask me the reason for my request."

"That does not sound like something lawful. Tell me," he said, twisting in his saddle to face me.

"Can you arrest Master Heathcote? You will find him at Guildhall. Oh, and once it's done, please arrange for someone to bring me his stock."

From the top of his horse, Richard lifted his brows. "You said I cannot ask why, but have you talked to Edward about it? I can't see him refusing you anything."

"I cannot ask him."

"Let me get this straight: you cannot trust the man you sleep with, but you think you can trust me, his brother?"

"Firstly, I do not sleep with your brother, and secondly," I brought Boudicca closer to his horse and placed a hand on his arm. "I know you have a good heart. Not always a good judgment, for sure, but you mean well, which is why I can't ask anyone else. You're the only one I trust at court."

"If you want that man out of the way, you could always hire someone to do the job. To be honest, that would be easier and knowing you, you certainly have the right contacts to proceed."

"It would be indeed the quickest way if I did not want to access his entire stock."

Again, Richard shot me a quizzical look, and although he did not speak, his eyes begged for more details.

"Fine," I said, "Heathcote stole my stock when Robert Woodville arrested Willem Cloppelin. The stock in Master Cloppelin's warehouse was mine, and they sold it to Heathcote with the king's agreement."

"Was Edward aware it was yours?"

"Without a doubt. Edward wanted me to have no fortune, no stock, no associates."

"And you want me to give you back the stock so you can build a fortune to continue lord Hampton's work against my family? I am your friend, but my family will always come first."

"Even before your mistress?" I asked, annoyed that he almost fathomed my aim.

He looked down. "Yes, even before Estrilda."

"I am certain she would be pleased to hear about that. Anyway, you are wrong. I do not intend to pay men for a rebellion, I want Heathcote to stop trading with my stock. I only want what is mine. What is wrong with that?"

"I shall see what I can do."

"Thank you, you never fail me. Now that business is over with, let's have fun. What about racing past the oat fields?" I suggested, and without giving him a chance to respond, I spurred Boudicca to a canter.

THAT EVENING, KNOWING I would soon retrieve my stock, I felt much better, was relieved, for soon the queen and her enormous family would pay for their evil actions. It had been a long time since I was enthusiastic. I noticed that my grin irritated more than one person that night, but I did not care, on the contrary.

Edward let a loud sigh of relief when I returned to my bedchamber and rose to his feet to take me into his arms as if he had not seen me for days.

"Edward, you must stop coming to my bedchamber every night; people are talking too much about us," I said, putting a finger to his lips to stop him from trying to kiss me.

"Why are you refusing me? Surely you are not worried about your reputation."

"No, I must admit that I find it quite empowering that people think I am your mistress," I said, removing my cloak and throwing it on the chair.

He grabbed the pitcher of wine on the side cabinet and poured two goblets.

"How long are you going to keep me longing? I cannot bear it anymore. I need you, Alys. I want you to be mine."

"As long as necessary," I said, eschewing another embrace.

"Why? I know you love me, even if you do not want to admit it. Why do you deny yourself the happiness you deserve?" he asked, and this time I let him wrap me in his arms, but I could not answer. He was right. I deserved to be happy and loved. But not with him. I could not love Edward, for he was the cause of my misery.

Then he let me go and took the wine. "There is something I meant to talk to you about for a while," he said in a rather severe tone as he brought me the wine.

Alarmed but doing my best to hide it, I sat on the bed and took the goblet. "You should not listen to gossip. I am not preparing a rebellion," I said.

"No, no, it's not that. The queen is getting edgy, and I believe we should try not to upset her more than necessary."

"Are you asking me to return to Wales?" I asked with a mixed feeling of sadness and relief. Undoubtedly, I would miss his company, but he was not Hampton. Thus it would not be too painful Edward could never equal him, and being away from him would help me keep the promise I had made to Hampton. Never to let anyone other than him touch me.

For some time, I doubted my ability to resist Edward much longer.

"No, I'm not asking you to go to Wales."

"Oh..." Now Edward had aroused my curiosity, and I moved to my feet.

"Mayhap, the time has come for you to remarry," he said, not even daring to look me in the eye.

"What!? I'm a widow. You've no right to force me this time."

"I don't, but the queen has asked me to stop seeing you. She can sense my love for you."

"But that is no reason to force me into marriage."

"I do it to protect you. If you marry, she will be at peace."

"You want to imprison me to please your wife! Remember, she tried to marry me off in the past, and we both know what happened." I paused for a while. "I refuse." I stood firmly on my feet and defiantly crossed my arms.

"Unfortunately, you cannot. I have decided you will marry, and you will."

"Are you sure you are doing this to appease the queen or is it to ensure that I am not doing anything against you? I don't know what people have told you about me, but you should not believe anything they've said. It is all lies."

"What are you talking about?" he asked.

For a second, I wondered if appeasing the queen was really all he wanted.

I moved by the window, looking out at the torches that lit the courtyard and the people coming in at out at this late hour. "I thought people would have said things about me. They always do."

"Hmm." He paused. "Anyway, my decision is made, and I will speak to lord Fullerton. I am sure he will be delighted to have you for a spouse."

"Never heard of him."

"That is why he's the perfect match. I don't believe he knows much about you either."

"Has he got any title?"

"Baron Fullerton."

"Is that it? A baron!" I said and wrapped a shawl around my shoulders and walked closer to the fireplace.

"Well, there aren't many bachelors or widowers available."

"What makes you think I would accept such a low union?"

"Because you love your children. You wouldn't like us to send them away from you."

"You would not dare."

"They are of noble blood, even if not legitimate. They must learn about their duties."

"I am dealing with their education."

"You have raised those boys against the York house. They must learn where their loyalties should lie."

"Do not worry about their loyalty. They know whom to be loyal to," I said and moved closer to the door, ready to leave, for I had enough of his conversation, but Edward stopped me and took me in his arms.

"Alys, Alys... Please. If you marry, you will keep your children."

"And if I don't?" I asked, pushing him away with both hands.

"Then you know what will happen."

"Fine, but do not expect me to ever become your lover if you force me to marry that lowlife," I said, raising my voice. "And find somewhere else to sleep tonight. I do not wish to see you for a while."

Edward tried to put a hand on my shoulder, but I stepped back and opened the door, inviting him to leave.

CHAPTER TWENTY
October 1473, London, Estrilda

King Edward, who needed Francis Burley's services more frequently, offered Francis a house in London. The freedom from the court and the fact that Estrilda could remain in London had delighted her.

Until last month, she had thought this would have brought her closer to Richard, who had been devoting his time to the She-Devil of Dudllan, but then Estrilda realized she had missed her course. Francis was overjoyed by the news, and, to be honest, so was Estrilda. She would have to wait a little longer for Richard. However, it was in vain, for by the time she would give birth, it would be almost a year since Richard and she had been together. Estrilda should have accepted Richard was in her past.

The gardens were not as large as Westminster's, but still of a decent size, and they even had a little orchard, a small one but still delectable. Especially at this time of the year when the scent of ripe apples and pears lingered everywhere. Their head cook would prepare some delightful sweet, which reminded Estrilda of her childhood with Lysbette. Estrilda had spent all afternoon picking apples and raspberries, ready to make some confits and conserves by Vesper time, but when she came back into the house, she saw Richard in the corridor. In shock, she dropped the basket of apples, and immediately he bent to help her pick up the fruit.

"What are you doing here? Aren't you supposed to be with your wife?" she asked.

Francis appeared at the door. "Estrilda, Richard has come to congratulate us."

"How does he know?" she asked as she approached her husband, took his hand and placed it on her belly. "My wife is expecting my heir," Francis said to Richard, who did not seem pleased by the news. His gaze became darker.

"Your Grace..." Estrilda said as Richard said nothing. "Aren't you happy for us?"

"Yes... Yes, that goes without saying, I'm pleased for both of you."

Then he clapped Francis on the back, and afterward he kissed Estrilda's hand. As she felt his lips on her skin, it was as if a barrier had fallen. All the desire she had tried so hard to suppress came back in a burning sensation.

"Francis, my friend, I actually came here to see my son, if I may."

"Of course."

As Francis passed through the door, Richard took Estrilda in his arms. "I've missed you so much."

How could she respond to that when her husband would be back any moment? Frozen by fear that Francis might return at once, Estrilda said nothing but did not move either.

"Don't you love me anymore?" Richard asked.

"You're married, remember? And you've also found me a wonderful husband, it should not surprise you if I tell you that I enjoy my husband's company. Anyhow, do not tell me you aren't enjoying your wife's bed every night," she said as she stepped back.

"Anne is nothing like you. Sometimes I regret..."

"Like me or like the countess of Dudllan?"

Richard did not reply.

"I know you love her more than you love me," she said. "Do you realize how much it hurts to see that when you are not with your wife, you are with Her?"

"There is nothing between Alys and me."

"With the familiarity you're using to speak about her, it won't be long before it happens."

"Don't be jealous. Al... lady Alys has suffered a lot, and she is lonely. All we do is go ride in the forest; we both enjoy our outings, that's all."

"Doesn't the king satisfy her, that she needs you too?" she asked as she picked up the basket of apples and hastened out of the parlor with her face flushed and heartbeat faster than usual.

Richard followed Estrilda through the corridor. "Wait!" he said and grabbed her arm. "Do not react like that," he said. But as he pulled her closer, she tried to avoid his gesture but she lost the grip on the fruit basket. The apples bounced and rolled down the stairs and some well-ripened ones splashed in a puree all over the staircase that descended to the kitchen.

"Look what you've done. They are ruined. Because of the evil countess of Dudllan!" Estrilda yelled and attempted to slap him, but as she swung around, she slipped on some apple puree, lost her balance, and then everything went fast. Although it seemed to be slow at the same time. She saw herself at the bottom of the stairs before it happened, but even though she held her arm out to grab Richard's tunic, she flew backward in the air, then banged the back of her head against the stones and rolled down to the entrance of the kitchens.

A FEW DAYS LATER, ESTRILDA opened her eyes to see Francis kneeling by the side of her bed. His eyes were puffy, and he looked exhausted.

"How are you?" he asked.

As she attempted to sit back against the bed frame, she realized she was aching all over. Then everything that happened sprung from the back of her mind: the apples, Richard, the staircase, and lady Alys.

"Sore," she said, and lifting the sheets, she put a hand on her belly. It was still a little puffed, but it felt empty and saggy, like an empty bag of oats rolled into a ball. Francis did not say a word but shook his head as she stared at him inquisitively, slowly understanding the words his silence conveyed.

"No, no!" she shrieked.

"I am afraid you had a big shock and quite a fall," he said, laying his hand on hers.

"Couldn't we have saved the child?"

Again, he shook his head. That was the last drop. Reality hit Estrilda like a cannonball, she wailed and screamed hysterically, life was suddenly unbearable and she slammed the bed with her fists several times as it this would ease the pain in her heart. Francis took her in his arms and patted her back gently, and then she melted into a waterfall of tears.

Later on, Estrilda recalled the last words she had with Richard before the accident. The evil countess of Dudllan. It was her fault. This would not have happened if Estrilda had not argued with Richard about lady Alys. The She-Devil would not get away with this. She was responsible for the death of Estrilda's child, and she would pay for it.

CHAPTER TWENTY-ONE
November 1473, London, Alys

For the last few nights, eaten up by anxiety, I could not sleep more than a couple of hours at a time. Once again, I had been blackmailed into a marriage, but I refused to resign myself to my fate, and it was not the many gifts Edward had sent me, in an attempt of reconciliation, that would change my mind. I had sent them all back, even if some of the jewels were absolutely magnificent and worth a small estate.

When everyone was asleep, I slipped out of the palace in a barge and let it flow downstream. Past Baybridge, I stopped and walked for a while along the deserted banks. It was scarily silent, not even a dog barking in the distance. Then I sat on a pile of crates and stared at the moon's reflection on the water.

Repressing tears, I gazed up at the sky. "Oh, Hampton, if only you were here. None of this would have happened. Look at what you have done to me! Look at my life," I cried towards the sky as if he could hear me.

An old man in rags approached out of nowhere, and I instinctively stood up, stepped back, and started to walk back to the barge.

"Don't run, my lady, I wish you no harm," he said.

I stopped and attempted to see his face. He was probably right; besides, he was limping.

"What do you want from me?" I asked.

"This is my dominion. No one comes here unless they have something for me."

"Forgive me; I did not realize." I dug into my purse and got a coin out. "Here, for your trouble. Again, pardon me. I needed to get away for a little while. Bad nightmares. Sometimes wandering by the river helps me find peace."

The man took the coin and, without looking at it, put it in his cloak pocket. "You're a brave lady to venture on your own in the middle of the night. Fear you not to be attacked? Some areas are full of cut-throats. You shouldn't travel alone at this time of the night."

"I can defend myself if necessary; besides, I have no fortune."

"Muggers don't only want your fortune. You're a beautiful woman, lady Dudllan. If someone were to deprive the king of his beautiful mistress, he'd pay a generous ransom to have her back."

"I am not the king's mistress," I said. Suddenly it dawned on me that he had used my name. "Wait... How do you know me?"

With the help of a walking stick, he moved closer to me. At each step, he paused, caught his breath, then moved again. I still could not see him properly. As he neared, I said: "Remove your hood! I'd like to see whom I'm talking to."

"People fear me in daylight. I only come out at night nowadays. You don't want to see my face, not a pretty sight."

"Why?"

"I was in the old king's army, a long time ago. Got injured in a battle; that's where I caught a nasty disease. I don't know why I am still alive. This is God's will. My face will always remind me of my past. I can't run away from it."

"Surely it can't be that bad. Remove your hood and let me see. I'm sure I have some potent herbs that could relieve your pain. Let me have a look," I said, holding out a hand, but he shook his head.

"No, thank you, my lady. You should go back to Wales. You don't belong here."

"What do you know about where I belong? Perhaps like you, I belong nowhere but in the streets."

"You don't mean that," he said, sat down, and beckoned me to do the same. Without a word, I obeyed.

For a moment, we both stayed silent and listened to the calmness of the night, breathing in the freezing air of this late autumnal night. Strangely, the cold did not bother me, and I must admit that the presence of this old stranger had something reassuring. After a while, he broke the silence.

"Tell me, aren't you happy at court?"

"I don't believe this should be your concern, but yes, I am happy at court if you must know," I lied. In fact, it had been a long time since I had been truly happy. Now my days were a matter of survival and hope.

"If it were the truth, surely you'd be in his bed and not by the river in the middle of the night talking to an old man like me."

"Couldn't sleep."

"Something's worrying you?"

"Obviously," I replied, without looking at him but staring at the ripples on the Thames.

"Sometimes talking about it can help."

"Thank you, but I don't think this would do anything. Nothing on earth can salvage me anymore."

"You'd be surprised. Perhaps I can do something for you," he said and leaned against the wall.

"I am sure you have many contacts here, but no, thank you. I must deal with this myself."

"Pretty stubborn lady, Hm."

"I've been told that before." I paused, and he remained silent. "Very well," I continued. "The king wants me to marry, and I do not want to. If I don't obey the order he has threatened to take my children from me."

"The king wants your land too."

"Dudllan is useless to him. No, the queen wants to torture me, and she put ideas into the king's head. He always agrees with her."

"You knew that before you became his mistress."

"Will you stop saying that! I am not his mistress."

"You're only lying to yourself when you say that. Everyone knows. But perhaps you feel less guilty if you convince yourself that you are not his mistress. Tell me honestly, would you be here now if your conscience was clear? Please don't deny it again; you're only tormenting yourself by denying it."

His voice was soothing and something about this old man almost made me at ease to confide in as I would have done with any old friend.

"I am doing nothing wrong." Which was entirely true, as all did I was to entice Edward, and even if we had kissed passionately on several occasions, I was determined not to let it go any further.

"Then why do you deny it?"

"I don't love him."

"And still, you are his mistress," he said as if almost angered. At that point, I noticed a change in his voice, and it became somewhat familiar.

"Who are you? Do I know you?" I asked, now intrigued by the tone and the melody of his voice.

"No, I don't believe you," he said, now with a voice that sounded slightly different, as if he had forced himself to change it. "Go back to Wales. It is your land now, and let no one take it from you," he said as he stood up with the help of his walking stick.

For a moment, still seated on the pile of timber, I thought about what he'd said. That man was no fool, but I wondered why he knew so much about me, and I did not even know his name.

As I turned to face him, I asked: "What is your name?" But he was gone.

Vanished, like a ghost. Strange! I had not heard him walking away. Was I losing my mind? It had felt real; I had thought I was awake. Was it another dream? Another ghost? But then a noise of crashing wooden boxes that collapsed at the corner of the small courtyard resounded, a few yards behind me. Thus, I rose to my feet and headed that way and saw the shadow of a man in a cape running away. The old man was right. I did not belong in London. It was a treacherous place, and I had enemies lurking out for me, but I remained troubled a little. Who was that man who had given me some sound advice and then withdrew before

I could find out his name? Perhaps it was a warning from Heaven. I had to retire to Wales. I had to leave London.

CHAPTER TWENTY-TWO
November- December 1473, London, Estrilda

The gossip about the imminent marriage of lady Alys and lord Fullerton was spreading fast. Everywhere in the castle and even at the market, it seemed to be the subject of conversation, unless lady Alys was around. Then everyone talked about the weather and how cold it was for the season.

The joy of Queen Elizabeth illuminated her ladies' days, which was a big change to their usual routine when they used to refrain from laughing or smiling too much in case it would irritate the queen. None of them could recall a time where Elizabeth had beamed so much.

"It seems that you will soon have your husband back in your bed," Estrilda said as she helped Elizabeth out of her gown.

"Yes, my husband has found a man who has heard little about the countess. We must ensure that they get marry soon before he finds out what a behemoth she is. Arrange for him to be at the banquet tonight; I want to speak to him. Lord Fullerton will fall in love with the countess of Dudllan."

"It would be better if it was her who falls in love with him," Estrilda said as Elizabeth lifted her arms so she could help her slip into her nightdress, perfumed with lavender and rose water.

"I doubt that would ever happen. The countess has a heart of stone. Nothing matters to that woman if it is not her children or her dead lover."

"Pardon my boldness, but don't you think she loves the king?"

"No, she does not, and he knows it. That is why he became so infatuated with her; the less she respects him, the more he worships her."

"I am confused. Why is he so obsessed by that insignificant woman when he has such a beautiful wife who cares for him?" Estrilda said as the queen sat at the dressing table for Estrilda to brush her hair.

"Men enjoy hunting and playing with fire. I do not doubt that my husband will hurt himself and return to me one day, but this takes too long for my taste. We must give Cupid a helping hand."

"You don't mean... using the forbidden craft?" she asked and put the brush on the side.

"Oh God, no! I would not know how to do it, but some plants to stimulate his desire... This might be the solution."

"Is that what you've used when you met King Edward?"

"No!"

"Pardon me again for asking, but if you think this will work on the countess's future husband, why don't you put any in the king's wine for your benefit?"

"Because he spends little time with me, and I would worry about making him fall for her even more. Since he started that affair with her, he has had no other mistresses. I could excuse him for following his male instincts, but this has turned into love, and I cannot want to forgive that."

CHAPTER TWENTY- THREE

December 1473, London/ Middleham, Alys

"Robyn, wake up..." I whispered, shaking him on his pallet. At first, he moaned and then when he saw it was me, he jumped out of bed. And I beckoned him to stay quiet so as not to wake up the other squires and groom in the dorter.

"Could you give me my breeches?" he asked, before I realized he wore nothing.

Flushed, I turned and picked the garment up and passed it back without looking behind me. I heard the rustle of his leather breeches as he put them on. Then he said, "What is happening?"

I waited until we were outside before replying, for I did not want anyone to hear my intention. "Prepare our horses; we are leaving at once." The air was chilled and soon, the ground will be frozen, but I could not delay our departure.

"Have you decided not to marry and to return to Wales?"

"No, we are going to Middleham," I whispered as he brought our horses into the stable yard.

"What for?"

"I need to see someone—well, I'm hoping to see someone," I said. "We must leave at once before anyone notices my departure."

He did not question me. He rarely did and immediately helped me on the saddle.

"I'll meet you by the gate shortly. I've got to get some provisions for the journey."

Dawn had not yet risen, so it was still hushed, which made our departure smoother. Once we reached the sentries, I made up a story, and it looked as if they had believed me, letting us to depart without question. Perhaps they were more worried that I would complain about them to the king, but anyway, we were now on our way to Middleham.

As we rode along the Great North road, wrapped up in fur coats and wearing leather gauntlets to protect our fingers from freezing, it felt like old times, except that we did not have to hide or steal food this time. We stopped at some inns for the night, and we ate proper meals.

"Now we are far enough from London. May I ask whom you are expecting to see in Middleham?" Robyn asked as we approached the town of York.

"Do you remember the Old Witch?"

"Aye."

"Well, I hope she is still alive, for I must speak to her urgently."

"Has the queen tried to poison you?" Though daylight had not yet pointed its nose through the night sky, I saw Robyn lifting his brows.

"No... Uhm, I hope she has not. That did not even cross my mind. No, I have seen a ghost... I think... and I want the Old Witch to read my palm."

"Are you serious? You don't have to travel for days to have someone read your palm, I could have found you someone in London for that."

"You don't understand. The ghost..." I paused for a moment. "Please, promise me you will not laugh at me or think I have lost my mind. I was lucid when it happened."

Robyn stared at me and did not say a word or even smile.

"Right, last night I could not sleep, so I went out of Westminster and walked on the riverbank and then I met someone. Some who told me to go back to Wales. He was very enigmatic. Something about that man made me feel safe, just as if he was..." I could not continue. "Anyway, he disappeared. I am not even sure it was a ghost, but he reminded me so much of Hampton, older, and this man appeared to be injured. I can't help thinking Fauconberg might have told me the truth, but why hadn't Hampton come to me if he's alive?"

"This is not the first that you have had dreams about him. Perhaps you fell asleep on the banks, and that is why."

"I was not asleep! Honestly, I wonder why I even told you. No one would ever believe me. That is why I need to see the Old Witch. She might be a fool, and most of the time makes little sense, but in the past, she had told me things that came true."

"You should have sent someone ahead first."

"No, this would have taken too long. The king wants me to marry, and I do not want to marry if..." I paused. "If he is alive."

Thinking back to the time I went to St Paul's, I was unsure if it was him I saw that day. I was too distressed to think properly then. Now, only the Old Witch could help me; she would tell me the truth.

AFTER A FEW MORE DAYS, we finally reached the outskirts of the village of Middleham. When I stopped in front of the familiar old cottage, I was pleased to see that the door was open.

The Old Witch was ancient, but when she appeared at the door, she welcomed us and took my hand in hers. Though, she made even less sense than in the past.

"I am lady Alys. Do you remember me?"

Then she passed her hands over my face, and I noticed a grayish filter over her eyes. Robyn passed a hand in front of her eyes, and she did not blink.

"Blind," he mimed.

"It's me, Alys of Lochlainn. A long time ago, you helped my son Edmund. Lord Hampton had even threatened to impale you if..."

"Oh yes, lady Alys. The stubborn Irish girl who used to climb up trees to annoy the countess of Hampton. Sit down," she said. "I'll get you some ale. Is that Richard with you?" She walked around the room as if she could see, with only a hand in front of her as she reached the table.

"No, it's Robyn."

"It's been a long time. I was told they killed him. Oh, poor Robyn. I am sorry, I know how much you loved him," she said.

Shooting a quizzical glance at Robyn, I also beckoned him to leave, as he gestured that the Old Witch had lost her mind and I did not want her to notice she was not taken seriously.

"Is your sight fully gone?" I asked as she poured the ale into a cup with a trembling hand but an accurate aim.

"I see shapes, that's how I get around."

"Sorry."

"Old age, nothing I can do. None of the potions worked. Anyway, why are you here? No one lives at the castle anymore."

"No, this is for you I traveled. In fact, I was hoping you could read my palm, but I guess you can't," I said, incapable of hiding the disappointment in my voice.

She sat down opposite me, held out her hand, searching for mine, then she took my hand and traced her nail across it.

"How can you? You can't see."

"I don't need to."

"What can you tell me? I need to know if he is alive."

"I know who you are talking about. He's never been dead."

Immediately my heart sank, but then it quickly flipped into my chest. With the Old Witch, nothing was ever clear and straightforward. "Who has never been dead?"

"Robyn, of course."

"I know that!" The sliver of hope had now left place to irritation. "Robyn is with me. I must know about lord Hampton," I said.

"Who?"

"Geoffrey Neville, the earl of Hampton, the master of Middleham, remember? He was killed on the battlefield a few years ago."

"Oh yes, nasty story. Got killed by Margaret of Anjou on New Year's Eve with the duke of York and his son... the poor girl. She was crying for days. When it happened, she rode barefoot across the moors when she heard the news. It was heartbreaking."

"No, not that lord Hampton. His son, the earl of Hampton. Is he alive or dead?"

"I don't know him."

"Of course, you do. You used to say he was a sheep. Look at my palm: What do you see? Should I marry? What about France? My love? What do you see?" I asked, sitting on the edge of my seat.

She lifted her hands. "You ask too many questions. It's not clear, it's all misty, and there's a ghost... I am sorry, I can't see."

"Mist and a ghost. Is that what you see? Is it a real ghost, is he dead?"

"I don't know."

All those days of travelling to the north to realize that I had wasted my time. She did not know what she was talking about anymore. Thus, deflated, I handed her a few coins, but she refused them.

Robyn jumped off the sidewall that surrounded the cottage when he saw the door open.

"What did you find out?" Robyn asked as I got out of the cottage.

"Nothing, come. We must return to London, and I guess I have no choice but to marry."

Disheartened, I returned to Westminster before Edward would send his army after me. It was surprising that he had not done so already, for I had been gone for over three weeks, but as soon as we entered the courtyard, Edward dashed to my side and helped me dismount. People had gathered in the courtyard, braving the strong winds that blew leaves and straw all over the ground, but only because they expected to witness the king's wrath and my disgrace. How wrong they were.

"Where the hell have you been? I was so worried about you. Did you go back to Wales again?" Edward asked, holding me in his arms as if he would never let me go, and so as not to disappoint the throng of courtiers, I wrapped my arms around his neck.

"No. In fact, I traveled to Middleham."

"Why?" he asked as we drew apart.

"Not to prepare a rebellion if that is what you are worried about. I went to see an old friend before you make a prisoner out of me again."

"A prisoner?" He lifted an eyebrow and put an arm around my waist, leading me indoors.

"You want me to marry, don't you?"

"Still, you'll be free; you will not be house-jailed. Come, I would like you to meet John of Fullerton."

"Is he here?"

"He has been here for a few days now, and I had to lie. I told him that you were unwell. I could hardly tell him that I did not know where you were. What would have I looked like if I had told him the truth?"

"A fool?" I smiled.

"You're impossible, but that is why I love you so much."

He squeezed my hand, but I could not return the feeling. How could he say he loved me when he was about to force me to marry? When I entered Edward's private chamber, lord Fullerton was there, standing by the window with his hands behind his back.

I studied him from head to toe. He had a sympathetic beefy face, but there was something about him I could not quite figure out. I knew he was a very faithful man to the king, but he also had been against Hampton.

"Sir John," I said and inclined my head. Then I stayed silent.

The atmosphere was quite palpable. I had nothing to tell that man, but Edward looked at us as if we were young people who had just been introduced. A future groom and his future bride. It wasn't the same now.

"May I speak to lord Fullerton in private, Your Grace?" I asked Edward.

He bowed and left the room. Lord Fullerton did not speak, but he looked somewhat embarrassed.

"Why do you want to marry me?" I asked once the door was closed.

"You or someone else, it doesn't matter. I just want to remarry," he replied, waving a hand.

A snorting laugh escaped me. "Just like you would buy a cow or a goat."

"When I spoke to the king a few weeks ago and told him I could do with a wife at the castle, he said he will ensure that I get an excellent one to reward my loyalty."

"But you do not seem pleased with his decision."

"My wife died a few months ago, and I loved her very much. However, running a household and spending time in London is quite challenging. I cannot manage on my own."

"Why don't you hire a steward instead of marrying?"

"Well, I have a steward, but a wife would be an ally I can count on," he said as he approached me.

I stepped back. "Is that what you think? I know we have never spoken before, but I have heard about you, and I know you were against lord Hampton. Do you really think that I will ever be your ally?"

"I have heard that you were quite indomitable, and that will be another challenge, but when you are my wife, you will have no choice but to obey. That is a wife's duty."

I looked at him in dismay. "You are right: a wife must obey her husband, but would that make her your ally? How can you ensure your wife will not plot behind your back against you or take a lover?"

"Because if it were the case, I would ensure that she gets the right punishment." He snorted.

"I see." Then I glanced at the door. At that point, I decided not to marry that man, who no doubt would turn into another Ratcliffe, and I would not let any man treat me that way ever again. "If you excuse me, lord Fullerton, I must go."

Lord Fullerton grabbed my arm. "Wait! We have not discussed our wedding arrangements. There are things we need to sort out before we make it official. What dowry will you bring?"

"Lord Fullerton, do you honestly think a woman like me would marry a man like you? I am a widow, and unlike a young damoiselle, I can have a say on whom I will marry, and you will not be that man."

"I don't believe any of us has a say in the matter. It is an order from the king."

"The king has made a mistake... again. Look, I will not marry you. I will never be your ally, and I will certainly not bed you, so you'd better tell the king that you wish to find another lady. I am sure that you will find one that is willing to obey and give you more heirs. Why don't you look at the queen's family? They have so many daughters; there must be still one that is not betrothed."

He looked taken aback. "Oh no, I am not worthy of being part of the queen's family."

"Commoners! Those girls are commoners! If you think you are not worthy of them, then you are certainly not worthy of my noble Irish blood. I am the daughter of an earl and a countess myself. My blood comes from a long generation of noblemen and women. If there is something unworthy, it is you, not me."

With my heart thumping and a jerky breath, I rushed to the door. "Call the king," I told the guard who stood outside the solar.

Edward had been waiting in the corridor and immediately stood up and joined us in the room.

"So, is everything in order? What day did you pick for the wedding?"

"What do you think?" I replied before lord Fullerton had a chance to open his mouth.

"What is the matter?" Edward asked.

"This man thinks he is not worthy of marrying one of your sisters-in-law who have squire's blood running through their veins but sees no objection in marrying into pure, noble blood. Did you find that man to insult me?" I asked Edward, ignoring the presence of lord Fullerton.

Edward looked at lord Fullerton. "Leave us, please," he said.

Once lord Fullerton was gone, Edward took me in his arms, but I moved away.

"Alys, please, you must remarry. For us."

"I have not disagreed with marrying; I only disagree with marrying that... ruthless man whom I am sure has no manners either. How dare he insult my bloodline? That man does not want a wife, but a servant who will agree to every word he says."

"You might be of a higher bloodline than the queen, but look where you are now. A widow with five bastards and no fortune."

"Well, this is all your fault. You forced me to marry the wrong man once, and you've killed the man who was protecting my fortune. If you want me to marry, find someone more suitable. Someone who will adore me and respect me; someone who will make me feel worthy and someone who will give me more pleasure than anyone else has ever done."

"If I could marry you, I would."

After I chortled, I said: "Well, I would not. I declined the offer once and would do it again. Wales is where I belong and where I am heading now!"

"You will stay here until I say you can leave."

"Do not do this. You know that it is not the way to treat me. I'm free to choose my own life, and I could get a lover if I wanted to."

"But you will not, you enjoy my company too much. I know that deep down you love me," he said as he moved his arm to enfold me.

No, he was wrong; I did not love him. I would never love anyone ever again... but when I abandoned myself to his embrace, a warmth crossed my entire body and this feeling scared me. Was I falling for him? No, I was not. I was a strong woman, and I would take control of my senses and feelings; I would not fall for anyone again. I forbade it. Perhaps the way to avoid falling for Edward was to marry that horrible man after all.

"Get changed, I'll see you at the banquet later," he said and left me alone in his parlor.

To my great astonishment, Anne of Gloucester smiled broadly before I entered the great hall and she even waved to acknowledge me. I glanced at Estrilda, whose expression I could not read. The last time I saw both at the same time, Hampton was alive. In regard to Anne, it was when Hampton announced her about her wedding to the Prince of Wales, the son of Margaret of Anjou, which would have made her the future queen of England if we'd been victorious. She was not yet twenty years old, and already she had suffered a great deal, and if it were not for having a husband she loved, she'd have no one in life. Even her sister was not acting like a family should. Both girls were so different. Anne was a strong woman and would stand against any man if necessary, while her sister was frail and submissive, and she would do whatever her husband asked of her, even betray her own father. My blood curdled by the thought. I was glad that Isabel was nowhere to be seen, nor George.

The hall was already full of revelers, related in one way or another to the queen's family. All of them talked so loudly that it covered the sound of the music, but I did not care anymore. I had enough of the banquets and the idle life of the court full of hypocrites, traitors, and back-stabbers. Standing at the back of the hall, I glanced around, enjoying the faint sound of music and the remainder of roast swan and boar aroma. Then Anne and Richard came towards me so I moved closer to the center of the room.

"Lady Alys, I am so pleased to see you," Anne said as she hastened to meet me, ignoring the frosty regard of the queen.

"And you too, Your Grace," I said and curtseyed. Now she was married to Richard, she was a duchess and fifth in line to the throne. "I see that you've finally found your happiness with Richard."

Anne took my arm and pulled me away from the crowd. "He is a wonderful husband, but life at court is not what I was hoping. When Richard saved me from the convent, I was hoping life would be like before, but the queen and even my sister have been awful to me. And I have strong suspicions that the queen is dealing with witchcraft. Her family rules as if they were of royal blood themselves. It is unbearable. Every day I am begging Richard to go back to Middleham. My poor father would turn in his grave if he could see what the court is like now."

At the name Middleham, I felt a pinch in my heart. It was painful enough to speak to Anne without thinking of Hampton, and now that she mentioned the name of the place where I fell for him, it was excruciating.

"If you had not betrayed your father, things would be different now."

"I have always been loyal to my father, always did what he told me to; even when he forced me to marry that horrible boy, I respected my father's will. We all did. And I have gained the respect of people in the North for the name I bear."

"Do they respect your sister as well? Do they know that she betrayed him to favor her husband? If she had informed your father that George had joined Edward with his army, your father would still be with me now."

"I... I did not know."

"Without a doubt, I trust you. Seeing you remind me of your father." Tittering, I continued: "I'm expecting to see him burst into the hall and have one of his infamous outrages." Strange how the idea made me smile, while I would certainly react differently if he were to appear and bawl.

"Mother always said that you took him from us to satisfy your thirst for power. I did not realize you loved him so much. She thought you were using him to suit your own plans and that you were no better than the queen."

"I'm afraid your mother was wrong. Your father and I never planned to fall for each other. If we'd been sensible, I would have married Edward, but I was young and foolish then. I haven't received the same education as you. After my mother died, my father neglected my education, and I was quite content with it. I'd never thought that one day I would live in England. Then I always lived my life as I wished, and I did not savvy women have not much say in this world. I learned the hard way."

"The queen speaks her mind, and she does not hide it. We all know that she governs through Edward."

"We both know why and how she does it, don't we?" I whispered.

"So, do you think the rumors are true?"

"How else would an older woman have power over a man like Edward? Until he met her, he had never stayed away from any nice-looking woman, peasant or noble. Since the king met her, he is besotted and only listens to her. That is not the Edward I knew."

"There are other rumors... about you and him."

I laughed. "As you said, they are rumors. Edward and I are... sorry were, friends. I could not love him, even before your father. I did not want to marry him, for his brother Edmund and I were... Anyway, this was a long time ago. How is Richard? And when are you planning to start a family?"

"When my husband stops seeing his mistress."

"Oh... I'm sorry, I did not mean to pry."

"That is quite all right. No one knows apart from the people who live at court, as he does not hide her very well. I am sure you will meet her at the banquet later. I am praying to God every day for her disgrace, but..."

"Praying to God for someone's disgrace is not very Christian," I remarked.

Anne lowered her eyes. "I cannot help being jealous. I've loved Richard all my life, and now my life is not what it should have been."

"It never is."

LATER, AS I WANDERED through the corridors looking for Richard, I noticed Estrilda coming toward me; I hid behind one of the tapestries and called to her as she passed by.

"Estrilda, come here, I must speak to you."

"Lady Alys?"

She hesitated, then after having looked on both sides of the corridor, she passed behind the tapestries to join me.

"Do you remember where you come from? If you do not intend to return there, I suggest you keep a low profile and stop this stupid affair with the king's brother," I said, pointing a threatening finger to her face.

"I do not believe that what I do in private is any concern of yours. I am highly regarded at court, while your presence is only tolerated by the queen, and since she now knows the reason you are here, it won't take long for you to be sent back to your countryside."

The woman in front of me had no resemblance to the little girl I had known. Lysbette was right, living at court changed people for the worst.

"What have they done to you? Where is the little girl that was so shy and pure?"

"I guess I had no choice when you put me with the Cloppelins, I had to obey them if I did not want to live in the streets, but now that I am at court and have a second husband, I am a countess like you and you've nothing to tell me. We are equals now!"

I chortled. "Is that what you think? Open your eyes, we will never be equal but, if this is your opinion. Be careful, some old stories might come back to the surface, and then we will see how long your highly regarded presence at court will last."

"I don't believe you would dare, as there are things I could repeat that would darken your name forever."

"My name can't be darkened any more than it already is, but tell me what could possibly cause me any more trouble?"

I pushed my way past her when she said: "I'm aware that you've met with King Louis and that you are secretly preparing a rebellion by supporting the cause of Henry Tudor."

I spun and for a brief instant, I was glad she could not see my face. With a tremendous effort, I regained control of myself. "Nonsense," I said. Fortunately, Hampton had taught me to keep an impassive face when telling a lie, but deep down, I was shocked that she would dare use this against me. And moreover, how did she find out? Unless, of course, it was her imagination, and she knew nothing but only guessed.

"You might think that Lysbette and Willem were loyal to you, but I was their daughter first and they were loyal to me only. Lysbette never forgave you for having placed me at court."

"Under another name. You seem to forget that."

"I know who I am," she said with pure hatred in her eyes.

"Do you really? So why were you parentless in the street? You've no idea who you are or where you come from. You might be one of those bastards from a drunkard and a whore, like the ones you hold so much in your esteem."

"Like your sons!"

I slapped her. "Never ever again speak about my sons, you are not worthy of polishing their boots."

As I returned to my chamber, I was still a little shaken by the conversation I had with Estrilda. Was she under a spell or had she turned evil? I'd never expected Estrilda to be my enemy, but now there could be no doubt that she was no longer on my side.

She was probably angry that I had never been close to her, but how could she do that to Lysbette? How could she pretend to love her when she used her? This was horrible. I had never been perfect, and I had done a lot of bad things myself, but I had never used people for my benefit. I had never abused people's trust. My enemies knew where they stood, and well, until now I believe I knew who they were... Estrilda had unsettled me. How many people pretended to be my friends and were not?

Oh, Hampton, life without you is too difficult. If you're alive, please come back.

THE NEXT DAY, MY MOOD was rather melancholic. I spent all night reminiscing on the past and all the what ifs, and now I had no reasons to stay in London. As I dashed across the long gallery, paying no attention to people or to the expensive tapestries that decorated the dimly lit corridor, I walked past by Edward's door, when I heard him calling me in.

"You look so pale, are you all right?" he asked as he stood from his desk, pushed the door close once I was inside. He kissed me warmly as if reading my dearest wish to escape London and its people.

"I can't. Please, let me go." I tried to move out of his arms, but he held me strongly.

"When will you finally let me taste you the way I desire?"

"I cannot love you. Please, do not force me, or you'll only hold a dead soul in your arms."

"Alys, I thought we had made peace," he said, releasing the pressure, "and that you loved me like before."

"It can never be like before." I sighed and stepped away from him. "Don't you see it? Your wife will always be between us, and there's also Hampton's spirit. I can't do that to him. I am sorry, I will return to Wales. That is better, and I shall not marry. Wales is where I belong."

"I forbid you to go there again. If what you want for your sons is a high place in this society, then I suggest you stay here and do what I say."

"Edward, you cannot order love. Regardless, it is not because I do not love you that I want to leave, but because I fear I might fall for you."

"You..." he paused. "What did you say?"

"Please do not ask me to repeat it. I was not conscious of this until a short while ago; but I realized that I would hurt both of us. I cannot be unfaithful to Hampton; that would not be fair to him. If it weren't for you, he would still be alive now." I sat on the chair before his desk and brushed some inexistent dust from the desk.

"He would not want to see you sad; on the contrary, he'd be pleased to see you've found your smile."

"If I fall for you, I will be hurt again. All the men I loved were killed in a battle for the throne."

"Those battles are over; I am the king now. No one will push me over," he said, now standing behind me, he put his hands on my shoulders.

"Do not be so certain. It's never over. One day someone will champion you."

"Trust me, no one will dare; I am too powerful."

"England might be supporting you, but Wales and Scotland never will. England is not prospering; the country might be at peace, but you know your people and how easy it is for them to turn their coats." Sensing danger, I stood up and paced to the window that overlooked the front courtyard. Children played with the puppies, trying to track them like game while merchants and visitors journey to and fro. Life inside the palace seemed peaceful. "People want more land and fewer taxes, and your wife's family is far too powerful for the likes of some people."

"You talk like Hampton used to, just as if you were preparing a rebellion. Is there something you wish to tell me?"

"Please do not ask, just trust what I'm telling you."

"Is it your doing?" he asked, raising his voice.

I remained silent.

"Speak!" he bellowed. "You're like Hampton, and I am sure you have something to do with it, but how? I've cut your income. How could you support a rebellion against me?"

I did not tell him that even if he had cut my trades, I had restarted others, which he did not know about; and I felt guilty that soon England would be under attack because of me.

"Alys, something is not right, and guilt reeks across your entire body."

"Very well, I've met King Louis," I finally admitted, too cowardly to dare meeting his eyes.

Edward lifted an arm as if about to hit me, so I stepped back, protecting my face with a hand, but instead of lashing down on me, he slammed his fists on his desk and cleared everything from it in one sweep. "Damn it! How could you do this to me?"

Reassured that he would not become physical with me, I found the courage to defend myself. "It was before... when I was angry with you... when you ordered the murder of my friend Fauconberg. I had sworn that I would revenge him and Hampton. You brought this upon yourself."

"Well, you've got to stop them."

"I don't think I can."

"Is that why you were leaving? You were abandoning me like a coward; that is why you wanted to retreat to Wales. Well, go! You're nothing to me anymore and do not count on my help for your bastards. You can rot in Wales as far as I am concerned," he said and turned back toward his desk with both fists on it.

I stepped towards him. I was about to put a hand on his shoulders, but I dared not. He did not move, nor did he say a word. When I left his study, I passed by the queen in the corridor. I did not stop or even look at her.

"I am your Queen," she shouted, but I ignored her and headed to the stables where I joined Robyn.

"Get my horse ready, we are leaving at once."

"Are you all right, my lady?"

"No. We're returning to Wales."

Even if he tried to hide it, I saw the joy that the news brought to Robyn. We would finally leave this nest of vipers and return to the quiet life of Dudllan. Robyn enjoyed battles and action, but he hated this place, which reeked of backstabbing and hypocrisy when he could not do anything to shut them up.

To go back to Ireland and forget about England was my dearest wish, but that would never happen. My father and I had not been in touch for years, although he was still alive. I knew for I had had regular contact with my brother Finnian. If anything had happened to my father, Finnian would have informed me, for I had never found the courage to contact my father and tell him how sorry I was for having disappointed him. But I was no longer the innocent and stupid girl that embarked on the boat all those years ago;

little did I know then that I would never return to my homeland again. I had destroyed everything I had touched, hurt people I had loved, and lost those whom I had loved the most. Could I pursue Hampton's dream? Should I continue, or should I just retreat until death calls for me? What would become of my boys if I were to do that?

I had no one to turn to, no confidante left. I wished I'd known where Lysbette was hiding, she would have comforted me, if she was alive. Did she even know what Estrilda had become? Better that she did not, or she would have put the blame on me. Now Wales was my only hope, unless I decided to flee to France like everyone else did.

CHAPTER TWENTY-FOUR
December 1473–January 1474, London, Estrilda

Something had happened between lady Alys and the king. It was evident, for she made no appearance at the banquet on Christmas Day, nor the day after. No one knew where she was. Rumors that she had left were circulating; nevertheless, the reason was entirely different depending on who delivered the news. The king was in a foul mood and sent back the minstrels a short while after they'd started playing their instruments, which was a shame as it ruined the whole atmosphere. King Edward even left before the last courses were served, asking his brothers and Robert Woodville to accompany him to his private chamber.

After the meal, Estrilda and her companions followed the queen, who instead of going through her pre-bed rituals paced the room as if she was waiting for some news.

"Your Grace, please sit down, or I'll not be able to brush your hair," Estrilda dared say.

Without a word, Elizabeth sat, removed her headdress, and let her hair fall over her shoulders, leaving a whiff of rose and lavender in the air. However, Estrilda barely touched her hair with the brush when the queen shouted and beckoned Estrilda to move away and accidentally tipped over the burning scented oil over the flagstones. Immediately, Estrilda bent to wipe up the oil and the scent of sandalwood and myrrh impregnated on the cloth and her hands, making her slightly dizzy.

Afterwards, Estrilda joined lady Spencer in the corner of the chamber by the prie-dieu and asked: "What is going on?"

"All I've found out was that the countess of Dudllan and the king had an argument and that she left London immediately after. The king wasn't aware she had gone; he heard it from one sentry."

"There must be something else. The queen would not be so anxious if it were just about the departure of the countess. She wanted her out."

"Do you think it has something to go with her going to France?"

"I heard people talk about it, but it was ages ago. Has she been there again?"

"Well, someone on the market said that she met the king of France. Since her return, she has been trading wine. Malmsey. And she is the only one who may trade it in England. It's the queen's favorite."

"I know, but that only would not create such a turmoil."

"Ask Charles Turnbey. The man always knows everything, and he's on duty by the king's study tonight," Estrilda said.

"No, you do it. Charles Turnbey has wandering hands, and his breath stinks of ale and cheese," Jane said.

"Oh please, he won't tell me anything, but he's got the beguine for you."

"Fine, but next time remember, you owe me a favor."

"Promise."

Lady Spencer did not find much. Eventually, the following morning, both Richard and Francis left with the king and his entire army. Some talked about France, but the men had been sworn to secrecy. Thus, even Estrilda's husband did not confide in her about his destination. Inclined to trust her instincts, Estrilda's guess was that perhaps they were going to Wales—taking the army was a distraction. That thought only angered Estrilda, mainly because there was nothing she could do to prevent Richard from going there.

CHAPTER TWENTY-FIVE
February 1474, Dudllan, Alys

I wished Hampton was here again. My savior and protector, the man I once hated the most, a man I had thought capable of every form of scheming. Not that I was wrong about him, but at the time I did not know his intentions were always right, even if it did not look so most of the time. I missed him every single day.

The weather got cold again, and the deeper the coat of snow on the ground, the bigger my guilt at having beguiled the king became, for even if I had not bedded the king, I had betrayed Hampton in a different way. If it wasn't for my sons, I would have attached a rope to a large rock, wrapped it around my waist, and thrown myself over the cliffs into the sea to never come back again, to be with my Love for eternity. I'll always remember the first time our eyes met— Hampton's big blue eyes. It was not love at first sight; it was nothing. I had mistaken him for a traveler when I met him in the village inn. And I recalled the day he came at Lochlainn, he acted like a king, but I hated him then. He was my enemy. I laughed. Who would have imagined he'd become my lover? Certainly not me. Our first kiss—when he tried to stop me from speaking and revealing myself to Edward and his secret bride.

I wished I could turn back time and change it all. I'd tell Hampton to kill Edward when he had a chance. He should have taken the throne for himself. No one would have minded, and the country would have been much better. Since I came back to Wales, I even attended church a few times, hoping God would grant my prayers. It was stupid. Why would God be impressed by my sorrow and regret? I was not worthy of him after all the blasphemy I had proclaimed.

"A message, Mother!" said Geoffrey, getting me out of my thoughts, and I looked at the missive he held out. Then I turned it to see the seal; it was from Jasper Tudor.

Immediately, I broke the seal and began to read. "Oh no, it is all my fault," I said aloud as I sat straight on the chair.

"What is it?"

"Edward has sent an army to France, and they've killed every single inhabitant of many villages. All innocents. Killed because of me."

"Why would it be your fault?"

"Edward knows I've met the king of France, and he was furious. That is probably why he sent his men over there."

I sat back in the chair, thinking of all the wrongs I had once again caused many people.

CHAPTER TWENTY-SIX
April 1474, London, Estrilda

When the herald announced the return of the king, the queen jumped to her feet and rushed into the courtyard with her ladies following. Eventually, they'd discovered through some indiscretion of the king's chamberlain that the king had gone to war with France. Or at least tried. From the moment the ladies heard the news, they worried for their men, but today was a triumphal return. The men were joyful, and each lady could not contain their happiness to see their knights had returned. Like most of them, the great joy of seeing her husband safe took over Estrilda's heart, and she threw herself in his arms.

"I've prayed to God every day for him to keep you safe."

"So, you care for your husband after all," he said, looking all tender and loving.

"I do," she said, feeling the heat on her cheeks.

"I thought Richard had taken your heart."

"Please, let's not talk about him now," she said as she glanced towards Richard. Their eyes met, and then he embraced his wife.

It was strange that just the idea of losing her husband had brought Estrilda closer to him, even though it had not weakened her love for Richard. After a few days of having her husband back, Estrilda had to concentrate hard not to throw herself into Richard's arms each time he walked by.

Francis never elaborated on what happened in France, but Estrilda did not care as long as he was back. She couldn't have faced being a widow for a second time. Anyway, today, Francis would teach her how to ride. Under a glorious spring sky, Estrilda made her way to meet him at the stables with her heart full of anticipation, admiring the blossom on the trees and calming her thudding heart by breathing in the perfume of the daffodils and the faint green smell of the bluebells.

"Are you sure you want to do this?" Francis asked as she joined him in the yard. A large horse stood next to him and suddenly, all the pleasant odor of the spring vanished when the horse pooed as if to warn her not to approach.

Estrilda brought a hand to her nose. "Yes, all the ladies do horseback riding, and I cannot."

"Why has your father never taught you?"

"He said ladies did not need to ride," she replied, briefly.

"We'll use the old palfrey. He is a good horse, and he'll teach you everything about horseback riding." Francis tapped the horse's neck.

"Oh..."

"Old horse to a new rider, a young horse to an old rider... we teach them, and they teach us. That's how it works. Some horses have the fire in them, but you'll be fine with this one," he said as he lifted her onto the horse's back.

"Oh... I am not sure I will enjoy this very much. It's ever so high." Estrilda gripped the saddle with both hands, but when the horse moved, she shrieked.

"Don't scream. He might be an old palfrey, but there's still life in him. Right, the first thing you must remember, a horse is a living creature, it can react to anything. So, you must always keep calm, as if you are not, your horse will feel it."

"All right." She tried to breathe out, to steady her heartbeats as they walked toward the small arena.

Once they reached the arena, Francis turned the reins in and placed her hands over them. "This is how you hold them. Pull the right to go right and left to go left."

"That sounds simple enough. I think I can do it."

"Yes, almost. But for the moment, just remember that."

Francis took hold of a rope and attached it to the bridle. "We will walk a little, so you get used to the movement and try to not show him you are worried."

"If it was only that easy."

"It is."

To distract her and ease her tension, Francis talked about the weather and some people from court, and it worked as Estrilda started to feel more at ease with the jolting movements.

"The view is so much better from there, and it is much easier to travel; you won't damage your pretty shoes walking in the city from now on. So, what is the latest news from the queen's private chamber?"

"She is still worried about the king and his mistress. Even if she is not at court at the moment, he has spent more time with that woman than he should have."

"Which one?"

"What do you mean which one?"

"The king has more than one mistress at a time."

"Beyond doubt, the one who threatens the queen the most is the She-devil of Dudllan."

"People are so unfair to her," he said, and Estrilda could not help but feel a little upset that he, too, would take her defense. But he did not notice her reaction and continued: "She followed lord Hampton till the end. Whatever he did, honorable or evil, she never failed him; moreover, she still praises him at each opportunity, but believe me, she is not a bad person at all. Even if the newsmongers of the court pretend that lady Alys was the one who had encouraged lord Hampton to rebel against Edward, I don't think it is true."

"I heard that too, but what I don't understand is that if that is true, why would she now be the king's mistress? Unless that's why they argued before you left for France."

"Good boy," he said, tapping the horse's neck. "You see, you've been walking and did not even worry," he continued without acknowledging her comment.

"Oh ... I did not realize."

"We'll walk a little longer, and then I will let the rope go, and you will be in charge."

"Are you sure? Isn't it a little too soon?"

"You'll be fine." Without telling her, he untied the horse and continued walking as if he was still in charge. "About the countess of Dudllan, the only thing I wonder is if she really loves our king or if she is using him," Francis said.

"Using him, for sure. No one can be that much in love with someone and suddenly fall for someone else."

"In her defense, and I am not supporting her at all, she has been alone for a few months. Don't forget she was engaged to Edward before he married the queen. They have been friends in the past, but still, I can't quite figure out what's going on between them."

"Do you know what happened, why did they not marry?"

"Someone said she got pregnant, and the king canceled their wedding, so lord Hampton took her under his protection."

"No one can blame the king if she was bearing someone else's child," she said without realizing that she was talking to her husband, who probably would think the conversation was leading to their own situation with Richard.

"Well, bearing someone else's child doesn't mean you have to abandon your plan. I've accepted you with someone else's offspring. Does that make me a fool?"

"Are you angry about this?" she asked, almost forgetting she was on the back of a horse for the first time.

"Not at all. But I'm saying that perhaps the king should have married her whether she was with someone else's child. They could have given the child to another family to look after it."

"If this is your way to say that I should give my child away, you are wasting your time," she said, and in her agitation, Estrilda gesticulated and scared the horse. Without warning, the animal swerved, and she screamed while gripping the saddle with both hands, but mercifully, Francis was quick to take hold of the horse's bridle and rescued her.

"You nearly killed me!" she shouted.

He chuckled. "Hardly. You must get used to that reaction from a horse; use your thighs to stay on the saddle, and your body. It will come with time."

"I don't think I will be able to ride like the queen," she said, holding the saddle with both hands while her heart was still rolling like a drum before an execution.

"We'll practice a little every day, and in no time, you'll ride on your own everywhere."

AFTER A COUPLE OF WEEKS, Etrilda's riding skills improved, and her daily riding lessons with Francis brought her much closer to him. And she even got used to the smell of the horses. At first, she had poured a mixture of different flower oils over her clothes to ensure the odor of the hay and dung disappeared, but now she did not care. Not that she would ever tell Francis, but she started to like horses. However close they had become, her heart still leaped out when Richard was around and guilt was soon replaced with her wild and sinful imagination.

"I have the impression you've forgotten about me," Richard complained as they met each other one afternoon in the gardens of Westminster. When she heard his voice, she started and glanced around to ensure Francis was not in the area.

"How could I?" she asked and approached Richard but refrained from putting her arms around his waist.

"You seem pretty close to Francis now."

"He is my husband. What do you expect?"

"I did not realize you loved him," he said, ripping a white rose from a bush and grazing his index at the same time.

"Well, you know him better than I do. How can one not love a man such as him? I cannot help it."

"Try not to forget me when I leave with the king," he said, giving her the rose stained with his blood. Estrilda took the flower and attached it to her gown, then she got a kerchief out and wiped the blood off his hand while avoiding looking him in the eyes.

"So, you're leaving again?"

"My brother requested that I accompany him to Ludlow. He wants to see his son, and then we will tour in Cornwall."

"And Wales?"

"No, it is not in the plan."

"Has he finally ended his affair with the countess of Dudllan?"

"It wasn't an affair. Anyway, the argument they had seemed serious; we will not see her again in London. Where is your husband?"

"I don't know. I've not seen him since the morning mass."

Richard smiled, put his arms around her, and brought her close to his chest. Like before, Estrilda's heart pounded, and dizziness took control of her. Because he was to leave soon, she was a little sad, but at the same time, she rejoiced that lady Alys would never come to London again. Richard brought his lips to her in a sweet and deep kiss, and her promise to be faithful to Francis vanished into oblivion.

CHAPTER TWENTY-SEVEN
April 1474, Dudllan, Alys

A few months after my return to Wales, I received a message from Edward. Without delay, I paid the messenger and took the letter. The contents could only be bad news, and I was in no rush to open it. I slipped it into my sleeve for later, much later.

"My lady, the king instructed me to wait for a response," the man said, still on his horse.

"You must be tired from the travel; I will read it later and give you a response in the morning."

"I am afraid this cannot wait. I must be on my way today."

"Does the king expect you to travel non-stop for two weeks? You will do me the favor to rest here for the night and to share our dinner, and then you can give me all the latest news. It is not that often that we get visitors here. Is the war with France over?"

"Not a war. Merely a warning, if you want my opinion."

"Come, you'll tell me all about it while you eat."

"The king wanted to warn France, or at least show them that England is mighty and will let no one invade it," he said as he dismounted.

"Geoffrey, give the horse some hay and rub his back with straw, he's dripping with sweat." Immediately, Geoffrey took the horse's reins and let him to the stable while the messenger and I headed for the keep.

"I've heard that English soldiers looted many villages and that in some places, the entire population was slaughtered."

"No, no. Just a few."

"What about the French army?" I asked as we entered the kitchen and before he could answer, I asked the domestic to prepare something for the messenger, then I turned back to the man and we both sat at the oak table. "So, about the French?"

"Nowhere to be seen. King Edward's army fought against a few mercenaries and not all were French, but King Louis's army did not turn up. The mercenaries were led by Jasper Tudor."

"And?"

"King Edward was victorious by far."

"What about Henry Tudor?"

"Probably dead."

"Henry is dead?" I asked, dropping the loaf of bread on the floor. Immediately some domestics rushed to pick it up before I had time to do so. I sat and leaned my back against the chair and tried to compose myself. Henry was too young; he could not be dead.

"Did you know him?" the messenger asked, whilst ripping a morsel of bread.

"He grew up here at Dudllan with his uncle."

"I am sorry to give you the bad news."

"Are you sure he is dead?"

"Almost certain. There was no one standing on the battlefield when King Edward's army left."

While the man ate, I took the letter, moved away from the table and began to read.

MY DEAR ALYS,

First, let me apologize for my appalling behavior. Your revelations devastated me, and I probably overreacted when you were only trying to make your peace. While I would prefer to speak to you directly, I feel my unexpected arrival would not receive a warm welcome. Therefore, I am sending a messenger to ask for your permission to visit. I am in a village nearby Dudllan and will only call if you allow me.

Please, I'm begging for your forgiveness. I've missed you and cannot live with the thought you might hate me.

Yours truly,

Edward

Feeling disturbed by the apologies Edward sent, but more so by the news of Henry's death, I realized that King Louis had been right; I did not know where I stood.

Again, I'd got accustomed to the idea that I would live here with no splendor and no friends other than the ones who lived within these castle walls. But now, it was up to me to make up with the king or to arouse his anger. The response he was expecting was obvious, but it frightened me. My son, Geoffrey, hated Edward, and I did not want to hurt my son, but deep down, a part of me desired to see Edward.

However, agreeing to let him come to Dudllan was a dangerous game, for it was not without risk. I could not fall for Edward. My will was resilient, but my weak heart often took control of me. Perhaps I had given up on all hopes that Hampton was alive. Oh, God knew I would have given everything for this to be true! But if it were true, Hampton would have contacted me, and he had not.

"Tell the king it would be an honor to receive him at Dudllan, but also tell him not to expect a luxurious banquet. We do not have the means."

Immediately after the messenger's departure, I rushed to my bedchamber and examined my gowns and jewelry. The king would be here in less than an hour. I picked up my favorite one, but then I recalled the last time I wore it a few years ago—I couldn't. Putting it back, I scrutinized my collections of gowns and choose a simple one and a pearl necklace. I braided my hair and hid them under a simple headdress. My attire was austere enough to prevent any gossip, but still pretty enough to show Edward that I had made an effort for him, without trying to entice his manly instincts. No one at Dudllan had heard the rumors drifting around the court. At least I hoped they hadn't heard them, and I wanted it to stay that way.

"Why is the king coming here?" asked Geoffrey.

"I'm not sure, but we must be polite to him. Receiving the king is an honor."

"That man killed my father. He's a murderer," Geoffrey said with an attitude and gesture that reminded me of Hampton.

"I know, but what choice do we have? We've no ally, thus we should be grateful that he deigns to visit us. No other noble people treat us with the respect with which they treated your father. You might have a title, but most English people will never accept us as their own, even if our bloodline is nobler than most of them. Please, try to be polite when the king and his retinue arrive."

He nodded and took my hand in his. I squeezed it. "We'll be fine. They won't stay for long. Come. I must ask the domestic to prepare the hall."

Geoffrey was thirteen; many young men of his age had squires' positions and were well educated. People were right, I'd neglected my children's education. All the same, Geoffrey trained with Robyn daily; just like Robyn, probably hoping to become a great warrior. Geoffrey wanted to be as grand as his father was, if not better.

"The king," the guards announced, and we all gathered in the courtyard to welcome him and his men. When they entered, I noticed Richard and Anne behind him. Anne was the only lady among two dozen men.

At first, it surprised me, as Edward had not mentioned them in his letter. Perhaps he took them with him as an excuse so that the queen would not suspect the real reason for his travel.

I bowed to Edward, who then kissed me on both cheeks.

"What a pleasure," he said.

And strangely enough for me, the real pleasure was to see Anne and Richard. "This is a nice surprise," I told Anne. I was truly content to see her, for we had a substantial thing in common and since we had seen each other back in London, I felt closer to her than I ever did, and I suspected she thought the same way.

"When I heard the king was visiting Ludlow, I convinced Richard to let me accompany them. Anything to get away from London and HER... but also away from my sister and her husband. They are unbearable but so well suited for each other! Father could not have chosen a better husband for Isabel."

"Indeed. I hope this long journey has not made you too tired. And I must apologize, for you will not find the luxury you are used to at Middleham castle. No minstrels here or any entertainment. But also, no embroidery class," I said, and we both laughed, recalling the many hours where I had to sit with her mother to learn embroidery.

Who would have thought that one day Anne and I would get on famously? However, the reason was that we both hung onto a past we refused to let go of, but still, I did not dare to mention what Fauconberg had said. Until I was sure, there was no need to give her false hopes. This would only have tormented her, like it did me.

"I will get the cook to prepare something, but I am afraid we won't have much," I said, addressing all my guests.

"Do not worry. We've eaten already, just some of your private reserve of French wine will do. Oh yes, I got winds of your special reserve of this delectable nectar," Edward said.

Slightly reluctant to let my reserve go with the king and his men, I asked: "How would you know?" Everyone laughed apart from me.

"I am the king; it is my duty to know."

As we walked along the corridors towards the great hall, I held Edward back and immediately he took me in his arms. I moved away.

"If you have come here to make me change my mind about getting married, you are wasting your time. Besides, I am furious that you sent an army to France and that you've killed Henry."

"Henry Tudor is not dead. He and his uncle ran away like cowards, but what is sure is that they have no army left. All the same, I did not come here to talk about France."

"I will not marry, if this is the reason for your trip."

"That is not why I am here either. We can talk about it later, but I will not try to force you. I have missed you so much," he said as he took my hand. He pushed me against the wall and tried to kiss me.

"Not here," I said, pushing him back. "I do not wish to give the people of Dudllan a reason to gossip about me."

While some domestics brought in wood for the fire and installed long trestle table, others brought white tablecloths.

"I am sorry, your visit was a little short notice," I said as we entered the hall.

As soon as one of the tables was set, we took seats and the wine was served, along with some food platters. Then we all gathered by the fireplace, and for a moment, it was almost as when we were younger at Middleham when we used to sit on deep sheepskin carpets by the fireplace to read or play chess. Except that tonight, we sat on chairs and drank non-diluted wine. Edmund, Louis and Arthur were absorbed in the stories Richard told them about London. Geoffrey did not speak much and stayed in a corner on his own. My heart went out to him. His solitude was not caused by anger due to the king's presence but more because of his father's absence. He needed a man to admire and whose example he could follow. Geoffrey had the habit of hanging onto Robyn each time he was at Dudllan.

I opened my arms for him to come and sit on next to me to listen to our guests' stories, but he declined, probably embarrassed that I still treated him as my little boy in front of our visitors. "I'll check on the horses and see if Robyn needs me," he said and walked out.

Nodding my approval, I smiled as I watched him leave the hall.

"What's wrong with him?" asked Edward.

"Your presence. Have you already forgotten you've killed his father?"

"I see," Edward said and stood up, heading for the door, and I looked at him quizzically.

"I think it is time that I have a man-to-man conversation with the young earl," he said.

"Suit yourself," I said, and then I turned my attention to Anne and whispered, "Are things better between you and Richard?"

Before replying, she shot a glance towards Richard who now stood and demonstrated his exploit as if he was reliving them. My sons looked at him in awe, and then Anne lowered her eyes. "Not really, I am hoping this journey will help us. In London, he's always with her, and when he joins me in bed, he's too tired to do his duty."

"Would you like it if I had a word with him?"

"I doubt that anyone can get her out of his mind. She probably gave him a love potion provided by the queen," she whispered to ensure that Richard heard no word. We laughed, but, unwilling to let the thought of Estrilda or the queen spoil our peaceful evening, I changed the conversation and focused on our past.

"Did I ever tell you about the first time I met your father when he came to Ireland?" I asked Anne, but I got interrupted by Louis.

"Mother, can I get my lute to show Richard?" Louis asked.

"Of course, but you should not say Richard, you should address him as either His Grace or the duke of Gloucester."

"So why did you call him Richard?" Louis replied, and I bit my lip not to laugh.

"Just get your lute," I finally said and returned my attention to Anne, who also tried not to laugh at Louis's remark.

"I have heard about the story of my father in Ireland, but not from you, and to be honest, I am never tired of hearing good things about my father," she said, putting her hand on mine.

In no time, Louis was back in the hall and the proud little cockerel stood in front of the small audience and offered us quite a spectacle., At that point, I realized that I did not know how talented my son was.

Later, Edward returned with Geoffrey, and whatever he had told him seemed to have transformed my eldest son. "Mother, do you know that King Edward is organizing a jousting tournament in the summer and he's invited me? He said he can help me train so that I could take part."

"You might be slightly too young to take part in a tourney," I said as Edward took a seat and brought it closer to mine.

"My opponent will be of my age; I won't be fighting against Robyn or Richard."

"I don't believe Richard would fight against Robyn ever again," I said, recalling the disaster that happened a few years ago.

"With equal arms, I can take your man any time," Richard said, perking up his head.

"In that case, I am sure that can be arranged," I said, thinking that Robyn would be more than proud to have his revenge in the jousting arena, especially now that he was even more experienced.

"That's settled then. Young man, you will begin your training at dawn," said Edward.

"I want to train, too," said Louis, leaving his lute on the table.

I opened my mouth to reply, but Edward spoke first.

"Master Louis, I shall arrange that you are sent to the best family in England where you will be a page first; if you are proving your value, you will then become a squire. And I am sure you will make a valiant knight one day, but you will have to work really hard before."

"I always work hard, Sire," he said and bowed. "When do I start training?"

I sighed, but I was pleased to see that happiness had returned to Dudllan, and then both Geoffrey and Louis sat next to the king and swallowed every word he said for a good hour or so. Now and then I caught glimpses of their conversation and heard some of Hampton's exploits.

When everyone had gone to bed, only Edward and I had stayed behind and retreated into the solar where the chairs were slightly more comfortable.

"What did you tell Geoffrey for him to come around so quick?"

"I told him how much I loved his father and I explained what happens on a battlefield and how men can be different, fighting for our side is our duty. I think he understood. Also, I explained that I did not want it to end like it did, but that's what happens during battle. He understood that everyone who takes part in battle knows it can be deadly. I promised Geoffrey to show him everything Hampton taught me."

"But it will take years before he will be able to take part in a tournament. Did you also tell him that?"

"Well, you should have sent him to a home to be a page a few years ago. Richard will take him into his service and teach him everything to become a squire in no time. We will add a little show for the young men to compete what they have learned, so if your son is a fast learner, he might even take part in the summer tournament. He knows it depends entirely on him," he said, wrapping his arms around me, and then he teased my neck with his lips. "Why did you wear this old gown?"

"This is not old."

"You have many more beautiful gowns, but you wore this one on purpose, to push me away, but it will not work," he said, strengthening his embrace, which I must admit felt safe and peaceful. But I was fooling myself and had to regain control.

Instead of listening to my reasoning, I closed my eyes and for a brief moment, it felt like Hampton was with me again. Not that I would have admitted it to Edward. Edward's hands slid down my back, while his breathing over my neck warmed up my entire body. Then his lips pressed against mine, giving me a sense of pleasure I did not want with him, and suddenly I worried that if I were to look at Edward at this instant, I'd fall for him and forget about Hampton.

Edward was still handsome, but I could not love him. Even if it was hard to ignore the burning desire that crept inside my mind and body. I could not. Time had not faded my love for Hampton. It was if I was his prisoner for eternity. I could never love another man like I loved Hampton, and did not want to forget him either, but Edward seemed so perfect, so attentive, so delicate, as if he was trying to heal my wound. I wondered if he felt the sorrow in my embrace.

Why was Hampton obsessing me so much? If he was alive, he obviously had no interest in me, and if he was dead, I was free to do what I wanted. I had to stop thinking about Hampton; this was too painful and tormented my soul.

Shivering, I woke up in the middle of the night by the dying fire in the solar. Both Edward and I had fallen asleep on the sheepskin in front of the fire in each other's arms.

"We should go to bed," I said.

"No, I am good here," he said, keeping his protective arms around me.

"What if someone sees us, like this?"

"There is nothing to feed rumors here, we are both clothed, and we were just talking."

I laid my head back on his chest and closed my eyes. "And kissing," I said.

"You can have so much more if you wanted," Edward said as he caressed my hair.

WHEN I WOKE AT DAWN, Edward was no longer by my side. For a fleeting moment, I worried that he had left Dudllan. I rushed to the window and could see many people in the courtyard. At least he was still here.

Once I got changed, I crossed the stable yard to join Richard by the training arena. He was watching Edward as he showed Geoffrey the primary use of the quintain. Edmund, Louis, and Arthur were sitting on the wall that surrounded the arena, all encouraging their brothers with, probably, a pinch of jealousy, but also admiration.

"What a beautiful day for a young squire to take his first lesson," Richard said.

"Indeed," I replied, then we both watched Geoffrey for a while. "May I be honest with you?"

"Always," he said with his eyes on my son.

"Do you remember when I advised you to wed Anne? I thought you loved her, or at least that you would love her after you marry her. She is not as strong as she seems. You should care more for her. That mistress of yours, I don't believe she is right for you. I think she will hurt you and it will destroy your marriage with Anne. You have a beautiful wife; you should have heirs. Anne loves you very much. She always did. Do not spoil your fortune for someone who is not worthy."

"You do not know Estrilda. She is so fragile; she is a wonderful woman. In fact, she reminds me of you."

"How could you say that? We could not be more different. My blood descends from a noble Irish line, and she is... from Flanders," I said after I had to control myself not to reveal where she came from.

"Like you, she is alone in a country where she knows no one. Her husband, whom her father forced her to marry, has passed away."

"Hasn't she married Francis? Let them be happy. Even if sometimes I wonder why Francis accepted. Honestly, it was a stupid idea, and I thought Francis would have been clever enough to refuse. But I guess I was wrong."

"Francis is no fool. Besides, may I remind you that you are the one who suggested that she marries Francis."

"I had no idea you were going to ask him. He is your friend; doesn't he deserve a faithful wife? You are forcing him to be the accomplice of your sin."

"You're in no position to talk about sin."

I squeezed my fists, angered by his remark. "I don't need you to judge me. We are talking about you and your lover, and you should leave her, now!"

"No."

"Why? Because you want to keep her for yourself? If you really love her, then you should wish for her happiness."

"Why would you care?"

The clash of the quintain and a loud thud attracted our attention to the training arena. Geoffrey was on the ground, but as I saw him scrambling to his feet and climbing back on his horse, I shouted, "Be careful." Then I returned my attention to Richard. "I do not do this for her, but for you and Anne. You're hurting her."

"I cannot help it."

"Try harder. I don't believe Hampton would have been pleased with how you treat his daughter."

"I never thought you cared much for Anne when Hampton was alive."

"Well, I do now. No one else would take her defense and if you, her husband, do not protect her, then I will."

He did not reply and stared blankly at Edward and Geoffrey.

"Richard, I know you are a good man and that you love Anne. Please, leave Estrilda and Francis to live their lives without you."

"I cannot bear the idea of him touching her. I should not have asked him to marry her," he said without looking at me.

"If you want to keep her for your mistress, then you should try to make it less obvious. And in public, put your wife first."

"You're not really the person who should give advice about putting a wife before a mistress when you've done the opposite all your life. First, with Hampton. You relegated his wife to a mere domestic role, and now with the queen."

"What are you talking about?"

"Everyone knows you are Edward's mistress."

Then, as Geoffrey eschewed the quintain after many trials, I clapped and shouted, "Well done, Geoffrey!" Then I turned my attention back to Richard. "Everyone is wrong. There is nothing between Edward and me; we enjoy each other's company, nothing more."

"If that is what you call enjoying each other's presence. I'm not blind. I can see how you both look at each other, and I know he spent last night with you."

"He did not."

"You need not lie to me. I'll never betray your secret, but I saw you in the solar last night."

"And? We were just talking."

"Of course, you were talking. It must have been an intense discussion for both of you to fall asleep on the floor in front of the fireplace in the solar."

"Are you spying on me?"

"No, it was a coincidence."

"If I did not know you better, I'd say you were jealous. You accuse me as if it was you, I've cheated on."

"I... yes, I am."

"Oh, not you, Richard. We are... we were friends."

"Aren't we anymore?"

"Well... time has passed. We both got older and... I've always liked you as my little brother. For heaven's sake, Richard, I am just telling you to take care of your wife, and you are trying to show me you care for me more than you should."

"I can't help it."

"What about your mistress, Estrilda?"

"As I said, she reminds me of you. A long time ago, when I first came to Middleham, there was this beautiful lady, she was a little older than me, but she was the most beautiful girl I had ever seen. She used to climb up the trees, and she rode her horse like a man. She was different from all the other ladies I had seen, and I fell in love with that lady. I tried to tell her once, but she just mocked me, as I was too young. I've never dared to tell you before... I've never stopped loving you." He stared at his feet as if I had caught him.

I wrapped my arms around him. "You'll always be my little brother. That is the best love I can give you, and that is a love that no one in the world will be able to destroy. No man or woman. Stay faithful to your wife. Don't be cruel with her, or with your mistress. Promise me that when you return to London, you will tell her it is over, and you will start a family with Anne."

"How could I not obey you?"

We both embraced each other.

"Am I disturbing something?" Anne asked as she joined us.

"Not at all," I said and wiped tears at the corner of my eyes. Then I nodded, and she understood I had spoken to her husband on her behalf.

Without a word, we watched Geoffrey, who had great success with avoiding being knocked down from his horse by the quintain, train. When they had finished, both Geoffrey and Edward joined us.

"Geoffrey will come to London so he can train for the tourney. I think I've found a little genius here," Edward said, stealing hold of my waist while I discreetly tried to push him away.

"I will not let him go alone to London. Without me, his life would be in danger."

"Please Mother," Geoffrey said, stepping forward. "I must train if I want to win. Don't you want to be proud of me?"

"I already am, my son, and besides, you can train here with Robyn."

Richard joined in the conversation. "Anne and I can take him under our protection if that reassures you. Geoffrey will be safe with his sister to look after him."

Then I approached Anne. "Will you care for him like your real brother? Promise me you will not let the queen go anywhere near my son."

"Geoffrey has always been the pride and joy of my father. I'll do everything to protect him. I swear," she said and took my hand warmly.

Reluctantly, I agreed to let Geoffrey go to London to live with Richard and Anne, and a few days later, the time for him to leave had come.

"Mother, please," he said as I hugged him, refusing to let him go. It was not the first time we were separated, but usually, I was the one leaving for London, and my children were safely guarded by my men and their nursemaid at Dudllan and not at the mercy of any witches or jealous women.

"Look after yourself; I could not bear to lose you."

"You won't have to. Besides, you'll come to the tourney. I'll show that I am capable, like Father. I know he won many tournaments in the past, Edward told me. This is going to be fantastic; the best knights of Christendom will take part."

"Come on, then, I will tell you all I know about our father," Anne said, opening an arm to invite him to follow her, and he mounted his horse.

Seeing my eldest son leave was more painful than I would have thought. Edmund, Louis, Arthur, and Alienor stood by my side in the courtyard and waved as their brother, who was now a grown-up and looking forward to his new life. All of them seemed so proud of him. We waved until the cloud of dust behind them disappeared and until we could no longer hear the clip-clop of horses.

CHAPTER TWENTY-EIGHT
June 1474, London, Estrilda

When the king had left for Ludlow, he was accompanied by Richard and his wife. It did not please Estrilda very much, but Francis was relieved to see that Richard had left, which was an opportunity for them to spend time as husband and wife. Her attitude was undoubtedly hurting her husband more than he would admit, but he had been warned before their wedding. Love was not part of the arrangement. This was something Estrilda had reserved to Richard, even if each day she grew a little fonder of Francis, it wasn't the same kind of love.

The day the king returned, almost two months after their departure, the entire court gathered in the courtyard to welcome him and his retinue; even the weather seemed to rejoice his return. The queen's joy when her husband entered was heart-melting, and King Edward seemed pleased to see her, too. Maybe that was all they needed; the departure of lady Alys had brought back peace and respite at Westminster. Perhaps now things would be back as they should be.

King Edward embraced the queen and kissed her passionately. Estrilda stood among the ladies who were all pleased for the queen, but she could not share her joy with them. When Richard dismounted, Estrilda was about to move forward so he could notice her presence, but he walked straight to his wife's horse and helped her to dismount; then he kissed her hand and walked with her towards the stairs. Estrilda froze when she detected something which did not rejoice her: contentment and even possibly the glow of love in his eyes.

What had happened?

Then she noticed Anne putting her hand on her belly. No, this could not be: she could not be with child! He had said he was not bedding her. But if she were with child, that meant he would put Estrilda's child second. Even if Anne's belly was still as flat as unraised bread, there was no doubt in the way she shone. The duchess was expecting a child. Richard's legitimate child would have all the honor it was due. All Estrilda could do now was hope and pray that it was a girl so that Richard would soon forget about it.

When they walked past Estrilda, Anne stopped and glared at her. Estrilda lowered her eyes and curtseyed, and then she saw Anne's feet moving away. Humiliated, Estrilda tried to hide her pain, but there was no time to rest for the queen ordered everyone to busy themselves with the preparations for a last-minute evening feast.

After an exhausting afternoon, Estrilda was pleased to sit at the table. Though she tried on several occasions to attract Richard's attention, he ignored her, for he seemed to enjoy the wine, the food, and his wife's company—a little too much for her taste. Never before had Richard failed to come to her within the hour of his return to the palace, and she did not understand why it was different this time. It could not be the child, indeed.

The music floating around the hall, the extravagant food that lay on the long tables, and even the sugar violets scattered across it did not lift her spirits.

When everyone raised their goblets to celebrate the king's return, as if he had returned from war, it was in a halfhearted way that Estrilda followed everyone's gesture, keeping her eyes on Richard at all times, hoping that he would feel her insistent gaze. She secretly prayed that in the evening he would call her to his bedchamber. But to no avail. Not once had he looked in her direction, and the only person who noticed her attitude was Francis.

"I believe we will finally be able to live as husband and wife from now on," he whispered.

"Why are you saying that?"

"For it looks like the countess has finally reasoned with Richard. Whatever she told him, it has worked, and now the duke and duchess are expecting their firstborn."

"The countess? Which countess?"

"Dudllan, of course, where do you think they went?"

Estrilda nearly choked on a piece of heron when he said that. "They were at Ludlow and in Cornwall, not in Wales, were they?"

"I am afraid that is where they were. Ludlow and Cornwall were just an excuse, and taking Richard and Anne was a diversion so no one would suspect where the king was going."

"But I thought lady Alys left because she had disagreed with the king. I thought their affair was over."

"Edward will never let her go. Can't you see that?"

"But she is a traitor."

"He's a forgiving king."

"She has been plotting against him with the king of France."

"You should not speak so loudly. The countess of Dudllan is in favor with the king, and if he had any doubts about her, he would have done something about it. As your husband, I'm asking you to keep your nose out of other people's business. Besides, it was not entirely the countess's fault. She has always supported lord Hampton, and no one can accuse her of being a traitor. When her heart is set, she is the most faithful person I've ever met. The woman would fight anyone who would dare to disagree with what she thinks right. Better to be on her side."

"It seems that you admire her. I really don't understand how this woman wins people so easily. Are you bedding her, too?" she asked, her breathing getting louder, and she bit her tongue for showing her vulnerable side.

"Why would you care with whom I am sharing my bed?"

"I do not care," she said and turned her head to avoid meeting his eyes.

"If I did not know you so well, I'd say you care at least a little." He kissed her hand. "But I would like to thank you, for you could not have given me a better proof that I have done well to be your husband."

His remark made her feel hot and sweaty, so she removed her hand from his.

"Do not build yourself false hope, husband. Now, if you'll excuse me, I am a little tired and would like to retire to my chamber."

"Are you joining the hunt tomorrow?"

"I would love to, but you know that my riding skills aren't yet at a level where I could safely follow a hunting party."

"Most of the ladies will go on foot for falconry."

"In that case, I shall be there."

Throughout the night, Estrilda waited for a sign from Richard, but nothing came. Exhausted and out of tears, she eventually fell asleep. Even Francis did not come to her chamber that night, but although this was unusual, she did not worry, for she doubted that he had a mistress. Francis was constantly caring for Richard, and this gave him no time for a mistress. Besides, sometimes she did not think she would have been bothered very much if it was the case. True, her husband was handsome and had allure, but he had not her heart entangled in passionate love.

When Estrilda joined the queen and her retinue for the hunting in the courtyard, which was packed with people chattering, horses thumping their hooves on the ground ready to go out, and dogs barking as if to summon the riders to make a move, she was shocked to see that Anne Neville was part of the riding group.

"Why is the duchess riding with the men?" she asked.

"Anne rides as well as any man," one of the ladies said. "Her father put her on her horse before she could even walk."

"But isn't she with child?" Estrilda asked, both shocked and deep down, hoping for something to happen to the child.

"That would not stop her."

"What if she falls? She will lose her child," she said, making a face.

"She won't," someone else replied.

"Let's hope she does not," Estrilda said. But deep down, she shamefully prayed for the opposite to happen. If Anne were to lose her child, Richard would come back to Estrilda. Then she noticed him, and she excused herself. She could no longer bear it; she had to speak to him.

On horseback and waiting for the hunt to depart, Richard was in discussion with Francis and a young lad Estrilda did not recognize at once, then Francis mentioned his name. The bastard of Dudllan and Hampton acted as if he was of noble blood and high importance at court. How the queen suffered his presence among the courtiers was beyond Estrilda.

"Your Grace," she called out. Richard turned and looked briefly in her direction, then his attention returned to his companion as if he had not noticed her. What did she do to deserve less attention than Hampton's bastard?

Despite being hurt by his disinterest, Estrilda strode to Richard and grabbed the bridle of his horse. The animal reacted by rearing, which made her stumble, and then she fell on her backside in front of the court. Immediately, squires and grooms came to her help.

"I am fine," she said, more irritated by the humiliation than by the pain in her bones. The last thing she wanted was to attract the attention of other people who had, fortunately, missed the incident.

"Estrilda, didn't I tell you that horses must be approached with care? Thank our Lord that the duke is one of the best horsemen in the kingdom; you could have caused him a serious fall," said Francis.

"That is fine," Richard said as if to take her defense, and that brought her a sliver of hope.

"I did not mean to cause any trouble, Your Grace, but I must speak to you," she said, unable to look him in the eyes.

Richard did not seem pleased, but nevertheless he dismounted, and they both walked away from the hunting party. "What is it?" he asked in a rather cold voice.

"Richard, what is going on? Why are you avoiding me?" she asked, but as she saw Francis staring at them, she stepped back to hide behind the stable walls and pulled Richard toward her.

"I can't bear life without you. Why haven't you come to me? Why haven't you spoken to me since your return?" she continued.

"To keep a promise."

"Because your wife is expecting a child, is that why? Soon she won't be able to satisfy your thirst; she will be too big and-"

He put a finger to her lips. "Please, you have a husband who loves you, and I a wife whom I love. We should accept this blessing from God."

"But you can't love her. It's me you love; I know because you told me you love me," she said, sounding a little as if she was begging and losing all dignity.

"It was lust and not love. I enjoyed every moment I have spent with you, but I cannot continue. Please do not address me again unless I speak to you first. When I want to see my son, I will deal with Francis. I am sorry," he said, as coldly as if he no longer had feelings for her. He had probably been manipulated by someone in Wales.

The shock from the news kept her frozen. There was no way she wanted to join the party now. Her throat ached and her eyes watered. Estrilda swallowed her pain and leaned against the wall. Then she let herself slip to the ground. It did not matter that her gown was soiled with horse dung. It did not matter if someone was to see her in that state. Alys of Dudllan had humiliated her without even being present, and she had dared to send her bastard to make sure her deeds were accomplished.

Then Estrilda heard a voice. "Oh, there you are," said lady Spencer. "The queen is looking for you. Are you all right?"

Estrilda nodded.

"Look at the state of you! You certainly cannot go looking like this. Hold on." She took her kerchief and wiped Estrilda's tears. "Oh, what have you done? Your skin is all soiled, and you are so pale." Then she bit her lips until blood came out and passed a finger over her lips and then tapped it over Estrilda's cheeks and above her eyelids. "That is better. Come now. The queen is waiting for us, and she doesn't like sad people, you know that. Have you ever done falconry?"

"No, I've always avoided hunting so far."

"This can be fun, and I guarantee it will bring a smile to your face, but please, until it comes naturally, force yourself. We do not want to worry the queen today; she is so glad that her husband has returned to her bed... You should have heard them last night; worse than rabbits, they were."

Estrilda smiled and followed her.

Lady Spencer was right. The hunt brought fresh intentions in her head. Still, all her fantastic ideas evaporated the moment they arrived back at the palace.

By the time everyone had returned at the end of a pleasant afternoon and had gathered in the courtyard, George of Clarence stepped down the main staircase and advanced towards the hunting party.

"You've killed her!" he bellowed. "You've killed her, and now it will be your turn, you witch!" He drew his blade out and pointed it at the throng of courtiers who suddenly ceased all conversation.

Everyone stared in horror in his direction, but no one was quite sure whom he addressed.

Then Richard and Edward rushed before him. They said something which Estrilda did not hear, but George shouted and jabbed his fingers towards the queen and her ladies: "You know she is a witch. She's poisoned my wife. And you've done nothing about it."

Both men took hold of George and dragged him away. Then Anne ran in their direction. It turned out that her sister, George's wife, had suffered some fever after giving birth while the party was out hunting and now, George was accusing the queen of having poisoned Isabel but a few days later, his wife had recovered which calmed the rumors of poisoning quickly.

The next day, George was gone. Lady Spencer said that the king had ordered him to return to the North until he accepted that the queen was in no way responsible for his wife's illness.

George hated Elizabeth so much that he never missed an opportunity to spread rumors about her. If the queen were responsible, she would have poisoned him, not his wife... Anyway, this was ridiculous. Queen Elizabeth was not a witch. If she were one, the first victim would have surely been lady Alys of Dudllan, who was still well alive and full of ill-advice, and that Estrilda was sure of.

CHAPTER TWENTY-NINE
June 1474, Dudllan, Alys

Only a few weeks after their return to London, Anne sent me a letter to inform me the incident that happened in London and the fear she had had for his sister's life. Although, this must have been stressful for Anne, I could not feel an ounce of sadness. Isabel had betrayed her father and I had never forgiven her. Because of her betrayal, Hampton had been killed in battle. This would have been another of my enemies out of my way; shame it was her and not George, though.

Memories of that fateful day at Barnett replayed in my head when my steward announced the approach of George of Clarence. I frowned. George had never come to Dudllan before, not even when he pretended to be on Hampton's side. Immediately, I put the letter away and rushed to the courtyard.

Taking a deep breath, with Robyn on one side and four of my men on the other side, I glared at George as he waited before the portcullis with only one of his trusted men.

"Let him pass," I said.

George dismounted, and, taking long strides, he hastened towards me. "I need your help," he said, without even greeting me.

"Pardon my surprise, but should I remind you that not that long ago, you've tried to take me to the scaffold and have me executed?"

"It was a mistake. Forgive me."

I curled my lips for a brief moment. After a short pause, I said: "Your excuses come too late."

"Would you at least listen to what I have to say?" George looked pale and devastated—actually defeated. Not the proud George he used to be, but more shockingly, the man before me was sober, which was unusual and suspicious.

"Fine, speak!"

"Inside," he said, in a tone that sounded as if he was ordering me.

I hesitated for a moment, then beckoned Robyn and my men to follow us.

"Leave your sword here," Robyn told George.

He scowled. "I'm not here to harm the countess."

"Either you do as my man tells you or you can return to London at once."

With a loud, exaggerated sigh, he unbuckled his sword and carelessly threw it to the ground.

"And your dagger?" I asked.

Angered by the second request, he sighed even louder, but still, he obeyed, and threw his dagger on the ground again.

As we climbed the steps to the keep, George said: "My wife was poisoned."

"If you've come here to accuse me of having poisoned your wife, you are wasting your time. It has nothing to do with me."

"It's the queen, she has tried to kill Isabel."

I stopped and swung around to face him. "Aren't you and the queen no longer on good terms now?"

"Never. She still considers me responsible for her father's death."

"Which is true. Haven't you yet realized that you must watch your back when you change sides all the time? Anyway, I still don't understand why you came here to inform me of Isabel's illness, for I've not forgotten she's betrayed Hampton. So, pardon me for not shedding a tear. Without her intervention, Hampton would still be with me."

"She had no choice but to follow me. I was... I am, her husband."

Shrugging, I continued silently to the solar. Only our footsteps echoed through the corridor, which was making our meeting very tense.

"What do you want from me?" I asked as I entered the room. Then George, followed by Robyn and four of my guards, ready to intervene if George were to attempt anything against me, joined me inside.

"I'm hoping you can help me."

"Against the queen?" I lifted both eyebrows. "If there were something I could do, I would have done it already. Anyway, what makes you think that the queen is responsible? I've heard that your wife had a fever after giving birth which can be natural and not thus exceptional."

"She was poisoned and has lost our child as result," he said as he poured himself a goblet of wine from the side cabinet.

"I cannot help you. I don't deal with witchcraft."

"But you have knowledge about herbs, don't deny it. Perhaps you could give me something."

"Couldn't you find a bonesetter for that? Why are you asking me?"

"I am the king's brother. If I see someone like that, people will talk, and it will come back to Edward. I've kind of accused his wife of witchcraft publicly. It would be in bad taste if people were to hear that I am mingling with that sort of people."

"What if people hear about your visit here? That would cause much more talk, didn't you think of that?" Incapable of calming down, I paced the room from the window to the wall and back to the window, now and then lifting my head toward George.

"No one knows I am here; Edward sent me to the North."

"Seriously, George, I'm not keen on helping you. For months, I've been a prisoner in my house because of you," I said, raising my voice. My heart sped up as if ready for battle. "You've ruined my life, you've deprived my children of their father, and you've killed my best man. Now leave my land and stop wasting my time!"

"Hampton used to say that when in need, joining forces with an enemy is sometimes necessary."

"How dare you remind me of what Hampton used to say?" I turned to face him and squeezed my hands to the point that my nails entered my palms so deeply that they bled.

"Because it is true. Help me get rid of the queen, and after that, I promise we will be enemies again."

If it were possible at all, I would have been glad to help him, but I loathed him as much as I hated the queen.

"Oh, it is so very tempting; I'd love nothing more than being your enemy."

"So, do we have an agreement?"

Before I replied, I cast a quick glance at Robyn, who shook his head. "Let me think about it," I told George.

George clapped his hands together. "Good, I assume that means you will."

"I don't know yet, I don't know if I can trust you."

"During our truce, and until our common enemy has paid, I give you my words. After, it will be like before!"

Or until you change your mind without warning, I thought. "I shall inform you of my decision in due course."

"When?"

"Next time you see me at court. But we need a plan. Go back to London before rumors about your visit here start spreading; you'll inform me of your plan once I am there. Now go!" I said, and so Robyn opened the door for him to leave. George walked out with a grin on his face, and he deliberately elbowed Robyn as he passed the door. With trembling hands, I took the jug of wine and filled my goblet to the brim.

Once George was gone, I stared out the window, cogitating on the insane proposal I'd accepted. Deep down, I could not deny that George was right, together we would be more powerful, but it was George... Could I be on his side without repulsing myself?

"Do you seriously intend to help him?" asked Robyn as he returned from having seen George out of Dudllan.

"It pains me to admit to it, but he's right. Joining our forces will help us. Hampton never had issues with that."

"Hampton was a man of honor. George is not. He'll never keep his word; as soon as he'll get what he wants, he'll turn against you."

"George is too scared of Edward; he won't do anything against me anymore."

"But he will do something against his wife."

"No," I said and put my goblet of wine away. "George is willing that I do something against Edward's wife. He's too cowardly to act himself. So as long as Edward supports me, I will be safe."

"On that subject..." Robyn said, looking uncomfortable. He sat on the chair by the fireplace, grabbed a book on the side, opened it, and flicked through the pages without reading.

I observed him silently and then he continued: "What do you think Hampton would say if he knew you were the king's mistress?"

"What is wrong with you all? I am not the king's mistress."

"I'm only assuming by what I've observed in the last few months. Pardon my honesty, but tell your tall story to others. I am not judging you, but..."

"Mayhap Edward and I have kissed now and then, but it is not at all what it looks like."

"So, what do you think what Hampton would say?"

"If I were to find someone to love, I am certain Hampton would be pleased to see someone has brought me a taste of life again, which is not the case with Edward. We are friends. Nothing more," I said, staring out the window. "Hampton is dead! Do you honestly believe he'd want to see me sad for the rest of my life?"

"In this case, why are you hiding your friendship from everyone and especially from your sons?"

Trepidation crept inside my mind, but I stayed silent.

"I will make it easier for you," he continued. "It is because you feel guilty for having turned your attention to Hampton's enemy, for, deep down, you know that Hampton would be unrestrained if he were to find out about you and the king. He would feel betrayed," he said, and then Robyn left the solar as if content to have played the role of Fauconberg for the first time.

All my friends were concerned that I was bedding the king, but I was not. I had always kept enough distance between Edward and me, but I guessed I had done nothing to stop the gossips. On the contrary, I had enjoyed their empowering effects. Anyway, I was a widow and therefore free to do whatever I fancied. Apart from the queen, I was hurting no one by enjoying Edward's company.

First, it was Fauconberg, then Richard, and now Robyn. The loss of Hampton had also hurt Robyn, I knew, but their anger and persistence increased my sense of betrayal.

What would Hampton say? I wished people would stop asking that question. It made me feel contrite. Of course, I knew the answer. It would outrage Hampton, and I would have to face an outburst even if I was not Edward's lover.

Hampton would have considered a passionate embrace a step too far, and I knew it.

CHAPTER THIRTY
July 1474, London, Estrilda

The constant aloofness of Richard was a little... no, was highly excruciating, and it was all lady Alys's fault. The more Richard ignored Estrilda, the more she became obsessed with him, and the more she hated Alys, and feared Alys would reveal her secret. Estrilda had to keep Richard on her side. For a fleeting moment, she even considered visiting a wise woman who would have the perfect potion to bring him back in her bed.

"Estrilda, the queen is waiting," lady Spencer said.

"Hmm?"

"Stop daydreaming and hurry!"

"But I am not on duty until four o'clock. What does she want?"

"The queen has called for you. The countess of Dudllan is back at court, and needless to tell you how the queen reacted when she heard about it."

"Why is she calling for me? I've nothing to do with the countess of Dudllan's presence at court."

"I do not know, but do not make her wait any longer, or her wrath might turn against you."

With no more prompting, Estrilda scrambled up to her feet, let her work fall on the chair, and hastened through the corridors. Taking a deep breath before entering the queen's private chamber, she peered through the gap by the door and saw Elizabeth pacing the room and twisting her necklace between her fingers.

The meeting happened so quickly that Estrilda was still troubled by the conversation when she got out. It even felt like a bad dream, except that it was not a dream. Fear of becoming a bad Christian stirred her loins, but above the eternal flames of Hell, she was more terrified to disappoint the queen.

A refusal to obey would have been interpreted as treason. True, Estrilda would have loved to have lady Alys out of Richard's life and she wanted to make sure Alys would never reveal her origins to anyone, but Estrilda'd never wished for anyone to die. However, she was now in a tricky situation where she had to obey the order or be the dead one.

"Estrilda, Estrilda," lady Spencer called her from the other side of the corridor.

She could not speak to Jane now. To avoid her, Estrilda quickened the pace towards the courtyard. Her heart was pulsing fast as if she was in danger and she started to shake, and thus she found refuge in the chapel where she prayed all afternoon. Before Vespers, knowing that everyone would attend the service but lady Alys, Estrilda headed for the stables. After that, she sat on the mound of hay in the corner of the stables and waited. As she composed herself, the sound of horses' hooves came closer. So, Estrilda hid behind the feed and did her best to stay calm while squeezing the dagger the queen gave her.

"Oh, this was fantastic. You will soon be as fast as your father," lady Alys said to her son as they returned from an outing. "Richard, you are a wonderful tutor. I could never thank you enough."

"It's an honor to help young Geoffrey. After all, his father taught me everything I know."

Lady Alys removed her saddle and put it on the floor; next, after tethering her horse on a hook, she walked in Estrilda's direction. Holding her breath, Estrilda tried to move back, but there was no more space.

"My lady, let me do this for you," a groom said, rushing to help Alys as if she was the queen. She stopped and swung around.

"Thank you, I must admit that I am a little exhausted. You help is more than welcome," she said. "Oh, I've left my saddle over there."

"Come," Richard told her, and he wrapped an arm around her waist. Estrilda squeezed the queen's dagger in her palm so much that the blade cut the skin slightly and pearls of blood fell on the floor.

As soon as the three of them passed the door, Estrilda came out of hiding and for a second, she stared at lady Alys's saddle. That was the solution! If lady Alys were to have an unfortunate accident, no one would accuse the queen or Estrilda of being responsible. But as she approached the saddle, the groom picked it up.

"Sorry, my lady, I shouldn't have left it there. You could have tripped."

Estrilda said nothing and was about to leave, but then she had a second thought. "Would you like that I take it to the saddle room for you? You already have a lot to do looking after the horse of the countess."

"No, thank you, I will do this myself," he said.

"Don't worry, I will tell no one."

"I will do it," he said, then he hesitated. "Were you looking for someone, my lady?"

"Er, yes, my husband, lord Vancey. Have you seen him?" she asked without thinking.

"Lord Vancey is not in London," he replied, looking at her suspiciously.

"Indeed. How silly of me to have forgotten," she said, feeling as though the ground was shifting beneath her feet, and then she rushed out before the groom became any more suspicious.

Hanging around in the stable courtyard, she waited for the grooms and squires to move on to other tasks. Once it was all clear, Estrilda ventured into the saddle room. A place larger than the Cloppelins' house with a floor as pristine as the great hall before a coronation day. On the walls were hanging saddles and bridles under which were gold name tags for each horse. Estrilda approached the one where it said Boudicca and looked around. As she took the dagger out, a thought crossed her mind; thus, she returned to the door and barred it. Reassured no one would disturb her, she headed for Boudicca's saddle and pulled the stirrup down; she lifted the flap and then took the dagger out and begun to cut through the leather strap.

But not all the way through, just enough so it would not break until lady Alys would be out in the woods.

Satisfied that she would not be directly involved in lady Alys's death, Estrilda left the saddle room.

Dusk had settled, and she had to rush back to her duties. The stable yard was rather dark now and was only lit with a few torches at each corner, but at least the grooms were in their quarter, for she could see the light and heard the hubbub of their conversations. Estrilda brushed her gown with a hand to ensure that she looked presentable.

As she walked through the alley, footsteps echoed behind her. She turned around but did not see a soul. As she continued, the sensation of being followed remained. Probably a trick from her guilty conscience. She hastened her footsteps, and then she lifted her gown and ran. Now she knew someone was behind her, for she saw a shadow reflecting against a wall. At the corner, Estrilda hid behind the wall, but a man caught her and squeezed his hands around her neck. A hood pulled over his head hid his face.

"Leave the countess of Dudllan alone!" the man said with a strong French accent.

"Let go of me, or I shall call the guards," she said with a trembling voice.

"All I have to do is press a little harder on your pretty throat, and you won't be able to call anyone. I'll let you go, but if you attempt to hurt lady Alys once more, I shall find you and I promise I won't be so delicate next time. Understood?"

Estrilda nodded, and the man scurried away, but she did not move. Her whole body trembled; she brought a hand to her throat and massaged the skin to ease the pain. Unwilling to see the queen now that she had failed in her mission, she stayed in the gardens for a while, but eventually the cold pulled her to her bedchamber, where she prayed for forgiveness from both God and the queen.

CHAPTER THIRTY-ONE
July 1474, London, Alys

When I accepted Edward's invitation to attend the jousting tournament festivities, I had almost forgotten that I had also given my word to George. Now I was in London, he would think I had agreed to help. I had no idea how he planned to get rid of the queen, nor was I sure that I wanted to be the accomplice of his dirty deed. But I admitted that joining forces with an enemy against a common one was necessary. Nevertheless, I struggled with the idea of having to smile at George. I'd never been good at showing sympathy towards an enemy.

The morning after my arrival, as I returned from a stroll in the gardens, George shouted from the other end of the corridor: "How can you parade at court as if you were the queen? You've no place here."

A few people were around when George shouted and I knew he was enjoying humiliating me in public, especially now that the attention was on us. But he was pushing the situation a little too close to the border of my tolerance, for I had agreed to help him, not for him to treat me as a lowlife.

"I am here by invitation and therefore allowed to walk where I wish, Your Grace!" I said. Then, as I approached through clenched teeth, I added: "Should I remind you that I could have married your brother. That would have made me a queen, and you would have bowed to me! But he was already married."

In a moment of misplaced pride, I had spoken of a secret I had promised never to reveal. Too late, I had said it. Perhaps it was a mistake, but I had to get rid of the queen, and even if I hated George from the bottom of my guts, I knew he was idiot enough to play into my hand and serve me, even if unintentionally.

"What did you say?" He called me back, grabbed my arms, and pulled me into another corridor.

"It does not matter what I said, you've heard me. But you must tell no one."

"Is it one of your lies?" he asked, then paused for a brief instant. "After all, it does not matter if it is true or not. We can spread the rumors, and it will be just the same."

"No. It is not the same. Hampton would have never done anything like that."

"He has done something very similar in the past."

"Hampton was honest, and he would have never done anything like that," I repeated, raising my voice, which echoed against the bare walls of the gallery.

"Is that what you think?... If I recall correctly, this was your idea, again. Do you remember the story about Edward being the bastard of an archer? It wasn't very nice towards my mother, and we all knew it was a lie, but people had believed it, and it served us well for a while."

"But..."

"Don't thank me. Your idea is astute."

"Never tell anyone it was my idea, it was not."

"Are you worried Edward will no longer be interested in you, or that you will be accused of treason?"

"Of course, you're an expert at treason."

"I thought you came here to help me, not to insult me," he said.

"If you want me to keep my word, then you should watch your attitude with me, George."

"It would not sound natural if I had welcomed you as one of my equals, or as if your presence were agreeable. This would look too suspicious."

"Well, considering that I am here on the king's invitation, I believe everyone knows I am welcome at court."

"Not everyone would agree with you."

"I do not care any more about what other people are saying. Now, will you please get out of my way; I must see the king."

THE CLATTER OF BOOTS nearby made us both jump, and we quickly went both our own way, but I caught sight of the queen with a few guards and many ladies behind her. No doubt Queen Elizabeth did not appreciate seeing George and me together. Hmm.

I turned around and caught back up with George.

"My dear George, would you like to join me later?" I asked loudly enough to ensure that the queen would hear it, and I took his arm in a friendly way in case she turned to look at this. I could feel the reticence in George's arm, but like me, he loathed the queen, so he played along.

"Want to poison me, do you?" George murmured.

The idea rejoiced me, but I was no longer the young and innocent girl who had poisoned Edmund of Rutland for revenge. I had learned my lesson... at least when it came to people I wasn't well acquainted with, but for George it was different. He was a monster. Why should I care about not poisoning him? He deserved it more than anyone else.

"That would be a pleasure," I whispered through clenched teeth. "I will see you tonight, and we can talk about it. I might even prepare you a nice concoction," I grinned.

George lifted an eyebrow as if I was insane. Then he shrugged and continued in one direction while I, satisfied, turned around. As I passed by the queen in the corridor, I pretended to be surprised and embarrassed.

"Lady Alys," she said.

"Your Grace," I replied and curtseyed.

"If I were you, I would choose my relations more carefully."

"Well, Your Grace, you are not me." I rose, smiled broadly, and moved away, leaving her speechless.

Even if I had temporarily agreed to be George's ally, I could not tell him about my visit to King Louis and that there were plans to place a new king on the throne. In a way, I was relieved that the king of France had not shared his projects with me, as I would have fretted constantly. I was just hoping that the day they'd attack, I would be away from London, but I also knew that it would be a few more months before it could happen.

Later that day, I found an excuse to leave the court and return to our London house. I had not had the heart to go to the house on my previous visits. The last time I was in that house, Hampton was still alive. Actually, it was the last time I saw him.

When I walked into the house, apart from the dust, the many cobwebs, and the overgrown shrubs in the courtyard, the place was almost as we had left it. Next, as I walked from room to room, I realized that people had been into the solar. It was a total slum, and some tapestries were missing. I would have to leave people here permanently to prevent more theft in the future. I did not want to stay in this house ever again, for it held too many memories, but I did not want people to steal my souvenirs.

As I continued through the corridors, I heard footsteps. Then spurs clanging against the stone floor. I closed my eyes. It felt like Hampton would appear around the corner, but it was all in my head. Then I reached the kitchen. A basket of dried herbs was overthrown on the flagstones, the hooks hanging on the ceiling were all empty. Then a rat brushed my feet. "Shoo!" I shouted and grabbed the broom.

The place was filthy, it smelled damp and dusty, and there were for sure many rat carcasses lying around the kitchen. I pushed open some coffers. In one of them were still a few vials of tinctures and pouches of herbs.

"What are you doing here?" a man said.

Suppressing a shriek, I spun around to face Robert Woodville.

"I've every right to be here, but you have not. Get out of here, murderer! This is my home!"

"Not anymore. This is my home now. In his great generosity, the king has thought this house would make a great reward for my services to this country. After all, this is one of the best houses in London."

"What are you talking about? It's impossible. This house was not his to give."

"When a traitor is arrested or killed, the king is entitled to do whatever he wants with his properties. I requested this one, and King Edward gave it to me without hesitation. Not even a second thought crossed his mind... his great friendship of the past forgotten as quickly as the tip of my blade entered Hampton's back," he said with a sadistic smile.

"Why did you want the house if you do not even live here? You've left the place to rot."

"I do not really need it. Let's say it is my trophy for winning over a traitor."

"Get out of here before I do something I might regret," I said.

"As I said, this place is mine; I could have you arrested for trespassing onto my property. But to prove to you that I am a good man, I will give you one hour to gather your belongings, and if you are not gone when I return, I will have you arrested," he said and left.

Speechless for a moment, anger and disappointment mingled in my head, then an idea spurted out. I reopened the coffers and picked up all the vials.

One of them was labeled as Cicuta Atropa. I squeezed my fingers around it. Thinking of Edmund, tears came to my eyes. I shook my head. Now was not the time to let myself reminisce.

I slipped the Cicuta and other vials into my purse, and after one last look, I left the kitchen and headed for the solar.

There I picked up this and that, then as I was about to return to Westminster, I saw George entering the courtyard.

With long strides, I hastened towards him. "You knew it was no longer mine!"

"No, I've only heard it now and believe me, I am not pleased, for this is my wife's inheritance."

"In this case, that gives us another enemy in common."

"What about our little conversation in Wales? Do you agree to help?"

"Yes, I agree, but do not think this is to help you. Oh, Hampton was so right about the Woodvilles," I said as I recalled the many times he had told me that they were the sources of the canker that ate England.

"How do you plan to get rid of the queen?"

"Oh no, I do not want her to die. In fact, I want her to live a long life." I walked along the corridors, looking around to see what I could salvage from the thieves.

"Have you gone mad?" he asked, grabbing my arm.

I shook him off and stepped away. "Not at all. I want her to suffer more than I have. She took the people I love away from me. I shall do the same to her."

"Watch out, Dudllan. There are limits I will not accept to cross. Edward is a fool, but he is my brother, and I will not let you harm his children."

"That is not my intention."

"What, then?"

I lifted a hand. "Do not ask questions. I cannot trust you, George."

"I said you could trust me until I have my revenge."

"And then you will turn against me. That is the reason why I will not inform you of my decision. Now I must leave, and if I were you, I would leave now, as Woodville will return shortly."

FOR THE NEXT HOUR OR so, I ambled through the streets of London, glancing at several stalls at the market, dodging people who seemed to be in a rush. A merchant sold me a piece of freshly baked honey cake with very little persuasion—still a little warm when I took it. Daydreaming, I ambled to the riverbank and sat on a wall where I savored the sweet treat while I wondered what I should do with my life... I would have gladly gone back to Wales at once, but I had taken all my children to London and Geoffrey was so looking forward to the joust. I could not deprive him of that pleasure; he had trained so hard. Reluctantly, I returned to the palace.

"Where were you? You've a bad habit of disappearing," Edward said when our path crossed in the entrance gallery later that evening.

"How could you have done that to me? I was in London, and I know what you've done."

"Done what?" he asked as he approached me.

"You gave my sons' house to Robert Woodville."

"When Hampton died, everything he owned was mine to deal with. I am the king, and therefore I may give whoever I want some land or property. Now, come, my dear, I've got some minstrels from Provence in tonight." Edward put his hand under my arm and led me towards the hall. As we walked past people, they stopped and bowed.

"But why Woodville?"

"He serves me well," Edward replied as if this was of no importance.

"Robert Woodville does not deserve that house. He killed Hampton and shouldn't receive any reward for his evil acts," I tried to stop, but he invited me to continue. Even the delicious smell of the food that whiffed across the corridor did not change my mood.

"It was war."

"If you do not take the house back from him, I will leave England forever."

"And where would you go?" Edward asked, pulling me into one of the receiving chambers along the corridor.

"To France." I crossed my arms and stood firmly by the door.

"Do you think the king of France needs a mistress?"

"King Louis is always looking for allies, and he always gets what he wants. He's not the sort of king that would betray a friend," I lied. King Louis was nothing but disloyal to people and turned his coat as often as the wind changed direction.

Edward chuckled. "You have nothing. The king of France will not give you a helping hand."

"I might have no lands, but I know a lot about you."

"Be reasonable. I cannot anger Robert Woodville. He is the brother of my wife. She is not happy that you did not marry as she wished, so please do not force me to do any more to hurt her."

"Why should I be concerned about her feelings? She has none for me."

"I am not asking you to do this for her, but for me. You know I love you," he said, stopped, and enfolded me in his arms.

"You do not love me, please do not say that." I pushed him away. I did not want to hear him telling he loved me, for I worried that his tenderness and kind words would be the end of me if he said it too often.

But he did not listen to anything I had said and drew me close to him and pressed my head on his chest. That was so unfair. His woody and herbal smells were like a soothing decoction and a powerful charm that could have easily made me fall madly in love with him.

"You are stubborn, Alys of Lochlainn," he said in my hair. No one had called me by that name for years, and the sound of it brought lots of memories and regrets. "Why do you entice me and then rebuke me at the time?" he continued.

Retaking control of myself, I moved away from him. "Because I respect myself, and I am afraid I cannot love you. Not when I see that you favored murderers over me."

When Edward left, I returned to my bedchamber and paced the room, squeezing the bottle of Cicuta in my pocket. I then looked at the crucifix that hung on the wall opposite my bed. I kneeled on the prie-dieu.

"My lord, I know that I haven't been a very good Christian and you've probably decided to abandon me, for I abandoned you many years ago, but I am asking for your guidance for what I am about to do. I had promised Edmund of Rutland that I would never do this again, but I cannot see another solution. Please, Lord, give me your blessing for what I am about to do."

I crossed myself and walked out of the bedchamber.

"Ah, Robyn, I need your help." Then before I continued, I ensured no one was around. "Can you create some distractions during the banquet tonight?"

"What kind?"

"Total chaos so that no one will notice if I move from my seat for a brief moment."

CHAPTER THIRTY-TWO
August 1474, London, Estrilda

The banquet tonight was gigantic, in preparation for the big jousting tournament that would take place in a few days. Lady Alys was even more resplendent than usual, and her smile was magnificent, which did not please the queen, of course. Also, lady Alys had the seat of honor between the king and his brother George. For the first time, she and George seemed to have a civilized conversation, which was rather odd.

Once everyone took their seat, the king raised a hand, and the music started. Then shortly after, loud screams and shouts reverberated in the hallway, the doors flung open and in came a few dozen geese that escaped the kitchens, followed by four pigs and a countless number of chickens, and then the scullions and cooks rushed after them, trying desperately to catch the loose animals. Some of the birds flew onto the top table, disturbing the guests. Terrified, the queen moved out of her chair and hid in a corner of the hall when a pig came and sniffed at the bottom of her feet. Next, half a dozen cows, sheep, and goats also invaded the great hall. There was a mixture of panic and amusement from the guests, but when many dogs came in and jumped all over the tables and ate the poultry from their trenchers, the guests did not find the scene amusing. Only lady Alys stayed at the table with a placid face, as if not disturbed at all.

Every guest attempted to help the domestics re-establish order in the hall. Shortly after this incident, the feast resumed as if nothing had happened. But halfway through the evening, Robert Woodville, the queen's brother, felt unwell and collapsed on the table.

"Have you any more entertainment for your guests?" Lady Alys asked, rather loudly. Several domestics helped lord Woodville to his chamber. Estrilda was sat too far to find out the king's response, but the look on the queen's face was far from gladdened by that remark of lady Alys's.

The rest of the evening continued on as usual but the queen, probably exasperated by lady Alys's attitude and worried about her brother, retired earlier, and apart from this little incident, everyone else reveled as if nothing had happened. Estrilda must admit that the evening had been quite a pleasant one in the end.

IN THE MORNING, ESTRILDA learned that the queen's brother, Robert Woodville, had passed away. Queen Elizabeth, in great distress, was furious, for she was sure that lady Alys had somehow something to do with the death of lord Woodville. But how could she have been responsible? She was at the banquet with everyone, and she did not even approach lord Woodville during the feast, and then he was in his room with the doctors and his wife. Lady Alys would not have been able to approach him.

Not that Estrilda was defending lady Alys at all, but on this occasion, nothing would convince Estrilda that Alys was involved in this tragic incident. The queen's hatred for lady

Alys was blind and unfounded, but Elizabeth was stubborn, and nobody could reason with her.

When Elizabeth called a man into her private chamber in the middle of the night, Estrilda became suspicious that the queen was going a little too far.

"Ensure that I shall never see the face of Dudllan again, and you shall be a rich man."

"Do you mean you wish her... dead?"

"Preferably, yes. But if you are too scared, then I shall do it myself, and I am sure it would be easy to find a reason to lock you in the Tower. For a long, long time."

"I shall do as you wish, Your Grace," the man said, bowed, and retreated.

IN THE NEXT FEW DAYS, more knights arrived from all over Christendom, all eager to take part in the tournament. Most countries had sent representatives, but France sent more men than all other countries together; if they had invaded England, they would not have sent more men.

All this great animation made Estrilda almost forget about Richard for a brief moment. But even if she felt at peace with her love affair, she could not help but worry for lady Alys. Estrilda had failed to obey the queen's order when she was asked her to get rid of lady Alys, but the man Elizabeth had hired would for sure succeed, for he would not be intimidated by her protectors. Besides, if he were to fail, his life would be in danger.

However, so far, he had not acted for lady Alys was still parading around the court, laughing and behaving as if she cared about nothing else but enjoying the presence of the foreign knights, which also enticed the king's attention.

Looking at all those handsome knights everywhere, Estrilda was surprised not to see lady Spencer around. This was somewhat unusual, but the strangest thing was that she did not attend church in the morning. Jane was not a faithful wife, but she was a devoted Christian, and all those years Estrilda had known her, Jane had never missed an office.

So, after the service, Estrilda visited lady Spencer's bedchamber, thinking she might have reveled in carnal pleasures and had overslept, but she wasn't there either. Her bed had not been used. Therefore, Estrilda assumed that Jane had spent the night with one of the French knights who camped outside the palace's walls, by the stables, so Estrilda carried on with her duties, no longer worrying about her friend.

That evening, before the banquet started, the king and queen sat on the throne, welcoming each knight who was to take part in the tourney, and then someone entered with a large coffer and gave a letter to the queen. She smiled, thinking it was some presents from France or Spain, but once she read the letter, she dropped the parchment to the floor and rushed to open the coffer and closed it immediately. She became pale and sat down.

Discreetly, Estrilda picked up the letter and read:

"If you touch or attempt anything on the countess's life ever again, your children will pay for your actions. They will be next. Enjoy the present."

Then Estrilda attempted to look in the coffer, but her stomach churned when she saw the contents, and she rushed out of the hall before she became sick. Her friend lady Spencer and the man the queen had hired to kill lady Alys had been murdered. Both their heads were in the coffer.

Estrilda's heart was longer rejoicing at the feast and animations of the palace, and she did not intend to return to the banquet hall; she stayed outside for a while, hoping the fresh air would soothe her pain.

Her dear friend Jane Spencer was gone. What would she do without Jane to reprimand her, to make her laugh, to comfort her?

As Estrilda sat on a bench by a rosebush, she heard laughter and saw lady Alys and Robyn walking and undoubtedly rejoicing at their evil actions. Murderers! Estrilda's blood boiled, and she scurried after them. How could they laugh after having murdered two people and butchered their bodies? They were malicious people, and they did not deserve their freedom.

The moment Estrilda grabbed lady Alys's shoulders from behind, Alys turned in shock. The She-Devil stayed speechless, and before she had time to react, Estrilda slapped her. Alys said nothing, just stared at Estrilda blankly as if she did not know the reason for the gesture. As Estrilda was about to reiterate, Robyn grabbed her arm.

"That's enough!" he said. "Don't you have respect for the lady who saved your life?"

"Saved my life? That woman has done nothing for me, and now she has killed my only friend."

"What are you talking about?" Lady Alys said.

"My friend, lady Spencer. I know that it is you who killed her, and if that was not sick enough, you've beheaded her and sent her head to the queen with the head of the man she paid to kill you."

Again, Alys did not respond, but she sat down as if she was thinking about what Estrilda had said.

Then she said: "Sit down, Estrilda."

"So you can kill me while I am off guard," Estrilda said as she tried to free her arm from Robyn's grip.

"No one wants to kill you," she said. "Sit down!"

So, Estrilda did, but Robyn still held her, and when lady Alys nodded at him, obeying like a puppy, he let her arm go.

"Now, tell me calmly what happened, and what is this story about a man who was hired to kill me?"

Did she really ignore it all? Could it be that the Frenchman who menaced Estrilda was the one who killed her friend? But why kill lady Spencer! What did she do?

Taking a deep breath, Estrilda said: "The queen hired a man to kill you, as she is certain you have caused her brother's death, but I am not sure why lady Spencer was also killed? Anyway, someone sent a letter to the queen and a coffer. The letter was a warning that her children would be next if the queen attempts anything against you. In the coffer... there were two heads... it was horrible."

"Estrilda, I have killed no one. But lady Spencer was not your friend. She pretended all right, but she was using you. Surely you must remember her... In the past when I lived in London, my boys' nursemaid was lady Jane, whom I thought was my friend too, but she betrayed me. She was the same person. She knew who you were, and she was only pretending to be your friend so she could get her revenge on me. I admit that I would have gladly killed her myself if I had

had a chance. Someone did me a favor. But I am afraid I have no idea who my benefactor is."

"Then if it is not you, I think I know who did," Estrilda said, but then she realized that she should not have said that. How could she explain her encounter with the Frenchman, for she too had received the mission to kill Lady Alys, and she had accepted at the time? Through no choice of her, but she had not refused to obey the queen.

"Oh, and who is that?"

"I don't know his name, but there is a Frenchman who protects you," Estrilda said, hoping Alys would not ask any more.

"Hmm. Well, it is nice to know that France is still on my side. Look, try not to worry about what happened and go back inside and enjoy the banquet," she said, as if it was easy to decide to enjoy it.

AFTER A WHILE, ESTRILDA returned to the hall. Every lady attempted to attract a knights' attention and those very handsome men tried their best to draw the ladies to be their champions. However, the queen had retired and refused to attend the evening ceremonies. King Edward was angered that her absence might offend the knights. Nevertheless, he explained her mourning, and Estrilda believed that they all understood, and to be honest, most of her ladies were relieved that they could enjoy the evening knowing that Queen Elizabeth would not be observing them.

Among the ladies looking for a champion was lady Alys, even more resplendent than usual, and she attracted the attention of most the knights present with her gold gown set with rubies. A fortune! Of course, this came straight out of the royal cassette. Then Estrilda heard a voice with a strong French accent, and immediately she recognized the man. The one who had menaced her. He asked lady Alys to dance, and she even embraced him as if she knew him. The king did not seem pleased with her behavior and for once, nor was Estrilda. Alys had said she had no idea who had killed lady Spencer, but she seemed to know him very well if it was that man. But what angered Estrilda the most was when Alys danced with Richard.

CHAPTER THIRTY-THREE
August 1474, London, Alys

The first day of the greatest joust ever organized eventually arrived, and my son Geoffrey could not hide his excitement when he woke up, well before dawn. He had crossed the palace to run to my bedchamber to remind me it was the day; in case I had forgotten. Bless him. And then he had disappeared as quickly as he had arrived.

The tower and the riverbanks had been transformed for the week: merchants had set up their stalls, hoping to flog some of their unwanted goods for triple their price, others were preparing small braziers where they would roast sausages to sell during the day. There was a mixture of nobility, English and foreign-born. Many brigands would not miss an opportunity to relieve the richest of their heavy purses.

As I entered the tent where Geoffrey was getting ready, followed by my three other boys and daughter, a squire helped him with his chain mail armor. "Let me do it," I said and approached. The squire bowed and stepped back.

"You look like a man with this on. Do you think you are ready?" I asked as I secured the leather strap on his shoulder.

"Richard and I trained twice a day. He taught me the tricks Father knew," he said, and as I noticed pride in his voice, I also noticed Louis making a long face, and I tapped his shoulder.

"Well, as long as you concentrate and respect the rules, I am sure you will do very well. Remember, no ducking!" I told Geoffrey.

He took his helmet under his arm, and as we passed the entrance, side by side, we joined the nursemaid who had waited outside. It seemed that the crowd was growing by the minute. The hubbub was getting louder. From a distance, we could see the French camp where many knights were getting ready to show their prowess.

"One day, I will beat them all," Geoffrey said.

Louis was already running towards the French camp. "Come back here, little devil," I shouted, but he had disappeared among the throng, and I decided not to worry too much; he'd be back when the tournament would start.

Then I returned my attention to Geoffrey. "You've still a lot more to learn before you can beat the enemy of England. Until then, try to stay on your horse and do not let the quintain hit you. When I was young, the only time it hit me was on my first day of training."

He looked at me suspiciously.

"True," I continued, "My brothers and I used to play a lot in the arena, and once I knew how it worked, I always managed to avoid it, which annoyed my brothers very much."

"Jousting is a sport for men," he said, as if to tell me off.

"I know, but there was no harm in playing in the arena. Anyway, try to concentrate. Good luck, my little man. I shall support you from the king's stand," I said, and then I removed one of my foulards and attached it around his arm.

"You shall be my champion, Geoffrey of Dudllan." I kissed his forehead and let him join Richard and his squire.

As I watched Geoffrey moving away, I could not help but worry, but at the same time, I was proud of him. He was so much like his father; shame Hampton wasn't there to see him. Holding Arthur and Alienor's hands, I headed for the king's pavilion to take my seat before the parade began, and then I spotted Gérard.

"Take the children to the pavilion," I told the nursemaid as I strode after Gérard.

"So, you did not reply last night when I asked who had sent you to Dudllan?" I asked as I reached him.

"No one. I came to England with Margaret of Anjou's army, and after the defeat, I hid in the woods. When I heard about you, I knew you would open your door to anyone who was on Jasper and Henry Tudor's side."

"Really? But then why did you come so late after Anjou's defeat? Why didn't you try to return to France?"

Before Gérard could reply, drum rolls announced the start of the parade was imminent.

"Go, or you'll miss your son's performance," he said.

"That suits you. You still have not convinced me," I said as I headed towards the king's pavilion.

"I'll see you later, but I promise this is the truth," he said.

I shrugged and hastened the pace.

WHEN I REACHED THE Royal Pavilion and took my seat next to Edward, I could not help but noticed his wife pretended to ignore me. Today was all about the tournament and being proud of my son. I would not let her presence spoil it for me.

The young men were the first ones to parade on horseback around the arena. As they approached, I stood at the edge of the pavilion and clapped to encourage my son. Once all the boys had paraded, they took their place in the center of the arena, and it was now the turn of the knights to march and be introduced by their respective herald. All of them praising their master, who of course were the best—further to them, anyway. There were almost as many as one hundred of them, all hoping to capture the top prize and the heart of a lady at the same time. The ladies behave in what lady Beaufort would have called a very inappropriate manner, even the married ones. The most popular knight came from Spain, Lord de la Santa Montagon: his black horse's caparison was covered in a devilish red, the man had everything, and he made a great impression at the banquet the night before with his charming accent, his beautiful face, and the way had swirled around the dancing floor. Of course, all the knights looked the part, and at that point, anyone could have won, but I must admit that I too had a preference for de la Santa Montagon.

After every single one of them had been introduced which took more than a couple of hours, the tournament was about to start when a French knight cantered into the arena, and joined the procession, while his squires and a herald ran behind him and rushed over to one of the line marshals and spoke to him. The marshal then consulted his colleagues, and the master of tournament nodded. Then the herald shouted for everyone to hear:

"The earl of Etrilly from France, unbeaten champion. This noble knight and his—"

The master of the tournament waved to stop the French herald and beckoned the knight to join the others. The French knight's horse's blue caparison was decorated in Fleur de Lys; his rider dressed in black and had a black helmet. Both looked beautiful and mysterious, a little like Lancelot, except that his horse was black and had a much shinier coat than all the other horses out there.

The earl of Etrilly... for a brief instant, that name troubled me a little. It was familiar.

Suddenly, Edward took my hand even if his wife was next to us, and probably furious, but she showed no sign of being annoyed.

"Frogs! They think they can do everything, even come in at the last minute," Edward murmured in my ears, and I laughed. With my new gown of Venetian fabric and gold thread, I felt resplendent and even happy, probably because I had drunk quite a lot of wine already. Then as all the knights cleared the arena, the French knight, the earl of Etrilly, turned his horse and stopped in front of the pavilion with his herald, who spoke on his behalf.

"Madame, the earl of Etrilly is requesting the honor of wearing your colors."

"Oh..." I then looked at Edward, who nodded his approval. Hence, I stood up and removed my scarf and approached the balustrade. As I moved closer, the knight tilted his lance, and I attached my foulard on the tip of it, while I tried to look at his eyes through the tiny opening in the visor. I could not really see his eyes, but I felt them on me as if he was undressing me. My entire body warmed in embarrassment.

"Monsieur, honorez les couleurs que je vous offre," I said. He nodded and waved with his free hand, inclining, his head

I waved back at him. Edward then stood next to me and took hold of my hand and kissed it. I glared at him, surprised. Why was he acting so in public and with his wife next to him? It was well that he took my hand while she sat on the other side; she could not notice, but now that we both stood before her? I removed my hand from his and waved again at the earl of Etrilly to encourage him to win. The man straightened his lance, and his fiery horse reared before they cantered into the arena.

"This French knight seems to have turned your head," Edward said.

"Absolutely not. He requested my colors, and that is normal that I give him my support. What is wrong with you?"

"Nothing." Then he whispered in my ear. "Have you met Etrilly? Perhaps when you traveled to France."

"No, I have never heard of him before today." But as I spoke, I recalled that indeed that name was familiar, but it was a name I had not heard for many years, and it was not a real name either. At least I had thought it was not a real one, for I had made up the Baron of Etrilly when I forged Hampton's handwriting when I was still at Lochlainn. At the time, I had hoped to get rid of the duke of York. Was it a coincidence? Or was it a secret sign someone special wanted to give me publicly? Did Fauconberg tell me the truth?

Was Hampton alive? Was he the earl of Etrilly? My head fuzzed with questions and memories. I could not put my thoughts in order. Edward placed a hand on my shoulder, and I moved sideways.

"Not now, please."

He said nothing, but I noticed suspicion in his eyes.

Then the master of the tournament announced the start of the next round.

Each day, knights were either injured or eliminated for not having enough points to go on with the contest. The first round was like a slaughter for the less experienced riders. None of the opponents of the Spanish knight resisted his powerful strikes— all of them got unhorsed. And it was the same for my champion's opponents, who all got blown off their horses with one strike in the abdomen, apart from one of them who did not have the guts to ride along the rail and pull his horse to avoid an impact. Edward was furious, for that cowardly knight was English, and for the moment, it was clear that France and Spain were far better.

The excitement and the claps were louder each day, and also the crowd seemed to grow as the tournament went on. Londoners were climbing flag poles and walls to steal peeks at the event. It was as if the entire city had stopped its usual activity to assist the tournament. Well, the only thing that had not changed was the merchants not missing an opportunity to make more money. The banks were transformed into a massive kitchen that spread the smell of fried sausages, burning wood, and fried sweet pastries. As soon as we approached the gates, the empowering food smell mixed with the ones of burned hoof where the horses were being reshot before the next round invaded the air. But overall, the atmosphere was of good humor.

On the third day, after sitting for a few hours in a row in the pavilion, I ventured out on the pretext that I wanted to get some sweet pastries. In fact, I just wanted to enjoy the crowd, but mainly I wanted to see the earl of Etrilly. Every knight competing had approached the arena with their squires holding their helmet and gauntlets, and my champion had been the only one to hide his face.

"Madame, you should not venture on your own in this area. You might cause some accident, for your beauty is blinding."

I turned around to see the person who had spoken.

"Oh, my dear Lord de la Santa Montagon, what a pleasure to see you. I must admit I escaped the king's pavilion to experience the tournament like everyone else, but... Actually, perhaps you could indicate to me where I could find the earl of Etrilly."

"Alas, Madame. It would have been a pleasure, but my duties are calling me, or I would have taken you there myself, as I too would be interested in meeting him. Tomorrow, perhaps? Why don't you meet me after mass, and we can go there together?"

"What do you think the countess of Norfolk would say if she were to find out I am parading at her champion's arm in the morning?"

"I do not believe the countess of Norfolk would dare to venture into this filthy place," he said, holding out an arm to prevent someone bumping into me. "I must go, my lady, be careful here."

"Good luck, Sir."

The Spanish knight was about to leave, but then he turned around and asked: "Will you attend the fest tonight?"

"I wouldn't miss it for the world."

As I continued ambling around the people, hoping to catch of glimpse of Etrilly, I noticed his horse near a blacksmith. The magnificent animal snorted, flaring his nostrils, and tapped his front hoof impatiently on the ground.

"What a beautiful horse," I said as I approached and gently patted the horse's neck.

"Be careful, Madame. He bites."

I removed my hand and study the horse for an instant; he was still young and had powerful haunches, but I also sensed he had a good spirit, so I brought my hand to his forehead and caressed it.

"Don't say I haven't warned you," said the French squire who, although he had a strong accent, expressed himself in a relatively good English for a Frenchman.

"No, he won't bite me; he knows I mean well. Where is your lord, I would like to meet him... to encourage him and congratulate him. He has honored my colors well, so far."

"I am afraid this is not possible; he is preparing for the next round and cannot allow himself the distraction."

"Lady Alys?" Robyn called and joined me. I looked briefly at him and then turned to the French squire.

"Tell your master I wish to see him at the banquet tonight."

He bowed, and I bade him farewell before moving away with Robyn.

"What are you doing here, my lady?" he asked.

"Like everyone, I am curious. Look at that horse, isn't he magnificent?"

"Yes," he said absently. "The king might not appreciate you wandering here on your own."

"Well, you are with me now, so the king shouldn't worry about my safety."

"This is not a place for a lady, tis full of-"

"People? Fine, spoil-joy, take me back to my goaler," I said, putting my arm under his.

That evening, even if he had beaten all his opponents, yet again, the earl of Etrilly made no appearance at the banquet and nor on the last evening. His rudeness infuriated me a little more, and on the last day of the tournament, I felt like walking to the arena and retrieving my scarf. At least the Spanish knight had kept me company during the last two banquets, and he had been charming and an excellent cavalier to dance with. Something about him attracted all the ladies, and I even caught the queen staring at him a few times.

After another eventful day, the earl of Etrilly, who had beaten Lord de la Santa Montagon, the favorite, was the victorious champion. The master of the tournament announced him as the grand winner. All his opponents ended on the ground, which aroused Edward's wrath against the man whom I could not see the face of, and reminded me of a powerful man. A man whose embrace would make me feel like a protected woman. At last, I would finally see his face when he'd come to collect his prize.

Edward must have seen something in the way I looked at the French knight, for I sensed jealousy in the way he squeezed my hand. In truth, it was not Etrilly I was admiring, but the man I wished he were. As the earl of Etrilly approached the pavilion and the officials to receive the winner's goblet, Edward interrupted the Master of Tournament and said to Etrilly:

"You fought valiantly, but before you receive your prize, I would like to give you one more challenge, and this time you can name your prize."

The crowd was in shock, for the king had just broken the rules of the tournament, but the French knight whispered to his herald who then said:

"The earl of Etrilly requests the countess of Dudllan to be his prize."

Suddenly the entire arena became silent before the buzz of conversations became louder while I stumbled, put my hand on the seat to steady myself, and then rage took control of me. Now I knew that this rude Frenchman was not Hampton, for Hampton would not have humiliated me by trading me like cattle in front of so many spectators.

Edward frowned and put a hand on my arm. "Don't fret," he whispered.

For the last few days, I had admired the elegance and virility of the French knight, I had encouraged and clapped him, but that did not mean I wanted to leave England with him. However, my thoughts mingled in my head and I was confused, not knowing what to think anymore. I wanted to see the face of Etrilly. I wanted him to be Hampton so I could run away with him. Well, that was what I had dreamed secretly, but his audacity was too disrespectful to my rank. Who did he think I was?

Shaking my head, I whispered to Edward, "Tell the French man I refuse. I am not some stupid common wench one can trade to please a man."

But all Edward did was to take my hands in his. "I will win. He won't take you from me."

"Are you saying that the challenge is you fighting him on the arena?"

Edward nodded.

"Did you pay any attention over the last few days? You have no chance. The man has even beaten de la Santa Montagon."

Edward shook his head and for a brief moment, I glanced at the queen, who smiled as if she had something to do with this, as if she was certain Edward would lose and I would never be seen again.

"Why did you have to challenge him?"

"Because I dislike the idea that a French knight would defeat the English ones. I will beat him," he said and then turned around and continued: "The countess of Dudllan accepts. If you win, she will be at your service, but if you lose, all your men will be at my service, and I will take your lands in France."

The crowd exclaimed in shock at the king's announcement while many English clapped and roared to encourage their brainless king. The earl of Etrilly inclined his head and pulled his rein to move away while Edward left to don his armor and I dropped back on my seat, full of rage.

A few minutes after, my son Geoffrey rushed into the pavilion. "Mother, what is this that I've heard?"

"I am not quite sure, but do not fret. All will be well." I said and stood up. We stayed together hand in hand at the edge of the balustrade, looking at the center of the empty arena where the sand was being raked before the last challenge.

"Which one do you want to win?" Geoffrey asked.

"The king, of course," I said, but deep down I could not decide on the ideal outcome. Edward was a little too arrogant, and he deserved a lesson, but not at my cost. Hadn't he paid attention to how well the earl fought against the other knights? That man was valor and strength incarnated, and I doubted very much that Edward, who spent more time drinking wine than training his horse, stood a chance.

When both riders were in place on each side of the arena, my heart thumped hard and silence felt over the entire town. All we could hear was the horses snorting. Edward had chosen a gray stallion with a magnificent gray coat that shined as if it had been polished, while Etrilly's horse looked a little more dull and tired after a week of intense effort.

At the blast of trumpets, the line marshal lifted his arms, preparing to give the signal, but before he had dropped the flag, Edward spurred his horse and charged towards his opponent. Then the black horse of Etrilly reared and with his powerful haunches charged towards Edward. Both lances aimed precisely at the other rider. The moment Edward approached, for some reason he moved his lance horizontally and next he hurled it toward the ground on the other side of the railing. The French horse tripped and propelled his rider in the air, before falling himself to the sound of cracking bone. We all heard the snap as his bone broke under the lance which had snapped in two bits under the impact. The crowd cheered when the French knight landed on the ground in a loud, clanging thud.

I gasped in horror.

I could not believe that Edward had done that in front of everyone— cheating and not even hiding it. It was so disrespectful. Now, both French rider and horse stayed on the ground. The French horse did his best to get up, but he could not; while the earl of Etrilly was still immobile on the ground—I expected the worst and my heart went out to him. That was not fair.

When Edward roared his victory and brandished the remains of his lance as he had won a war against France, my heart skipped a beat. I released my son's hand and hastened to the arena. Lifting my skirts for speed, without caring about the mud and horse dung, I trod on. All I worried about was the black horse; one of his front legs was broken, and I knew what it meant. The French knight was still on the ground with his men around him, but no one seemed to pay attention to the horse, so I bent close to the horse and glanced in the direction of the knight. One of his squires lifted the visor of his helmet, and for a split moment, I thought I had seen Gérard coming to the rescue of the earl.

Then the horse neighed and tried to move, but he was hurting himself even more at each movement. Thus, I returned my attention to him and caressed his head. "Hush, hush, you'll be fine. I am sorry, this is all my fault," I said and thought, yet again. Then I turned to the squires, and shouted: "Get me some comfrey, resin, and clay. Hurry, and after you'll arrange for the horse to be taken to the stables."

"My lady, we need to put him down to end his suffering," one of them said as he approached.

I stood up and placed myself before them. "You will not. If any one of you attempts to kill this horse, he will have to taste my blade first. I can cure him. It will take a long time, but I can do it. Now, do as I ask, and hurry!"

As I sat on the ground next to the horse, visions of Tristan came into my mind. The good times we had together. I recalled the day he was born and that dreadful day when Robyn took his life away from me. The night I spent by Tristan's side until Fauconberg came and buried him. I would not let them do this to this beauty. This horse was young; he could recover, and his injury was less grave than Tristan's.

"You'll be fine. Just hang on with me, and I promise you will canter through your French fields again." I caressed him from the top of his head to his croup. As if he understood, or was giving up, the horse laid his head on the ground.

"The horse is lost," one of Etrilly's men said.

"Do as you're told, or I will not be responsible for my actions. I can use a sword, and I will not be afraid to employ it in public, and I will ensure you suffer very much. Now get the horse in the stable and get me what I've asked for," I shouted.

Then Edward approached. "You are safe now," he said, but I leaped onto my feet and slapped him.

"You cheated. Look what you've done! You've injured an innocent animal. How dare you?"

"I had to," he said as he dismounted, and then he attempted to take me in his arms. "I did not want to lose you. I had to win, but as Etrilly approached, I could see he was in a better position than I was. He would have unhorsed me. I had no choice. I had to do that, for you."

"No, you did not have to. You should have admitted defeat instead of cheating. Hopefully, your people have seen what a cowardly king is ruling them. I will make sure that it's spread across France too, and I shall speak to Etrilly later and tell him to report this to King Louis. We will see if you are still as proud when you've become the laughingstock of the French court. Look what you've done to the earl." I waved in his direction. "You'd better go and see if he's still alive and if he is, apologize for your behavior. Even if I don't believe it is possible to forgive such an attitude, for I will not."

"Why are you defending the French earl? You said you did not know him, but you lied, didn't you?"

Finally, a squire brought me the potent herbs I needed, and I kneeled again next to the horse without responding to Edward. I was not defending the French earl, but there was something that was telling me that I should have trusted the Frenchman, and what Edward had done to that poor horse was unacceptable. The grooms and squires passed a hessian cloth under the horse's belly and used ropes to lift him onto a cart and took him to the stables. I caressed his head and whispered in his ear to keep him as calm as possible.

"What are you doing? This is a French horse. You lied to me! You know that man very well and perhaps you are in connivance with him," Edward said as I climbed onto the cart, next to the horse.

"I do not know the earl, but this horse is injured because of me, because you are a coward. How do you think it makes me feel? I can heal that horse. For your reference, I'm not on his master's side at all, but I am no longer on your side either. How can I respect you, knowing what you've done?" I said and beckoned the cart driver to make a move, and glanced at the earl of Etrilly, whose squires were lifting on to a cart.

At the royal stables, as the squires moved the horse, I followed them, and we put him in a separate area. The horse master's decision, although an excellent one, had not been for the horse's best interest but because he did not want a French horse to mingle with his own, in case it would have brought some disease.

Once the horse was supported by a brace, I prepared a poultice of clay and resin, mixed it into a paste with the comfrey, and clad his leg, and then I strapped planks of wood around his foreleg. "Now we've got to help him stand up."

A few grooms, a squire, and the horse master pulled the rope to lift the horse off the ground and secured him so he could stand without putting too much pressure on his leg. The poor animal was trembling, not knowing what was happening to him.

After all that, I gave him some water in which I had poured some valerian decoction, hoping to relax him a little.

"Well done," the horse master said. "How did you know about that? Do you think it will work?"

"I sincerely hope it will. Last year my horse had an accident and broke a leg; I could have helped him, but they put him down. I have repaired broken legs on wild rabbits before, so I would have tried on Tristan, but it was too late. But I know this will work for this horse; he's young," I said as I caressed his neck. "Will you arrange for someone to bring me something to eat? I must stay here."

"It looks like he's already adopted you," the horse master said while the horse nipped gently at the end of my braided hair. "We can look after him now. You deserve a little rest."

"Thank you, in that case, I'll sneak into the kitchens quickly. Just keep your eye on him. I shouldn't be too long. Oh, have you any news about the earl of Etrilly? Is he all right?"

"His men took him to his tent, but I know nothing more, I'm afraid."

"Oh, I'd better go and tell him about his horse and apologize on behalf of the king, for I know he will not. This would not have happened if it was not for me."

"Take as much time as you need. Don't worry about the horse, I'll ask someone to stay with him in your absence."

The French camp was close to the stables and not in the best part of the castle grounds. There were more than enough chambers at Westminster and the Tower to lodge every single knight and their squires, but the king had not even had the decency to offer the earl of Etrilly a chamber to help him recover. I hoped that he had at least sent him a physician.

As I approached the tent of the French knight under the bright sunshine of the late afternoon, I saw Robyn coming out.

"What are you doing here?" I said as I tiptoed behind him.

Startled, he turned around. "Lady Alys, what are you doing here?"

"I believe I've asked you the same question first."

"I... I wanted to see how the earl was," Robyn said as he continued walking across the camp.

"Do you know him?"

"I've met him when I was in France," he replied sheepishly.

"Oh.... But you did not say when I asked you the other day. Anyway, how is he?"

"He'll recover."

"Good. Now I'd better offer him my apologies."

Out of nowhere, Robyn took hold of my arm. "I don't think it will be possible; he's resting. You should come back later," he said, trying to force me to walk with him in the opposite direction.

"That is fine; I won't stay long," I said as I stopped, but Robyn still held my arm. I glared at him. "What's going on? You're acting oddly. Please, let my arm go!"

"I'm sorry," he said, removing his hand most awkwardly, and I moved away from him, heading back to the tent.

Pulling the flap of the tent and before entering, I said. "Hello, I'm lady Alys of Dudllan, I'd like to see the earl of Etrilly; I must offer him my apologies. Is he decent? Can I come in?" I asked, attempting to approach slowly.

Immediately, one of his men came in front of me and blocked the access.

"Sorry, ma'am, the earl is resting."

"I shan't stay long, I just want to apologize."

"We will inform him of your visit," he said, beckoning me to get out of the tent.

Resigned not to see the earl, I agreed to leave, but since everyone seemed to be eager to stop me from seeing him, I became very intrigued. The earl had not removed his helmet at the tournament, and I recalled that when his men attended him in the arena, they did not remove his helmet either. This was odd, as removing a knight's helmet is the first thing people usually do when a knight is unhorsed. Did the man have a monstrous deformity he was ashamed of, or was it something else— like the man wasn't who he pretended to be? Someone who should not be of the world. Perhaps... No, it was impossible.

"Very well," I finally said. "Tell the earl I will be back on the morrow. Oh and tell him his horse will be fine." I turned, pretending to leave, then I swiftly swirled around and tried to enter. I was no longer sixteen and no longer as agile as I once was, but I ducked to avoid the Frenchmen and skipped under one of the men's legs to finally succeed.

Behind a thin veil showed the shadow of a man lying on a bed.

"Madam, please, the earl must rest," a young Frenchwoman said as she put a bowl of some sort of tincture from which the pungent and bitter aroma rose to my nose. She was dressed like a rich lady, but the fact she cared for the earl's health made me think she might have been a wench or mayhap his mistress. Placing herself between the earl and me, she thrust her body as if this would scare me from approaching any closer. If I had managed to escape three of his guards, it was not that frail French girl who would stop me.

"Get out of my way. The earl doesn't have the plague. I just want to give him my apologies."

"C'est bon, laissez-là passer."

"The earl doesn't speak English," she said.

"It's not a problem. Je parle français. Have you any more excuses to stop me, or can I finally speak to Monsieur d'Etrilly?" I asked, and she reluctantly stepped aside.

I lifted the veil and a man in his thirties laid on the bed, an arm in a bandage. He had a pleasant face, a thin nose, and an unshaven beard. Hmm, perhaps I should have run away with him before he and his horse got injured. However, in a way, I was a little disappointed, for I had never met that man before.

With all that happened, I had almost convinced myself that the earl of Etrilly was Hampton, and the word of Fauconberg had hung in my head every day of the tournament. How stupid of me. The man in front of me was not Hampton. I had to come back to reality. Hampton was dead.

"I'm sorry to force the entrance to your tent, my lord, but I had to give my apologies and give you news about your horse."

"Merci, ça va aller," he told the lady who curtseyed and stepped back. "Have they killed my horse?" he asked in French.

"No, your horse has a broken leg, but he will survive. Although I should warn you, you won't be able to ride him for a long time, and after that, it would be better if you only let ladies or children ride, at least for a while. I promise to care for him until you can take him back to France."

"Thank you."

We both stayed silent for a while, only looking at each other. I had never seen his face before, and I did not understand why he hid his face at the tournament. Did someone know him, and he did not want them to recognize him? If he had shown his face, I probably would not have been worried to follow him... well, maybe not, as I would have been furious about the way he went about it.

"May I ask you a question?" I finally said, breaking the awkward but somehow peaceful silence.

He nodded.

"Why did you ask me for your prize? Don't you think it was a little rude?"

"Taking away the king of England's mistress is the best prize a French knight could get."

"Monsieur, you are fortunate enough to lie convalescent on your bed, or I would have slapped you for the insult. For your information, I am not the king's mistress. How could you say such a thing when you know nothing about me?"

"I did not mean to offend you. Forgive me, Madame."

"I hope you are," I said as I was about to leave, and then I turned around. "And just so you know, no man will ever possess, and certainly not you."

Thereafter, I passed the flap of the tent. Someone darted off as if they had been spying on our conversation. Probably one of Edward's man ensuring that I would not give myself to the French knight.

Men! All the same, thinking we belonged to them. Well, that was true for their wives, but I was a widow and, therefore, a free woman. The only man who'd ever had the honor to have me as his possession was Hampton, but now no man would.

AS SOON AS I LEFT THE knight, I returned to see the black horse. It did not occur to me to have asked Etrilly the name of his horse.

"How are you?" I said as I caressed his forehead. You'll be fine, I promise I'll do my best. When spring comes back, you will run in the fields. Shame you cannot come to Dudllan, we have the sea there that would have been perfect for you. I am sure you have lovely pastures in France, but you will not see them for a long, long time."

As I spoke to the horse, his ears moved as though he was listening, as Tristan used to. Tears came to my eyes, and I wrapped my arms around his neck and closed my eyes.

"I wish I could keep you forever, but your master will want you back when you are healed. Shame, I am sure that you and Boudicca would get on well." Then the horse stiffened his neck and neighed.

As I opened my eyes, still hugging the horse, I noticed a shadow reflecting against the wall, projected by the moon. It looked like Hampton. His ghost was watching over me, as if to remind me of my oath to him. I had almost been unfaithful to the man I had loved, and I had let Robyn killed my horse. The shadow was still there. I could feel someone watching me. Someone who obviously did not want me to know he was there, or he would have spoken to me. Intrigued, I turned around to see a man brandishing a dagger and suddenly he leapt out of the darkness and dashed over to me. I screamed and tried to avoid his blade, but I fell to the ground. Out of the dark alley, another man appeared and fought my aggressor. My savior had one arm in a bandage, but still, after very little struggle, he took control and killed the man.

As the body of my aggressor fell to the ground, my savior caught his breath, and I could not keep my eyes off him.

"Hampton...?" I asked, paralyzed by stupor.

For a second, he stared at me and then he disappeared as if he did not want to speak to me.

I was not mad. It was him!

CHAPTER THIRTY-FOUR
August 1474, London, Alys

After a sleepless night, looking after the horse, renewing his bandage regularly while thinking about Hampton and why he'd disappeared after saving my life, once the groom came over to release me from my duty, I headed towards the kitchens.

"Alys," Edward said as I rushed across the corridor, following eagerly the smell of freshly baked bread.

"I've nothing to say to you," I said. "I only came here to get a piece of bread and cheese. Then I must return to the horse that you've injured, remember?"

"Please, I am sorry. I'm just so taken by you that imagining that someone could take you away from me frightened me."

"You've been perfectly capable of doing that with no one's help. How could I respect myself if I were stupid enough to fall for a man with no courage?" I asked as I walked on.

"I was an idiot, I admit. Look," he said, taking my arm to stop me, "Would it make you feel better if I were to repent my fault in public? I will offer the earl another chance, and I swear not to cheat."

"Should I remind you that his horse is injured much more than the rider?" I pushed him away and continued to the kitchens.

"How do you know?"

"Because I've seen him. All right, it won't be long before he's on his feet, but for his horse, it will take much longer."

"You've met him?" he asked as we passed the door.

"With a few difficulties. But eventually, they let me see him. The man is better protected than you are," I said as I sat at a table and ripped a piece of the freshly baked loaf of bread.

"I'm surprised you are so calm about the situation. I expected never to see again if you were to find out."

"Well, I will no longer stay at the palace nor show my face by your side in public if that is what you are thinking about, but I promised the earl of Etrilly I will care for his horse until he is fit enough to go back to France, so you will suffer my presence a few more months and then I'll return to Dudllan."

There were so many domestics coming and going in this infernal kitchen that no one noticed the king's presence but when one of the scullions tripped over Edward's leg, he yelled at the domestics and asked them to leave. In no time, in a cacophony of panic, everyone abandoned their tasks, and we were on our own.

"I'd always felt you were strong-minded, but I did not realize you were without feelings," he continued.

I lifted my eyebrows. "Pardon?"

"At first, I wasn't sure if it was him or not. But when he asked for you, there were no more doubts in my mind. Still, I wondered why he took so long to reveal himself. It might be because he's heard you were my mistress."

"I am not your mistress!"

"Most people trust you are."

"That does not make it true," I said, taking a juicy plum from one of the abandoned baskets and bit into the fruit, savoring the sweetness of the plum.

"You must admit that you are just as good as my mistress. You've let me embrace and kiss you and even shared your bed many times."

"That's all it was—you never took my body, and you never will. You knew I was missing Hampton, and I needed a man by my side, and you've made the most of it to satisfy your own needs. But I will never be your mistress. What happened yesterday made me realize why I did not want to love you. You are an egoist, and you've killed the one I loved, and now you assume you have all the rights over me."

"I could not let him continue his rebellion; I had to neutralize him, so when the opportunity arose, we captured him and locked him in the Tower."

"Edward, what are you talking about?"

"Hampton. Didn't you say you met him?" he asked, and for a second, my head whirled, and my legs wobbled a little, probably with the rush of sugar in my blood.

"Have you abused the wine already? I've never said I've met Hampton," I said.

"You said you went to Etrilly's tent and met him. I expected you saw him."

I stared at Edward, bewildered. "Are you trying to tell me that Hampton is alive?" I asked. Suddenly I realized that I had not been mad. My mind was sane. What I had taken for visions or imagination was real. Hampton was alive, and that was him I'd seen the night before. That was him who saved me.

"Yes. I am sorry, I thought you knew," Edward said, sitting next to me and pouring two cups of ale. "At Barnett, Hampton was badly injured, but I did not want him dead. We took him to the Tower and spread the rumor he was dead. So that people would stop fighting for his cause. But for people to stand by us, we had to show them a body. So, we found someone of the same corpulence and hair color; all we had to do was to cover his face and body to ensure no one would see it was not him, not even you. After a while, Hampton escaped, and the guards informed me he had been killed during the escape. I truly believed he was dead until-"

"Is he accompanying the earl of Etrilly?"

"He is the earl."

"But it can't be, I saw the earl, and he's too young."

"He might have fooled you."

"If you knew he was alive, why did you let me believe he was dead? How could you even look me in the eye? How could you let me fall for you?"

"Having you was a small victory. Let's call it revenge. Remember what happened over ten years ago; you were never to be his, but mine. That's what our fathers wanted."

"I was never yours, and never be."

"You do not mean that, or you would not have enticed me for over a year. I recognize you love me."

"No, I was just a woman who needed attention and love, but you've abused my weakness. You disgust me." I slapped him and headed for the door.

He grabbed my arm. "Where are you going?"

"To find him. What do you think?"

"When he escaped, he chose the life of an outlaw. He abandoned you and your children. His life in England is over. Forget about him. He remarried and rebuilt a life in France."

"You're lying," I said and tried to leave the room

But Edward swiftly rushed to my side and barred the way.

"Let me go."

"No, Hampton is part of your past. Pay no heed to him anymore."

"How could you ask such a thing of me? It was unbearable to consider he was dead; now that I'm certain he is alive, I will not give up on him."

"But he forsook you. If he wanted to be with you and your children, he would have come to you, but he has not. He does not want you anymore. I've found out that the earl of Etrilly is married. You must have met his wife. She is travelling with him."

"If this is true, why did he ask for me for his prize? Now, that is the proof that he has not forgotten about me."

"Alys, if Hampton wanted to be with you, he would have come to you earlier; he would have tried to see his children. But he has not, has he?" Edward raised his voice. "Hampton only asked you for his prize to humiliate me. He does not love you anymore, and deep down you know that I am right. Nothing was stopping him from going to Dudllan."

"Perhaps because your spies are everywhere," I said, but in reality, Edward was right. If Hampton had loved me, he would have braved any danger to be with me. He would have revealed himself and stopped my suffering. Perhaps Hampton was hurt, maybe someone had told him I did not love him anymore. Hampton was proud, but he was a clever one; he must have known I would never forget him.

"Did you tell him anything about me?"

"I might have mentioned something, but do not fret about that; when I told him we enjoyed spending the night in the same bed, my dear cousin thought it was a lie, for he said you would never lower yourself to become my mistress."

Unable to look him in the eyes, I realized what happened and why Hampton had avoided coming to Dudllan. He was disappointed. Somehow, he had heard the rumors out about Edward and I and felt betrayed. Both Fauconberg and Robyn had tried to warn me, but I did not listen. I never did.

Worried about my reaction, Edward placed his hands on my shoulder. I moved back.

"Sorry, I must go. Now there is hope. I must find him."

"No, please."

"You will not stop me this time, no one will," I said and scurried out to find Hampton.

CHAPTER THIRTY-FIVE
August 1474, London, Alys

My heart was light and full of hope but also full of anger as I rushed through the corridor to reach the stables. Then as I continued across the stable yard towards the French camp, I noticed soldiers and carts leaving clouds of dust behind them. The musky smells of the dying campfires rose into the air. Closer to Hampton's encampment, I realized they had dismantled every tent, and the last few men were heading away from London.

"Hampton," I shouted. "Come back! Come back," I screamed again, running towards the last few men I could see.

Why did he run without talking to me? Puzzled and defeated, I glanced around the site, unable to understand why the men were leaving without warning. Of course, the tournament ceremonies were finished, but I was sure they would stay a few more days.

"Countess of Dudllan?" a man asked.

I spun around to face a man who handed me a letter. "From the earl of Etrilly," he said, and as he was about to leave, I called him back.

"Wait! Where is he? Tell him I want to see him."

The man stopped. "The earl left a few hours ago. You'll have to go to France to see him."

Without a word, I stormed off and headed back to the stable yard.

I approached the black horse with a trembling chin. "Your master left without you. Don't worry, he might have abandoned both of us, but I will look after you," I said as I sat on the wall next to the stable door and unfolded the letter.

My dear Alys,

Pardon me. At the tournament, my heart melted at the sight of your happiness with Edward. I savvy that Edward told you I was alive. I did not want you to know. Please, you must forget me. There is no place for you in my new life in France. Go back to Wales with your children and forget that I ever existed. The Hampton you knew no longer exists.

The more I read, the more my pulse sped up, and my nostrils flared while I crumpled part of the paper.

Do not run after me. I recognize that this will not stop you, but I am requesting you not to. We have no future together.

Please forget me.

Geoffrey

"I will not," I said out loud as I ripped the letter in pieces and threw it on the floor, and then I rushed out to the stables, shoving a squire without even apologizing. After a few more steps, I turned around and returned into the stable to pick up the pieces of the letter, stuffed them into my purse, not wanting anyone to recompose the letter, and went out again and headed for the squires' quarters.

"Robyn, Robyn," I said as I came out of the stable. "Get Boudicca ready, now."

"Where do you want to go?" he asked, removing his satchel from his shoulder and held it in one hand. As I noticed his bag looked pretty full, I wondered if he, too, was leaving England without telling me.

"You know where, probably the same place as you, traitor!" I said and slapped him.

"Traitor?"

"Etrilly, eh? I only wanted to see how he was," I said as I tried to imitate Robyn's voice.

"Forgive me, I swore I would not tell."

"But you are my friend, my confidant. Or did you only come back to spy on me, on his orders? It is probably you who told him I was the king's mistress. Now he is gone and doesn't want anything to do with me. Because of you! I must catch him before his ship leaves Southampton. Arrange for someone to look after the black horse while I am gone."

"No."

His word was as snappy as if he had thrown a bucket of ice-cold water in my face. "Are you refusing to obey?"

"Pardon me, but I obey the person to whom I swore an oath. I promised I will not let you go after him."

"Then you will go yourself and bring him back here."

"I will not."

"In this case, you leave me with no other choices. I shall speak to the king and ask him to send his army after Hampton," I said and waited for Robyn to change his mind, but he said and did nothing. He shrugged, threw his bag back on his shoulder, and headed towards the stables.

Furious, I followed Robyn, but as he entered the stables, I continued towards the palace. With or without Robyn's help, I would go to Hampton. He would not leave the country without me.

As I headed towards the guard's room, someone seized me and hauled me into the saddle room. A man's large hands covered my mouth, and with an arm, my aggressor thwarted my movements. When he swung me around, my heart stalled.

At first, I gasped, then felt a little dizzy. My first instinct was to step back and though I wanted to scream or shout and hit him, I remained speechless and motionless. Still, my pulse raised to an alarming speed, filling me with a strong desire to embrace him. I was dreaming- surely. I stared. Hampton! No mistake. His hand on my lips was real. I could feel the strength, and this special ambrosial smell did not lie to me. Not a ghost. My breathing was jerking faster and would reach a point where my heart would explode like a cannonball crashing into the side of a ship. I trembled. All the same, I found it difficult to compose myself and instead of yelling at him, I let myself fall in his arms and embraced him with all my strength.

"Why?" I asked and as I squeezed him, closed my eyes, and rested my head on his chest, feeling his heartbeats echoing inside of me as he wrapped his valid arm around me and instantly three years of pain evaporated and warmed up my entire body. His neck was not as ambrosial as I first thought., it was more sandalwood- probably the mark of his new French wife- still, it aroused a feeling I thought I would never have again. Then I lifted my eyes to look at him, and without realizing his sweet minty lips caressed mine. Anger, jealousy, treason, everything disappeared in this deep, tender kiss that I had been longing for the last few years. And I pressed against his torso crushing his wounded arm.

"Ouch."

"I'm sorry," I said, immediately releasing my pressure

"That's all right, only badly bruised."

I smiled. It was a lie, but as always, he was proud and would not admit how badly Edward had injured him. I glanced at the bandage. It was pretty good, and somehow, it made me angry that even his new wife was better than me at it.

"Never abandon me again, this was so cruel." I moved to kiss him again and but he stepped back a little.

"Alys, this is not reasonable. I've nothing to offer you anymore," he said, caressing my hair.

"I need nothing else but you. Do you realize how painful it was? Every single day since that dreadful letter, I had to summon the courage to live. Why did you let us believe you were dead?"

"Because in a way, I am. That's what Edward wanted."

"And you were going to let him win?" I asked, slapping his chest with a fist.

"I would not have, but you did. It did not take you long to fall into someone else's arms," he said, pushing me away.

"You were dead! Everyone told me that I should not hang onto a ghost, and that I was on the losing side. I've tried to continue your work. I have tried. But I was lonely, and Edward was the only friend I had; he has been tender and kind to the boys and to me." I placed a hand on his good arm.

"Do you love him?"

"No! I've only loved you—no one else. You were always in my thoughts, but I needed to feel loved. I am sorry, my love. If I had known you were alive, I would have gone to you."

He stepped back and turned on me; when I tried to put my hand on his forearm, he pushed me gently and fidgeted with a saddle "I was Edward's prisoner for a few months, and when I escaped, the first thing I did was to go to Dudllan. It was just after he ordered your house-arrest. I know you saw me, but you thought it was a ghost. I didn't want to put you in danger, so I left. I regretted later and I came back you weren't well then, it was just before the birth of our daughter. For a few nights, I watched you sleeping, but I could not stay for I knew Edward would send someone to Dudllan, so I went to France, and the next time I came back to you, you were there with him. You looked happy." Hampton frowned.

"But I was not. I was lonely, and I needed to get my trades back, and I knew that seducing the king was the only way to get back my money."

"When he returned your fortune, why did you continue to entice him?"

I had no answer to that question, at least not one that would not have upset him, so I twisted the conversation to focus on him. "You have no right to be bitter. You were dead, and I was free to court whom I wanted, but if I had known you were alive, I would have done everything I could to find you. How dare you judge me when you are the one who forsook your sons and me? You have no right. You've let us all down."

"As I said, when I escaped, I came to you, but you were in someone else's arms!"

"It was months after I thought you had died. It took me a lot of courage to survive without you, and Edward helped me, but I do not love him. And you are not in a position to discuss my love life when Edward said you were married. What is that all about? Who is she?"

He did not reply, and as he used to when he wanted me to stop talking, he brought his lips on mine. And then he moved away, as if guilty or ashamed. I could not quite figure out his gesture.

"Alys, I must leave. Please don't get angry but you must stay here. You've no place in my life now."

"What about your sons, have they no longer a place in your life either? Is your new wife so precious that you're abandoning us again?"

"I am not abandoning you. All I wanted was to spare you more pain. I am no longer the powerful man that I once was."

"We could go to France with you. Don't forget Geoffrey owns lands there."

"Didn't you agree to give them back to the king of France?"

"How do you know?" I asked, incapable of keeping my eyebrows still.

"Because I intercepted your letter."

"You were spying on me?"

"No, I was trying to protect you."

"So, you care about us after all." I approached, unsure whether he would push me away or not. He took me in his arm.

"Come." He took my hand and led me through a passageway I knew nothing about.

Feeling his hands in mine brought me confidence and strength. I had no idea where he was taking me, but I beamed and felt as if I was bouncing on my feet behind him. The passage led us to a chamber behind the stables, an empty room with only a small window at the top of one of the walls.

As we were alone in the stables, he took me in his arms. "You're impossible to forget, Alys of Lochlainn, but I've nothing to offer you now. If you leave with me, the king will seize your land and your trades, and you will have nothing left," he said, caressing my hair and drew me closer to him.

"As long as I am with you, nothing else matters." I squeezed my arms around him, wanting to make sure it was not a dream.

He chuckled. "You would not say that if you were to live in a tent all of your life."

"I'll survive. It's not like I have not been used to the rough life." I lifted my face to look at him and then rested it against his chest. "We have a daughter," I muttered.

"Yes, I have seen Alienor. She is beautiful, like you." He put his hand on my face, and I approached my face closer to his. I wanted him to kiss me, but he moved back.

"King Louis gave us what we needed, and even if Henry Tudor is not yet ready, we will act, regardless. There will be another war soon. You must take our children back to Dudllan immediately."

"No, we can't have another war. Come with us to Dudllan?"

"Not after all those years. But if I get killed..."

"Don't say that, please." I pulled him against the wall and wrapped a leg around his waist as if to prevent him from leaving.

"That's not the behavior of an English Lady."

"I've been waiting for this moment for the last three years what do you expect?"

He lifted an eyebrow. "So, you're gagging for it." His voice was as suave as always.

"Aren't you?" A pinch of jealousy and an image of that young French woman I saw in the tent cross my mind. Was she his wife? Was he really married? I cupped my hands around his buttocks. As he entered me savagely, I realized that perhaps he had not been near a woman for a long time.

"Gosh. Those French women must be queuing at your door..." I gasped. "If you're so rough with them too."

"Sorry. Can't help. I wanted this for so long." A movement of his hips and the jealousy vanished, leaving me gasping for air.

As we readjusted our clothing, I laughed out loud. "Not that I am complaining, but you did accustom me to much better in the past. Must be the French wenches."

He brought his mouth to mine and kissed me, and my heart melted. It was a farewell kiss. The most passionate kiss he had ever given me, a kiss impregnated in my soul with love, forever. A cascade of tears rolled down my cheeks as my heart burst into thousands of pieces.

"Listen to Robyn. He's a good lad."

"Will you not speak to your sons before you leave?"

"No, and I do not want them to hear that I am alive. There is no need to give them false hope in case something happens to me on the battlefield."

"Why did you come to England and ask me for your prize?"

"It was reckless but seeing you and Edward so close fired me up. When I saw in your eyes a look I recognized, I thought you loved him. I was jealous," he said, looking down.

"How could you have forgotten how much I love you?"

"I know." He held me against his chest.

"Now, I must go."

"Will you ever come back?"

"It won't be for a few months. Edward must suspect nothing. He cannot think I am preparing something against him."

"He's the one who told me you were alive; he also knows you are the earl of Etrilly."

"It doesn't matter. Go back to Edward and tell him you want to retire to Dudllan, but make sure you keep him happy. He must not think about a war for the moment."

"You're asking me to bed the king? What if I enjoy it?"

"You already are," he said with an apparent resentment in his voice.

"Why do I suspect you are using me? I know exactly how you work; using people and having them do things to serve your interest is what you've always been good at."

"And disobeying is what you're good at."

"You are right. I will not go back to Edward. Never! Now I've found you, I will stay with you, and you won't get rid of me even if you want to."

"Stubborn as a mule!"

"Just like you."

"Oh, Alys, you've always been my weakness."

"And you, my strength."

"Come on, go and pack and meet us at Southampton, I'll have a ship ready for you. I'll instruct Robyn."

"The little traitor."

"Robyn is one of my best men."

"Hampton, what about your wife in France? What is she going to say when she sees us all?

Again, he took me in his arms, and I felt my anger and relief turning into a lush desire. Both our breathing became stronger, but time was running out, and we could not waste it. Not even after so long.

"I must go," he said.

"Wait! You did not tell me. How did you escape?"

"It took a while to recognize the guards' routine, and some of them used to be in my services. Fauconberg helped. I'll tell you more. Now, I really must go. My men have been waiting for too long." He kissed my forehead and escaped through the passageway.

After a short moment of recomposing myself, I walked out to find Robyn.

"Get my children out of here and ensure no one notices. We are meeting Hampton at Southampton."

"But-"

"Gérard? What is he doing here?" I asked, interrupting Robyn as I saw him approaching.

"That's all right, he's with us," Robyn said. "Lord Hampton sent him to Dudllan."

"You knew?"

"No."

"Pardon me," Gérard said, then took my hand and kissed it. "I had sworn silence. Not even Fauconberg knew who I was."

"Hampton is fortunate to have such faithful men behind him. Now, we need to transport the black horse to Southampton."

"Are you sure it is safe to do so?"

"What other choice do we have? He will die if he stays here with no one to care for him."

"I've prepared some herbs to calm him, I will give him a little more so he will be able to lay on the cart. Hopefully, if the winds are on our side, we can transport him safely back to France. I'm not leaving him here. I've lost Tristan, and I will not lose that one."

"Never seen anyone care so much for horses," Gérard said.

"Gérard, take care of the black horse. Robyn, get my children while I get Geoffrey out of Richard's house. We'll all meet at Southampton. Hurry."

We scampered in different directions. Before I was to get my son, I had to write a letter to Edward, to ensure he would not think that I had followed Hampton if he decided to chase after me. So, I returned to my bedchamber and wrote.

Dear Edward,

You were right. He is the earl of Etrilly, but you were also wrong, for he is not the man I used to know. Because of you. You knew he was alive, and you still tried to seduce me so you could win over him. You've never loved me. As always, you've used me, and now the man I love refuses to see me because he thinks I was your mistress. You stole him from me. Twice! And I will not forgive you. I am returning to Dudllan with my children and the black horse. I do not want to see you ever again. Please never come to Dudllan. There is no need to spy on me either, I will just be living a peasant's life in my castle, and I recognize that you are the victor and the king of England, but I don't want to see you or talk to you ever again. You've broken my heart, and I want nothing to do with you. I am sure your wife will rejoice at the news. She won, and I've lost. It is time for me to leave London for good.

I will never forget that once we were friends, we were betrothed, once we were enemies and that now we are nothing.

Alys of Dudllan

AS I HURRIED ALONG the corridors with the letter in my hand, I passed by Estrilda. I stopped. What if she was to report my escape? I could not risk her alarming the king.

"Estrilda."

"Lady Alys."

We both stared at each other in silence.

"What happened for us to become enemies?" I asked.

"I am not your enemy."

"It's even worse than I thought. Estrilda, you have been spying on me, and you've reported my moves to the queen. Please do not deny it, for I know it is true."

"I..."

"Do not give me excuses either. But tell me what I have done wrong to you, as I have never meant to harm you. I always wanted what was best for you."

"Richard... you convinced him to marry someone else than me."

"I did not know you loved him when I advised him to wed Anne, but when he mentioned your name, it was too late; he had decided to marry her. I am sorry, but it is not my fault he married another woman. Look, you have a great husband, you should care for him."

"Yes, Francis is a great man. I don't think I could have asked for a better man."

"Then what is stopping you from living in your country home with him?"

"I cannot bear the idea of not seeing Richard. My heart is torn between the two of them."

"I understand, but one day you will have to decide which one you love the most, and you will have to make a choice."

"Is that why you are leaving in the middle of the night? Have you made your choice to follow lord Hampton?"

"What?"

"He is alive, but don't worry, I've told no one, not even Richard."

"How do you know?"

"I saw him a few nights ago as I was walking around their camp. He has not seen me, but I recognized him at once."

"And you did not think of informing me?"

"As I said, I've told no one."

"But you should have told me, I've only found out a few hours ago."

"I thought you were happy with the king."

"No, I was not. Estrilda, I know you are angry with me, but please promise you will tell no one about lord Hampton. No one must know about it. Especially not the queen."

"You have my word. I will keep that secret," she said, but although she seemed sincere, I still could not be sure whether I could trust her or not.

"I'm sorry, I never meant to do you any harm. Lysbette was right; court is not a good place to live. It changes people."

"Thank you," she said and then unexpectedly, she took me in her arms as if she still was the little girl I had known a few years ago, and after a moment of hesitation. I embraced her sincerely.

"I must go now," I said, drawing apart.

"May God accompany you in your journey. And if you go to Flanders one day..." she paused and drew an inward breath before continuing, "Lysbette lives there. I am sorry she came to see you a few months ago, but I... she left without seeing you. She had something important to tell. I guess she had heard that lord Hampton was alive. I am sorry I did not let her see you."

The news brought a smile to my face and lifted a big weight off my heart. I could not believe that life was finally turning in my favor; after all those years of suffering, I received two pieces of excellent news in a day, and I suddenly worried that I would wake up and it would all be in the past.

"Why are you suddenly so kind?" I asked, still incredulous.

"Because now I know you did not mean to hurt me. I was so angry and even more when I lost my child... I thought you wanted to take Richard from me."

"Estrilda, since the day I met you, I've cared for you, and all I wanted was your happiness. Honestly, I did what I thought was best for you at the time. All I cared about was to do the right thing for you."

"I know," she said and then she kissed me on both cheeks, and I embraced her.

An hour later, Geoffrey, Robyn, and my children were traveling at the speed of the devil towards Southampton, while Gérard and the black horse had a couple of hours ahead of us. The wind in my face gave me the sensation I was seventeen again, when life was full of hope, when I was innocent, when life was good.

Memories rushed in my head as we reached the port of Southampton. Expecting Hampton's reaction, my heart drummed wildly, giving me a jerking breathing sensation. The shadow of Hampton appeared on the deck against the morning sun. I smiled. At first, I worried he would have changed his mind, but to my great relief, he beamed at the sight of us and dashed down the footpath to embrace our children. Then he gazed at me and lifted me off the ground and twirled me around as if I was as light as a bunch of hay.

"My stubborn Irish lady, what a joy to see you again! I am so pleased you disobeyed my orders."

"And I will never let you out of my sight ever again," I said and embraced him.

We both smiled.

For the first time in a long time, life was good, and hope was shining over the horizon for a new life in France.

THE END

No part of this publication may be reproduced, stored in a retrieval system or transmitted in any form or means, electronics, mechanical, photocopying, recording, or otherwise without prior permission of the author. Thank you for respecting the work of this author.

ACKNOWLEDGEMENTS

Thank you for reading this book. I hope you have enjoyed it as much as I enjoyed writing it.

I would also like to thank my wonderful daughter, who has been very supportive throughout the writing of this book.

The War of the Roses' story inspired me to write these books because it is my favorite period in History. However, I took the liberty to replace the character of the Earl of Warwick with the Earl of Hampton, mainly because it suited the purpose of the Series. I hope you will forgive this. You will see familiar players in this period and new characters I have created across the Series.

One of my favorite ladies in the Wars of the Roses is Elizabeth Woodville, even if in this Series, she does not have the best role. I think one day I will have to write something from her point of view.

If you would like to keep in touch and find out about the next books, please join me on Facebook or on twitter; I'd love to hear from you. You can always send me an email at

Thank you. Keep reading and I'll keep writing,

FLEUR DE LYS- Book 3

Alys of Lochlainn thought she had finally found happiness with Hampton, but when she arrives at Plessis with him, she discovers that he has remarried. Furious, Alys sets out to get revenge on his new wife. But when their daughter is kidnapped, she has to put her plans on hold and help Hampton find her. Alys eventually returns to England after a heated argument with Hampton, but will they ever have the chance to be together?

SHAMROCK - Prequel

She has a heart of gold... but poor instincts. When an attempt to save her family sparks disaster, only her wits can set her free.

Ireland, 1459. Alys of Lochlainn craves her father's attention. Neglected since her mother's death eleven years ago, the seventeen-year-old heiress is most displeased when an English earl and his son arrive to recruit allies for war. Determined to prevent her only remaining parent from dying on the battlefield, she concocts a desperate scheme to drive the foreign nobles from their land.

Attempting to scare them off with poison, Alys unintentionally almost kills the handsome young Englishman. But after an unscrupulous commoner's blackmail forces her to nurse the dutiful man back to health, she's alarmed when she finds herself falling for her brave patient.

Can Alys choose between her family's safety and her heart's calling?

Shamrock is the dramatic prequel to the Lochlainn medieval romance novels. If you like historical fiction with a touch of love story, fast-paced twists and turns, and breathtaking mystery, then you'll adore Augusta Gosling's suspenseful series starter.

© Augusta Gosling 2022

Don't miss out!

Visit the website below and you can sign up to receive emails whenever Augusta Gosling publishes a new book. There's no charge and no obligation.

https://books2read.com/r/B-A-KJAT-FOIAC

BOOKS 2 READ

Connecting independent readers to independent writers.

CPSIA information can be obtained
at www.ICGtesting.com
Printed in the USA
BVHW071139131022
649366BV00009B/607